AF270120

A

FRIEND

INDEED

BOOKS BY ELKA RAY

THE TOBY WONG VANCOUVER ISLAND MYSTERIES
Divorce Is Murder
Killer Coin

STANDALONE NOVELS
A Friend Indeed
Saigon Dark
Hanoi Jane

SHORT STORY COLLECTIONS
What You Don't Know

A FRIEND INDEED

ELKA RAY

BLACK STONE

PUBLISHING

First edition: 2024
ISBN 979-8-200-96019-4
Fiction / Thrillers / Psychological

Version 1

Blackstone Publishing
31 Mistletoe Rd.
Ashland, OR 97520

www.BlackstonePublishing.com

*For my childhood friends, C and JR—
whose husbands, like mine, remain very much alive.*

It's the friends you can call up at four a.m. that matter.
—Marlene Dietrich

CHAPTER 1

Jo: That night

The phone's buzz jolts me awake. I hesitate. Good news never comes in the dead of night. Unless . . . I reach for it. For one stupid second, I'm convinced it's my ex, Trevor.

"Hello?" It comes out a thick mumble.

"Jo? It's me!" Not Trevor but Dana, my best and oldest friend. Her words are jerky. "Jo, I need your help! Can you come over?"

I find my glasses. The '80s clock radio that came with my basement apartment blinks 12:09 a.m. "What? Now?" I say, incredulous. "But I have Ruby. And I have to teach in the morning. What's happened?"

"I . . . Please!" says Dana. "I just . . ." She's gulping too hard to get the words out.

I sit up. Holy shit. *Something's* happened. The last time I heard Dana cry was well over a decade ago, when Owen started acting out as a toddler. I click the light on. "Dana? Are you okay?"

"Please, Jo." A sob breaks free. "I really need you!"

I fight back a sigh and kick back the covers. Is saying no an option? She's my best and oldest friend. She's sobbing hysterically. Plus, I owe her.

And she *needs* me.

This last thought brings a tiny lift like I've been chosen first for softball. Pathetic, but there it is, even at my age. That's a first in thirty years of friendship. Even as a young girl—no, especially as a young girl, Dana never needed me.

I stagger out of bed and head for the bathroom. "Okay," I say. "I'll be right over."

———

At this time of night, the Oaks lies deserted. It's the most exclusive part of town. Immense trees flank the road as if to keep me in line. High walls guard old mansions with spiky black rooftops.

It starts to drizzle. The ornate streetlamps are feeble. I fight back a yawn and click on my wipers. The left one's wonky. It squeaks and smears the wetness. Yet one more thing that needs fixing.

I turn onto Elm and check my rearview: Ruby's fast asleep in her booster seat. Poor kid, hauled out of bed past midnight. Tomorrow's Monday. A school day. She's in kindergarten. This had better not be some pointless drama.

I should have refused. But how could I? Dana sounded desperate. And she's done so much for me, especially after Chicago. No, I won't think of that. Of course Dana helped me. That's what friends do. We're here for each other.

I slow at a stop sign. Now it's my turn. She said she needed me. Might her twins be in trouble, or little Zoe, who's the same age as Ruby?

I turn onto Beach Drive. By the water, the lots and mansions grow even bigger, the walls and gates more imposing. Those gates represent their owners' egos. No one *needs* a gate as tall as a double-decker bus. No one *needs* a twelve-thousand-square-foot mansion.

A sigh escapes. What I need is sleep. And a new car, preferably one made this millennium. An ex who paid child support would be a bonus. Fucking Trevor. How idiotic to think he'd actually call me.

I slow and turn into Dana's driveway. The wrought-iron gates rise before me. In the back seat, Ruby mumbles in her sleep. I pull up and type in the security code. The gates slide open. Modern magic.

I hesitate. *Need.* What an odd thing to say. And Dana's tone. She sounded almost . . . scared. She's normally cool and collected.

Is she in danger? Am I putting Ruby at risk? This thought shrinks my chest. But no. Dana would have called the cops instead of me, which means it's some domestic drama—maybe an argument with Stanley.

I was a bridesmaid at their wedding, going on two decades ago. Even so, I don't really know him. By the time Stan moved here, I'd left town. We've barely spoken since I moved back two months ago.

What I do know is that I don't trust him. He runs a hedge fund and is utterly convinced he deserves his good fortune. He's too rich, with all the confidence that breeds. Men like Stan lack imagination. Maybe Dana caught him cheating and that's what prompted her hysterical call to me. Yes, Stan's just the type to find someone younger and blonder.

I jolt forward, past the graceful hemlocks, our state tree. The gates glide shut behind me.

The driveway's so long it's got speed bumps. Oregon oaks, Douglas firs, and Pacific rhododendrons line the road, all native to the Pacific Northwest. The wiper's squeak is increasingly shrill. I grit my teeth. It's like nails on a blackboard.

Damn. I regret coming over. I shouldn't have caved. I'm due in early tomorrow for a tutoring session. Ever since I lost my last job, I've had trouble sleeping. I wake at four like clockwork, debts and fears pressing in. I should have told Dana to take a sleeping pill and that I'd call her in the morning.

As I round the bend, Winderlea looms into view, dark and brutal over the treetops. The grounds are magical, overlooking the Strait of Juan de Fuca. But that house! Even by Scottish Baronial standards, it's an eyesore. The porch is as dark and deep as a cavern. And its ominous chimneys look like watchtowers. You couldn't pay me to live there— and I live in a basement.

I'm not sure how Dana stands it.

———

I reach in to undo Ruby's seat belt. She smiles in her sleep. The sight softens my jaw. There's nothing as precious as a sleeping child. Nothing as fragile.

She murmurs and twitches as I struggle to lift her out. "Shhhh, baby." I balance her on my hip and slam the car door.

At five, Ruby's too big to comfortably carry. Her chin grinds my shoulder as I plod up the cobbled path. The air smells of cedar and the ocean.

As I approach the house, I stare at the huge blocky thing, its tall windows aglitter. Built in 1908, it's the real deal, one of those grand old piles with a name, not some pseudo-aged plywood McMansion. Tonight it's unlit, which is odd, albeit a blessing—it's even uglier floodlit. Normally, come dusk, Winderlea lights up like the *Titanic*.

In my arms, Ruby startles, as if the house woke her. I shift her weight and stroke her hair. It's silky in my fingers. Her breath's warm on my neck. I keep stroking her hair. Her stiff body loosens.

I'm climbing the never-ending stairs to the front porch when Dana appears, a thin, ghostly blur. "Jo?" she calls. It's too dark to see her clearly. "Oh, thank God!" she says. "Come inside!"

Thighs straining, I stagger on.

I'm at the lip of the porch when some faint light paints Dana's face. Shock stops me. One eye's puffed half shut. Her top lip's busted. This wreckage is tear-stained.

My voice rings loud in the silence. "Jesus! Did someone hit you?"

Was it Stan? That bastard! Unless it was Owen? But no, he's not had an outburst in years. I teach Owen tenth-grade English. He's an odd kid but okay, with an underdog's knack for ironic humor. He'd never hurt his mother. Nor would Chad, his golden boy twin brother.

"Shhhh," hisses Dana. She steps back and inside. "Lock the door."

I lean back to balance my sleeping daughter and push the heavy door shut. High overhead, a chandelier twinkles. Its glow doesn't reach us. This house absorbs warmth and light.

I shiver. It's colder inside than out. "Dana?" I say, alarmed. "What's going on?"

Instead of answering, she retreats. Her voice floats free, a ragged stage whisper. "This way. I need to show you."

I hesitate, then follow. With each step, Ruby feels heavier. Like the driveway, the hall is endless. I hurry to catch up. Dana's barefoot, but my shoes clatter.

Far ahead, a door opens and pale bluish light paints the floor.

"In here," calls Dana. Her voice echoes. "In my studio." She disappears through the door.

Dana's a florist—or, as the papers say, "a celebrity floral designer." Her clients include politicians and pop stars. I step into her studio and stop. Along two walls stand blue-lit coolers full of flowers: pom poms of peonies, banks of blood-red roses, spiky birds of paradise, vicious as medieval weapons. Thanks to the coolers, the room is less dark than the hall.

My breathing has shallowed. The smell's sweet and heavy, with an odd rusty tang.

Dana walks to a workbench and stops. Her back's to me. In the eerie light, her fair hair shines blue. "There," she says, her voice strangled.

A marble bench blocks my view.

I step closer and halt. Stan's face down on the white marble floor. I bite back a gasp, mindful of waking Ruby.

He's clad in boxer shorts and socks. His skin is raw-chicken pale. A Turkish towel's slung over the back of his head and shoulders, like he just stepped from a sauna and collapsed. A black puddle, shiny as ink, surrounds his head and chest. A large broken vase rests nearby.

Absurdly, I focus on the towel. That stain! What a waste! Turkish towels cost a fortune. I twist to Dana. "Is he—?"

She looks my way. Horrified eyes drop to my sleeping child. Her swollen mouth stretches. "Oh my God! You've got Ruby!"

I blink, slow and stupefied. She's right. I must get Ruby away from . . . that. Yet my feet feel part of the floor. Stan can't be dead. Is this a bad prank? That spill could be oil. Or molasses. Or . . .

"He's dead!" whispers Dana.

My lips are numb as I ask, "Are you sure?"

No response. I force my eyes back to Stan. His back . . . there's no rise and fall.

I inch his way. "Stan?" He doesn't move. I nudge his leg with my foot. My loafer leaves a smudge on his pale, meaty calf.

I should kneel down, try to find a pulse. But I can't. Not with Ruby. I stare at his socks: red, with a print of tiny footballs. I was with Dana when she bought them. We were shopping with our daughters.

Zoe must be upstairs, asleep. She's five, the same age as Ruby. I sway. Poor Zoe, losing her daddy. And Dana's twins. They're fifteen. A tough age.

To avoid looking at Stan, I step back and focus on the flowers in the closest cooler. White roses so perfect they look fake. Tiny wicked-faced orchids. And those Queen of Night hybrids, the darkest of all tulips, disgusting things, full and fleshy as internal organs. I feel dizzy.

Was it a heart attack? Stan had the type A personality I associate with coronaries. Is it too late to try CPR?

Dana gags. This rouses me. I spin to her: "Where's the ambulance, Dana?"

She must be in shock. Instead of answering, she sobs.

"Dana?" I try the stern, slow voice I use with daydreaming students: "Dana, did you call 911?"

When she doesn't respond, I thrust a hand into my coat pocket and extract my phone.

"No!" shrieks Dana.

I pull back in alarm. Dana never yells. She doesn't need to. She's got other ways to keep people in line: a look of ice, a jab of side-eye. Now her eyes are wild.

"What?" I snap. "Stan's dead! We need help! Why didn't you call?"

Her head shakes, eyes blazing blue in her lopsided face. "No!" she cries. "No police! You don't get it! I killed Stan!"

CHAPTER 2

Jo

I'm shaking so hard my legs are unsteady. I lurch from side to side down the dark tunnel of a hall.

Dana's behind me. She calls out, beseeching. "Jo! Stop!"

I ignore her and stumble toward the den. My phone's still clutched in one hand, pressed to my sleeping child. I'm scared I'll drop Ruby. She's increasingly heavy. I must put her down—*now*.

I shoulder the den's mahogany door.

The room smells of cologne, sporty and manly. My throat clogs. It smells of Stan.

I swish the wall with tingling fingers until I find the switch. The sudden light is blinding. Ruby twitches in my arms. I hug her. "Shhhh," I whisper.

The den's very much Stan's room, all chrome and black leather, with the world's biggest flat-screen and a bookshelf full of golfing trophies. There's a larger-than-life-sized closeup photo of Stan snowboarding: neon coat, flashing teeth, and shiny goggles hiding his eyes.

I stagger toward a massive sofa. Everything in this house seems made for giants, like some master race lives here. The ceilings are fourteen feet high.

Dana's still behind me, still pleading: "Please, Jo! Please! Let me explain!"

My arms quiver as I release Ruby onto the couch. Her little face screws up, then smooths over. Thank God my daughter's a deep sleeper.

Without Ruby's weight, my arms feel floaty. I reach for a blanket neatly folded on one armrest. It's printed with an image of Disney's Little Mermaid. It must be Zoe's. I want to cry. I shake out the blanket and allow it to settle gently over Ruby.

Phone in hand, I cross the room.

"No!" shriek-whispers Dana. "No! Don't call!"

I stop. Even in the dark, Dana's face looks blotchy. I gape at her, uncomprehending. "What the fuck happened?" Instead of answering, she stares straight ahead and wraps her thin arms around herself. I bark out her name: "Dana!"

She collapses onto another sofa, a wasteland of shiny black leather. Her bottom lip trembles. "Stan hit me."

"What?" I recoil.

To say Dana is beautiful is an understatement. She's ethereal, Grace Kelly in a wedding dress. Cinderella at the ball, graceful despite high-heeled glass slippers. And she's not just a pretty face. She's smart and successful. In her quiet way, she's commanding. Her life's always been charmed.

Dana brings her hands to her face, covering it. "It wasn't the first time. Stan . . . He . . . It's . . ." When she looks up, I hardly recognize her: she looks haunted and ghastly, a cowed, hunted creature. Her voice is tortured: "It's been going on for years."

I can't move. Years? Jesus Christ. How could Dana have settled for that? She could have had anyone!

A memory floats free: me, walking from the bus stop and seeing Dana up ahead, outside our middle school.

"Dana! Wait!" I called, and ran to catch up.

She slowed but didn't stop.

Up ahead, some older boys stood, slouching. Upon seeing Dana, they straightened: an honor guard at attention. Her effect on them was comical. What wouldn't they do to impress her?

Meanwhile, none of them saw me. I was an accessory, like her school bag.

I shake my head, back in Stan's ugly den. That bastard! "But . . ." I blurt. "Why didn't you leave?"

She flinches and looks at her hands.

Guilt strikes. What's wrong with me? This is the oldest story in the abused-woman book. Victims of domestic violence get gaslighted and blame themselves. They hope things will improve.

I'm her best friend. I've known her since we were twelve. Yet here I am, doubting her. And turning the blame onto her. Stan hit her! One look at her proves that. I feel sick. Oh my God.

Dana twists her pajama top's hem. "Before . . . He just never . . ." Her voice breaks. "Not my face."

I recall her long-sleeved, ladylike blouses. The endless Hermès scarves, even in summer. I fell for it, deceived by overpriced finery. What a fool. Some best friend I am!

I take a deep breath. "We need to call the police, Dana. This isn't your fault. You didn't mean for him to die!"

Her head snaps up, eyes fiery again. "No!" Her vehemence shocks me. "No, Jo! I did! Tonight, when he punched me, I lost it. I bashed him. Repeatedly. With a vase."

I shake my head, stubborn. "So you snapped. He beat you. It was still self-defense!"

Dana stands. She doesn't look cowed now, her back straight and regal. This is the Dana I know, able to still a room with one airy glance. "Jo," she says softly. "You're my best friend. You believe me. But no one else will. I spent all those years playing Mrs. Perfect. Even you thought my marriage was perfect!"

I can't answer. Her life did seem perfect. And all along, Stan was hitting her . . . Trying to grind down her shine.

Dana steps toward me. "The police will crucify me," she says. "They'll ask our neighbors. And our friends." This last word's spoken with a hitch. "None of them will back me up! They never saw him hurt me. The cops will say I set this all up. What will that do to my children?"

Again, I can't disagree. Dana's the queen of Glebes Bay high society. Anyone who's ever been jealous will say she's a cold evil bitch, who planned this. Her ladies-in-waiting will be lining up to throw knives at her. It'll be an orgy of schadenfreude. Even I feel a trace of it. Don't I?

I do not. But I should have known.

"There's no way you planned this," I say. "Why would you?"

Her shoulders slump, and fresh tears fill her eyes. "There was someone else. Stan wanted a divorce, and I signed a prenup."

I blink. An affair? A prenup? What the fuck? That's not part of the fairy tale.

"They'll say I did it for the money," she says. "For all of this." She waves a hand at the corniced ceiling.

I'm too stunned to reply. A savvy prosecutor would paint her as a jealous aging wife on the cusp of losing her looks, desperate to keep her claws on her husband's hard-earned money.

"It gets worse," she says. "He wanted custody . . ." A sob escapes. "Of the kids. Zoe's only five!"

I can't swallow. Holy shit. I don't know what I'd do if Trev got custody of Ruby. Kidnap her, probably. Go on the run.

Tears spill down her mismatched cheeks. "He—Oh God, you know him, he's ruthless! And he has endless money for lawyers. He claims I spoil the kids, that I'm a bad mother!"

I blink, my phone still clutched in my hand. She does spoil her kids a bit, but Dana's not a bad mom. She's just busy and distracted, a common story at Stanton House, where I teach. Half my students' parents are missing in action, too busy redecorating their second homes or organizing charity balls, while the other half are helicopter parents.

"Oh, Dana . . ." My words sound hollow. I tell her everything about my life—or nearly everything. How could she have hidden all this? "Why didn't you tell me?"

"I just . . . I felt pathetic." Her voice quivers. "I should have left him, but I couldn't. We have three kids! I kept hoping." She licks her split lip and winces, pulls herself back together. "Plus . . . You know." She shrugs. "You have your own problems."

I'm taken aback. It's true though. I've had more than my share. Fucking Trevor and his debts. That ugly business at my last school.

I shake my head and crack a wry smile. "No shit. But compared to *this*? It kind of takes the cake!"

She smiles too. A giggle breaks free. Soon, we're both cackling hysterically, not laughing because this is funny but because it's not.

"I've had a crap year," I say between snorts. "But you . . ." I flap a hand in the direction of her studio. "Jesus Christ, Dana!"

She wipes her eyes, not laughing now. "I win," she says, "first prize for the biggest fuckup." Her voice is wry.

"You always win, Dana."

She steps closer and sinks down beside me. "I need your help," she whispers.

I wait. After that manic laughter, I feel unsteady. I remember my dad learning English idioms from a textbook: *There's no free lunch.* He'd say it again and again. Those *r* sounds are tricky.

All these years, Dana gave me things: hand-me-downs, gifts, and cachet. She plucked me out of preteen-loser-land. She made my adolescence bearable. And she got me hired at Stanton House—no easy task after Chicago. She had to pull strings, my very own fairy godmother. Beautiful, magical Dana.

On the sofa, Ruby snores softly. Dana's gaze is imploring. I take a deep breath and look down at my sleeping daughter. "Let's get out of here," I say. We can't discuss this near Ruby.

Dana rises shakily. She precedes me into the hall.

I look toward the front door. I could walk away. Grab my daughter and run.

Yet I won't. Dana's my best—indeed, only—real friend. It's too late to leave. She needs me.

I square my shoulders and turn toward her gigantic kitchen.

CHAPTER 3

Dana

I need a drink to quell my panic. I open the fridge. Thanks to Gloria, it's sparkling, with Tupperware stacked like building blocks, all neatly labeled: *Carrot sticks*, *Pastrami* . . . There's a half-full bottle of Chablis in the door well. I extract it.

"None for me," says Jo, her tone implying I shouldn't.

She's right, but I don't care. Wine's nowhere near strong enough, but now's not the time for oblivion. As it is, I'm not thinking straight.

I pull a can of San Pellegrino from the fridge and set it on the counter. Jo ignores it. She turns to glare at the picture windows. It's too dark to see the gardens or the sea.

When I pour myself a glass of wine, I can barely keep the bottle steady. One sip, then another. It's good wine, bought by Stan. The thought of him shuts my gorge. I splutter and squeeze my eyes shut.

Stan, my husband of sixteen years, some of them happy, is dead. I recall him lifting me over the threshold when we were newlyweds. How big he felt. How solid. He pretended I was too heavy and collapsed on the bed. Even when my dress was off and his pants down, we couldn't stop laughing.

Fresh tears fill my eyes. That was so long ago. We'll never laugh that way again. Not that we laughed much in recent years. I'm sick to even want him back. Stan got what he deserved.

Tears squeeze though my lids. They say it takes hours for the soul to leave the body. Where is he now? I picture him in my studio, hovering near the ceiling and watching us—spread out like board game markers from Clue: Ruby in the den; Zoe and the twins upstairs in bed; me and Jo freaking out in the kitchen.

Jo's voice snaps me back: "The longer you wait, the worse it looks. You need to call the police *now*."

In the light off the stove, she looks old, eyes cupped in shadows, glasses slightly askew. She used to have that sexy librarian look. Now it's plain old librarian: hair in a sensible crop, clothes dull and practical. The divorce from Trevor took its toll.

Jo's always been her own worst enemy, one of those supersmart women who makes inexplicably dumb choices—like Trevor Gregory, his smile a lasso. Champion bull rider and bullshitter. Who marries a cowboy?

I recall Stanley and shake myself. Jesus. Talk about stones and glass houses. "I can't go to the police," I say. "They won't believe me. You know that. My only chance is to hide his body."

Hide. This word shames me. You hide things you plan to find, as in hide and seek. Even now, I can't be honest with myself. Dump. Dispose of. Bury. I must get rid of Stan.

Jo glares at me. One hand's in her short hair. She tugs at it, something she's done her whole life when she's stressed or frustrated. "How?" she asks.

I have no answer. Every thought's a deer trail, leading off into dark woods and petering out. I keep getting turned around, panic-stricken. I was hoping she'd know what to do. What if I've misjudged and she won't help me? But she *must*. Jo owes me. My voice quakes. "Bury him? In the woods. I could be out of town in thirty minutes. Find an old logging road . . ."

Jo snorts. From the shine in her eyes, I know her mind's reengaged. Jo loves nothing more than a problem to solve. A chance to show how smart she is. "Do you know how hard it is to dig a grave in the woods?" she says. "All those rocks and roots. Just last week two hunters found human remains near Gladwell Falls. It was this girl who went missing three months back. She was coming home from ballet when—"

I cut her off, my voice shrill. "What should I do, Jo?"

Jo's scowling so hard there's a crack between her brows. She chews her bottom lip. "I told you. Call the police. Get a great lawyer."

"I can't!" It's a desperate shriek. "I kept bashing him! It was beyond self-defense!"

Jo inhales. I hold my breath. We're both quiet. I feel ill. I shouldn't have called her.

Jo's gaze veers back to the windows. "You have a boat, right?" she asks.

I nod and stare into the dark, hardly daring to hope. Does this mean she'll help me? "The yacht's at the Yacht Club, but there's a small motorboat down at the jetty."

"It's risky. Bodies float. You know, like those detached human feet?"

I don't have time for Jo's stories but can't not ask: "What feet?" She's full of facts, mostly useless but occasionally vital.

"In the past decade, at least a dozen human feet have washed up around the Pacific Northwest. They float because they're in sneakers."

I grit my teeth. "Stan's not wearing sneakers."

Jo looks at me, derailed from her train of thought. "We'd have to go out to where it's deeper. And weigh him down."

I nod, feeling shaky. She said *we*. That means she's in. Oh, thank God.

Jo reaches for the San Pellegrino. I'm startled by the pop of the tab. She's glaring at me, obviously waiting for some reaction.

"The ocean," I say. "You're right. The ocean's better." It's right out back. Stan is—*was*—a water sports fanatic. He loves—*loved*—the ocean. It's a better resting place than some shallow grave in the woods. More respectful.

I sag against the fridge. Is there no end to my bullshit?

"Dana, do you have a tarp?" asks Jo. Now she's decided, she's all action. Her voice is grim. "Moving him will be messy."

My stomach lurches. Messy. "I . . . yeah. In the shed. And a wheelbarrow."

"Right then." She eyes the clock on the stove. "First things first. Where's his phone?"

I blink. "What?"

"If he left, he'd take his cell."

"Oh, right," I say. "It's charging upstairs. Beside our bed."

"Go and get it and turn it off," says Jo.

I nod. We must get rid of it.

"Are there security cameras?" she says.

"Outside," I say, shocked I'd forgotten this too. "Front and back."

"Go disarm them."

I hesitate. "Won't that seem suspicious?"

Jo snorts. "Not as suspicious as footage of us dumping Stan!" When I don't move, she clucks. "Come on, Dana. It's time to get moving."

She sounds matter-of-fact, like we're discussing a school fundraiser, not the disposal of my husband's bloody corpse. But then I see her eyes, wide and bloodshot behind her unflattering glasses.

Fuck. This is bad. Jo's as freaked out as I am.

———

Thank God my studio's got a service entrance. It'd be hard to fit Stan out a regular door. And forget stairs.

The wheelbarrow lurches over the cobbles. In the drizzle, the stones are slippery. It's hard to see where we're going with all the outdoor lights off.

Jo's pushing and I'm walking sideways, near the front, trying to hold Stan steady. It takes ages to reach the back of the house. The wheelbarrow rattles and tilts. I grab the tarp. It slips in my gloved hands.

While Jo fetched the wheelbarrow, I wrapped Stan in layers: towels, sheets, and this tarp, now tied with rope. He's six foot one and 190 pounds. An enormous blue mummy. There's no way I could manage this without help.

To our right lie a row of pines and the dark roof of the guesthouse. "Left," I whisper.

Jo's panting behind me. Her job's harder. I look back. Her arms are wobbly. "Jo?" I say. "Want to trade places?"

She shakes her head and steers left, her neck cabled. We cross the stone terrace just below the front patio.

Below this lies a huge lawn, then a lower Japanese garden with a lotus pond. At the far end of the house, a sloping path cuts down to the boathouse on the rocks. Last of all come the dark pebbled beach and the jetty.

The steeper the slope, the jumpier the wheelbarrow. It's getting harder to hold Stan steady.

"Stop," says Jo. She sets the wheelbarrow down and straightens, swivels her wrists. "Shit. Look at that boat ramp."

I twist to follow her gaze, eyeing the steep angle. If we lose control, he'll shoot off the end of the dock. Imagine that: Stan found right out back in shallow water, gift-wrapped.

"What if I walk in front?" I say. "I could slow the wheelbarrow." Or would Stan mow me down? He'd surely want to.

Jo doesn't answer. She's probably trying to work out the physics. Her hair sticks up where she's been tugging at it. That, and her round, worried eyes, make her look younger, almost childlike. She grinds her teeth, thinking.

"Jo?" I say, to bring her back. We're exposed out here on the rocks. What if that old busybody Harold Attwater's awake, two doors down? There's not much Stan could be besides a corpse. A rolled carpet? A pile of two-by-fours in a tarp? Harold Attwater reports jaywalkers. I fear he's on the phone to Crime Stoppers this very minute.

Jo's eyes snap to mine. "Let's get him to the top of the ramp and tip him, then drag him down."

"Okay." Thank God for Jo. I'd be even more screwed without her.

She positions the wheelbarrow at the top of the ramp. "Come on this side and help me."

There's a dreadful thud when we drop him.

Long after we've dragged him down to the jetty, I can still feel that thump in the pit of my belly.

CHAPTER 4

Dana

Dark water slaps the boat's sides. I use a paddle—taken from one of Stan's countless kayaks—to push us away from the jetty.

The boat is small. It came with the house when we bought it. Now and then, Stan used it to motor to the Yacht Club. Mostly it sat by our dock, neglected.

I start to paddle.

It's stopped drizzling. The wind's dropped, and the ocean's glassy. This is lucky: Jo gets seasick. And this boat's too small to handle bad weather.

I'm crouched in the back, behind three built-in bench seats. Jo's kneeling in the bow, also wielding a paddle. Stan's mummy lies across all three seats. He's taking up most of the space. As usual. I can't bear to touch him.

When I yank on the paddle, the tarp crackles. My gut heaves. It's like a message. Even dead, trust Stan to be obtrusive. He had a loud voice, a loud laugh. He snored. He sang in the shower. And he yelled a lot, especially lately. Tears flood my eyes. I can't stop shaking.

"Dana?"

I look up. Jo's twisted my way. She sounds irate: "We're not moving!"

I look around. Shit. The coast lies far too close. We've hardly made any progress.

We decided to paddle out a ways because the motor would be noisy. While the Oaks looks deserted, plenty of people could be watching. The woman in the Dutch Colonial on the corner is a night owl. Teens often hang out on the public beach, just up the block. My own sons could be watching!

"Paddle harder!" I say. My arms are burning. I'm getting blisters. The motion takes me back to summer camp—in a canoe, on a lake. Jo couldn't come. Her mom couldn't afford it.

"I'm trying," gasps Jo. "We're getting nowhere."

Again, I look over my shoulder. Winderlea and its grounds lie dark. Some of the neighboring mansions have outdoor lights on. Trees shine green-gold. Light ripples on the smooth water.

I inhale. It's lovely. Why did Stan and I never come out here in the boat at night? All this beauty lay right outside our door. My paddle splashes. The tarp crackles.

I shake myself. What the fuck. Now's no time for nostalgia. I could end up in jail! I need to focus. I slice my paddle into the water and pull.

"Dana?" Jo sounds strangled. She's stopped paddling. We start to turn in a circle.

"Jo?" I say, alarmed.

Her head's between her knees. She squints up at me. "I'm okay . . . Just out of shape." She's pale as putty and breathing like Darth Vader. "Hurry . . . up! Start . . . the . . . fucking . . . motor!"

I start it up and we head for the mouth of the bay. The wind's cold against my face. It takes a while for Jo to stop wheezing.

The farther we get from shore, the bigger the waves. The boat's bouncing. I slow us down.

I keep my eyes on the islands: four low black mounds, at least another ten minutes' away. They're uninhabited, home to dry grass and rocks, plus mounds of bird shit.

Some years back, a stray cat was found out there. It must have swum out. It made the paper—front page news in Glebes Bay. They printed its photo, a mangy old tabby. Someone adopted it, named it Molly Brown. Of course Jo later explained why.

We hit a big swell, and the boat bounces. Cold spray blasts my cheeks. My teeth clack. Jo turns, her face greenish gray. "Slow down," she rasps. Poor her. She's seasick.

I ease back on the throttle. "Where to?" I ask.

Jo turns again, one hand clamped to her mouth. "Port, twenty degrees."

I'm surprised. So far as I know, she's never been on a boat in her life. But I shouldn't be. She's a teacher and well read, after all. She'd know the right terms. I turn as directed.

Jo speaks through splayed fingers. "They'll have divers in the bay. We need to go out a ways, past the islands."

We motor on in silence.

As soon as we pass the first island, the sea gets rougher. Even I feel queasy. I slow further. I'm cold. We've been out a good thirty minutes. We bounce onward.

"Okay, here," says Jo. Her voice sounds squishy.

I slow down, then stop. Jo leans out, over the side, and retches. Her short hair's sticking up. Her back shudders. I catch a sour whiff of vomit.

When she's done, I motor on a bit to evade the smell. We can't drop Stan near Jo's slick of vomit.

"Enough," says Jo. "Here."

I cut the engine. The sudden silence feels overwhelming. Jo's hunched in the bow, head in hands. We slowly drift toward the biggest island. The boat sways gently.

Jo turns and removes her glasses. Her face looks naked without them. "Dana?" she rasps.

"Yeah?"

She rubs salt spray off the lenses. "You sure you want to do this?"

I look back to shore, starred with tiny cheery lights. We could turn around. Take him back. I could call the cops, admit everything.

"Yes," I say. There's no going back. I know exactly what would happen.

Jo opens her mouth as if to contradict me. I lay a hand on Stan's body and close my eyes to shut her out. I bow my head, aware Jo's watching. I try to breathe deeply.

When I raise my head, Jo looks away. Maybe she thinks I've been saying a prayer or goodbye to my husband—*late husband*. Why does late mean dead?

"This is the only way," I say.

She nods. "Okay."

Stan's tarp crackles as she shifts. She pulls Stan's iPhone out of her pocket. I'm lucky she remembered it. Stan never went anywhere without his cell.

There's a plop when she drops it overboard. It disappears fast.

I reach for the broken vase lying in a plastic bag in the boat's bottom. It's heavy.

At the last minute, Jo remembered this too. I ran back to get it. She's good with details.

I drop the bag overboard. There's a heavy plop. We both watch it sink. It feels like a test run. God, Stan would hate this: more plastic pollution.

Up near Jo's end lies a length of chain, each link almost as thick as my wrist. Jo found it in the shed, along with the tarp and the wheelbarrow. It's hellishly heavy. Her idea is to wrap it around Stan.

She picks up the chain. "You'll have to come forward."

I crawl up by his chest. It's lucky he's off the ground, balanced on the benches.

Jo ties the first loop and passes the chain under him. I reach beneath him to grab it. We both pull, hand over hand, until the loop's tight. We manage five loops, Stan trussed like a pot roast. Sweat coats my back. I unzip my dark jacket.

Jo secures the chain's ends with an old bike lock, also found in the garden shed. She thought of everything. She swivels her wrists and sighs: "Now for the hard part."

My stomach sinks. Moving him without the chain was hard enough. And that was on dry land, not in a small, tippy boat. How will we manage? Thank God he's not heaped in the bottom. We don't need to lift him, just roll.

Jo takes his head-end. I crawl down to his feet. "On the count of three," she says. I nod. She counts slowly.

We both heave. Muscles I didn't know I had are straining. It seems impossible, but he's moving. When he's poised on the rim, I'm scared he'll roll backward. But no, there's the tipping point.

"Push," grunts Jo.

He flips and topples over.

There's a sickening lurch. The boat tips beneath us. There's a splash.

Dark water rushes up. We did it! He's in the water! Fuck! The boat's flipping. I shriek. Without thinking, I jump back to counterbalance us. Jo also lunges backward. The boat rocks madly. Cold spray hits us.

Sick and stunned, I lie curled in the boat's flooded bottom. Water sloshes. The boat's still rocking.

Overhead, the clouds have thinned to reveal a white hook of moon. I sit up and crawl to the side. My jeans and jacket are soaked. I don't want to look but must. This is it.

Goodbye, Stan.

The sea's darker than the sky. Ripples break its surface. In the depths, something blue flashes. I jolt back. What was that? We haven't stopped rocking.

I grip the boat's side and peer back into the black water. That blue spark! I look at the veiled moon and my ring. Was it the diamonds catching moonlight?

Even when Stan proposed, sailing on Lake Como, and I was thrilled, I disliked this ring. Not just one humongous diamond but three. So flashy and ostentatious.

I touch it. The stones are cold and hard. The last ripples hit the boat in accusatory slaps. I start to twist at the ring.

Jo hisses: "What are you doing?"

"I don't want it," I say. "I'm throwing it in. With Stan."

I keep clawing at the ring. I know it's an empty gesture. Am I ridding myself of this symbol of marriage or trying to show I don't care about its worth, don't need Stan's fortune?

Jo grabs my arm. "Stop it!"

I blink at her vacantly, still wrenching at the jutting stones.

"The cops will be over you like a rash!" she says. "They'll notice everything! Your ring disappears, they'll ask where it went."

I stare at my hand. The moon's disappeared. Yet even in the dark, the stones emit light. "I'll say . . . I threw it at him during our fight. Maybe he took it . . ."

"No!" says Jo. "You'll lie as little as possible. And not about stupid shit! That's how you'll fuck up!" She sounds livid.

I'm not thinking straight. What we've done is too awful.

I stop twisting the diamonds and look out at the ocean. It feels alive: a vast roiling beast flexing its muscles, our boat a flea on dark skin. I shiver. Thick black blood flows beneath us. My eyes glitch on the spot where we dropped him. There's movement in the blackness. I gasp and point. "Look!"

It can't be, yet it is: Stan's blue tarp, rising up. Any second now, he'll lunge out of the water.

"What?" gasps Jo.

"It's . . . He's . . . floating."

"What?" She twists around. "No, he's not!"

"But I saw . . ."

She throws up her hands. "There's nothing there!"

I can't move. Am I seeing things?

"Dana?" She sounds scared. I know she feels it too, a curse upon us. We've unleashed something. "Come on, Dana! Get moving!"

I want to move but can't. Every nightmare feels possible. The boat won't stop rocking. Or is it just me? The biggest island looms closer; the surf seems louder.

Jo crawls back and shakes me. "We're near the rocks! Start the fucking motor!"

I jolt back and reach for the starter-rope's toggle. One tug. Two. My blisters burn. The engine sputters.

Jo gasps: "Don't flood it! Fuck! That's all we need!"

I imagine us shipwrecked and stranded like that scrawny old cat. I let go of the toggle. "Fine." I sound twelve, scared to my bratty self. "You try."

Jo crawls over the bench and squats beside me. One sharp yank gets the motor going. "I'll drive," she says tightly. "Move to the middle. And keep an eye out for debris."

I crawl to the central bench and sink down. Jo turns us toward shore. Distant lights twinkle. Wind catches my hair.

It's a relief to be moving, to flush my lungs with cold air.

I pull my hands into my sleeves. I'm wet through and chilled. My teeth chatter. For some minutes, we ride in silence.

"Dana?" Although she's driving slowly, we've started to bounce again. Jo sounds ill.

"Yes?"

"Did you love him?"

I look back, over my shoulder, toward my huddled friend and the black knuckles of islands. I find the spot we left Stan. I bite my lip, hard, and spin the way we're headed. "Yes. I *still* love him."

It's the truth, isn't it? Or it's part of the truth. My eyes fill with hot, angry tears. I hate that I loved him, just like my father. How could I have repeated that stupid, dreadful pattern? My head hangs.

I never told anyone about my dad, not even Jo. Not even now. I'm still not sure why. Shame, maybe.

In kids' stories, people are good or bad, all neatly labeled. The Wicked Witch. The Good Fairy. Real people are jumbled, like that monster in England who raised millions for cancer while molesting sick children. Even bad people have some good in them, and vice versa.

Stan had big helpings of both. He was the life of every party. He fought ocean pollution long before it got trendy. He was brave and sentimental. He once jumped into a filthy drainage ditch to save an old lady's labradoodle.

I sound bitter: "I didn't marry him for the money, if that's what you think."

Jo snorts. "I never thought that."

I hug myself. "Most people do."

"Well, fuck most people, Dana."

I smile. Jo's always been loyal. That's why we've stayed friends for so long.

It's hard to forge friendships when you're richer than everyone you know. There's the uneasy sense that people want something from you— maybe not money, but the glamour they think it brings. Beauty's the same. People think you think you're hot shit. They assume things about you. And they get jealous. But not Jo. I think back to the day we became friends:

For some reason, I was late for PE on the second day of sixth grade. When I entered the gym, I found the girls divided into small groups: two on the mats, wrestling, with a third meant to referee.

I slowed to watch. The teacher, Mr. Granger, was at the far end, instructing his favorites. Closest to me, Kitty Myers was grappling with the weird new girl—the one with the home hack-job haircut.

They stumbled backward and forward, locked together. From Kitty's flushed cheeks, she was obviously trying. This was interesting. While Kitty had twenty pounds on her opponent, she was soft. The new kid looked wiry and feral.

"Dyke!" grunted Kitty.

The new girl pushed her down and held her.

"Let go of me!" squealed Kitty.

"Stop!" said Angie Zukovitch, who was reffing them. She raised her hands above her head in an X, like it was the WWE. The new girl released Kitty and stepped back. By then, I wasn't the only one watching.

When Kitty sat up, she was red-faced and snake-eyed. "Did you see her grope me?" she hissed to Angie. "No wonder her name's Jo Dyke-stra!"

The new girl blinked in shock. She opened her mouth to protest, but I beat her to it.

"You wish, Kitty," I said. I smiled at Jo. "I need a wrestling partner."

Jo flushed with embarrassment and relief. She clearly knew who I was. "Um, sure. Okay." She dusted herself off, then followed me to another mat.

"Ignore them," I told her.

"Okay."

We got into position. She was skin and bones in my arms, like I was hugging a wild bird. It didn't take long until I'd pinned her.

"You didn't even try," I said as I let her up.

She flashed a half smile. "No point, was there?"

I smiled back. She played that well. I liked that. That's when I decided she would be my best friend.

The boat jolts over a wave, bringing me back to the moment. My teeth clack.

Behind me, Jo's retching again. Poor Jo. Nausea's awful. I had terrible morning sickness with the twins. I stare at the horizon, then check my watch. We only have about two more hours of darkness.

The boat smacks down hard. Shock waves hum up my spine. Cold spray hits like bird shot.

Behind me, Jo groans. I twist to look at her, neck rigid and mouth puckered.

"Jo?" I say.

She grunts.

"I . . ." Gratitude overwhelms me. I can barely speak. "Thank you."

"Oh, fuck." She leans over the side and retches. A streamer of vomit flies behind us.

I wince. She gags again, then straightens. "Look where we're going! There are deadheads." Her voice is raw. She wipes her mouth with her sleeve.

"Jo? I'm sorry."

Her nostrils flare. "I know." She takes a deep breath. "I know you're sorry. Just . . . keep it together." She slows the boat and spits over the side. "You can thank me when this is all over."

CHAPTER 5

Dana: The next morning

Cleaning up took longer than expected. We worked through the night. Jo and Ruby just left. It's already 6:00 a.m. and not yet light.

I'm freshly showered and dressed in dark jeans and a navy sweater. I sit on the edge of our bed in the near-dark, an ice pack clutched to my eye. I threw back the sheets so the bed would look slept in. I even rolled on my side and punched dents in the pillows.

I look around. This room has the impersonal elegance of a decent hotel, all icy white and dove gray. Stan loved modern decor. He liked the contrast with the house's rough, ancient exterior. I find it jarring, an old lady made up like a young girl. I reposition the ice pack.

Normally, if I were up this early, I'd be curled in the bay window, waiting for the sunrise. No, I'd be waiting to take photos of the sunrise to post on Instagram, along with some inspiring quote. *Every day is a fresh start!*

What a fraud.

This thought starts me sobbing. I don't understand it. I'm not a crier.

Through streaming eyes, I peer out the window. It's hard to distinguish the sky from the ocean. I look down. Stan's out there somewhere. On the seabed, dragged this way and that. God, he'd hate that. Going with the flow was not in his nature.

I get off the bed and yank the drapes shut. No, that's not right. I deserve this. I tug them back open. I must face reality. Stan's out there, rotting.

I lean against the cold window.

The sky lightens so gradually it hardly seems real. Gray turns to silver. The islands take shape, forever tainted. A blush lights the horizon.

The scene's prettiness can't touch me. I wish it would stay night forever.

I turn. Are those sirens? They grow louder, drawing near. Their shriek fills my head. The police are coming for me! Although they can't be. Not yet. No one knows. Unless Jo told. But she wouldn't.

The sirens reach a climax and pass. They grow fainter and less piercing. My chest loosens. I bow my head. What have I done? This is my life. The life of an outlaw.

My eye throbs. I shift the ice pack and turn my back on the window.

Instead of standing here weeping, I should be rehearsing my story. Jo made me go over it several times. I can't fuck it up.

"We argued," I whisper. "Stan hit me." My voice shakes. Do I sound melodramatic? Or not distraught enough? I clear my throat. "He hit me. No! He's never done that before! He'd been drinking . . . He felt terrible! He ran off—to think, I guess." I add a bewildered head shake. "I don't know where he went."

On the bedside table, my phone alarm dings. I'm startled. The sound worsens my headache. I rush to turn it off. It's time to wake up my children.

The police are one thing, but the kids . . . What should I say? Zoe's young enough to believe Mommy tripped and slammed her face on a door, but the twins are a different story. Whatever they know or don't know about last night, I must convince them to keep quiet.

I retreat to the bathroom.

As I scour my face, I picture Jo getting ready in her poky apartment. Poor her. She's teaching today. I'm not sure how she'll manage. But Jo's tough. She often pulled all-nighters back in college. Although that was a while back.

I'm padding down the long hall when the sirens start again, now headed in the opposite direction. Ambulance. And police.

Sirens mean one thing: someone's in trouble.

Outside Zoe's door, I pause, then shuffle on. Owen and Chad are across the hall from each other. They're not identical twins but fraternal. Right from day one, they couldn't have been less alike: Chad straight off a Pampers ad, Owen scrawny and screaming.

Between their doors I stop, unsure which way to turn. Into Chad's room, with its smell of mouthwash and its gleaming sports trophies? Or into Owen's, piled high with musty comics and toys, the curtains always drawn so it feels like the nest of some small woodland creature?

It's cowardly, but I turn toward Chad's door. He's my easier son, for whom things come easily. Not that I don't worry for him too, fearing cracks beneath the gloss. No one's life is that perfect. Look at me, for God's sake.

Chad reminds me of myself at that age: too careful. Sometimes I want to shake him and say, "You're fifteen. Have some fun. It's okay to screw up."

Although I guess he did a bit, with Gemma Costin. The pair of them were suspended only last week. It was actually Jo who caught them cheating on an English exam. We had to troop in to see the principal. Chad was mortified. I know Gemma put him up to it. Stan was livid.

There's a window at the end of the hall. As I raise a hand to knock on Chad's door, my ring catches the light. I remember last night in the boat, wanting to toss it. Part of me still wishes I had. I'll never look at this ring without thinking of Stan. "Diamonds are forever"—the ultimate marketing bullshit, and yet . . . My throat's tight. Poor Stan.

A memory glitters: Stan teaching me to snowboard, off-piste, in Chamonix. The sky was bright blue, the snow dazzling.

"It's too steep," I said, staring down, my gut knotted. "I can't do it."

"You can, Dana." Surrounded by gingery stubble, his smile blazed white. "Just relax. You're a natural. I'll stay right beside you. Trust me."

I did. He was right. Powder sparkled around us. The fear in my belly gave way to wild, swooping excitement. I was a natural. He helped me feel that.

Those early years, we fit together. Him, loud and boisterous. Me, cool and classic. We were yin and yang. So what happened?

Did Owen's issues get between us? He was diagnosed with a whole rash of things: ADHD, anxiety, OCD. We got pills but no real answers.

Or was it moving here? I thought a small town would help Owen, but Stan was bored here. Despite his outdoorsiness, he was a big-city person.

I'm too tired. My face throbs.

I lower my hand and lean against the wall outside my sleeping son's door. More light shines in through the window. The diamonds flash as if in warning. I twist the ring so the stones are hidden. I make a fist. The gems jab into my palm. To punish myself, I squeeze them into a blister.

CHAPTER 6

Jo

What the fuck have I done? Seeing Dana's bruised face and Stan's body, I panicked. I should have forced her to call the cops. I should have called them myself! I can't believe we actually dumped him. And that cleanup! Just the thought speeds my breathing. I've been too busy to think clearly.

Now, as I drive tiredly home, my head swarms with misgivings. I must be in shock. The whole night has the feel of a fever dream, fantastical and disjointed. I feel seasick all over again, like my Toyota's rocking. I should have talked Dana out of it.

It's 6:10 a.m. Behind me, Ruby's snoring in her booster seat. She woke up when I carried her to the car but has nodded off again. Outside, dawn's breaking. The sky's an eerie blue gray. I'm too strung out to be driving. Thank Christ the Oaks is deserted.

I turn up the heater, which barely works. It throws out lukewarm air with a burnt chemical smell. My eyes feel pried open. It's drizzling again. My left wiper's squeaking.

I've got talk radio playing—softly, on account of Ruby. I'm not listening to the DJ's banter. I turned it on to help keep me awake, although adrenaline's still pumping. Questions chase each other through my head. What if someone saw us out in the boat or burning the bloody rags? Will the smell of bleach linger in Dana's studio?

I turn onto Marlowe Street, as tired and wired as a kid before an exam, full of crammed facts and coffee. Except now the facts are risky. It's the lies I must remember. Our story.

In the half-light, the streets look haunted. Mist hangs between the houses, which lie far apart. Dark trees twist overhead.

Most homes in the Oaks date from the early 1900s, built in the same era as Winderlea. Each one's different and impressive, full of Edwardian architectural wizardry: pointy witches' hats, arched windows, and turrets. It's strange to think that real people with real problems actually live in them. The Oaks has a movie-set feel.

I grip the wheel with sore fingers. I check the clock on the dash. Shit. I need to be at school by 7:30. The thought drags me down. I force my spine straight. At least I'll have time for a quick shower.

While I long to call in sick, I don't dare. It might look suspicious. I must stick to my routine. I'm new at Stanton House, still on shaky ground. After what happened in Chicago, I really need this job.

Staring into the fading dark, I'm back there—in the most prominent private school in Illinois, flanked by a pair of policemen. They escorted me toward the front doors. All around, staff and teachers looked shell-shocked. And the students, with their sly smirks and whispers.

And then. Checking the joint account, all my savings gone, pilfered by Trevor. The eviction notice, taped to my door as I stood there slack with dread, Ruby's small hand in mine.

I called the only person who might help. By the time Dana picked up, I was sobbing.

"Jo? Hey. Where are you?" She turned down her radio. "What's happened?"

"I . . ." Tears were pooling in my glasses. "I . . . I'm still in Chicago." My voice was raw with panic. "I've been fired."

"What? Why?"

"They accused me of—Oh God, Dana. It doesn't matter. It's not fair!" I was crying so hard my words were garbled. "I'm a good teacher! I really am!"

"Jo? Calm down. Just tell me what happened."

"I can't calm down! I'm going to be homeless!"

"Homeless?" Her incredulity jumped down the line. "What do you mean?"

"I'm being evicted. Me and Ruby. I have no job. I could lose my teaching license. They'll make sure I'm never hired in this state again!"

I could hear her clippers snipping stems. "Come here."

"What?"

"My kids' school is great. Very exclusive. I can get you a job."

Her certainty took my breath away. "What? How? You don't understand. I've got no references now. And if they dig into this—"

She cut me off. "They won't. You're a good teacher." All the while, her clippers kept clicking. "You can come stay in our guesthouse till you're back on your feet," she said. "Just leave it to me. It'd be great to have you back in Glebes Bay."

I'm so distracted by this memory I don't see the stop sign's approach. I coast into the intersection at Elm. High beams blind my tired eyes.

I gasp. It's a car coming downhill fast. It has the right of way. In the glow of the streetlamp, I see the driver's face: a young man, shocked and livid.

Instinct saves me. I hit the gas. The car swerves behind me. My eyes stay glued to the rearview mirror.

Two shadows—one small and one larger—emerge from the bushes to cross Marlowe. The car swerves again. There's a squeal of brakes and a thump. Something thuds—a jack-o-lantern tossed off a porch. Nasty rotten-vegetable sounds. Celery snapped.

I brake in the middle of the road. My car jerks to a stop. I twist in my seat and gape back.

Ruby's sitting up in her booster seat. She's been shocked awake. "Mommy?"

"Don't worry," I say. I look out the back window.

The other car stopped too. It's half turned onto Marlowe. Near the curb lies a long black lump. Oh my God. He hit something.

I wait for the car's door to burst open, for the young man to stagger out. Instead, he turns off his car's headlights. The car accelerates and skids around the black mound. It speeds down Marlowe, then swings, fast and loose, onto Beach. Its engine revs and grows fainter. I sit rigid, disbelieving.

Holy shit. Still twisted back, I squeeze my eyes shut.

As kids, Dana and I used to watch bad horror movies, the kind where everyone dies in grisly ways. The plots were all the same: a bitter madman picks off a bunch of dumb kids. Knowing what was coming didn't help. I'd still sit there, hiding my eyes.

This feels the same, except now I'm an adult. And it's no movie.

"Mommy?" says Ruby. Her voice cracks, plaintive. "What's happening?"

I open my eyes. Ruby's staring around the car, as if surprised to be here. "Nothing," I say. "We, um—we slept at Auntie Dana's. She felt sick, but she's better. Don't worry."

Rain drums against my car's roof. My heart's trying to escape from my chest. I peer through the deluge. The dark shape in the road hasn't moved. It's small. Someone's child! Like Ruby . . .

Without thinking, I grab my bag off the passenger seat. I find my cellphone. My fingers stab 911. "Hello! I need help!" I rasp. "I'm in the Oaks. The intersection of Marlowe and Elm. There's been a hit-and-run! Someone's hurt! Badly!"

The operator drones out questions: my name, the victim's condition.

"I don't know! I don't know!" I say. "They're in the street, not moving! Hurry!" All the while, I'm aware of Ruby. I don't want to scare her. She turns to gaze out the window.

"Stay on the line," the operator instructs me.

The phone falls from my grasp and lands in my lap. "Are you there?" asks the operator. Her voice is faint but sharp, grating in the darkness. Holy shit. It's hard to breathe. I stare at the phone but can't pick it up. "Hello?" she says. "Hello? Are you there, ma'am?"

I feel faint with panic. What have I done? Surely my number's been recorded. I'm not meant to be here! I should be home, asleep. Or getting ready for school. I'll have to admit to being at Dana's. And I ran that stop sign.

I unlatch my seat belt. My cell phone slips to the floor. How much dumber could I get? I just dumped a man's body yet felt compelled to call 911. My breaths start skipping. I can't believe I did that! Yet how could I not? Anyone decent would get help. Someone's lying there, injured.

I nip my bottom lip, teeth sharp and reproachful. What's done is done. It's time to move. I can't just sit here.

I jam the car into reverse and back closer to the curb. I cut the engine. The car fills with silence. I reach for my phone and bring it back to my ear. "Hello? I'm here."

"The ambulance isn't far," says the operator. "Is the victim breathing?"

"I'm going to check."

I twist to see Ruby, still staring blankly out the window. Apart from the rain, all is quiet. What if I'm wrong and it's not human? It could be a deer. Or nothing at all. After tonight, that feels possible. I might have imagined it all.

I yank my hair hard, to rouse myself. An ambulance is coming. And the police. I need to check, *now*. That person—if it is a person— needs help.

"I'll be right back," I tell Ruby. I stagger out of the car.

The rain's icy. It flickers orange under the streetlamps. Beneath my feet, the asphalt glistens. I cross the intersection. With each step, the truth lies closer. That dark shape's no animal. No figment of my crazed imagination.

Some feet away, I stop, a fist clenched tight to my mouth. Oh my God. She's tiny. A child of ten or eleven. Someone's baby.

Wobbling closer, I see I'm wrong. Relief wells in me, then sloshes. I sway. It's not a child but a woman. She's unusually small and looks Asian. She lies on her back, arms flung wide: the *Y* in YMCA.

"Hello?" I sound pathetic. Do I really expect an answer?

Above a dark coat, her face is slack. Her eyes are shut. She looks peaceful, like she's sleeping.

She's not.

As I bend toward her, a little dog starts yapping.

I spin to see a Yorkie lunging at me. Its tiny teeth flash white. A leash drags behind it.

My heart twists at the sight: small and fierce, trying to protect its fallen master. "Shhhh, boy," I say, and crouch beside the woman. The

Yorkie darts back and forth, yapping. Its dark eyes bulge. It's clearly terrified. I've always loved dogs and wish we could have one. "Good boy," I murmur. "Yeah. There's a good dog."

I touch the woman's arm and shake it gingerly. Her chest rises and falls, but she doesn't react. As I reach for her wrist, some light I was blocking finds her head. Her dark hair's spread out.

I slap a hand to my mouth. That's not hair. There's a dark halo of blood on the asphalt. Blood. Just like Stanley's, pooling on the white marble.

The puddle's expanding. It shines black under the streetlight. The dog's stepped in it. Oh Jesus. It's leaving tiny paw prints.

The operator's voice squawks in my pocket. I ignore it and squeeze the woman's small hand. She moans. I wonder if she can hear me.

"Help's coming," I tell her. Guilt and horror shake my voice. Did she see me run that stop sign? What will she tell the police if she wakes up? "Don't worry," I say, as much to myself as to her. "It will be okay."

As the sirens draw closer, the dog growls at me. It's like it knows I'm complicit. Is my guilt that obvious?

"Mommy?"

I look up. Ruby's managed to roll down the window. She's trying to open the door.

"Stay there!" I shriek. My voice is shriller than it should be. Ruby freezes. "Just . . . please. Sit tight, hon." I've scared Ruby.

I must get a grip. I can't admit to any of this. Yes, I missed that stop sign, but I was driving well below the speed limit. This wouldn't have happened if that prick hadn't been speeding down the hill. And he drove off, when I didn't. This wasn't my fault. I got sucked in, like at Dana's.

The dog yaps at me.

"Stop it!" I cry. "Stop!"

It backs away with a snarl.

Turning, I can see blue and red lights. I stand and wave my arms. The police. And an ambulance right behind. "Here!" I call. "Help! Help! Over here!"

I'll admit to nothing. Deny, deny. But my legs feel weak. I'm shit scared they'll see right through my lies.

CHAPTER 7

Dana

My head bows, and my knees quiver. I can't do this.

I'm at the sink, washing blueberries, the latest superfood. The kids are at the kitchen table, in their school uniforms, eating granola—the healthy kind, without too much trans fat or sugar.

The only way to get away with this is to act normally. Walk and talk, smile. Turn on the tap. Pick out the bad berries.

A clatter makes me turn. Zoe's spilled her almond milk. A pool of white spreads across the glass table.

"Zoe!" snarls Chad.

My daughter's round face collapses. "It was an accident!" she wails.

I grab a cloth and move their way. "Chad," I warn him. He curls his lip and lifts his glass so I can wipe under it. His gaze remains glued to his phone.

I return to the sink and rinse out the cloth. That done, I stand, swaying. What was I doing? Right. Blueberries. Antiaging. Packed with antioxidants. I retrieve the colander. A few berries bounce out when I transfer them to a bowl. I don't retrieve them. Thank God Gloria will be in later to clean up.

I set the blueberries on the table and sit down. I should eat something.

My swollen eye pulses. I touch it gingerly.

Since I couldn't hide my injuries, I told the kids I ran into my closet door in the dark. I laughed about it, said it looked worse than it felt when the opposite's true: it hurts more than it should. Everything hurts.

Zoe believed me. At five, she's easy to fool. But the twins? Doubtful, despite their lack of reaction. Owen's not a morning person. He never talks before 8:00 a.m. This morning he looks especially morose, slumped over his bowl, chin in hand. And Chad? Well, Chad's the star of his own show, too intent on some text drama to spare much thought for his mom.

Only Zoe seems glad I'm here. Clad in gray tights, her short legs swing beneath her Starck chair. "Annie got a new bike," she informs me. "It's pink. With a white seat. And a bell."

"Oh yeah?" I manage. I pick out a blueberry and eat it. It's sour and dry, hard to swallow.

"Her new helmet's purple." When I fail to respond: "Sparkly purple."

"Mmmmm, purple."

"Do you like purple, Mommy?"

"Me? Ah, yeah, sure."

"As much as pink?" she asks.

"Um." I force down another blueberry. I've forgotten her question. "Yes," I venture.

"Why?"

"Er." I'm screwed.

At this age, all conversations with Zoe involve whys. Normally, I try to answer. Conversations with small kids can be curiously philosophical. Each *why* leads to another. Why must I go to bed now? Why does the time on the clock matter? Why can't we choose a new time, to start now?

This morning I can't think. One terrible question fills my head: How did last night happen?

I stand up. I can't eat. I check the clock. Time to get moving. Return the yogurt to the fridge. Put Zoe's lunchbox in her *Frozen* backpack. Remind Chad to pack his water bottle. Ask Owen if he's got chess club. Pour a bowl of kibble for our fat orange cat, Toonces. Find Stan's raincoat and hide it in my pink Marni tote bag.

After dropping off the kids, I'll toss his coat by the sea cliffs in Norman Gaynor Park. The area's popular with dog walkers, bird watchers, and suicides. A red herring. Part of Jo's plan.

Behind me, Zoe's still chattering. I zip up my bag. Toonces crunches his cat chow.

"It's getting late," I say tiredly. "Eat up, Zoe."

She sounds cross. "Owen's not eating."

I turn and sigh. "Please Zoe. Just eat. And you too, Owen."

From beneath his long bangs, my son glares at the cereal. "I don't want it."

I stay quiet, unsure how best to respond. Owen always eats this brand. He's a creature of habit: same cereal, same bowl and spoon. It was worse when he was small. Even tiny changes—new branding on the milk carton—could send him ballistic.

Owen pushes back his bowl. "I don't feel well."

I hesitate. Should I keep him home today? No, routine's better.

"I'm not hungry either," pipes up Zoe. "Why can't we get Lucky Charms? Annie gets those." Her voice is dangerously whiny, as if tears are looming.

Owen rouses himself and leans closer to his sister. His tone's confiding, like he's letting her in on a big secret. "Did you know that Lucky Charms are colored with unicorn poop?"

Zoe makes a face. "Unicorns aren't real!"

"Are too," says Owen. "And they poop sweet rainbow-colored goo." His voice drops further. "But it's really sad. They're kept in these giant factory farms and hooked up to machines that milk their magic poo!"

Zoe looks doubtful until Owen winks. She giggles.

I'm grateful to Owen and surprised he's so chatty.

I check my watch. "Go brush your teeth, everyone."

Zoe's eyes widen. "But . . ." She picks up her spoon. "I'm not done with my breakfast."

Even Owen manages a few more mouthfuls before dumping what's left in his bowl into the garbage disposal. He shuffles off to the bathroom.

Ten minutes later, I manage to herd the kids toward the Range

Rover. Toonces follows us outside and vanishes—a flash of orange in the cedar hedge.

I pull out of the garage and steer slowly down the long drive. Despite my dark glasses, the sky's cruelly bright.

Chad is moaning about slow Wi-Fi. Zoe's complaining she's too big for her booster seat. Nobody has asked about Dad.

I'm relieved, and sad. If I vanished, when would they notice?

After exiting the huge gates, I stop and squint both ways. The road's empty but for one parked car: Ralph Isles's new Porsche. It's unmistakable, some fancy model that was specially ordered. In the weak sun it looks extra tacky: bright midlife-crisis red, the only one of its kind in Glebes Bay.

I blink. Why is it here, across the street, a bit to the right of my driveway?

"Mom?" It's Chad, riding shotgun. He sounds impatient. "What are you waiting for? The road's clear."

Just then, I see Ralph Isles jogging our way, feet flashing in white sneakers. Even dressed in shorts and a sweatshirt, he looks dapper, a trim man with a neat beard and short-clipped gray hair. A silver fox. I've never liked him.

I turn left and pull up in front of Ralph. I lower Chad's window and call out. "Hey, Ralph."

An MD, Ralph Isles is Stan's business partner in a health care investment fund. He's listening to music and must not hear. I try again, louder.

Ralph's eyes hit mine. He looks startled and displeased, obliged to stop but obviously keen to jog on. Decorum pulls him closer. I am Stan's wife, after all.

He pops out his earbuds and leans down to Chad's window. "Morning." Seeing my bruises, he frowns. "Oh dear. Dana, what happened?"

"Hi Ralph. I . . . ah . . . I had an accident. I'm fine. Really. You?" I sound disjointed. I hadn't planned what to say. I just need to know why his car is parked out front of my house this morning.

"I'm fine," says Ralph. He looks away, toward his car. "I stopped by last night to see Stan but realized he was, ah . . ." He pauses. "Busy."

I cringe, icy ants up my spine. Ralph knows the gate code, as do all Stan's buddies. He must have come by during our fight, in which case he heard us screaming.

"I decided another time would be better," continues Ralph. "But realized I'd left my car key at home." He shakes his head, like it's funny but not. "You know, it's that kind you push to start? I started the car, stuck the key in my jacket, went back inside, and left my jacket in the front hall."

Some response is expected. "Oh, right," I manage.

"I walked home, figured I'd jog over this morning. No big deal." This is emphasized by a fake smile.

I nod. Ralph lives only a few blocks away, in a fussy Queen Anne, also in the Oaks.

He looks toward Winderlea. "Is Stan around?"

I take a deep breath, shake my head. "Ah, no." I want to say more. I should admit to the fight, explain that Stan stormed off. Yet I don't want to say this in front of the children.

"Ralph?" I let go of the wheel. "Can we have a word, please? In private?"

In the midst of his neat, silver beard, Ralph's mouth purses. "Ah, sure," he says, clearly reluctant to get embroiled in our domestic drama. He checks his watch pointedly and jogs on the spot.

I undo my seat belt and open my door.

Chad, who's been intent on his phone, looks up, aghast. "I'll be late, Mom!"

"No you won't," I say. "Just give me two minutes."

Zoe's in the back, watching *Peppa Pig*. Massive headphones are clamped over Owen's ears. Despite the thumping bass, I'm sure he's tracked my every word. He always does when I'd rather he didn't hear.

I check for traffic and climb out of my car. Ralph joins me on the curb. We walk a few slow steps in tandem, heading toward his Porsche.

I stop. He frowns at me. "What's happened, Dana?"

I don't know Ralph well. Nor do I trust him. He's got pale lizard eyes. He's unmarried but has a son from a brief, long-ago union. This boy's also at Stanton House, a year ahead of the twins.

Ralph looks anxious, thin lips pressed together. Is he repulsed by my injuries? My held-back hysteria?

He's the most fastidious man I know, his nails manicured, his man bag packed like a bento box. I suspect he views women as disorderly.

"I can't find Stan," I say. "We argued last night. He left. He hasn't come home."

Ralph's frown deepens. He leans away from me and my messy theatrics. "Oh dear. What time was this?"

I shake my head. "I don't know. Late. Past eleven." I want to ask when he stopped by but can't get the words out. The police will interview Ralph, ask him about my demeanor. Everything I say and do matters.

He looks toward my house. "I've been trying to reach him."

"Why?"

He waves a hand. "Oh. Business matters." His tight voice and stiff hand flick leave me convinced: there's trouble.

Perhaps Stan's fortune is disintegrating, all that theoretical money—stocks and bonds, numbers on a screen—popping like soap bubbles. Normally I'd want to learn more. Now I don't care.

I lick my scabbed lip. "If he calls back, can you let me know? I guess he needs space, but I'm getting worried."

Ralph nods. The man's perpetually tanned, his skin usually so flawless he could be wearing foundation. Yet today he looks pale and drawn.

He's still jogging in place, but it seems halfhearted. "I will," he says. "And please tell him to call me when he gets in touch."

"Of course." I head back to my car.

The second I'm in my seat, Zoe asks the dreaded question: "Mommy, where's Daddy?"

I reach for my seat belt, buying time. "He went out early."

Her eyes, brown like Stan's, meet mine in the rearview mirror. "Where to?"

I say the first thing that pops into my head: "Um, jogging." This is pathetic. Even Zoe looks skeptical. Stan goes to the gym but doesn't jog.

My insides curdle. I must do better with the cops.

While the twins don't react, I feel them listening, feel the tension in the car. Owen's music thuds from his earphones. Chad's jabbing violently at his phone.

Before pulling away from the curb, I check my side-view mirror just in time to see Ralph Isles fold into his ludicrous car. When did he stop by last night? How much did he see and hear? Despite my glasses, I squint. My bashed eye throbs.

"Mommy?" It's Zoe again.

"Yes, hon?" I pull away, feeling shaky.

"Annie Welland's parents are divorced. That's why she got a new bike, from her daddy. She already had one from her mom. But the new one's better." All of this is said matter-of-factly.

I try to answer but can't. I know Annie Welland's parents from the PTA. They're embroiled in a bitter divorce, poor Annie a pawn in a hideous battle of "he said/she said."

I want to cry. Would things have gotten that ugly between me and Stan? Maybe. Probably. He seemed determined to divorce me, convinced I was ruining our offspring, who needed what he called "tough love." Stan wasn't one to shy away from a fight. And I'd have fought tooth and nail to keep my children.

A breath rattles out of me. Poor Annie Welland. At least Zoe will be spared that.

CHAPTER 8

Jo

The interview room feels like a sketchy elevator: small and bright, with a cable that's ready to snap. Across from me sit two detectives, an older guy named Farley and a young one named Morton. They're both pale, haggard, and look sleep-deprived. I imagine they live here at the police station, surviving on mistrust and bad coffee.

Morton's pallor is broken by freckles. He's got shockingly bright red hair. The other guy, Farley, must be near retirement. He's hunched and overweight. He reminds me of a toad. A freakishly smart one.

My left foot starts to jiggle. Why the fuck did I call 911? These policemen—no, all policemen—scare me. I hate their sharp gazes, their unconcealed suspicion. They hold all the power, while all I have are my wits, which are dull from being up all night doing unthinkable things.

If I say the wrong thing, I could lose everything. My liberty. My reputation. But most of all, Ruby. The extent of the risk I've taken is sinking in. I've got the shakes. I've had no sleep, no breakfast, and far too much coffee.

A paper cup sits in front of me, half-full, calling out. I reach for it but stop. Too much caffeine might make me blab. I can't have more, no matter how tempting.

When the attending officers let me leave the accident scene, I raced home to feed and dress Ruby, then dropped her at school.

I had to call Stanton House to say I wouldn't be coming to work today. While helping the police is my civic duty, the sour-voiced school secretary implied I was playing hooky. Cow. It's not like I chose to be here.

To stop myself from grabbing the coffee cup, I sit on my hands.

"Would you like a fresh cup?" asks Detective Morton.

"No, thank you." Damn. He noticed that weakness. I press my thighs together to stop my foot tapping.

Despite a quick shower, I'm scared I smell of bleach and fear. I'm sure my eyes are bloodshot. And I wore this coat last night. It looks clean to the eye, but what if they test it for bloodstains? I'm hot but keep it on. The silence stretches. I can't stop staring at the damn coffee.

Both detectives wait. I know it's a ploy to increase the tension. The younger one, Morton, crosses his skinny legs. "Ms. Dykstra, let's take it from the top," he says. "Tell me exactly what you saw."

I swallow. We've been through this before. And before that. I know they're hoping for inconsistencies, trying to trip me up. They'll compare this statement to the one I made at the scene. I know they suspect me.

I take a deep breath. "I was stopped on Marlowe." I don't like how my voice has gone phlegmy. "A car was coming down Elm, fast. As it turned left, it swerved and hit that poor woman."

Morton nods. "The victim, where was she in relation to you?"

"Behind me," I say. "He hit her when he was making the turn."

Morton's pale eyelids flutter. He's got blue eyes like a white rabbit's. His eyelashes are as red as his hair. "This speeding car, what color was it?"

I grab my bangs and pull. He's asked this before. And the uniforms asked too. "I . . . I'm sorry," I say. Should I make something up? "I don't recall."

Morton winces. "Two doors or four?"

I wince.

"Old or new?" He sounds increasingly desperate. "Hatchback or sedan?"

I rack my brain. Nothing. "I'm sorry," I say, again. "I'm not a car person."

The old guy, Farley, is tapping his pen as if he'd like to stab me with it.

I could invent a car, just to appease him. But that would be wrong. "I was looking at the driver," I say. "Not the car. It was a young guy. With fair, longish hair."

Farley leans in. "Mrs. Dykstra?" No Ms. for him. In their saggy beds, his eyes are suspicious. "You live in Finley Cove?"

I nod cautiously, thrown by this change in topic. I live in a basement suite in Finley Cove, a nice, middle-class neighborhood that borders the Oaks. It's nowhere near as fancy but still pleasant, with some decent playgrounds and parks.

Dana grew up there. Her dad was an obstetrician, not rich enough for the Oaks but highly respectable. He delivered half the kids in our school. I chose Finley Cove for its good public school, for Ruby. It's where I went as a kid, back when children deemed "gifted" were sent out of their "disadvantaged" school districts.

I realize Farley's still waiting for me to answer. I'm so tired I'm wilting. "Yes," I say. "I live on Ross Street."

Farley shifts. His toad eyes glitter: "Why were you in the Oaks, early this morning?"

I hold his gaze. Dana and I talked about this. We knew I'd likely be seen going to or from her place. Maybe caught on CCTV. We planned my answer. Nonetheless, my chest tightens. I figured I'd have more time to get myself together. I'm not ready for showtime.

"My best friend lives there. She had a fight with her husband. She called me late last night, very upset. I went over to calm her down." All of this is true, yet it feels like a lie. My voice has thinned. I've started sweating.

Silence follows. I resist the urge to fill it. What if they dig up that bad business in Chicago? I give them Dana's name and address.

When the interview finally ends, they summon an artist to sketch a likeness based on my memories of the hit-and-run driver. She's an older woman in Birkenstocks and a nubbly red cardigan. She looks kind. I imagine she gardens and writes letters to Amnesty International.

She smiles as she sits: "You alright, dear?"

I nod. This small sympathy makes me want to cry.

Despite our best efforts, the results are laughable: James Dean with a perm and dentures. Even the artist looks skeptical. "You sure about that chin, dear?"

I shut my eyes and try to recall the young man in the car. I got a good look at him but no longer feel sure of anything. This police sketch is the sort of image that gets mocked on Twitter. All he needs are gag glasses and a fake mustache.

Finally, close to noon, Morton returns to say I'm free to go. Both detectives walk me to my car. Farley's got a slight limp. We walk slowly through the rain. I can't believe how good the air smells after the stuffy police station.

As we near my Toyota, I see the detectives eyeing it for damage. I bet it's already been swabbed. My head throbs. My car's in dire shape, full of dings and scuffs. And that rust . . . It does look a bit like blood. What if they impound it? How will I get to work without my car?

We all stop by the driver's side. "Thanks for coming in," says Morton. He extends a freckled hand. As we shake, I worry he'll notice my blistered palms.

Farley grimaces. Instead of a handshake, he gives me a tight nod. "We'll be in touch," he says darkly.

I nod. Is that a threat, or am I just overtired and paranoid? I want to protest my innocence, but that makes people sound guiltier. And the truth is I'm not innocent. Not at all. Last night I became an accomplice to . . . What? Manslaughter? Illegal disposal of a corpse? A felony for sure. Plus, I ran that stop sign. I can barely get the key in the lock. Good God. What a mess.

I fall shakily into my seat.

Before I can close the door, Detective Morton leans in. "Drive safely."

Farley nods knowingly, as though he's sure I'm a dangerous driver.

"Thanks," I say, then blurt out. "Um. What happened to her Yorkie?"

Farley's wrinkled forehead furrows. "Pardon?" He scratches his jaw. "The lady had a little dog."

"Ah. Don't worry," says Farley. His grin's wolfish. "The dog's fine. It's with its owner. The victim was her nanny, who typically walked it."

It's only as I'm driving away that I realize: Jesus. What must those detectives think of me? I didn't ask about that poor woman but about the *dog*.

CHAPTER 9

Jo

The hit-and-run is bound to be the top story until the press learns that Stan's missing. I check my watch: 8:03 p.m. I hope I haven't missed it.

I crouch before my boxy TV and click it on. The picture flickers. I only just got Ruby into bed and keep the sound low.

If this set ever had a remote, it doesn't now. It only gets a few channels. I don't usually watch it but want the local news. I dare not search anything on my laptop.

On screen, a female reporter in a red blazer is standing out in front of the local hospital. I turn the sound up slightly: "I'm here outside Glebes Bay General, where hit-and-run accident victim Alma Reyes is fighting for survival." She sweeps a hand behind her. The camera pans to some parked ambulances. A man in scrubs walks by.

I sit on the sagging plaid sofa. Everything in this apartment is at least three decades old. It all looks salvaged from Goodwill.

The reporter explains about the accident in the Oaks. While her mouth's solemn, her eyes shine. For her, this counts as *news*. "Alma Reyes's condition remains critical," she says, "with doctors unsure whether she'll regain consciousness or have lasting brain damage."

For a second, I'm relieved; if she's unconscious, she can't tell the cops I failed to stop. Except . . . What am I hoping for? That she'll *die*? I feel even guiltier.

The screen flashes to a picture of Alma, a plain, fortyish woman whose neat hair is center-parted. It looks like a passport photo. A male voice explains: "Filipino citizen and mother of three, Alma Reyes was working in Glebes Bay as a nanny. She was struck in the Oaks while taking her employer's dog for an early morning walk."

I shake my head, appalled. That guy left a mother of three lying in the street like trash! At least I stopped—even if it was a tiny bit my fault. Or would he have hit her anyway? He was driving too fast. Drunk probably. Maybe joyriding in a stolen car.

I shut my eyes and recall the brave little dog.

"The police have set up a tip line," says the news anchor. "They're pursuing several leads."

Shit. Several. That pops my eyes open. Am I one of them? What if someone else saw me run that stop sign? I rub under my glasses and pinch the bridge of my nose.

"Mommy?"

I look around, aghast. Ruby's in the doorway. She's got a limp toy bunny in hand.

I jump up and switch off the TV. Faced with Ruby, I feel guiltier about everything. That woman, Alma Reyes, was likely her poor family's main breadwinner. Is she a single mother? What will become of her children? "Baby, why aren't you in bed?"

Ruby scowls. "I'm not tired."

I sway toward her. "Well, I am." How long have I been awake? At least thirty-six hours. "Let's go." I usher her down the narrow hall. I may as well sleep in her bed.

I'm drifting off when Ruby says, "Mommy?" Her breath's warm on my cheek.

I try not to sigh. "Yes, Ruby?"

"That lady on TV, was she the one from this morning?"

My muscles tense. How long was Ruby standing there, listening in? I'm worried that accident scene was traumatic. I had to take Ruby out of the car when the uniforms quizzed me but tried to distract her from the paramedics working on Alma.

"Yes," I say. "But she'll be okay. She's in the hospital. With good doctors." I rub my sore eyes. "It's time to sleep, hon. I'm beat."

"Why? Couldn't you sleep at Auntie Dana's?"

"Not so well." I roll over. What does Ruby remember about last night? "How about you?"

"Toonces was meowing," she says. "I went to pet him."

"Oh," I say. Ruby loves Zoe's ginger cat. We're not allowed pets in our rental. I moisten my lips. "Where did you pet him?"

"The kitchen," says Ruby. "He was hungry."

My head throbs. Could she really have gone to the kitchen last night? If so, when? I'm scared to think what she might have seen. Or is this a memory from some other visit? I certainly hope so. She often feeds Toonces.

"Then what?" I say. I try to keep my voice soft and easy. I mustn't make last night seem important.

I can hear the smile in her voice. "Toonces slept on my feet. He was heavy!"

I smile too. The cat was not in the den when I woke Ruby this morning. That means she's recalling some other night. Relief leaves me weak. She slept through it all. "That's nice," I say. "Now it's time to sleep, Rubes."

I wait for her to talk back, only to realize her body has loosened. She's drifted off. I can sleep.

The single bed is cramped. I shut my eyes and wait. Despite my fatigue, my brain's buzzing. Has Dana reported Stan missing? If she cracks, I'll go to jail. What would happen to Ruby? How could I put her at such risk?

I inhale her sweet scent. She can't go to Trevor. He'd neglect her, probably dump her with his alcoholic, chain-smoking mother. Her taste in men is even worse than mine. Who knows what could happen to Ruby?

I gaze, dry-eyed, at the dark ceiling. While I can't see it, I can feel it, low and oppressive. The room's cold but airless. The bed's hard and lumpy.

I think of Alma Reyes in the ICU and the callous young man who hit her. I recall his sneering face. The fury in his eyes. My breath catches.

I've been so busy worrying about the cops tying me to Stan that I've failed to grasp this other danger. If I could see the hit-and-run driver, could he see me? He almost killed that poor woman. He knows I'm partly to blame. Could he track me down and make sure I couldn't ID him in the future? Maybe he'd try to pin the accident on me.

All of a sudden, I'm too hot. I push down the quilt. Beside me, Ruby grumbles. I hold my breath until she settles.

Outside, a car door slams. I twitch, startled. I've gone beyond tiredness to feeling so wired I could snap. I start to cry with frustration. This is all wrong. I should never have returned to Glebes Bay.

When I left town after high school, I swore I'd never return. This place is full of bad memories. I rub my eyes, see myself at nine years old.

I took my key out of my schoolbag and unlocked the front door. Stepping into our trailer, something felt wrong. I stopped and listened. Someone was crying.

I peered into the small living room, saw Mom huddled on the couch. She was never home at this time. Never sitting idle. And why was she crying?

"Mom?" I said.

In her hands, she was twisting a white hankie. "Sit down," she said. "It's Dad. He had a stroke. He didn't make it."

I didn't talk for three days. I couldn't eat either.

I massage my sore forehead. Heartbreak has a taste. There's still a trace of it in the back of my throat. All those years spent missing my father. Adults repeat the patterns they learn in childhood. No wonder I fell for Trev, a man who always had one cowboy boot out the damn door.

Ruby's snoring beside me. I pray her childhood is nothing like mine.

In the street, another car door slams. Are those footsteps? It's probably just the neighbors. But that rattle. Was that my front door? The sounds seem close. Magnified. Something thumps overhead. Adrenaline whips through me. I want to scream. I should've known it was unlucky to come back.

I flip over and try to unlock my muscles. It's not my fault. What choice did I have? Alone and broke. A single mom. My career in tatters. At least here I had Dana.

Staring into the noisy dark, the irony of my situation settles. Before moving back, I made two lists: Glebes Bay's pros on one side, its cons on the other. Dana, a job at Stanton House, and low crime were the town's only pluses. Yet here I am, scared shitless—and a criminal, thanks to Dana.

CHAPTER 10

Dana

The buzzer for the gate sounds, and the intercom crackles. It's the police.

I press a button to admit them.

I sit in the den, hands on knees, steeling myself. Any minute now the doorbell will ring. I'll rise and open the door, introduce myself. First impressions are everything. I must nail it.

My hand shakes as I reach for my wineglass. Just a sip to relax me.

The bell clangs, deep and doleful. I rise and smooth down my ice-blue cashmere sweater.

Zoe and the twins are upstairs in their rooms. I waited until Gloria had left before calling to report Stan missing.

At the door, I pause to take a deep breath. I check my watch: a simple Cartier Tank in white gold, a gift from Stan. It's 8:44 p.m. That makes it fourteen minutes from my call to the police's arrival. Not bad.

Jo warned me my call might be recorded. I think I struck the right chord. The officer I spoke with—a man—seemed to take me seriously, especially when I mentioned our address. If we were poor or Black, I might still be waiting.

I hide the watch under my sleeve and tug the door open.

A man and a woman stand waiting. He's tall and thin with short dark hair, mid to late thirties. The woman's older, closer to fifty. She's short but looks strong. Her hair's gray and chin-length. They both clock my injuries, unsmiling.

I freeze, aware of how bad I look. Thanks to the booze and the Tylenol, I'd momentarily forgotten.

I touch my bruised face. "Ah, come in," I say. Their probing gaze is unsettling. I've never dealt with the police, never had to. I'm not sure how to treat them—like guests or tradesmen? My eyes are watering. "I'm Stan's wife, Dana McFarlane."

They eye the entrance hall—designed by Jean-Louis Deniot—as if it were hiding a meth lab.

The woman extends a hand first. I shake it. Beneath heavy lids, her eyes are shrewd. "Detective Judith Shergold," she says.

The man's grip is softer. "I'm Detective Brian Bellows."

I offer them drinks, which they decline, and lead them into the den. It's a big room but smaller than the living room, which can feel overwhelming. Plus, I can't bear to look at the ocean.

"Please sit." I motion them toward a sofa.

They perch side by side. Shergold is where I sat last night when I told Jo about the violence. I take a seat on the other sofa.

The man, Bellows, delivers the prompt: "You called to report your husband missing?"

"Yes." I nod. "Last night. We had a fight. He left . . . He hasn't called. It's not like him."

Detective Shergold's face is blank. Her voice is neutral too. "A physical fight?"

I swallow. "Yes. He . . . he struck me."

"With what?"

"His hand."

Bellows frowns and sits straighter. "Is there a history of domestic violence?"

I shake my head, hard. "No! Nothing like that. I . . ." I twist at my ring, feel the diamonds' sharp corners. "He'd been drinking . . . And went a bit crazy. It's . . . He's not like that. He felt terrible, obviously. I mean, remorseful." My throat's gluey. I didn't want to admit that this was a pattern. My fear of looking pathetic is truly pathetic.

The woman, Shergold, sounds brisk: "When did you last see him?"

"It was late. Maybe midnight?" I force my fingers away from my ring. "I figured he'd gone someplace to cool off. Out for a walk maybe. And then this morning, I thought . . . We have an apartment in Seattle. Maybe he took a taxi. But I called the concierge and checked. He's not there. And he's not answering his phone." I bite my lip and wince. Shit. I've cracked the scab open. When I lick it, it tastes bloody.

"He left on foot?" asks Detective Bellows.

"Yes. His car, cars, are all here." That does seem suspicious. I clear my throat, offer an excuse: "Like I said, he'd been drinking."

Detective Bellows asks most of the questions—about Stan's job and habits. "Was he under stress lately?"

What's the right answer? "I don't know. Maybe. We don't discuss work much."

"Why did you argue?" This is from Detective Shergold. Her face is plain, with no makeup. What you see is what you get, although I doubt that. She's the one to watch out for.

I look at my lap. Should I tell them about Stan's affair? They're going to notice his credit card charges. I did.

They both wait. The house is quiet.

I rouse myself. I must focus. "Stan's been talking about divorce," I say softly. "I think he's having an affair. But we . . . we'll work it out, go to counseling. We've been together for sixteen years." My chest's tight. "We have three children."

Shergold's face doesn't change. "Who's his affair with?"

"I don't know. That's what our fight was about. I asked, and he denied it. He got angry." I take a deep breath. "We were both upset."

"I see," says Detective Shergold. One eyebrow lifts. "Did you also get violent?"

"No!" It comes out louder than I intended, although that might not be bad. I sound shocked at the concept. I shake my head. "Of course not."

"Well . . ." Detective Shergold eyes the portrait of Stan snowboarding. "He'll probably reappear."

"Yes." I nod, like I'm eager to believe this. "I just . . . It's not like him not to answer his phone. It's going straight to voicemail. I thought I should call you, just in case."

"You did the right thing," says Detective Bellows. His voice is soothing.

At some signal I miss, they both rise. "Chances are good he'll return," says Bellows. "But we'll look into it. If anything changes, please call."

I rise too. "I will." I follow them back into the hall.

"While we're here," says Shergold, "could we get a recent photo of Stanley?"

This takes me aback. Perhaps they really are worried. Have they sensed my demeanor's off? Or they might be ticking boxes. Stan's rich enough to get kidnapped. Maybe that's what they're thinking.

"Just a moment," I say, and retreat to Stan's study.

I crack open the door. His smell is stronger in here—cigar smoke and that spicy aftershave he's started wearing. It stinks. Did his girlfriend buy it? I click on the light and head for the bookshelf.

There's a row of framed photos, but none are recent. No one prints photos anymore. I should just email one to the detectives.

I'm turning to go when I see a snapshot of Stan on his desk. It's unframed, a standard four-by-six print. He's on his yacht, leaning against the rail. From his hairline it's obviously recent. I pick it up. Something's weird.

Then I realize: it's his smile, too wide and eager. His blue eyes twinkle, and his cheeks are ruddy.

Tears sting my eyes. I dig my nails into my sore palms. I mustn't cry. This shouldn't matter. But it does. My last photo of Stan was taken by his lover. I can't know this, but I do. The proof's in his smile: once upon a time, his face lit up like that for me.

Without thinking, I rip the print in half, then into quarters. I tear these pieces still smaller and toss them on his desk—a shower of bitter confetti.

I'm shaking the last shreds off my sweaty palms when a noise makes me look up. It's Detective Shergold peering around the half-open door.

She smiles tightly. "Mrs. McFarlane?" Her eyes drop from my face to my hands to the photo scraps littering Stan's desk. A gray eyebrow rises. "Is everything alright?"

I can't move. I know I look guilty. And crazy. Crazy guilty.

I spin to grab a framed photo off Stan's shelf. It was taken two years ago. He's got a big shit-eating grin and is cradling a giant gold golfing trophy.

I come out from behind Stan's desk and hold out this photo. "This is the most recent one I found. It's, um . . ." I stop. Everything I say sounds like a lie.

I stand in front of his desk, trying to block her view of the shredded photo.

Detective Shergold takes the framed portrait. "Perfect. Thank you. This is extremely helpful."

I sag against Stan's desk and try not to cry.

CHAPTER 11

Jo: Two days since Stan died

I need to make sure Dana's sticking to the story. I doubt her phones are tapped yet, but you never know. By now the police must have realized there's no surveillance footage for the night Stan went missing. That must have stoked their suspicions. It's safer to talk in person.

I walk fast. School just got out. I'm meeting Dana at the Stanton House football field. Chad's got a JV game.

I scan the field and pick out Chad. Even in his helmet, pads, and uniform, he stands out. It's like he's taller, straighter, and runs more smoothly than the others.

Eyes drift to Chad. He's inherited his mom's magic, yet he lacks depth, all surface dazzle. Or was teenage Dana similar, and I was too starstruck to realize?

A gust of wind catches my scarf. It's a typical autumn day, cool and blustery. The tight-packed pines on the edge of the field jostle and thrash, much like the players. My phone beeps with a text. I check it as I walk. It's from Dana: *I'm here—in the bleachers.*

Peering up, I see her in the stands. She's sitting way off by herself, bent over her phone, dressed in a smart navy trench coat. Big black sunglasses hide most of her face. Even from here she looks thinner than she did two days back.

I reknot my scarf. Has it been only two days? First Stan, then Alma.

Shock upon shock. How my classes dragged today! I kept forgetting what I was saying. My students got snarky. Kids are like dogs—they know when you're off and take the opportunity to harass you.

Something's happened on the field. The opposing team's fans are cheering. Dana glances around, looking fearful.

I walk faster, spurred by cold and unease. If I'm feeling the stress, imagine Dana. She's never had to deal with anything bad, except Owen's issues.

That was hard, but she had the cash to hire an army of therapists. She quit her job as a lawyer to manage his care.

Maybe Dana's determination paid off. Or else his problems were minor. Over the years, I've seen kids diagnosed with all sorts of crap. Many of them struck me as fine; they were the kids with spark, who couldn't be shoved in a box. What's normal anyways? Pick any trait of human behavior. We're all on some spectrum.

By age six, Owen was deemed well enough to attend a normal school—if you define a ridiculously expensive private school like Stanton House as "normal."

At fifteen, he's like many kids I've taught: somewhat awkward, which can make him seem shifty. He has a habit of nodding to himself. He's not fond of eye contact.

Despite his tics, I prefer Owen to Chad. Owen's creative. He enjoys making hanging mobiles out of wire and stacking things to make them balance. He carves scary wooden masks like relics of a lost civilization. He's good with computers and lousy at English which is what I teach at Stanton House. Chad wouldn't know a joke if it poked him in his perfect face. Owen's slyly funny.

In the bleachers, Dana's movements are jerky as she rewraps her camel scarf. My unease grows. What if she's not up to this? I'm fucked if she crumbles.

I start to climb. She's way up. Soon my thighs are burning. My tote bag's handles dig into my shoulder.

I'm close when she looks up, startled. Seeing it's me, her face softens. "Oh, Jo," she says. I sit beside her. "It's been . . ." Words fail her.

I set down my bag. "Tell me." I want every detail. Cheers erupt on our side. I see that Chad's got the ball.

"They found Stan's coat this morning," says Dana. "Near the cliffs."

I nod grimly. I heard that on the midday news in the staff room.

"That's ramped things up," she continues. "Before they seemed to think he'd show up, but now . . . The police came back twice today."

I sigh. It was my idea to plant his coat by those cliffs, locally known as Jumpers Point. Was that a mistake? It's hard to know what to do.

"They had searchers out in the park," adds Dana. She sounds tearful. "And dogs."

"We should print flyers," I say. "I'll help you stick some up tomorrow." That's what a distraught wife would do. Plaster the town with her missing husband's visage, go on TV begging for answers.

Dana nods shakily. "Okay." She rubs her forehead like it's throbbing.

"What are the cops like?" I ask. Are they the same two who quizzed me about Alma Reyes?

"There are two detectives," says Dana. "A man and a woman. The guy's maybe thirty-five. The woman's in her fifties."

I'm surprised. I'd expected it to be my two: freckled Morton and the old guy, Farley. Obviously, that was silly. Glebes Bay would have more than two detectives. And those two must be busy trying to catch Alma's hit-and-run driver.

Have they put two and two together and realized Stan's wife is the friend I was helping? I rub my hands together. "What have they asked you?"

"About our fight," she says. "Why we argued. If he'd hit me before. The same questions, over and over."

Her busted lip has scabbed over. There's a spill of purple beneath her giant glasses. I wonder if she bought them specially, to cover her swollen eye. Or were they laying around, left over from some tropical vacation?

I grip my knees. "Is it time to stop talking and call in your lawyer?"

After law school, Dana practiced corporate law for three years. She quit when Owen began having problems. He got thrown out of preschool. By then, Stan had gone from rich to super rich. Dana didn't have to work ever again. Nor did Stanley, for that matter.

Dana started Fairytale Flowers when the twins were eight or nine. I dismissed it as a rich lady's hobby. A misjudgment on my part. Dana's that rare combination: an artist and businesswoman.

"You're a former lawyer," I say. "It wouldn't be unusual for you to stop talking. Especially if the cops keep rehashing the same shit and you're starting to feel like a suspect."

Dana sounds frustrated. "I *am* a suspect. The spouse is always a suspect! And we fought." She gazes out at the field. "But if Stan really was missing, I'd do everything to help find him. I wouldn't clam up and call my lawyer."

I nod. That makes sense. Except if she's too overwrought, she'll mess up. The police will be looking for contradictions.

"They want to question the kids," she says quietly. I look at the field and spy Chad—number 12—in the midst of a huddle.

"The twins?" It comes out sharper than intended.

Dana tilts back. She looks even more stricken. "Should I refuse?"

I hunch forward, elbows on knees, thinking. My hands start to go for my hair. I force them down, into a steeple.

I've been worrying that her kids saw or heard something. "Have you asked them?"

Despite the dark lenses, I see her eyes widen. "What?"

"Your face. The bruises. What did you tell them?"

She twists her ring, the one she wanted to toss, the one that would pay off my debts—and then some. Her head dips. "I . . . I lied, said I tripped."

"You should ask if they heard anything that night. If you didn't know where Stan was, you'd ask them."

She takes this in, nods. "Yeah. Oh, Jesus." She bites her lip, then winces. "I'm doing this all wrong."

"You're doing fine." I reach for her hand and squeeze it.

I watched the twins in class today, looking for signs. They seemed normal. Chad was his glib, chatty self. Owen only spoke when he had to.

"Dana," I say, "talk to the kids first. Then decide if they should speak to the cops. And if they do, they definitely need a lawyer present."

If the police did decide Stan's been murdered, Dana might not be the only person of interest. Antisocial Owen would be a dream suspect for a policeman lacking imagination. I don't say this. Dana's already stressed enough.

She nods and opens her purse, extracts a tissue. "I . . . Just. Okay." This last word's extra quiet.

"You're doing great," I say. "It's normal for you to be losing it. Your husband's missing. Being distraught is a good thing. It's the ice queens who get persecuted, the women who don't cry and don't look broken enough. Remember Lindy Chamberlain?" Dana looks blank. "That Australian lady whose baby got stolen by a dingo? It got made into a movie?" She shudders. "Anyway, it'll be okay. Just stick to the story."

"Hello, ladies!"

I turn, aghast. We were so intent on each other we didn't notice her approach. Angie Costin shimmies toward us, all big hair and lip gloss. Did she overhear anything?

The bracelets on her waving wrist jangle. Her hair, distressed by too much bleach, flaps like it's trying to surrender.

Angie grins. "Mind if I join you?"

Dana grits her teeth into a smile. I don't bother.

We went to school with Angie, née Zukovitch, back when she was a chubby brunette with crooked teeth and a talent for digging up gossip. Only one of these qualities remains, which explains her presence here, hoping to mine shiny nuggets. *Oh, poor, poor Dana. I didn't dare ask about her face . . . Can you imagine?* I can hear her put-on pity in my head.

Angie slides onto the bleacher beside me but is careful to leave a good distance.

"How are you?" she says. The question is directed at Dana. I'm persona non grata.

"Um, okay," says Dana.

"Oh, you poor thing," trills Angie, her muddy green eyes fixed on Dana's. "Has there been any news?"

"They found his jacket in Norman Gaynor Park."

From Angie's lack of excitement, it's clear she already knew. She pouts, an affectation that probably looked cute when she first met Walt, her car-dealer husband, but these days it only emphasizes the grooves around her mouth, brought on by decades of menthol cigarettes and fake tanning. "Why would he go there?" she asks.

Dana shrugs.

"Is Gemma cheering today?" I ask, to change the subject. It's either that or tell Angie to fuck off, which I can't afford to do. Thanks to Walt's business acumen, she's a Stanton House parent. I'm a lowly teacher, the hired help. One step up from the janitor, Mr. Gomez.

"No. Wrist strain." Her words are spoken tightly to signal her displeasure that I exist and are directed at Dana to show I'm unworthy of an answer.

Angie's daughter, Gemma, is a cheerleader and the kid I like least in the whole damn school. She's a smarter, meaner, prettier version of Angie, all of which makes her more dangerous. She's also dating Dana's golden boy, Chad.

Gemma's obviously a rotten influence, talking Chad into slipping her answers. I turned them both in for cheating, more reason for Angie to hate me. Welcome to Glebes Bay, where six degrees of separation is shrunk to a big fat zero. We've all known each other since middle school, back when Angie was convinced she was Dana's bestie.

Angie leans in, her news trumping her dislike of me. She's so close I can smell her breath: fake mint over a sour base of coffee, guilty cigarettes, and venom. "The police interviewed Ryan Reeve," she says. "Down at the station."

Dana blanches beneath her film-star shades. There's excitement on the field, but we all ignore it.

"Who's Ryan Reeve?" I ask quickly, both to find out and to pull Angie's attention away from Dana.

Dana swallows hard. "He lives next door. On the left."

I picture the house—or rather its impressive fence. The house is set way back from the street, near the water. Did this Ryan see or hear something? I feel cold all over.

"I . . . I . . ." Dana sounds like she's choking. I want to pat her on the back but stay frozen. "I guess that's good," she says, finally. "Maybe Ryan saw which way Stanley went." She's hiding her shock well, maybe better than I am. "Do you know Ryan well?" she asks Angie.

"Nah," says Angie. "Not really. I know his parents, Mindy and Greg, through Walt. They buy their cars from us." Maybe it's the thought of Walt that makes her lips tighten. Or maybe she's annoyed to be giving out info while getting so little back. Fair trades aren't in the Costins' natures.

Angie sniffs. "For a while, Ryan was coaching Jordan in tennis."

Jordan is Angie's son, now in ninth grade. I dislike him marginally less than his sister. He's just as mean but less bright. I figure he'll do less damage.

"Ryan's fit, isn't he?" continues Angie. "Very sporty." This last part comes with a knowing smile.

While I miss the implication, it's obvious Dana doesn't. She looks frozen solid, her cheeks pale as ice. I make a mental note: Ryan Reeve, son of Mindy and Greg, Dana's rich neighbors.

I nudge Dana with my knee. Her head twitches, like she just woke up. Her mouth closes.

Turning, I see Angie watching her. The intensity of her gaze scares me. Angie Costin was never that smart, but she's got a nose for trouble. Shit. She's caught the scent of something.

Dana licks her lips. "I . . . Sorry," she says. "I have a bad headache. I didn't sleep. What were you saying?"

"The Reeves," says Angie smoothly. "Your neighbors. Ryan?" Her voice is a soft purr. "How well do you know them?"

"Ah, not well," says Dana. "We've met, of course. And I see them some-times, pulling out of their driveway and stuff. But you know how it is these days. Neighbors don't connect like they used to. And the lots are so big."

Angie nods. "We had to fire Ryan."

Again, Dana misses a beat. I jump in. "Why?"

Angie looks hesitant, like she'd rather not say. This is a well-practiced mannerism, one I remember from way back when. She blinks and straightens. Her voice is prim. "There was some trouble with Jordan."

"Trouble?" says Dana.

I'm trying to imagine Angie's idea of trouble. Maybe this Ryan guy just told Angie's brat to behave. Maybe he told him to stop being lazy.

"Drugs," mouths Angie. Her eyes jerk my way when she says this, as if because of my connection to the school I might somehow use this knowledge against her precious baby. Her nostrils flare with outrage. "He sold Jordie marijuana!"

A roar erupts. The announcer's voice whoops through the speakers. Our side scored a touchdown.

Dana leans back so abruptly it startles me and Angie. We all shift, like three birds on a wire, ready to flap but resettling. "That's awful!" says Dana. She looks ill. "Jordan's what, fourteen?"

"Fifteen in April."

I look at Dana. "We smoked pot at that age."

"It's just different when you're a mother," says Dana.

Despite myself, I laugh. "No shit," I say. "But we have to be realistic. Our kids are going to try drugs and get drunk. Not Ruby, obviously, at her age. But as teens? It's just . . . normal."

"Well," says Angie, still prim. She's got her hands clasped like a choir girl. Like I don't remember her plastered on Malibu with a glob of cum on her plaid top after giving Brent Dunkirk a blow job.

"I wasn't going to pay a dealer to meet with my son twice a week for tennis."

"Fair enough," I say.

Dana still looks oddly stricken. "Are you sure?" she asks Angie.

"Sure he was selling pot? Yes. I found it zipped into Jordan's racket bag. When I confronted him, he said he'd bought it off Ryan." Angie scrunches her tired hair. "You know he's almost thirty and still living with his folks, right?" She snorts. "What do they call them? The boomerang generation?"

"No, those are the kids who move out and then move back," I say. I'm pedantic by nature. It goes with being a teacher.

"He did move out for a while, to Japan," says Dana.

Angie spins her way. I start to turn too but stop myself. Dana said she barely knew him.

She must realize her mistake because her jaw clenches.

"So you do know him," says Angie. Her voice is saccharine—no, aspartame. Dripping with fake sweetness.

"We've met a few times," Dana says tightly. "You know, going in and out. I remember he mentioned Japan. I thought that was interesting." Her voice falters.

I catch a pleading look from Dana, like she's begging Angie to drop it. I tense. I thought we were hiding shit from Angie. It feels like *I'm* the one on the outside.

"Mom?" We all turn to see Gemma slouching our way, neon backpack slung over one shoulder. One wrist is wrapped in a compression bandage. Despite the weather, she's in tiny shorts and flip-flops. She looks petulant. "Can we go now?" Her eyes leapfrog me and land on Dana.

Angie smiles at her offspring. "You don't want to see the end of the game?"

None of us has paid the slightest attention to the game. I turn to squint at the scoreboard. Stanton House is killing the local public school. Our team's in the opposition's end zone. I'd give the game another five minutes, tops.

"I want to go," says Gemma. Speaking to her mom with that whine in her voice, she sounds like she's four years old. The rest of the time, she sounds forty.

"Um, okay," says Angie. She reaches for her purse.

Pussy, I think, then regret it. It's an unfeminist thought. But if Angie had stood up to her kid, Gemma wouldn't be such a monster. A scarily pretty monster, with legs so skinny, smooth, and long it's hard not to stare at them and a face like a Madonna's: big eyes, pert nose, chubby cheeks. She's got her arms crossed, pouting.

Noticing my gaze, she turns her back. Gemma Costin hates me.

Physically, she's a perfect match for Chad, the pair of them destined to be prom queen and king, to be just like their rich parents. They'll lead high-gloss lives, cushioned by cash and good looks.

Then I remember: Chad's perfect life has derailed. His dad's gone. Dead, although the poor boy doesn't know it.

Stan's disappearance is the talk of the town. Chad must be struggling to hold it together, and now his bitch girlfriend is mad at him. Otherwise she'd stick around to kiss the star player and pose for cute couples' photos. I wonder what happened. Typical Gemma to kick a guy when he's down.

"I want to stop at the mall," Gemma tells her mother. "I need a new backpack."

I glance at the one on her shoulder. It looks fine. New, in fact.

"Okay," says Angie. With a fresh pout, she stands up. Her coat—identical to Dana's except black—flaps open. They're both wearing slim dark jeans and ankle boots, like it's some rich-lady uniform. Who wore it better? Poor Angie. Dana will be eighty and still wearing it better.

"Bye, Dana," says Angie, with a sad smile. "Just hang in there."

"See you, Angie," I say loudly and sweetly. I do this for Gemma, who will be pissed at her mom for sitting with me. The thought of sowing discord between those two lifts my spirits, at least for a second.

Dana's goodbye to Angie is more subdued. She still looks pale, like she hasn't recovered from whatever Angie was doing here, asking about her pot-dealing neighbor.

I watch mother and daughter sidestep to the end of our row. They descend together, Gemma's pale, skinny legs in perfect sync with her mom's, marching to the same beat in their bitch army. Gemma tosses her hair and looks back at me, glaring. Her long hair is almost white, even paler than Dana's.

Still watching them, I speak out the side of my mouth. "Okay, what just happened?"

Dana's voice is high: "What do you—?"

I turn. "Don't bullshit me, Dana."

All around, people are on their feet, cheering. Stanton House won. Dana and I don't look.

Her head dips. A tear escapes from beneath her black Chanel glasses. She starts to quake. "Fuck. I've been stupid," my best friend whispers. "Utterly stupid."

CHAPTER 12

Jo

I'm rage-cleaning the remains of our dinner. Dana and I are in her kitchen. She's sitting on a stool at the counter, a glass of red wine in hand.

I followed her back here after the football game. I had to get to the bottom of the Ryan Reeve story. Not only was Dana cheating on Stan but Angie knew before I did.

The *Frozen* soundtrack leaks out of the den, where Ruby and Zoe are watching the movie. Dana's housekeeper, Gloria, collected the girls from school. Dana's twins are still out, Chad at a postgame party and Owen at chess club. "Let it go," trills the song. I wish I could. A lack of sleep, too much stress, and my fury at Dana have resulted in a brain-splitting headache.

I grab a dirty plate off the stack in the sink. Being here at Winderlea is not helping my mood. My mind keeps returning to my last visit: the pair of us dragging Stan's lifeless body. I scrape bits of lasagna into the trash compactor. While dinner was tasty, I could barely swallow it. Tomato sauce on white porcelain kept reminding me of blood on marble.

Dana takes a long swig of wine. She's had enough. Her gaze is vacant.

Catching the light, the wine in her glass is the color of blood: Stan's blood and Alma's. I shudder. What are the chances of two pools of blood spilling in one night? Stan's death freed some nightmarish genie from a bottle.

I look away. I'm being maudlin.

I jam the plate into Dana's supersized dishwasher and reach for another. Everything in this house seems inflated. Her espresso machine belongs in Starbucks. Her fridge could house a walrus carcass.

Dana waves a hand. "You don't have to do that," she says. "Just leave everything in the sink. Gloria will be in in the morning."

I reach for the next plate and scrape it. It's something to do, besides scream at Dana. When I do speak, it's through clenched teeth: "How does Angie know about you and this guy Ryan?"

Dana shrugs. "You know her, Jo! She probably saw me talking to him and sussed it out. And she doesn't know! She was fishing!"

I ignore this. Dana must have told her *something*. And if Angie wasn't sure before, based on Dana's reaction in the bleachers, she is now. "Who else could know?" My voice cracks. "Did Stan know? Is that why he wanted to divorce you?"

Dana looks away. "Of course not."

I knock the plate against a mug. Damn. I've chipped it. I'm not sure I believe her.

I run the tap and try to calm down. "You haven't seen Ryan since, have you? I mean, since . . . ?"

"No! I said no!" she says, nostrils flaring.

I inhale. "When did you last see him?" "See" is a euphemism, as I suspect "know" was for Angie when she said, "So you do *know* him." God, I hate Angie. Have the cops talked to her? Will she tell them about Ryan?

Dana crosses her legs, ladylike. She should have kept them shut. Her eyes skate left. "The day before Stan . . ." A hard swallow. "Saturday. Stan was in Seattle."

The plate I was scraping slides from my grasp. It clatters into the sink against the others.

Dana jumps and gasps. "Jesus! Would you stop cleaning?"

I can't help but sneer. "Well, someone will have to!" It would never occur to Dana that Gloria might prefer to start her day without a sink full of crusty dishes.

My mother, long since dead, worked as a cleaner at the Oaktree

Mall. Whenever I went there with friends as a teenager, I was morti-fied to see her. I often think of her when I'm cleaning, like right now, or when I mopped Stan's blood off Dana's studio floor.

People like Dana never think of the dirty work. They don't realize that garbagemen and janitors are the cornerstones of our civilization. They don't care about people like Alma Reyes, now on life support, an ocean away from her loved ones. These folk don't exist for Dana. They're machinery. A background hum. Is that how she sees me? Here to clean up her shit but not trusted with the details of her love life. I can't believe she told Angie!

Dana touches her forehead. She sags against the counter. "I'm sorry." Her voice shakes, contrite and exhausted. "Jesus, Jo. I'm so sorry."

"I know," I say. "I'm sorry too." Getting angry won't help. "Just . . ." I take a deep breath. "I'm sorry if I'm being intrusive. It's not like I'm asking for the thrill of it. I'm not judging you for fucking your neighbor. I only care about what the cops know! And what Angie might tell them."

She nods manically, tears in her eyes. "I know." She hides her face in her hands. "I'm just . . ." She gulps. "I'm embarrassed."

"Because you had an affair?"

"Because I had an affair with *him*." There are two bright spots on her pale cheeks. They make her look doll-like.

"Why?"

"He's . . ." She takes a swig, followed by a big breath. "He's gorgeous. I mean, seriously—" Her face flushes. "You should see him."

I hold my breath. Shit. Is she in love with this guy?

Dana shakes her head as if I'd asked out loud. "Physically, he's stun-ning. But he's twenty-eight and kind of a . . ." She swallows hard. "A bit of a loser, I guess. He doesn't have a real job. And he lives at home, like Angie said, with his parents."

"How long has it been going on?" I ask.

Dana stares into her wine glass. "Two months?"

Damn. I stay quiet.

Tears fill her eyes. "It looks awful."

I think back to that night, to Dana's claim that Stan was having an affair and that's why they fought. That's why Stan hit her.

Everything Dana told me could be a lie. Maybe she planned to kill Stan for the money. Dana wanted to keep her infinite riches and shack up with her hot young lover.

As soon as these thoughts bubble up, I shoot them down. I've known Dana for thirty years. So she didn't tell me about her affair with the young stud next door. If I were her, I might have hidden that too. It's too much of a stereotype, turning her into a cougar: a rich, fortysomething lady preying on the bad boy next door. She was silly to get involved with a guy like that: part-time tennis coach, part-time dope dealer. But she's not a cold-blooded killer.

I stick another plate in the washer. "Look, if Angie knows about you and Ryan, so will everyone else in town. She lives to gossip. Sooner or later, the cops will ask you about him."

Dana studies her wine. "What should I tell them?"

I adjust the tap. The water's getting too hot. "The truth. Having an affair isn't illegal."

She drains what's left in her glass. "I don't want to tell them. It's humiliating."

I fight a fresh urge to snap at her. There's more than her pride at stake here. There's the possibility of life in prison. Life without our children. "You have no choice. The police will interview all your neighbors. Do you really think this Ryan guy will lie about your relationship? He has no reason to! And if the cops know you're trying to hide an affair, they'll see that as another motive for killing Stanley."

"They'll see it as a motive anyway." Her voice is soft but clear. "I was cheating on my husband."

"Well, own up and act contrite. Say you only did it because you knew he was cheating on you first. That you hoped he'd notice and get jealous." I attempt a smile. "You know, all that good old high school stuff. Play the desperate, neglected little woman."

Dana doesn't smile. I study her. "You did think that, right?" I say. "I mean, that he was cheating?"

She frowns, perhaps hearing the doubt in my voice. "Yes! I know he was having an affair!"

"How?"

"I looked at his credit card bills," she says. "Coco de Mer lingerie. He wasn't buying it for me. And jewelry too." Her lip quivers. "She has expensive tastes, whoever she is. Like *really* expensive."

I rinse off the last plate. "You don't know who it is?"

"No clue." She looks glum.

I imagine the cops will find Dana's romantic rival. That could be a good thing. At least they'll have another suspect. It's lucky that Dana admitted her marriage wasn't perfect. Maybe that battered face was a blessing in disguise. It forced her to admit things weren't rosy. He was cheating. She was cheating. Maybe hot Ryan Reeve won't be too big of an issue.

CHAPTER 13

Dana

Detectives Shergold and Bellows are back, both in plain, neat clothes, like they're here to convert me to the Jehovah's Witnesses.

Jo left ten minutes ago. I didn't expect the police this late, at ten past eight in the evening. I guess that's why they've come now, to catch me unexpectedly.

"Detectives?" I say. There's a fresh glass of wine in my hand. I'm standing in the doorway. When the bell rang, I thought it was Jo, that she forgot something. Did these two see her leave? But so what if they did? She was my friend long before she became my accomplice. We have daughters the same age. She came over for dinner, as friends do. Still, I'm scared to draw their attention in her direction.

"Can we come in?" This is said by the woman, Detective Shergold.

I hesitate. Good question. Is this the right time to decline and say, "No, I'm not speaking without counsel"? Or I might be better off playing the sick-with-guilt wife who had an affair in a sad attempt to regain her adored husband's attention. While lawyering up might be smarter, it could also raise their suspicions.

"Okay." I step back. The wine has left me reckless. "Please, this way." I lead them into Stan's study.

Shergold's been here before, but Bellows peers around with interest. This room was decorated to resemble a swanky men's club, all hunter green and red hardwood. His desk's the size of a billiard table. Classic books Stan never read are arrayed on the shelves above photos in antique silver frames: the obligatory wife and kids. Stan holding a golf club, admiring his shot. Stan fishing. Stan with his best friends from college, heli-skiing.

I chose this room for three reasons. With the door shut, it's practically soundproof. Zoe's just gone to bed but could reemerge at any moment. Or the twins could come down for yet another snack. Second, I think choosing Stan's space makes me look less guilty, like I want to feel close to him, which I wouldn't if I'd killed him. Third, my studio is next down the hall. I didn't want to pass it with the detectives' eyes on me.

Rather than sit at Stan's desk, I motion them toward the far corner, where three low armchairs nuzzle close to a teak coffee table. I take the chair facing the door. The detectives take the others. The room still smells faintly of cigar smoke, one of Stan's affectations. He only smoked them with men he thought worthy of impressing.

Detective Shergold unbuttons her coat and smooths back her gray bob. Most middle-aged women around here who don't dye their hair are hippy types and wear it long and scraggly. Her haircut's as sharp as her eyes, studying Stan's fridge-sized humidor.

Meanwhile, I appraise Detective Bellows. He has a long nose and close-set eyes beneath wide eyebrows. It's not a pleasant face. He looks sneaky.

"We'll make this quick," says Detective Shergold. She smiles coldly. "Do you know Ryan Reeve?"

Despite expecting this question, I nod and feign ignorance. A double bluff. "Yes, he's my neighbor."

"What's your relationship with Ryan?" This is from Detective Bellows.

"We're friendly," I say hesitantly. I will put out, but must first play hard to get. It's more realistic.

"Friendly?" says Detective Bellows, this word as pointed as his schnoz. "You weren't sexually involved with Mr. Reeve, then?"

I feel myself blush. "No!" I blurt. I start to shake my head, then lean forward to bury my face in my hands. "We were," I admit. I've started crying.

It's partly real shame, but not for cheating on Stanley. I don't regret sleeping with Ryan. The sex was phenomenal. However, I do regret it coinciding with Stan's killing, forcing me to discuss it with horrible strangers. And I regret confiding in Angie. We had too many cocktails at some boring Friends of the Library dinner. I didn't tell her it was Ryan but did mention I'd caught the eye of someone super fit and younger. Fuck Angie for bringing it up when Jo was with me—trying, as usual, to drive a wedge between us.

"I see." Detective Shergold's tongue darts out, fleshy and pink between pale, thin lips. I look away. It was almost obscene, that glistening pink flash.

Now that I've admitted to cheating, the cops want details.

I'm suitably contrite. Jo would be proud of my performance. Yes, I'm a cheating wife, but I was doing it with good intentions, a desperate and admittedly misguided attempt to save my faltering marriage by trying to make my beloved husband jealous.

Detective Bellows looks serious and sympathetic, a young priest giving absolution. His hands are clasped. Sinner repent, and all shall be forgiven.

I'm feeling hopeful until I see Detective Shergold frowning beneath her steely gray haircut. It's like an ancient Greek helmet. My contrition pings right off her.

"When did you last see Mr. Reeve?" asks Shergold. I see Ryan in my mind's eye, tanned and naked.

I look away, despite knowing I shouldn't. Shergold's bayonet gaze scares me. She's the leader of this crusade. Is it ambition that drives her? Or a true desire for justice? Probably the latter. Just my luck.

To buy time, I wipe my eyes. "The day before Stan d—" I pretend to cough, blinking in shock. "Disappeared," I whisper. "Saturday."

My heart surges. My palms, ground hard against my thighs, feel clammy. I almost said "died." I almost blew it. To hide my shock, I talk: "Have you found anything yet?" I ask, shakily. "Besides Stan's jacket?"

"We're pursuing every avenue, Mrs. McFarlane," says Bellows.

I nod, woozy. I shouldn't have spoken to them, not after all that wine. That was close. I'm perspiring. "You . . . you don't think Ryan had anything to do with it, d-do you?" I stutter. I'm not trying to throw my pretty lover under a bus. It's just an obvious question.

Detective Bellows's head straightens. He's slightly cross-eyed, which makes his gaze unsettling. He's never looking quite where he should be. "Do you suspect Ryan had some involvement?" he asks.

I shake my head, hard. "No. Most definitely not!" But I sound worried.

Bellows looks somber: "Was Ryan jealous?"

I shake my head again but with less strength. "No. Not at all! It was just a casual fling. He's . . ." My cheeks flush and my eyes dip with self-deprecation. "He's much younger."

Detective Bellows looks unconvinced. How gallant, especially given my current appearance. Although I suppose they've looked up old photos where I look a lot better, pics from my website and the society pages.

"Ryan never said anything threatening?" asks Bellows. "He wasn't possessive?"

"No," I say firmly.

His frown deepens. "Was there anyone else with reason to harm your husband?"

They've asked me this before. I said no. I'm loath to point them straight to Ralph Isles, not when I'm afraid he heard us fighting. But the cops will get to Ralph sooner or later. I suspect something was up with their business. Something unpleasant. Ralph looked awfully shifty yesterday morning when he asked about Stanley.

"Did your husband have enemies?" asks Detective Bellows, as if voicing the same thing in a different way might help it get through my thick skull.

I shrug. The more avenues they have to pursue, the more chance they'll get lost down one. "Maybe someone from work." I say hesitantly, then hasten to add: "Which I know nothing about. I just didn't ask." I shift in my seat. "But I do know, well, not all investors were happy.

Some people." I wring my hands like I'm ashamed to express it. "Some people lost money. Lots of money."

Detective Bellows nods. He glances at Detective Shergold. She nods. She's definitely in charge here. "Thanks for your time," she says.

They both rise. I do too. My sore eye feels hot when I touch it. I follow them down the long hall.

"Ah, while we're here," says Detective Shergold, "when's a good time to speak to your children?"

My throat clogs. I should have been prepared for this. "I can't let you speak to them. It's too upsetting for them. They're struggling."

Detective Shergold's lip curls. "What if your children saw or heard something that could help us find their father?"

I shake my head and force my clenched hands to relax. "They're minors. My lawyer advised against it. I've asked them," I continue. "They heard nothing. Not even . . ." My finger finds my bruised eye. "Not even our fight." I drop my hand. "Thank God," I add. "I'm sorry, but they can't help you."

"Sometimes children remember things," says Detective Bellows. "When professionals ask them. Naturally, your lawyer could be present. And a child psychologist, if you like." He sounds sincere, like he's just trying to help us.

I feel tired and drunk. And increasingly rattled. "I . . . Let me think about it."

Detective Shergold nods. In the hall light, her face is grim. "Think fast. The first seventy-two hours are vital."

We've reached my foyer.

I nod. That deadline is tomorrow. And Stan is way beyond help. Before I can blink it away, a vision creeps into view: Stan on the ocean floor, crawling home toward Winderlea, bloated and battered.

"Mrs. McFarlane?"

Stan's ravaged face fades, leaving Bellows's. He zips up his coat. "There was no one else here Sunday night?" His voice is too casual. "Before or after your fight?"

They haven't asked this before, not straight out. I always stopped the story soon after Stan left.

I unlock the door and pry it open. They might already know Jo came over. It's better to just say so. "My friend, Jo, Jo Dykstra. She came over. I was . . ." I hold the door open. In my thin sweater, I'm freezing. The detectives don't move. "I was very upset," I say.

"How long did she stay?" asks Bellows.

"Most of the night," I admit. "Her daughter, Ruby, slept in the den. Jo sat up with me, trying to calm me down. It was late when they left. Or early morning."

"Morning?" says Shergold.

I'm still holding the door. I pause, considering. These detectives seem too interested in my best friend. While I don't know what Ralph saw, they'll question him no matter what. He's Stan's business partner. I may as well deflect them from Jo.

I look up, like I've recalled something. "Oh. And Ralph. Ralph Isles, Stan's partner, he said he stopped by Sunday evening to see Stan." I swallow, abashed. "I think he heard us fighting and left. I met him in the street yesterday morning."

Detective Shergold has been gazing out the door at the floodlit garden. Her eyes veer to me. "What time did Mr. Isles stop by?"

"I don't know," I say. "He didn't ring the bell or anything."

I think I've distracted her with this mention of Ralph. But a moment later her voice sharpens. "This friend of yours, Jo Dykstra? How do you know each other?"

"Oh," I say. "We're old school friends."

"Best friends?"

I nod warily. It's awful, having to answer all their nosy questions. Normally, I'd let my housekeeper deal with these people. Or my assistant, Daisy. "We're good friends. She only moved back here this summer."

"Old friends are the best, aren't they?" says Detective Shergold. "The ones you can count on in a crisis." Her smile gives me shivers. "What brought Ms. Dykstra back to Glebes Bay?"

"I . . ." The question's so unexpected I can't answer. Besides, I'm not sure of the details—just that Jo wouldn't want her to know. Does Shergold know more than I do?

I clear my throat. "She came back for her daughter," I say. "Glebes Bay's a good place to grow up. Beautiful nature. Small and safe." I realize what I've said and feel stupid. It's hardly safe when your husband's vanished.

Shergold pretends not to notice. She nods happily. "The sort of place where everyone knows everyone." She leaves "and every*thing*" unsaid.

"Goodnight," Shergold says briskly. She marches across the porch and down the stairs, Bellows trailing behind her.

"G-goodnight." The salutation sticks in my throat. I'm scared. They're going to talk to Jo.

CHAPTER 14

Jo

A loud knock on my front door startles me, and I drop my pen. I've finally settled down to grading papers.

My first thought is Dana, although that's unlikely. I just got home from her place forty minutes ago.

She's only stopped by here once, bearing a housewarming gift soon after I moved in. It was a basket of European cheeses, crackers, and chutneys from a deli I can't afford. Her visit embarrassed us both: me because my place is a dump, and her due to the contrast. After that, we've stuck to cafés or meeting at Winderlea.

Another knock. Perhaps it's my landlady, who lives upstairs. Although that's doubtful. She's a stickler for decorum and calls first.

I check my watch. It's past 9:00 p.m. Fearing the noise will wake Ruby, I scurry down the short hall. When I open the door, cool night air rushes in. I keep the chain on and peer through the gap, ready to slam the door shut.

Three concrete steps descend to my basement door. On the narrow slab out front stand two people, shoulder to shoulder. Dana barely described them, but I know who they are: the detectives on Stan's case.

I frown through the gap. "Can I help you?"

The man speaks. "Are you Joanna Dykstra?"

"Yes?"

He raises a badge, as on TV. "I'm Detective Bellows, and this is Detective Shergold." His chin tips toward his partner. "May we come in? It's about Stanley McFarlane."

I frown harder. "Dana's husband, Stan?" Although I expected them sooner or later, I feel unprepared. "I don't see how I can help you."

"It won't take long," says the woman. "May we come in, please?"

I unlock the chain and step back. "Please keep your voices down." I lower mine to demonstrate, my *please* as pointed as hers. "My daughter's asleep."

I have to press myself against the wall to let them squeeze past. "Straight ahead," I whisper. "Into the kitchen." I follow them down the short hall.

The apartment came fully furnished. The kitchen's much like my mom's back in our trailer: hotplates instead of a stove, a fridge that's noisy and narrow. I motion them toward the ugly Formica table, then offer tea or coffee.

"Just water, please," says Bellows. Shergold nods.

These cops remind me of some of my students' miffed parents who mask their complaints with passive-aggressive politeness.

I walk to the sink and wait for the tap to run clear. I fill three glasses with water.

Detective Shergold takes a seat. Made of aluminum, the kitchen chairs are flimsy.

"We'll be recording this, for our files," says her partner. He sits and places a device on the table.

"How old is your daughter?" he begins, after I've joined them. It sounds conversational, something to break the ice. Everyone knows women love to gab about their kids. He'd be complimenting my shoes if I weren't sock footed. He must be the Good Cop.

"She's five," I say. I suspect he already knows Ruby's age, knows far too much about me. Do they know about my tragic addiction to home decor TikTok? And how I still google Trevor? "The same age as Dana's daughter, Zoe."

"How well do you know the McFarlanes?" asks Shergold. Her eyes are bright and canny.

I reach for my water glass. She's the smart one.

The questions are what I'd expect: backstory of how I know Stan and Dana, inching toward my impressions of their marriage.

"Did they seem happy?" asks Detective Bellows.

"Yes. Sure." I say it with a touch of hesitation.

"Did Dana tell you she suspected Stan of having an affair?"

I shift in my seat, as if reluctant to break Dana's confidence, and yet . . . they are the police. I can't *lie* to them. "Yes."

"Did you believe her?" asks Detective Shergold. Her hands are neatly clasped on the edge of the table, like someone saying Grace before dinner.

"Absolutely," I say. "Dana's not the jealous type. If she felt something was up, I believe her."

"Did he ever hit on you?" asks Shergold, her eyes calm below those blunt bangs.

I snort. "No! I'm Dana's best friend. Of course not!" I'd also never be Stan's type. Not in a million years. He liked women who got noticed.

"Did you know they were discussing divorce?"

I take a sip of cool water. I could admit that I didn't know, but pride stops me. Why did she hide that? But I know why: even to me, Dana couldn't bear to admit things weren't perfect. Did she tell Angie? She wouldn't. They're not real friends. Dana didn't call Angie for help that night, she called *me*. I take a deep breath. Focus. "Yes. Stan told Dana he wanted to split up. She was . . ." I take another sip. It's vital to choose my words carefully, to paint Dana as heartbroken yet hopeful, not livid and vengeful. "She was hurt. But she didn't believe it. She thought they'd work it out." I believe this.

"Even though she thought he was cheating?"

"Lots of marriages survive that," I say. Although mine didn't. "They have three beautiful children. And they were a good team." How many clichés can I fit into this conversation? I decide to add one more: "Couples get through rocky patches."

Detective Shergold nods. Her face looks bland, her eyes on my scarred table. Suddenly they pop up to poke me in the face. "Why were you there that night?" she asks smoothly.

I flinch. Either Dana told them or they've spoken to those other detectives, the ones on Alma's case. If they've put things together, they must suspect me of *something*. It's too big a coincidence, me involved in both cases. Yet coincidence is what it is. What shit luck. Coincidences happen.

I try not to freeze, yet my jaw has locked solid. It takes a beat to unclench it. "Dana called me. She was upset. Crying. I drove over."

Detective Bellows smiles encouragingly. "What time was this?"

"I'm not sure," I say. "It was late. I was asleep when she called me." They can check our phone records.

A glare from Shergold. "And what did you find when you got there?"

"Stan was gone. They'd had a fight." I shake my head. "He hit her."

Detective Bellows looks suitably somber. He leans forward and quietly asks, "Did you know that her husband was abusive?"

I shake my head hard. "No!" This is actually true. "It wasn't like that. Stan never hit Dana before. There's no way she'd have put up with it. Dana's . . ." I throw up my hands. It's hard to put into words. "She's strong. And she knows her own worth. She'd never have stayed in an abusive marriage." Of all tonight's lies, these glide most easily off my tongue. Before I learned otherwise, I'd have sworn this was true. I take a deep breath, reel myself back. "That night. It sounds like Stan snapped," I say. "I mean, from what Dana told me, he lost it. I guess he'd been drinking . . ." I blink at Detective Bellows. "Not that that's an excuse. There's no excuse. You saw her face. But no, that was the first time he hurt her. Maybe Stan had some sort of breakdown. He wasn't a bad guy. Not really!"

They don't respond to this.

Shergold must make some sign I don't catch because Bellows pockets the recorder. "Thank you for your time." He stands up. Detective Shergold and I rise with him.

That went well, I think, which is when Shergold turns and asks, "Why do you think he's dead?" There's a smile in her voice when she says it.

Right away, I realize my mistake. I was speaking about Stan in past tense. The ultimate rookie-killer slipup. What a moron.

I'm short, but Detective Shergold is even shorter. I gape down at her: "Pardon?"

"You teach English," she says. "I'd expect tenses to matter to you. And yet you said they '*were* a good team' and he '*wasn't* a bad guy.'"

I give her my best "really?" scowl, the one I use when my students are trying—and failing—to be clever. "We were discussing the past," I say. "And he did have an affair, bash his wife, and abscond! I'd hardly say he's a great guy."

Detective Shergold smiles. "Abscond," she says, like I've used a good word.

We walk single file down the narrow hall. At the door, Detective Bellows stops. Shergold and I do too. She turns my way. "Where would he go, a guy like Stanley?"

"He's rich. He could go anywhere."

"Hmmmm."

Bellows opens the door. The night air feels good against my face. I realize I'm sweating. "Thanks for your time," he tells me.

Shergold smiles. "We've taken a lot of your time, of late. I mean, the police." She sounds anything but sympathetic. "What bad luck, you being the one to find Mrs. Reyes."

I freeze. A rush of heat travels through me. "I . . . Y-yes," I stammer. "That poor woman. It's just awful."

Detective Shergold buttons her coat. "You stayed at Dana's a long time, if you were driving home at six nineteen in the morning."

I nod, unsure how to respond. The silence hangs heavy.

Detective Shergold pulls her keys from her pocket. "What did you do all night long?"

"We sat up talking."

She tilts her head. "Yet you were meant to work in the morning." She tucks her hair behind one ear. It's unpierced, which is unusual. Most women have pierced ears.

I did mine myself, age thirteen, with a needle. I lacked the money to do them at the mall with Dana.

We all wait. The silence expands to the point where I can't bear it. "Dana was distraught," I say. "She kept begging me to stay."

Shergold's smile widens. "What a good friend you are."

I pretend to smile. I hate this lady.

With a nod, she steps through the doorway and precedes Bellows up to ground level. My front door is set on the side of the house, in a narrow gap facing the neighbor's. They have teenage sons. Music's pounding in their basement rec room.

Heart clattering, I watch the detectives walk to their car, which is as gray and unremarkable as Detective Shergold. I wait until it drives off. It has a powerful engine.

I shut and lock the door. I lean against the wall. Drawing breath, I tell myself to calm down. Those cops were fishing. Everything will be fine if we stick to the story.

If someone saw us moving Stan's corpse, we'd already be locked up. The police have nothing on us, not even a body.

As for Alma, I did the right thing by stopping. That should count for something. Some good karma, at least. God knows I need it.

CHAPTER 15

Dana: Three nights after Stan's death

Owen almost wrecked the vigil by refusing to come. He relented when I threatened to curtail his screen time. But his displeasure's obvious from his hunched, hostile posture.

We're in Norman Gaynor Park, between the parking lot and the sea cliffs. It's where Stan's jacket was found. Jo thought it was a suitable place for the vigil. It's freezing, with a savage wind off the water.

While we're all bundled up, in his ripped jeans, oversized coat, and dark hood, Owen looks ready to steal someone's car. At least Chad's dressed appropriately in a button-down shirt, navy sweater, and his fitted school raincoat. And Zoe, whose hand I'm holding, is stealing everyone's heart in her pink rain slicker and yellow hair ribbons.

The vigil was Jo's idea. She organized everything. Missing person flyers. Candles. Yellow ribbons. All I had to do was show up and play my part, plus drag my kids along.

Jo passes me an unlit candle. She's holding one too, along with a cordless microphone she borrowed from the school. She peers up at the sky. "I hope the rain holds off a bit longer."

I nod and check my watch. It's almost seven, and dark. I turn my back on the sea and clutch my candle.

More people came than I expected, especially given the weather. A hundred, at least. Or 150? I recognize most of them but not all. Kids, staff, and parents from Stanton House. Members of our country club. Ladies from yoga and tennis. Women from the book group I stopped attending two years ago. People I see walking their dogs or recognize from the local coffee shop. Clients of Stan's.

Everyone looks sympathetic and serious. Many come over to hug me or shake my hand. They're all kind, all offering to help. All these faces of people whose names I should know.

I feel everyone's eyes on me. Do I look like a fraud?

"You okay?" asks Jo.

I nod. People are still coming from the parking lot. Some are carrying bunches of flowers. A few hold yellow balloons. Jo's got my assistant, Daisy, passing out candles and flyers.

When the stragglers have been absorbed into the group, Jo pulls a lighter from her pocket. She lights my candle first, then Chad's. He uses his to light Owen's. I light Jo's. She turns to the young woman beside her. I recognize her: a waitress at Stan's favorite café. My throat shuts. All these people here to support us. It's touching. Or is she his lover? She favors low-cut tops. She's twentysomething and pretty.

My candle flickers. I cup it with my palm to block out the wind.

"Are you okay to say a few words?" Jo asks me. "Or should I speak on your behalf?"

I wipe my eyes. "No, I want to thank all these people."

Jo nods. Her hand's on my elbow. "Yes, good." She passes me the microphone.

I clear my throat. "Hello, everyone," I say. People look up. Silence settles. "I'm Dana McFarlane, Stan's wife. I want to . . ." Emotion overtakes me. I'm not putting it on. I'm truly devastated. I take a deep, shaky breath: "I want to thank you all for coming tonight, for caring about Stan." My voice disintegrates. Chest heaving, I hand the mic back to Jo.

She speaks well. About people coming together in tragedy. About community spirit. And how hope prevails.

I fix my gaze on my candle's flame and let Jo's words flow over me without thinking too hard. The flame's bright and fragile. I'm not sure what to hope for. Afterward, various people come forward to say they're sorry. Many offer to help. With what I don't know. I say thank you over and over. All this undeserved kindness. If only they knew. I start trembling.

I need a moment to myself. I turn and walk toward the sea cliffs.

I'm standing there, punishing myself by staring out to sea, when footsteps approach. I turn to see Chad.

"Mom?" He stops beside me.

I study him. His face is abnormally blank. "You okay, hon?" I ask.

He shrugs. "How can I be okay when Dad's dead?"

I'm so stunned it takes me a second to react. "What?" I gasp.

"Everyone at school says so." His voice betrays zero emotion.

Fear and anger flare through me. My God, kids are cruel. What awful rumors have the twins overheard? I should have pulled them out of school. I should have found a good counselor. I shouldn't have forced them to attend this damn vigil. Are people here to honor Stan, or did morbid curiosity attract them?

"You don't know that!" I say. "He's not dead!"

Chad bows his head. Tears fill his eyes. His lips squeeze shut. "Whatever." For once, he sounds like Owen.

A scuffling sound behind us makes me turn. I freeze. Maybe fifteen feet away stands Detective Shergold. I had no idea she was here. She's not looking our way but toward the crowd. Shit. What did she overhear?

I reach for Chad's elbow. "Let's get out of here," I say. I propel him along the gravel path, toward our car.

Up ahead, in the parking lot, engines are starting. People are leaving the vigil. *Good nights* ring out. Car doors slam.

I slow my pace. I'm too spent to talk to anyone else. I keep my head down.

"Mom?" says Chad. He sounds young all of a sudden, his voice high and breathy. "What's going to happen?"

Despite knowing I shouldn't, I look back at the cliffs and ocean, black and unforgiving. Detective Shergold is still watching the dispersing crowd.

"I don't know," I say. "But we'll find him. It'll be o—"

He cuts me off with a harsh laugh. "No, Mom. It will not! We both know Dad's gone."

I'm so shocked I stumble. He sounds angry and sure.

CHAPTER 16

Dana: Four days since Stan's death

The door to my mailbox is stuck. It needs oil. I should tell Gary, the gardener. Or is it Gerry? I ought to remember. I see him practically every day.

I tug at the door until it's half open. I squeeze my hand in. No one sends letters anymore. It's all bills and junk mail. *Wait. What's this?* I extract a folded piece of paper.

Two words are written with red Sharpie in thick block-print letters: I KNOW.

The words swim in and out of focus. This must be a joke. Some cruel prank. I feel lightheaded.

Maybe someone who heard about Stan on the news is trying to have some sick fun. Tragedies attract weirdos.

I look up. The road's empty. I feel exposed. Whoever put this here could be watching. I turn and flee through the iron gates and up my drive.

Rounding the bend, the wind sweeps in, cold from the sea. It tears at my clothes. The note flaps. I start to run. Overhead, the oaks creak, full of warning. And the house, tall and dark, judging me, like it knows about Stan. I run as fast as I can.

On reaching the steps, I stop, winded. My breaths come in jerky gasps. The pine trees rustle.

I sink onto the bottom step, gasping. Behind me, the sea rushes in and out. It hisses over the stones, gleeful.

I know, I know, I know.

I shut my eyes and cover my head with my hands. Stan's death was an earthquake. It triggered this tsunami. There's no way to stop it and nowhere to run.

CHAPTER 17

Jo

I have four missed calls, all from Dana. Between classes, I phone her back. I'm in the hall. Students rush by.

Dana picks up right away. Her voice is shrill: "Jo? I need to see you!"

My mouth's full of bran muffin. I gulp it down. The bran's mealy. I have to speak loudly on account of the noise. "What? Now? I'm at school."

"Don't you get breaks?"

I check my watch. "At two." I have a free hour for grading.

"I'll be there!"

She hangs up before I can dissuade her.

Last night I got no work done because of the vigil. Unmarked papers are like weeds, eager to spread. I need that hour to catch up. And yet. My throat's gone gluey. Dana sounded panicky. I hope she hasn't fucked up with those detectives.

I force down another dry gulp. The bell clangs. I toss the remnants of my muffin in a bin and head back to class.

I force myself to focus on Hamlet and his madness. Let's hope Stan's ghost isn't inciting his offspring to seek vengeance.

At two, I'm on the school's front porch, awaiting Dana. Her Mercedes pulls into the guest lot and parks crookedly, a bad sign. She stumbles out, designer clothes askew, an "it girl" on a bender. Even her hair looks awful.

I hurry down the wide stairs. "Dana?" I'm worried someone will see her this way, then I remember: poor Dana is allowed to be disheveled, distraught, and even drunk just past midday. Her husband—the love of her life—is missing.

She squints against the weak sun. "Jo?" Her face crumples. "Something's happened." She nods to her shiny car. "Let's get out of here! Go someplace private."

The way she says it takes me back to our senior year in high school. Dana's parents gave her a little white Mazda. Not often, because Dana was mostly responsible, we'd skip our last class and drive to the beach or the mall. I recall the freedom of exiting the students' parking lot: windows down, gravel crunching beneath our tires, music blaring.

I have no nostalgia for high school. My life started after leaving Glebes Bay. And yet, that buzz of escape . . . Feelings were stronger when we were young.

I rub under my glasses. "I can't leave the school grounds."

"Oh," says Dana. Her forehead lifts. "What? Really?"

If I weren't so worried, I'd laugh. Her surprise is comical. Dana forgets most people can't do as they please. Money brings freedom.

She peers up at the red brick school covered in ivy. It looks good in the glossy brochures, respectable and substantial. Her voice cracks. "Where can we talk?"

"The art room's empty." I'm holding a stack of papers. The assignment: discuss the concept of savagery in *Lord of the Flies*. I've read three of the papers so far, each of them so abysmal I was tempted to write LOC across the top in big letters—"laugh or cry"—my own private acronym. I could scrawl LOC across my whole life, really.

We don't speak as we head to the art room. "In here," I tell Dana. I pull the door shut behind us.

There are tables instead of desks, arranged in a U. Dana stops to survey the walls lined with kids' art, grades six through twelve. They represent a wide range of styles, subjects, and talent. Some of the older boys get quite dark. There's a lot of red and black. Perhaps she's scanning the signatures, searching for Owen's.

I pull out two chairs.

"Is it the police?" I ask quietly when we're both seated.

"No," she says. "Although last night." She gulps. "Did you know Shergold was at the vigil?"

I nod. "Yes. Cops also go to funerals, looking for anyone acting weird."

Dana's mouth tics into a quick, crooked smile. "Well, last night it was Chad acting weird. He told me Stan's dead. I'm scared Shergold overheard him!"

"What?" I say. The fear that one of her kids saw or heard something flashes back into view.

"It's what kids at school have been saying." Her voice falters. "But the way he said it, it was like he knew. Or I'm just paranoid."

"Jesus," I say. "But he can't know. Right?"

"No, of course not." The words are reassuring. Her tone isn't. She presses her palms to her temples. She must have forgotten about her injured eye because she flinches and drops her hands. "Anyway, that's not why I'm here."

The way she says it, without meeting my gaze, injects a nasty fizz into my belly. I feel bloated, like a shaken-up soda can.

With quivering hands, she reaches into her purse, withdraws a piece of crumpled paper, then smooths it out. She leans away from it like it might be coated in anthrax.

I take it from her. Thick red marker. Big block letters: I KNOW.

I stare as if the letters might rearrange themselves. Like I'm pondering options for Scrabble.

"Is this a joke?" I say softly.

"I wondered that too." Her cheeks are pinker, like sharing this has brought hope. "Maybe it's some nutcase who heard about Stan on the news and wants to make trouble."

I flip the note over. I KNOW. I lean back in my chair and use both hands to grab fistfuls of hair. "Maybe."

Her face falls. "You don't believe that?"

"Do you?"

Her eyes return to the note. "I guess not," she admits. "It's too big a coincidence."

I stay quiet.

"So . . ." She's dead pale again. Pearls, small and tasteful, shine on her earlobes.

"Someone knows," I say, "but what?"

The scrape of her chair brings me back to the art room, to the smells of dust and paint, to kids' drawings glued on construction paper.

A tear trails down Dana's good cheek. "What should we do?"

My eyes find a drawing of a boat on bright blue water. It's cheerful, by one of the younger kids, with a red sail and a yellow sun up in the corner.

"Fuck." It comes out breathless. "Who could have seen us?" I ask Dana.

"I don't know!" She tilts her head back, as if to return her tears to their source. A silk scarf circles her neck, paler blue than her eyes. She mops her face with it. She'll ruin it if she's not careful.

"Think Dana," I say. "Someone saw us!"

"The kids, I guess. But there's no way they'd—" She looks at the note. "Maybe one of the neighbors?"

I consider. "Ryan Reeve?" I ask.

Dana frowns. "No." She winces. "Maybe."

"He wasn't meeting you that night?"

"No!" She sounds irate. "Of course not!"

"Could someone else have been there? Was anyone staying in the guesthouse?"

"No." She almost laughs. "I'd have thought of that." She licks her lips. "Stan's partner, Ralph Isles? The next morning, I saw his car parked out front. He said he stopped by. I . . . I figured he heard me and Stan fighting."

Great. Another witness for the prosecution.

I know Ralph—or Dr. Isles, as he prefers to be known. His son, Emmett, is at Stanton House. The father's pompous, and the son creeps me out: pale, neat, and blank faced. Emmett looks airbrushed.

I yank at my hair. "What does this note-writer want?"

"Money, I guess," says Dana. "It's blackmail."

I nod. "Probably. Could it be something else?" It's like I'm prompting her to review for some upcoming test.

She licks her lips. "I don't know. Revenge?" She practically mouths this. "Like a poison-pen letter?"

I feel queasy. Money's cut and dried. A business deal. Revenge is something else. The desire to make someone suffer. "Revenge for what?" I ask. "Why'd you say that?"

Dana bows her forehead to her fist. "I don't know. It's just— Why not ask for money right away, from the start?"

"To drag this out," I say. "And raise the pressure. So we'll get frantic."

She looks up. The bruise framing her eye has purpled. It's a horrible color, rusty around the edges. "Maybe you're right." She takes a long, deep breath. "It's a game. An awful game."

"Yes."

Dana's chin lifts. Her eyes narrow. I hold my breath. This is the Dana I know, steel beneath silk. "They won't win," she says. "I'll find out who it is." Her lips tighten.

I nod, relieved. Thank God she's back and fighting. If she crumbles, it's all over. "This person doesn't know who they're messing with," I say.

Her eyes flare like gas jets. "It must be someone I know—someone *we* know."

I tilt my head, considering. It's hard to know what's worse: some shadowy figure or someone so familiar we assume they're harmless.

Dana shakes her head. She grabs the note and slips it into her lambskin Dior clutch. "It feels personal." She snaps her purse shut.

CHAPTER 18

Dana: Six nights since Stan's death

A sharp noise breaks the silence. An alarm? I blink. I'm in my bedroom, on Stan's side of the bed. My cell phone blares in the dark. It sounds angry.

I lean out and click on the bedside light. With clumsy fingers I pick up my phone.

It's not the police or Jo, who was my second guess, but Angie Costin. Her profile pic's a selfie of her grinning so hard it must've hurt. Some app has turned her skin to peach plastic.

I clear my throat: "Hello?" I sound scared.

She yelps my name: "Dana?"

"Angie?" I say, confused. We're friendly enough, or pretend to be, but don't call each other late at night. Something must be wrong.

Angie's voice is loud. "Have you seen Gemma?"

"Gemma?" I parrot. I rub my eyes. "Uh, no."

"Are you sure?" Her voice shakes. "I just checked her room. She's not here!"

I pinch my forehead, still struggling to wake up. "Have you tried calling her?" Chad's never far from his phone.

"I confiscated it," says Angie tightly. "After that exam trouble."

"Oh. Right," I say, abashed. I should have done that too, or found some other way to punish Chad. Instead, I let it slide. You know you're in trouble when Angie Costin outperforms you as a mom. "Um, sorry," I say. "I haven't seen Gemma."

For a moment, the phone's silent. The house is quiet too. I can only hear the ocean scraping the pebbles.

"Where could she be?" moans Angie.

Rubbing sleep from my eyes, I recall sneaking out as a teen—or telling my mother I was sleeping at Jo's place. Her mom was too tired to keep track of us. When she wasn't working two jobs, she was passed out on their saggy sofa.

Looking back, those teenage nights felt endless. Me and Jo, arms linked, stumbling through the dark town. Riding in cars with boys. Guzzling booze that smelled like cheap bodywash.

Despite our drunken stupidity, nothing really bad happened. I lost my new leather jacket. Someone's drunk uncle groped Jo. We weren't gang-raped or murdered.

Angie's voice cuts through my reverie. "Can you ask Chad if he's seen her?" She sounds accusatory, like my son's led her princess astray.

I sit up straighter and bite back a snappy response. Maybe I'm over-sensitive. My head's fuzzy. It must be those sleeping pills.

I swing my legs out of bed and stand up. The hardwood's cool and smooth.

Gemma's barely sixteen. Angie's right to be worried. "Um, yeah. I'll go ask him."

I walk to the closet and extract my robe. It's soft, a gift from Stan last Christmas. I want to cry. Grief's everywhere, ambushing me. It's like the water table in my head has risen, tears on the brink of flooding.

"Where is she?" rasps Angie, as I pad down the hall. "This isn't like her!"

Outside Chad's door, I pause. Should I knock or just look? He's almost certainly asleep. He looked tired today, like he's getting run down. It's a wonder the boys sleep at all, given the stress they're under. I still haven't booked counseling sessions.

I don't want to wake Chad. I try the door handle.

To my surprise, it's locked. When did that start? I press my ear to his door.

Angie's panting down the line. "Dana? What's happening?" Her voice is sandpaper against my ear. It triggers a memory of a junior high party. Then, like now, I was in a dark hallway.

In someone's parents' basement. An olive-green carpet. Fake wood-paneled walls.

I was walking past a half-shut door when I heard Angie's nasty titter—and Jo's voice, pleading and tearful. "Stop! Give me that!"

I pushed open the door.

Apelike Bryce Dyson was dangling a Polaroid just out of Jo's reach. Kyle Alberts stood by, a leer on his stupid, handsome face. In her tight angora sweater, Angie watched too, an overgroomed house cat.

Jo lunged for the photo. Her face was flushed and distraught, her hair messy. Her top's neck was stretched out. Again Angie tittered.

I stepped into the room. "What's going on?"

Angie scowled at me. Behind their efforts to look cool, Bryce and Kyle looked embarrassed. "Hey, Dana," said Bryce. "How's it going, eh?" He sounded drunk or stoned.

Jo had started to shake. She clutched her jean jacket shut.

I strolled to the boys, kept my face and pace casual. "Let me see." I nodded at the Polaroid. I held out my hand. I wasn't asking.

Bryce shook his head. "Aw. We were just having fun."

I plucked it from his grasp.

A quick glance at it: Kyle was pinning Jo's arms. Her shorts were down. Bryce was pushing down her panties. Her mound was shockingly pale and bare. Almost bald. And her breasts—exposed, since her top was wrenched up—were all but flat.

I tucked the Polaroid into my pocket and spoke slowly: "You guys are assholes."

"She was into it!" said Bryce.

I gave him a look that said save it. And Angie—I looked at her too, long and hard. Did she take the photo?

"Jo?" I said. Her cheeks blazed blotchy red. I didn't feel sorry for her. Not at all. I was angry.

She followed me down the hall. I walked fast. Not a word until we were outside, in the backyard. Jo started crying. Gluey, gulping sobs. "I . . . I thought he liked me."

"Stop," I said. She'd had a crush on Kyle for ages. But guys like that don't respect girls like Jo. They just use them for whatever fun they can get. Didn't she know that? That photo would have been passed all over school. Probably all over town.

"You went into a room alone with him. Didn't you?" I said. "And you're drunk! A dumb, easy target!" I pried out the photo and handed it over. "Burn it."

Her shoulders hunched. Her chin lowered. For a second, I thought she'd defend herself, say it wasn't her fault. Instead, she pushed it deep into her jeans' front pocket and nodded. "I . . . You're right." She hiccuped. "Thank you, Dana."

"Dana? You still there?" Angie's voice hisses out of my phone, bringing me back to adulthood. And to current problems.

"Just a second." I gently knock on Chad's door.

Maybe I imagine a muffled laugh and a soft scuffle. I knock again, louder. There's definitely movement in there, the bed springs shifting. My son's voice sounds sleepy. "What?" he says. "Who is it?"

"It's me, Mom."

"Mom? I'm sleeping."

I recall the fear in Angie's voice. It's 1:00 a.m. Her sixteen-year-old daughter is missing. "Chad, can you please open the door?"

He sighs so loudly I can hear it out here in the hall. This is followed by bumps and shuffling. It's a long time before the lock turns.

My son glares around the door. He's wearing boxer shorts and nothing else. "What's going on?" He yawns, or pretends to, then turns and totters back to bed.

I step into his room. It lies quiet and dark. There's a manly mustiness and something else. Is it just my imagination or does it smell faintly floral?

"Angie called," I say. "She can't find Gemma."

My son is sitting on his bed, his comforter pulled over his lap. For a flash he looks guilty instead of worried. His Adam's apple works its way up and down. I'm reminded of those carnival games where you hit a target with a mallet to shoot a light up and down a scale. Better Luck Next Time! Or red lights flash and bells ding: Congratulations, Strongman!

Chad fingers his fair hair. "Gemma?" he asks, like he's not sure he knows her.

"Gemma Costin. Your girlfriend?"

He nods. "I, um. No. I don't know where she is."

Even in the dark I can see him blushing. I'm surprised. Chad's always been a good liar. As a toddler it was always Owen who gave the game up, freezing when asked who'd gouged a crater in a newly iced cake or broke Daddy's new camera. Chad, meanwhile, would make doe eyes and look extra cherubic.

He's scarlet. "I haven't seen her," he mumbles.

I open his closet door.

"Aw, come on, Mom," he says. "What are you doing? You don't—"

I open the long drapes on the window by his bed.

There, her back pressed to the glass, stands Angie's missing daughter, wearing only panties, a crop top, and a look of utter disdain.

"Well," I say to no one in particular, then into my phone: "Hey, Ange, I found her."

"Jesus!" says Angie, voice tight with relief and fury. The relief's stronger. "I'm going to kill her! I'll be right over." Angie's house is only two blocks away.

"Okay." I hang up and slide the phone into my robe's pocket.

Gemma's arms are crossed below her small, high breasts. Her nipples are hard beneath her thin crop top. She makes a noise, part sigh and part hiss, and steps away from the wall. She looks neither contrite nor embarrassed, just defiant.

My son hangs his head. "Mom? I'm sorry."

I tighten the belt of my robe. Am I shocked that my fifteen-year-old son is sexually active? I wasn't at that age, although I wasn't far off it.

I hesitate, trying to work out how I feel. As long as they're careful, it's not the sex that alarms me. It's the sneakiness. The lying. I don't like Gemma much, don't think she's a good influence. She brings out the worst in Chad. If it were some other girl, some girl I liked, it'd be easier to accept. But he won't be with her forever. It's a phase. I take a deep calming breath.

"Look," I say, addressing them both. "With everything going on with Dad . . ." I look at Chad when I say this. "I'm too stressed to deal with this properly. I'm worried you're too young but . . . well, I guess not . . ." I rub one foot against the other. Without slippers, my feet are freezing. "Do we need to talk about safe sex?" I'm not ready to become a grannie.

"Aw, come on, Mom, we're not stupid," says Chad. He sounds mortified. Gemma's glaring at me.

I nod. "That's good," I say. "But I can't have you sneaking around in the middle of the night." My voice sharpens. "And lying." I look at Gemma. "How did you get here?"

"It's a short walk," she scoffs.

"It's not safe. Not alone. In the dark."

She rolls her eyes and looks like she wants to respond, but the bell sounds for my front gate. I buzz Angie in from my phone.

"It's your mom," I tell Gemma.

She flounces across the room and retrieves her clothes—jeans and a hoodie—from under Chad's bed, where someone kicked them.

I look away as she slips into her jeans. So does my son.

"Bye, Gemma," he says when she's at the door. He still looks abashed. "See you."

"Whatever." She says this angrily but has a change of heart. She stops to blow a cartoonish kiss. It seems directed at me more than at Chad, a final act of defiance.

When her eyes meet mine, there's a dare in them. She smirks.

I can't move.

Instead of holding her gaze, my eyes skitter to the window where she stood. I stride across the room and peer down through the glass.

Far below, the ocean shines like charcoal silk. I can make out the black triangle of the boathouse and our skinny dock, the bump of the motorboat.

Turning, I feel dizzy. I recall the red block letters—I KNOW—and hear Jo's angry question: who else could have been here? Did Gemma sneak over that night too? A chill whips through me.

The front doorbell sounds. It's Angie.

At Chad's bedroom door, I pause. My son still won't meet my eyes. "Go to sleep," I tell him.

Gemma is already stalking down the hall. In the dark, I see her blond hair swaying. She seems too old for Chad. Or do all moms see their sons as perpetually innocent?

I follow shakily. What if she saw us? Any upstanding citizen would have told the police. But Gemma's far from upstanding. First and foremost, she's her mom's daughter. Those Costins know the value of a secret.

CHAPTER 19

Dana: One week since Stan's death

I stand in the window, feeling tired and rattled. The cops just left.

They showed up early, before I'd even made coffee. Luckily, they didn't stay long and asked no tough questions. They came to tell me there's been a lead: a man resembling Stan was seen hitchhiking near Santa Fe. Reported by a "credible witness."

What a farce! I stare, lost in thought, out at the garden.

Beneath the terraced lawns, the maples are reddening in the Japanese garden. In the sun, the ocean shines navy. Two white sailboats chase each other past the islands. Closer in, seagulls hover.

I used to love this view. Now, I shudder. The sea's an ugly reminder of Stan. A seagull dives low, squawking. It sounds harsh and accusing.

I should yank the drapes shut, block it all out. But it's too much effort. There are too many windows.

I turn my back on the sea and take a deep breath. Today's tough. It's been a whole week, seven days of jumping at the phone ringing and listening for a knock on the door. Seven days of little food and no real sleep. I can't focus.

Coffee in hand, I collapse on the sofa. I pinch my forehead, trying to picture Stan as a hitchhiker, thumb out beside some desert freeway. This new Stan's not glued to his tablet. He doesn't care about the stock market or his son getting into Harvard. He's like a young man on an adventure.

I want to join him. I want to get suntanned and dusty . . .

As if, snaps Jo's voice in my head. Stan couldn't sleep in hotels with less than four stars. We had to stay at a Travelodge once, and he spent the whole night moaning like the damn princess with the pea.

I swig more coffee.

Gloria has placed today's paper on the coffee table, folded discreetly. I grab it and rip it open. The story's moved off the front page. Each day it creeps further back, shedding tired quotes and shrinking.

The cops are still ruling nothing out. Stan's wife, socialite Dana McFarlane, is still pleading for her husband's safe return. Stan's estimated net worth gets a mention, as does his jacket being found near a "popular" suicide spot.

There's a photo of me and Stan at a charity ball. He's holding a microphone. I'm at his side in a strapless gown, smiling vacantly like the magician's brainless assistant.

I throw down the paper. Why are socialites always women? What's the male equivalent? I've won the world's most prestigious floral design competition—twice. Clients book me at least a year in advance. Yet the *Glebes Bay Spokesman* only identifies me by Stan's money.

I get it. Stan's fortune is fascinating and the source of all this: the house, the grounds, the gardener—Greg?—now trimming the cedar hedge. I scrape back my hair. The high-pitched whine of his weed-whacker isn't helping my headache.

I haul myself off the sofa. Time to get moving.

The twins are at the mall. Zoe's at ballet. Gloria will collect her when she's done at the Gourmet Market. My assistant for Fairytale Flowers, Daisy—yes, her real name—is racking up overtime, desperately trying to complete all the orders I've failed to tackle. Rather than sitting here daydreaming, I should go and help her.

"Mommy?"

I turn, surprised to see Zoe. It must be later than I thought. She trots closer, her cheeks as pink as her tutu.

I smile. Thank goodness for Zoe. She's sunshine personified, right down to her sweet sun-kissed freckles. "You're home!" I say. "How was ballet?"

"Good. Chloe M. had an accident."

"Oh dear. What happened?"

"She peed her pants."

"Oh. Poor Chloe."

Zoe nods. "Yup. She asked to use the restroom, but Miss Alexa said no."

"Hmmm." I bet Miss Alexa won't make that mistake again. If a five-year-old says they have to go, they have to go *now*.

"Mommy," says Zoe, "will Daddy come to my dance show?"

Her show's in two weeks. "I, ah . . ." I'm not sure how to answer. "I hope so."

"I really hope he comes," says Zoe.

Tears press against the backs of my eyes. She misses her daddy. And it's all my fault. "Want to go for a walk?" I say, hoping to distract her. I need to check the mailbox. I've gotten a bit obsessive since receiving the note.

"Okay," she says.

"Go find your jacket. And rain boots."

In the hall, we meet Gloria, armed with bags of groceries. Seeing me, she looks startled, like she's guilty of something. Has she been talking to the press? Or the police? I can't manage without her, but she makes me nervous.

"Are you going out?" she asks. It could be small talk but seems nosy.

"Just in the garden," I say and step out the door.

The rain's stopped, but it's wet out. Zoe's hand is warm in mine. We descend the long front staircase.

The air smells of woodsmoke and damp, decaying leaves. Despite the weak sun, it's chilly. My windbreaker's flimsy. I should have chosen a warmer jacket. I zip up Zoe's raincoat. It's printed with ladybugs. Fly away home.

As we trail down the driveway, I think of last night: lithe Gemma Costin in my son's bedroom. Her pink crop top and panties. Her smug fuck-you expression. Just thinking about her makes me tired.

This is what I get for coming back to Glebes Bay. I should never have left Seattle. It was bad enough dealing with Angie and her ilk when I was young. Gemma's an updated version: mean girl, next generation. It figures she'd get her claws into Chad.

Zoe's skipping beside me. Sunlight glints through the oaks. I'm squinting.

Chad and I didn't discuss Gemma this morning, not with Owen and Zoe present. I'm not sure what to say or how to punish him. I should. He lied, after all. Yet I can't be bothered.

I'm being lame. I need to step up, start acting like a parent. Even Angie punished Gemma for cheating. What did I do? Nothing. Should I confiscate Chad's phone? I kick at a pebble. Perhaps I should leave it. Chad's dealing with major trauma. He's fifteen. Sneaking around with girls is normal, the same shit I pulled at his age. Maybe I should be happy he's distracted by Gemma, that he has someone to talk to.

I remember Gemma's sly fox face as she turned from his window. That staged air kiss. Only an idiot would be relieved about Gemma. You can't talk to a cyborg.

The wind catches my hair. It could use a wash. Another thing I've neglected. And I need fresh highlights. I push it back over my shoulders and sidestep a puddle.

The driveway's dark and wet. The lawn's as plush as a golf course. High in an oak, a squirrel chatters. There's a flicker of orange in the bushes. Our cat, Toonces.

Zoe's run on ahead. She's jumping over puddles.

A week ago, I'd have admired the scene's beauty. I'd have detoured to see the late-blooming begonias and the fiery-leafed maples. I'd have stopped to pet Toonces.

Last Sunday at this time, I was ignorant of what was coming. What was I doing? Probably working in my studio.

Yes, I remember: I was making a centerpiece for a wedding. I was miffed the orchids weren't the red I wanted: blood red instead of candy apple. I sent a message of clipped complaint to my supplier.

I stumble. How absurd. A bomb was ticking, and I was stressing about flowers.

There's a bitter taste in the back of my throat. I need to eat more, not just alternate wine and coffee. It seems the cops are looking elsewhere, but that could be an act to get my guard down. Jo keeps reminding me: I need fuel to keep my wits about me.

Zoe's stopped to peer at a snail. I click the gates open.

Stepping through them, my chest tightens. I managed to forget my mission, but now it's in sight: my mailbox. My feet feel heavy.

It's been three days since I found the note. The Note. It's sealed in a ziplock bag and hidden in a hollow tree near the guest cottage. I'm not sure why I kept it. It's not like I'll forget what it said.

No. I do know why I kept it. It's physical proof I'm not crazy. I can check it if I have to. This is not in my head.

Zoe catches up. She's carrying the snail. It's pulled back in its shell, its brown foot shriveled and slimy.

"It needs a new home," she says. She sounds solemn.

I nod and point to the huge slab of granite that bears the house's name. "How about there?" The gardener kills snails. They eat our plants, after all.

Zoe sets the snail onto the rock. It tumbles off. In the weak sun, the sign's letters glint gold: WINDERLEA.

Not for the first time, I wonder who named the place. Was it the coal baron who ordered it built, a one-time miner who clawed out a fortune? Or was it his wife, who bore nine children and died in child-birth two months after moving in?

Jo researched the house's history back when we bought it. Like any old place, Winderlea's had its fair share of tragedies. Two of the coal baron's sons died in the war. Another drank himself to death. The next owner, who was in timber, drowned in a boating mishap. His widow moved out, convinced the place was haunted.

Zoe's still crouched, watching the fallen snail.

I approach the mailbox as I would a wild animal. For three days, nothing's happened. It might be time. I reach for the door, full of an-ticipatory dread. This feeling's all too familiar.

My dad never snapped and hit me. I'd displease him somehow,

sometimes without knowing why. His head would rear back, and his eyes would narrow. "Just wait," he'd say softly. "You've got it coming."

That waiting was worse than being beaten. Sometimes hours would pass, even days, before Dad fetched the cane. My fear would build. I'd try to hide it, which only fueled his sadism. Still, I tried. I had my pride.

I pry open the mailbox's door. Dread churns deep in my abdomen. I feel trembly. I know it's coming. I want it over with. Now.

I wriggle my hand into the box and pull out a flyer. *Discount furniture. Buy now. Pay later.*

I try again. There's something else in there. I pincer out a piece of folded paper. The wind catches the furniture flyer, which slips from my fingers. I watch it rise, then plummet into the bushes. Normally, I'd pick it up. At this moment, it doesn't matter.

I unfold the note. Same red ink. Same block letters.

3 MILLION DOLLARS AND THIS GOES AWAY. GET IT READY.

I reread it. My gut's fizzing. Is this dread or relief? Relief, maybe? It's what I expected: a demand for money. Three million dollars. I do have it. Yet could I get it with Stan not officially dead, and the cops eyeing me? It's not like there's three million in cash in my closet or a cache of gold bars in the garden.

The fallen flyer lies a few feet away, amid the ivy, all screaming red and orange: *NO MONEY DOWN!* I bend to retrieve it and crush it in my fist. I want to tear it to shreds, rip it with my teeth. Eat it. Being helpless makes me feel crazy.

As a girl, I sometimes fantasized I'd kill my father. I imagined lying in wait with a bat. Or I could fetch the key to the gun safe in the basement. I still don't know what stopped me. Cowardice? Decorum? Love, even?

A breeze rustles dried-out oak leaves. I went from one bully to another. I broke all my own rules. Did what I swore I'd never do. How fucked up could I be? How could I have married Stan?

Still clutching that flyer, I pound the mailbox's stuck door. Pain explodes in my fist. The door doesn't budge. I smash it harder.

"Mommy?" Zoe sounds scared.

I spin. Shit. I forgot she's here.

She's twenty feet away, still holding that damn snail. Her mouth hangs open. "Mommy? What's wrong?" All around her, the hydrangeas—so blue and pretty in the summer—lie faded and ghostly.

"I . . . Nothing," I say, aware I look crazy. Jesus. I've lost it in front of Zoe.

Eyes wide with alarm, she starts running my way. Her pink tutu flutters.

I clutch my hurt hand and stagger toward her. I bend to embrace her. "Everything's fine! I just . . . I hurt my hand."

She leans back to examine it and frowns. "Poor Mommy. Should I kiss it better?"

A shaky laugh escapes me. If only it were that simple. I hold my hand up for Zoe to kiss it. "Thanks, baby." I mustn't cry.

I'm still kneeling beside her when a noise makes me turn. A man's jogging on the sidewalk. Mirrored shades hide his eyes. Is he looking at me strangely?

Behind him stands a parked van with a tinted windshield. What if someone's in there, watching? It could be the blackmailer, gloating. Or the cops, clicking photos. What better way to rattle me than to leave these notes and watch? An innocent person would head straight to the station.

I regain my feet and grab Zoe's hand. I can't stay out here. I pull her toward the gates but mistype the code. The gates stay shut. Thick black bars block our way. My injured hand throbs. I re-stab the numbers. Again, nothing happens.

Behind me, the jogger's footsteps pound closer. What if he's not some random jogger? My heart's a panicked bird against glass, thrashing. I jab in the code. Finally, the gates open.

We're hurrying up the drive when Zoe drops the snail. Its shell smashes on the pavement.

Zoe stops. "Oh, Mommy!" she cries. She squats and starts howling. "I've killed him! I've made him dead!"

CHAPTER 20

Jo

It's Sunday. I'm on hold with Glebes Bay General. I called to check on Alma Reyes's condition. I heard on the news that she needed more surgery. I've been worrying about her. And feeling guilty for running that damn stop sign.

My cellphone rings. It's Dana. I hesitate. I've been on hold for ages already. And they probably won't tell me anything anyway. Patient confidentiality. I hang up on the hospital and accept Dana's call.

"Jo?" she says. Her voice is high with distress. "I need to see you. I . . . I found another—"

I cut her off. I'm scared her phone's tapped. "Wait! I'll come over!"

"No," she says. "I had to get out of the house. I'm at the club with Zoe. Come here!"

The Oaks Yacht and Country Club is private. The family joining fee runs around my annual salary. Then there are eye-watering monthly fees.

For this insane sum, members get access to a gym, a spa, an indoor-outdoor pool, a thirty-six-hole golf course, tennis and racquetball courts, a restaurant, a café, and a kids' club, plus the chance to mingle with the crème de la crème of Glebes Bay. Why the hell would Dana want to go there?

"Ruby!" I call. "Go find your coat, hon. We're going to meet Zoe."

I'm helping Ruby tie her shoes when she says, "Mommy, why don't we have a real house like Zoe?"

I lean back and study my daughter. Should I broach this later? No. She deserves an answer. "You know, there will always be people who have more than you," I say. "A bigger house, better toys." I tie her laces into a bow. "But many people have much less. Kids who don't have a home at all. Some kids are even hungry. So we're lucky, Rubes. Most of all because we have each other." I tip forward and kiss her. "Right, love?"

She nods and looks solemn.

I hustle her out to the car. After that speech, I wish we weren't headed to rich-people central.

It's raining again. There's not much traffic. The Oaks Yacht and Country Club faces Norman Gaynor Park and sits on the bay. The clubhouse overlooks the moored yachts. I'm relieved to find the club's parking lot lies almost bare. The guest slots are way at the back.

Ruby skips beside me as I plod toward the club's entrance.

Its portico screams glitzy hotel, while the lobby features gleaming floors and too many pillars. The centerpiece is one of Dana's giant floral arrangements. She always does them. This week's features pink Easter lilies. They're vile, slutty flowers.

"Can I help you?" A woman in a teal suit appears out of nowhere. Tall and thin, of indeterminate age, her blond hair secured in an expert twist. Her teeth are scarily perfect. "I'm Sophia, our guest relations manager." She looks me up and down and winces.

My sweatpants' knees are baggy. I should have changed, but for fuck's sake, I can dress how I want. It's the weekend.

I scowl at her. Snobby bitch. It's not like *she* could afford to be a member here either. I unbutton Ruby's coat. "We're here to meet Dana McFarlane."

When Dana appears—dressed for yoga—she looks pale and fragile. A towel's draped over her spindly neck. She's clutching a Stella McCartney gym bag.

"Hello, darling!" she says to Ruby. "Zoe's upstairs in the Kids Club." Her fake cheer sounds painful. "Why don't you go find her?"

"Okay, Auntie Dana!" says Ruby.

We watch her bound up the stairs.

Ruby loves playing with Zoe. She loves the Kids Club. I try not to compare the girls, but it's hard, Zoe with the best of everything and Ruby with hand-me-downs. Not to mention Zoe's private school education. Expensive lessons and tutors. College tuition. Job prospects. In short, their vastly different futures.

My envy feels petty now that Zoe's lost her daddy. I sign my name in the guest ledger. Poor Zoe. Not that Trev would win Father of the Year. His efforts add up to the occasional ill-chosen gift and sporadic video calls: Trev grinning like a clown and referring to himself as "Daddy." What an ass.

I start to unzip my raincoat, but the zipper gets stuck. I yank at it. Thinking of Trevor never helps. His debts and deception. The feel of his lips beneath my ear. Even now, the thought stirs a tingle.

I grit my teeth, angered by my old longing. Did I love Trev this fiercely when I still had him? Maybe. But only because I never really had him. *That* was Trev's appeal. I don't need a therapist to tell me when I'm repeating a childhood pattern. Unfortunately, just because your brain catches on doesn't mean your heart ever will.

"Come on," says Dana. She plucks invisible lint off her Lululemons. "Let's go get coffee."

As we walk toward the café, I tell myself to stop dwelling on Trevor. He wasn't special. The world's full of men too selfish to behave like adults. Men who leave their children to be raised by women.

Dana opens the café's door. Soft rock wafts out. I follow her in.

I need to focus on the present, on me and Dana. Our big problem. If the police catch on, I could lose everything—even Ruby. Why didn't I say no to Dana?

Seeing her beaten face, I couldn't think clearly. It was like finding an injured stray. I had to help. She's done so much for me. Still, how could I have been so stupid?

Dana heads for a booth. I follow. The club's café does my head in. With all its ruffles and clashing florals, it's like the designer swallowed decades worth of Laura Ashley and spewed it back up.

Dana slumps onto a chintz banquette. She's white-faced—apart from her bruises, now faded to mustard and rust. They're ghastly, of course, yet they somehow accentuate her bone china beauty. Typical Dana. She pats her face with her towel.

I settle across from her. "What's going on?"

She looks around in case someone's listening. But the café's nearly empty: just two older ladies in the far corner, drinking Bloody Marys. They're both wearing floral dresses, as if trying to blend into the decor. The one facing us eyes Dana and says something to her companion. A moment later, that woman twists and pretends to stare out the back window.

Dana doesn't notice. "I found this in my mailbox." Her voice is ragged. She pulls a piece of paper from her gym bag and hands it over.

I flip it open.

THREE MILLION DOLLARS AND THIS GOES AWAY. GET IT READY.

"Huh." I swallow. "So it is about money."

Dana nods. Even her lips lack color. "I don't have it. I mean, I don't know if I can get it. Not without the cops noticing." I set the note face down on the table, between us. She takes a deep, shuddering breath. "If I could," she whispers, "do you think this would end?"

My mouth's gone dry. "I doubt it."

A crooked smile flits across her lips. "That's not how it works, right? At least not on TV. Blackmailers keep wanting more."

I shrug. My thoughts swirl.

A waitress appears. She looks about sixteen, with bad acne. Not a Stanton House student. She's got a sweet smile and demeanor. We both order chai lattes. "Put it on my account," says Dana.

When the girl retreats, Dana leans closer. "What if they go to the cops?"

"They won't," I say. "At least not yet. If they do, they lose all hope of getting money."

She nods mechanically. "Right. What should I do?"

"Wait?"

Dana blinks at the note, a tiny white square, like some evil portal. "But . . . I'm going crazy."

"Three million dollars," I say. It's hard to imagine that much money. "If you were sure." I swallow. "Like totally sure this would end." I study the tablecloth: a creepy print of red roses against a black background. "Could you get it?"

Dana tugs at her towel. "Maybe? Like if I sold some art, maybe?"

"Art." My eyes find the wall, covered in striped floral wallpaper. I look through it. I try to remember the artwork at Stan and Dana's.

A few years back, Stan realized investing in art could pay off. Maybe we all have a special talent, if we can find it; Stan's was making money.

Their whole giant house is full of ugly paintings—mostly abstracts, splotches and lines in primary colors. They're not Dana's style. Stan chose them because the artists were famous.

"There's a Van Dortmund in Stan's study," says Dana glumly. "It's worth about two million."

"What?" I blurt. Holy shit. "Dollars?"

I try to picture Stan's study. I haven't spent much time in there. From what I remember, it's like a cheesy men's club from the eighties. Stan modeled himself as a self-made man's man. He smoked cigars and drank overpriced whiskey. He had a vintage Harley he rode maybe twice a year. He liked to mention his "poor" childhood.

I met his parents at the wedding. They were both civil servants, far from rich, but Stan didn't grow up in a ghetto.

"The Van Dortmund," I say, "what does it look like?"

"It's of some gumballs. Kind of pop arty."

Seeing my expression, she snorts. "I know, it's ridiculous." She sighs. "No, it's obscene. Two million dollars. And I hate it." The anger in her voice takes me aback. "I hate pop art," she says. "It's tacky."

I nod. On that, we agree. If Stan had to collect million-dollar paintings, couldn't he have bought some impressionists, dreamy landscapes that one could get lost in? A painting of gumballs seems especially wrong in Winderlea. Dark scenes of massacres, maybe, but not fucking gumballs. I imagine the house was offended.

"There's also a Gustav Cleggs," continues Dana. "It must be expensive. Some dealer wanted to buy it last year, but Stan wouldn't sell. He said Cleggs was still gaining." She frowns. "I should find the dealer's contacts."

I nod numbly. The waitress reappears with our drinks. She sets them down. "I'll sign for those," says Dana.

After she's gone, Dana bites her lip. "Or could I sell some jewelry, maybe?"

My eyes flash to her ring. "The resale value on diamonds is lousy."

Her eyebrow lifts. "How do you know?"

I speak through an ironic smile: "Oh well, you know, with all the diamonds Trev showered on me." I shrug. "I read it somewhere." I point to her ring. "How big is it?"

"The center stone's nine carats."

I don't react. For fuck's sake. That's bigger than Meghan Markle's.

"It came with a certificate." She glares at her ring. "It must be worth *something*."

"Okay," I say. "At least there are options." I feel compelled to add: "Thank God you didn't toss it." I take a sip of my chai latte. It's sickly sweet.

"It was a stupid impulse," she concedes. "I sort of lost it." There's a bit more color in her cheeks. Being able to discuss things has calmed her.

Yet soon her face clouds over. "When I found the note in the mailbox, I saw a van parked out front. It had tinted windows." She chews on her lip. "I couldn't see inside. I wondered if it was the cops. You know, a sting op?"

Last week, this term would have been laughable on her lips; a sting op, like we're in an episode of *UC: Undercover*. Now, I can't help but worry.

"What if they planted the note?" whispers Dana.

"The cops?" I drink a bit more of my chai latte. Good God, what a thought. "It can't be them," I say. "Surely that's entrapment!" I squint. All these hideous patterns. And the music! A headache has flared out of nowhere.

"What if they suspect me and are leaving the notes to flush me out?" says Dana. "If I had nothing to hide, I'd show the police."

Yes, she would. Who wouldn't?

"*Should* I show the cops?" She sounds freshly tearful.

"If it's not the police, you'd just raise their suspicions," I say. "And what if they actually find the blackmailer and this person took pictures with his phone or something? He'd quickly confess to blackmail if he got accused of kidnapping or murder."

Dana picks at her French manicure. I can't remember the last time I saw her with chipped nails, despite all her flower arranging. Her hands look thinner and veinier. "What should I do?" she asks.

I take a deep breath. "We need to figure out who's sending these notes. To make sure they have no real proof we're involved."

"Okay." She still hasn't touched her drink. "And then what?"

I shake my head. "We need a list of suspects. Everyone who could have seen us, even if we don't suspect them." I nod at her gym bag. "Any chance you've got a pen?"

"No. Try the waitress."

I rise and borrow paper and a pen, then return to our table. The two older women drinking Bloody Marys eye my saggy track pants with a mixture of delight and horror. At least I'm giving them something to talk about. They can spend the next ten minutes speculating about why I'm here with glamorous and tragic Dana. What could we possibly have in common?

"So." I regain my seat and put pen to paper. "Did you check the security camera?" I know there's one by the gate since I turned off the system shortly after Dana showed me Stan's dead body.

"The CCTV's been off since—you know, that night," says Dana. "I forgot to turn it back on."

"Crap," I say. "Make sure you fix that. They might use the mailbox again."

"Will do," says Dana.

I think back to the two of us disposing of Stan's body. "Okay. That night. Who might have seen something?"

Dana twists her diamond ring. "Stan's partner, Ralph Isles," she says. "He said he came over that evening. I think there are business issues. Maybe a problem between him and Stan. Ralph could have come later. After . . ." She gulps. "You know."

I nod. After Stan was dead.

I imagine Ralph Isles watching me and Dana wheel a long bulky object through the dark garden. After Stan went missing, it wouldn't take a genius to put two and two together. I write RALPH ISLES.

"Who else?" I ask.

"Ryan Reeve?" Her cheeks have colored.

I write his name without comment.

"Gemma Costin," she adds.

I look up. My eyes narrow.

"She's been sneaking over to be with Chad. I found her in his bedroom last night. I guess she could have come round that night too." Her voice shakes into nothing.

"Shit," I say quietly. Dana should have told me sooner. If we all have a special talent, Gemma Costin's is leveraging off weakness.

I tap the pen against my teeth and picture Gemma in the dark, spying on me and Dana. She'd film us on her cell phone. That's what kids do. Every moment is documented with selfies and video clips. Any second now, it could go viral.

The pain behind my eyes has splintered. I reach up to rub my temples.

My hand shakes as I write Gemma's name.

Dana's voice has thinned. "Do you think she'd tell her mom?"

I consider. Gemma is sixteen years old. Kids that age don't tell their parents much unless it suits them. What might Gemma want? Power? Prestige? To make trouble? She's a vampire who feeds off frailty.

The pen's slippery in my hand. "I don't know." I add a question of my own: "Would she tell Chad?" My fingers hurt from gripping the pen so hard.

Dana doesn't respond. Her eyes look glassy.

I write Chad's name. And Owen's.

While Dana's lips tighten, she stays quiet. She swipes the note off the table and zips it into a pocket of her gym bag.

"I'm just listing everyone who *could* have seen or heard something," I say. "Everyone who could have sent those notes. I don't think it's the twins. Or Ruby or Zoe, obviously. Although I guess they could have seen something and mentioned it to someone else. A teacher at school? Or how about Gloria?"

Dana shrugs. I add her housekeeper's name to the list. Just in case, I add Zoe's and my daughter's names too.

Dana nods. For a second, she looks mollified, then her eyes narrow. "And you."

I look up, startled.

"Since we're just listing *coulds*," she says softly.

A sour taste fills my mouth. She won't meet my eye. I take a deep breath and add my name to the list. "Right." Does she really suspect me?

"I know it's not you," she adds. "Obviously." Her voice has that same conciliatory tone as mine when I'd assured her I didn't suspect the twins, not really.

The pen slips from my fingers and rolls off the table. I don't bother to retrieve it from the floral carpet. Surprise and hurt have tightened my throat. She's my best friend. I risked everything to help her, yet some part of her mistrusts me.

CHAPTER 21

Jo: Nine days after Stan's death

As if I don't have enough on my plate, someone's gone and stolen my stapler. To get a new one, I head to the office. The teachers' stationary supplies are housed in a big, locked cupboard. It's more secure than Fort Knox. The mad cow-faced school secretary holds the key.

I'm filling in a form for a replacement stapler when I spy Owen Mc-Farlane slouched in a chair in the narrow lobby separating the admin office and the principal's office.

The sight of him looking utterly wretched triggers a memory: the similar holding cell outside my high school principal's office. We referred to those chairs as Death Row.

Thanks to Dana, who always knew when to quit, I never landed there. But I came close that one time.

Some dumb jocks got caught smoking weed on the smelly high-jump mats stored behind the school's stage. This triggered mass panic and a search of students' belongings.

I'd asked to go to the toilet during History that day. The teacher, who looked exactly like the woman with the pitchfork in American Gothic, *almost refused, but when I whispered the word* period, *old Mrs. Gosford relented.*

"Be quick," she hissed, prune-mouthed.

I nodded sweetly. "I'll try, but I'm bleeding everywhere, and I'm out of quarters for the tampon machine. I'll have to get change at the office!"

At the word tampon, *Mrs. Gosford's bloodless lips lost more color. Had I proceeded to whip mine out right then and there, she couldn't have looked more horrified.*

Stepping out of the room, I saw a zombie army of teachers and support staff marching down the hall. Those who weren't moving were rifling through students' lockers. Holy crap. There was a baggie of shrooms in my gym bag.

I zipped straight past the can and up the side stairs. Luck was with me: the searchers hadn't reached my locker.

I found the magic mushrooms and stuffed them down the front of my jeans, then shuffled back toward the girls' toilet.

I didn't want to flush them. It was such a waste. Yet it was too risky to keep them on me. I'd seen the antidrug zeal in those teachers' eyes: they wouldn't stop with lockers and bags. The body searches could start any minute.

I continued down the hall, looking for somewhere to hide the baggie, somewhere it might be overlooked, somewhere I could return for it later. The school corridors were a wasteland. No potted plants. No ornaments. No handy nooks or crannies.

Up ahead, like an answer to an unspoken prayer, a vision appeared before me. At the base of her locker, neatly folded, lay Angie Zukovitch's cheerleading jacket. She must have forgotten it somewhere, and someone had kindly returned it. It shone like a beacon: cobalt blue with her surname in silver letters. The school colors.

I bent down and slipped the shrooms into the inside chest pocket. I'd been looking forward to them, but the sacrifice seemed worthwhile.

There was a spring in my step as I reentered History. Even Mrs. Gosford couldn't squash it.

Sure enough, later that day I saw Angie slumped on Death Row, pale beneath a layer of false bravado and pancake makeup. She never knew who did it or why: payback for her endless lame riffs on my surname, Dykstra, and for taking that nude Polaroid of me for Bryce and Kyle.

Plenty of people had reason to fuck with her back in high school. I didn't tell Dana until years later. I wasn't ashamed of setting Angie up, I just wasn't proud of it either. I even felt a little bad for not feeling bad when she was marched out of school, tearfully protesting her innocence between her loud, grim-faced parents.

I don't lack empathy. I just save it for those who deserve it, like Owen McFarlane. He looks pale and thin, a consumptive, tortured boy version of his mom.

Finally, the secretary hands me a new stapler. It's a tinny piece of shit. I'd better just go buy one. Crap stapler in hand, I walk over to Owen. "Hey, Owen."

He looks up. Beneath a mass of straggly curls, dark eyes take me in. Even in a school uniform of crisp white shirt and gray slacks, Owen manages to look goth. I like him. Someone in that family had to rebel. He shuffles his feet. "Hi, Ms. Jo."

In school, my name is Miz Jo. Back when I was a kid, we still called teachers by their surnames: Mr. O'Connor, Mrs. Dawson. I'm not sure when that shifted.

Outside of school, to Owen I'm plain old Jo. I met the twins as newborns. At that point, childless myself, I found them sweet but mind-numbing. It wasn't until I had Ruby that I understood Dana's obsession.

"You okay?" I ask. There's a geometric pattern drawn on the back of his hand in blue ink. It's like a starburst or a mandala using only straight lines. I wonder what it means and why he's here, looking like he's waiting—no, hoping—for death outside the principal's office.

Owen shrugs. He's not much of a talker.

I should go but don't. There are more questions I'd love to ask but don't dare: Did you see or hear anything that night? Do you know your mom's guilty as sin? Do you suspect I helped her?

Owen surprises me by saying: "The cops talked to me last night."

"Oh," I say. I thought Dana was against that. Was their lawyer with them? "Was it okay?"

Another shrug. "They asked a lot about you."

"Me?" I blurt before I can stop myself, then, in a more normal voice, say, "Really? What did they want to know?"

Owen sighs. "Just stuff."

I feel an urge to shake him.

I thought Owen was the honest twin, more straightforward and transparent than his high-gloss brother. But the way he hangs his head low and looks up seems covert. Is that mockery in his twisted lips or just his standard teenage-misfit expression?

I wrap my cardigan tighter. There's a draft in this office.

"Owen," I say, "why are you here?"

He blinks. His voice is soft. "I guess I'm in trouble."

"Why?" It comes out as a bleat. I want to shake him again. What's he done? His mom's under enough pressure without him misbehaving.

Owen's thin shoulders rise. His sandy curls obscure more of his face. "School searched our lockers this morning."

"Oh shit," I say. This word escapes through clenched teeth.

Again, I think back to my own narrow escape with the shrooms. How old was I? Sixteen. A year older than Owen. Evidently not old enough to know better. Who brings drugs to school? What was I thinking?

Owen swings his feet. When he glances up, he looks scared, arms clutching his belly like it hurts. His upper body is gently rocking.

The fear on his face fuels my own. I'm assuming it was drugs because of my own misspent youth. What if it's something else? Something worse. Something related to Stan's death.

"Owen?" I cross the gap between us and sidle into the chair beside his. "What did they find in your locker?"

He's rocking harder. "Spice," he mumbles.

Despite my relief, I'm outraged. "Spice!" I say. "Do you even know what that is?" I figured he might have tried pot, but this is worse. It's synthetic marijuana sprayed with God knows what. The effects are much stronger. And at school! Owen ignores me. I take a deep breath. "Where did you get it?"

He shoots me a sideways sneer that says I'm a moron. "It's everywhere."

I study my sensible work shoes tapping on the tiles next to Owen's scuffed loafers. Dana will lose it.

"Owen," I whisper. "It's illegal! The school might call the cops."

That gets his attention.

All motion stops. "The cops? But they barely found anything! It's not like I was selling it!"

"That's good," I say, somewhat relieved. At least he wasn't found with bushels. "But you're a minor. And it's dangerous. They'll want to know where it came from."

He rolls his eyes. "I'm not a narc."

My eyes follow suit in a jerky eye roll. What is this, a bad TV cop drama? First his mom talking about sting ops, and now Owen's contempt for narcs.

His gaze has reglued to the floor. He's stopped rocking, but his hands knead his knees. He's got big knuckles like his father's.

"Did you buy it at school?" I ask.

His lips twitch briefly into what could be a smile. "As if. Nobody sells anything here except shit."

"Such as?"

"Bobby Armstead's dad has a massive wine cellar."

I picture Bobby's good-old-boy dad when he finds his prized bottles of 1990 Château Margaux have gone missing. "Nice," I say. "Could you let me know next time Bobby's peddling his dad's premium hooch?"

If I was hoping for a smile, I don't get it.

Gazing at Owen, the truth hits me. I recall what Angie said about her son Jordan's tennis coach selling him marijuana. That coach lives next door to Owen. The smile dies on my lips. "It was your neighbor," I whisper. Dana's young lover.

Owen's whole body goes rigid. If he'd screamed yes, the truth couldn't be louder or clearer.

I shut my eyes. Jesus.

What a fucker, selling chemical-laced weed to his lover's vulnerable teenage son. I'd like to kick Ryan Reeve in the balls. As will Dana.

At that moment, Principal Bill's door opens. Seeing me seated beside Owen, his gray eyebrows rise, and the corners of his mouth shoot down. Principal Bill doesn't like me. He had no choice but to approve my hiring, not after Stan and Dana endorsed me. Not after their generous donation to Stanton House. They built the new science lab. So yes, I owe Dana.

"Owen?" says Principal Bill. A tall, thin man, his voice is unusually low. He's fond of western-style belt buckles and lariats. He moves and talks slowly. I suspect he does this to bore his opponents into submission. By the time he's finished a sentence, the will to live, let alone argue, is . . . long . . . gone. Strangely, kids seem to like him. He has a grandfatherly vibe.

Owen stands up. I stay quiet and seated.

"Jo?" says my boss. "Did you need to see me?" These six words last an ice age.

I shake my head. "No." There's no reason to pretend to like him either.

I stand up. "I was just speaking with Owen. About how hard it is with his dad still unfound." This is my reminder to go easy on him, to bear in mind what he's facing, and whose son he is. I click my stapler. "Have you spoken with Owen's mother?"

Principal Bill frowns. His head shake is stiff: "The secretary's been unable to reach her."

"She should be here," I say. "I'll try to call her."

Under their shroud of curls, Owen's eyes shift my way. "No!" he growls. "Mom makes everything worse! She's crazy! She's—" His voice breaks.

The panic in his eyes zaps me. Is Owen scared of—or for—Dana?

I quash this thought. That wasn't fear, just resentment. All teenagers feel misunderstood. And Owen has good reason to feel that way. No one in that family ever got him, with his pebble-towers on the beach, tribal wood carvings, and elaborate mobiles of found objects. Dana dragged him to all those doctors, made the poor kid feel defective instead of creative. No wonder he mistrusts her.

Owen is smart. All those therapists taught him was to hide himself better. I can't say those diagnoses were wrong, just that labels aren't always helpful.

"Shall we?" says Principal Bill. He motions Owen into his office.

Owen only half shuts the door.

Trying to listen in, I recall him, maybe age four, face blotched with fury because Dana had thrown out a mobile he'd fashioned from wire and seagull feathers. She said it was filthy, which it was. She'd urged him to remake it using fluffy dyed feathers from the craft store. What Dana didn't get was the purpose of that mobile. It wasn't decoration but protection, an attempt to keep his world in balance.

My memory is interrupted by footsteps. Principal Bill peers out, frowning, and shuts his door.

Damn. Did he know I was trying to eavesdrop?

As I stalk out into the hallway, I recall Owen's anger toward his mother. What if he knows the truth about his dad? The kid's fragile, maybe drug addled. I'm scared of what he'll let slip to that old windbag Bill.

CHAPTER 22

Jo

Phone pressed to my ear, I speed-walk to the art room. I have a free block between now and lunch. I'm so behind on my grading it's not funny, yet there's no way I can focus, not with Owen saying God knows what to Principal Bill.

Dana doesn't answer when I call. It goes to voicemail. I hang up and redial.

The art room's cold. I slip inside, shut the door, and dump my papers on a table. The parquet floor needs sweeping. It's covered in shreds of colored paper, chalk dust, and glitter. The room's utterly still.

Again voicemail. I lower my phone. Where the hell's Dana? If Principal Bill's reached her, she should be here already. Is she in his office?

I approach a window and scan the guest parking lot down below. There's a Range Rover, but it's not Dana's. There is no silver Mercedes. My frustration spikes. Where is she? Maybe her phone's on silent.

I send her a text—CALL ME!!!—and another: CALL ME ASAP!

If she sees them, she'll know it's urgent. I detest all caps.

The art room smells of gouache, an earthy scent like mud after heavy rain. It's giving me a headache. I pace before the tall windows. Glitter is stuck to my dark pants. Damn. That stuff never comes off; I refuse to buy it for Ruby. I recheck my phone. Where the fuck's Dana?

There's no way she wouldn't come when summoned by Principal

Bill. Unless she can't. This thought stops me cold. Dana's never without her phone. She even takes it to yoga. What if she's been arrested?

It's unlikely, yet I can't help but picture her in a cell, head in hands, her belongings confiscated, waiting—like Owen—to be summoned for interrogation.

I press my fingertips against the cool window. A man's raking leaves off the school's lawn and collecting them in shiny black garbage bags. The guest parking lot's almost empty. I look up. The wind's torn blue holes in the clouds.

I redial Dana's number, get no answer.

I stuff my phone and my unmarked essays into my bag. I'd better find her. Who knows what Owen's saying?

Teachers aren't meant to leave the school grounds during free periods. I need this job, need a good reference to help hide the blot on my name from Chicago. I don't want more trouble. But I have to find Dana.

I sneak down the back stairs and hurry to the staff lot. It's full of respectable cars, not as flashy as the parents' but none too bad, save for mine. A layer of grime coats my car. I wouldn't normally let it get this dirty, but I'm hoping the hit-and-run detectives have noticed I have nothing to hide—*ha ha*. I bet whoever struck Alma Reyes headed straight for the nearest car wash.

As I drive, the local news comes on. I don't pay attention until the announcer's voice says, "hit-and-run." I turn up the volume. "Alma Reyes, the forty-two-year-old Filipina struck in a hit-and-run in the Oaks early on the morning of October eighteenth, has succumbed to her injuries."

Shock locks my chest. I can't believe it. The poor woman died. She never awoke from her coma.

The newscaster's voice echoes: "There have been no arrests yet, although police report progress."

My eyes swim. Progress? I've been so consumed with worry about dumping Stan's body that I've barely thought about Alma Reyes. Or running that stop sign. Guilt churns my stomach. And now she's dead.

The news report ends as I approach Marlowe. I try not to look at the spot where she lay or remember her, frail and still, or that small, scrappy dog. It's not fair. I'm shaking with guilt, fury, and sorrow.

I was sure she'd pull through. How old are her poor children? I clutch the wheel, overcome with rage at the man who hit her. He was speeding. He left her for dead in the drizzle! And he put me on the cops' radar. Made me complicit. He obviously feels no remorse. I want him caught. And I want him to suffer.

The newscaster moves on to some local council meeting. Even he sounds bored stiff. I'm fighting back furious tears.

At Bennet, I turn right toward Beach, then left toward Dana's. I could turn onto Beach earlier but don't, out of habit. At this time of year, the road's empty. Come summer, Beach Drive is full of tourists driving twenty miles an hour.

Since the closing of the cannery and the mill, Glebes Bay depends on tourism. Weekenders come up from Seattle, lured by waterfront lodges, forest hikes, and a coastal town billed as "charming."

It *is* charming, yet there's much the tourists don't see. The off-season, for starters, when it rains nonstop. And the locals, scraping by in the poorer parts of town, like the Glebe, where I grew up, far from the movie-set locales of Beach Drive and Glebes Harbor, with its shiny white boats and flower baskets.

As I slow and pull into Dana's drive, I check the security camera facing the mailbox. Its green light is blinking. I'm glad Dana remembered to turn it back on. At least she's paying attention. Except where is she? I type in the gate's code, feeling shaky.

I'm worried about Dana—about us. And I'm still reeling over the news about Alma Reyes. She held on for nine days! I hate to think of her, turned and washed by strangers. The indignity! And her poor family back in the Philippines, undoubtedly praying. If she had to die, it should have been instantaneous.

Pulling through the tall gates, I swipe the tears from my eyes. The oaks lining Dana's drive are almost bare. Black branches reach skyward like charred witchy fingers. Through their lattice, Winderlea looks extra spooky.

I pull into a guest slot. Gloria's car, almost as crappy as mine, isn't here. It might be her day off. Where is she? I know nothing about Gloria. This is worrying.

Exiting my car, cool, damp air enfolds me. I zip my jacket. It's always colder near the sea.

The vast grounds lie still. I walk briskly to the front steps. In shadow, the house looks grim. The porch is a dark mouth. No lights are on. I trot up the steps and ring the bell. Its clangs echo. I try Dana's phone again. No reply.

Frustrated, I descend the stairs. Coming here was a waste of time. I should have stayed at school. I could get in trouble.

I'm near my car when a bird trills in the pines. It comes from the direction of Dana's guest cottage.

I stop, uneasy. The sound's odd, not quite a bird's cry. I stare into the trees.

Behind me lies the service entrance to Dana's studio. It's also unlit. Where's Dana's assistant? I know nothing about her either. What if Daisy found blood in the studio? We cleaned up in a hurry.

That weird sound comes again. I veer onto the path leading to the guest cottage. I pass dormant rose bushes and a red-skinned madrona.

Through the trees, the guesthouse comes into view. Unlike the main house, it's charming: a fairy-tale cottage with leaded glass in the windows. Its stone walls are embraced by climbing roses and ivy.

I'm a dozen steps away when the sound reoccurs: a short, shrill cry. I stop. Was it human? Or a bird chirping in warning?

I'm listening hard when movement yanks my gaze to a window. There's a gap in the sheer curtains. Something gold flashes.

Without thinking, I step closer, over ivy, between prickly rose bushes. Come summer, they'll be heavy with pink blossoms.

Just as I can picture the roses, I can picture the cottage's bedroom. I stayed there for a week with Ruby last summer, just after we moved back to Glebes Bay. The cottage is tiny but heavenly, with a view over the water. I'd gladly have stayed forever, but Dana made it clear that wasn't an option. It was hard to go from there to my dingy basement.

I peer through the leaded window.

Dana's hair cascades silver-blond off the bed. She's on her back, naked. Straddling her is a man with a photoshopped body. Caramel hair hides his face. His curls bounce as he thrusts. I've never seen him before, but who else could it be but Dana's hot young neighbor? Ryan Reeve, the gorgeous drug dealer.

Dana groans and grips his ass. His head rears back. Dana moans louder.

Holy shit! I jerk backward and sideways, out of the window. Shock's left me lightheaded.

I only saw his face for a second, but that was enough. I was wrong about never having seen him before. He's the hit-and-run driver!

CHAPTER 23

Dana

I stretch out my toes, painted black cherry red. I'm lying on the bed in a white robe. My hair's damp from the shower. Now that I'm alone, the cottage feels dreamy. The sun's come out. Dust motes hang in the sunbeams.

I scan the white walls, the white quilt, the gauzy drapes. It's like being on vacation in a secluded resort, someplace romantic. I imagine a tropical beach just outside the front door, with aqua water and coral reefs. I can hear the waves lapping.

Sometimes I come here to think. I'd love this cottage for my studio. I asked Stan, but he said no, we needed a guesthouse. We don't. It's rarely used.

I tip my toes back and forth, loosening my ankles. I feel good, less tense than I've felt since that night. After everything I've been through, I deserved this. It was worth it, though risky. I mustn't do it again—at least not in the near future.

Turning, I see my phone on the bedside table. I reach for it idly and tap in the code. I have twelve missed calls, all from Jo, and a slew of texts. Shit. I prop myself on my elbow. So much for feeling relaxed.

I think of the cops. What if they've shown Jo some proof she can't lie away? What if she's cracked under pressure? My throat's dry. What if they've offered her a plea deal?

I dismiss this idea. Jo's tough as nails and equally sharp. That's why I asked her. And she's loyal.

Still, my left eye, newly healed, starts to throb. I touch it, feeling the last hint of swelling. There's always a breaking point. If Jo were threatened with life in jail, life away from Ruby— Adrenaline whips through me. If she had to choose, she'd pick her daughter. What mother wouldn't?

I hit call. "Jo?"

She spits out her response: "Jesus! Are you done yet?"

"What?" I say, surprised. Have I caught her midconversation, talking to someone else? Whoever they are, they're in trouble.

"We need to talk," she says. "Now." This last word sounds vicious. "I'm on your doorstep."

I twist and sit up. "What?"

"I'm out front." She sounds livid.

"Um, okay." I smooth my hair. "Give me two minutes."

As I pull on my clothes—black pants, black silk top, and a long, loose charcoal cardigan—it's hard not to picture each item being torn off me. God, Ryan's hot. And he can't get enough of me. I smile. If I knew how, I'd whistle some jaunty show tune.

I slip into my shoes and go outside.

I walk quickly. The holly has a wealth of red berries. According to Jo, that means we're in for a harsh winter. The lights are off in my studio. Daisy must have left early for lunch.

Sure enough, Jo's car sits alone in the guest slots. Isn't she supposed to be at school? I hope she hasn't messed up at work again. I don't know the full story of what happened to her in Chicago—and don't want to— but getting Jo hired at Stanton House wasn't easy.

Rounding the house, I see her on a bench near the front steps. Nearby stands the wheelbarrow, heaped with bags of leaves. The gardener must also be on his lunch break.

The sight of Jo and the wheelbarrow stirs a shudder. I can't help but think of that night, how hard it was to move Stan. I pull my hands up into my soft sleeves.

Arms crossed, Jo watches my approach. The vertical streak between her brows looks deeper than ever. Without knowing why, I feel guilty.

I stop a few feet away. "Hi," I venture.

She doesn't answer. When Jo's angry, she grinds her teeth. She's doing it now.

I try again. "Jo?" What have I done? Or is she mad at someone else? No, this feels pointed my way. "What's going on?"

Again, no answer. She's scaring me. Have the police told her something?

She stands. "Let's go inside." She sounds grim.

I follow her up the stairs and open the door. Stepping inside, I gaze around like I don't live here. Floor so glossy it looks lacquered. Octagonal glass table. Blue and white Delftware vases. And that frozen waterfall of a chandelier.

Daisy's done the hall flowers: a solemn blue and white arrangement. Not quite funerary but appropriate for our situation. I turn away. The jasmine's scent is cloying.

Jo pushes past me and heads for the kitchen. I follow meekly.

I fetch two San Pellegrinos from the fridge—mandarin for me, bitter orange for Jo—and perch on a stool. Jo stands. The counters gleam, thanks to Gloria. Where is Gloria? Jo ignores the offered soda.

"What's happened?" I ask. Her silence is punishing. I'm scared and annoyed.

"That man," she says. "The one you were fucking. Was that your young neighbor?"

Shock pops my mouth open. Jesus. Jo was spying on me. I take a slow sip of soda. It's so cold it hurts.

"Was it?" Her voice rises.

I feel my cheeks color.

Jo throws up her hands. "What the fuck, Dana?"

She's right. It was stupid. I'm under police scrutiny. "It just . . . happened. I had to talk to him, to see if he knew anything about that night. If he could've been the one leaving the notes." That Night. The Notes. They've taken on capital letters, like horror movie titles.

Jo cuts me off with a snarl: "You weren't talking!"

I take a deep breath. Her anger is justified. If I fuck up, she's going down too. I clutch my cold can, feeling sick and ashamed—not for sleeping with Ryan, but for doing it now, with the cops hovering. What if they'd seen me? I'm meant to be the shattered wife praying for Stan's safe return, not some horny old housewife getting it on with my deadbeat neighbor. It looks bad. I can't meet her eyes. "It won't happen again. I just—"

"It was him! Ryan Reeve killed Alma Reyes!"

I look up and frown, lost by this change of topic. Jo's face has reddened. "What? Who?" I say.

"The hit-and-run!" Her voice shakes. "He drove over that poor woman, then took off!"

I recall straddling him, how good he felt. "That's impossible." My voice quivers.

Jo's eyes narrow into hazel shards. Her voice is shrill. "I have to tell the police! He did it!" She looks close to tears.

I look out the window. A strip of ocean sparkles navy. Could Ryan really have done what Jo said?

"Jesus," cries Jo. She starts pacing. "That poor woman! She's dead, Dana!"

Her hysteria surprises me. Finding that lady must have been more traumatic than I thought. I set down my can, clear my throat. "I guess if you're sure, you should report him."

She spins and screams: "I can't! That's the problem!"

When I don't respond, she spells it out.

"If he saw us schlepping Stan in a wheelbarrow that night, he'd get a plea deal. Alma's death was manslaughter. The police would claim Stan's was murder."

I feel ill. They'd do anything to get me. Could Ryan actually be my blackmailer?

Jo's face twists. She starts crying.

"You'll turn him in," I say. "Just not yet. Not until we're sure who's behind the notes." I grab a box of tissues off the counter and walk toward her. "I don't think it's him," I add, passing her the tissues.

Jo swipes at her tears. "He killed someone, Dana! You don't think he'd be up for blackmail?" She balls up the paper towel. "Christ. Of all the people you could choose!" She snorts. "I mean, look at you! You could have anyone! Some loser dealing dope to Jordan Costin and . . ." She stops, like she's remembered something. Her voice sharpens. "And Owen."

How does this involve Owen?

"That's why I came over," said Jo. "The school found drugs in Owen's locker. Spice. It's basically some plant laced with chemical shit. Kids smoke it. The stuff's bad news, Dana."

"I . . ." There's a surge of pain behind my left eye, so sharp and sudden I feel like puking. "Oh my God," I whisper. "Ryan sold it to Owen?"

Jo nods. "Yes. Owen's in the principal's office."

"Jesus!" I grab the chrome countertop to steady myself. I bend forward, dizzy.

Faced with my distress, Jo looks mollified. I've been punished enough. "You'd better get over there."

I can't even talk. Drugs. Owen. I look around for my car keys. Except I shouldn't. I had that wine earlier. I feel queasy.

Jo must know what I'm thinking because she grabs her massive tote bag. "I'll drive," she says flatly. "Come on."

I follow her shakily into the hall. The smell of jasmine's overwhelming. It's a relief to get outside. Jo grips my elbow as we descend the stairs. I gulp down cold autumn air.

"This supports the notes being from Ryan," says Jo as we walk to her car.

"Why?" I say. My brain's an overloaded washing machine, unbalanced but churning. My lover sold hallucinogenic drugs to my child.

"Ryan could have been here that night, selling shit to Owen," says Jo. She unlocks her car's door.

I pry open the passenger door. It's a relief to sink into the seat.

Jo's right, as usual: if Chad managed to whisk his girlfriend upstairs, Owen could easily have snuck out for a dope deal. For all I know, Owen and Ryan have been *doing* drugs together. I've been that oblivious. A terrible mother.

Jo jams the car into reverse, then pulls out and heads down the drive. Her car rattles. It's a wonder the thing's still running.

I consider buying her a new car. I've thought of it before, and of paying her rent for a better apartment. I never broached the subject because of Stanley. He wouldn't have liked me giving Jo money.

A few years back, Stan's younger brother went bankrupt. Stan didn't bail him out, said he'd gambled and lost, luck of the draw. Stan could be a real asshole.

I stare up at the trees. They look sad without leaves. Stan's gone. There's nothing to stop me from helping Jo out. Except no, that's unwise. A sudden change in her finances might interest the police. And she might think I don't trust her and am buying her silence.

The car jolts. I trust her, don't I?

Jo types in the gates' passcode. I hold my breath as they open.

As we turn onto Beach, I see a gray sedan parked across the road. Two men sit up front, heads bent, books in hand. Books? That's suspicious! Are they my blackmailers, waiting to see me collect another note? Are they plainclothes detectives?

I rub my forehead. My sore eye pulses. Fear's exhausting.

Looking up, I catch sight of Ryan on the sidewalk, jogging. His perfect ass is wrapped in tight red running shorts, like the tempting biblical apple in Eden. Hot damn.

Anger drowns my desire. He sold dangerous drugs to my son! I clench my fists, feeling sick. I read an article about spice. It can be laced with everything from fentanyl to embalming fluid.

Jo asks, "You okay?"

I study her. Peering straight ahead at the road, she looks tired and anxious. Deep grooves bracket her mouth.

I nod and twist my stupid ring. "Yes. Thanks for coming to find me."

"It's okay." Anger spent, she sounds done in.

Still ahead, Ryan bounds along the sidewalk. I try not to look his way as we pass. I dig my nails into my palms. This is typical. I'm seeing danger in all the wrong places. What kind of person has sex with a drug-dealing creep yet doubts her best childhood friend?

CHAPTER 24

Jo: Ten days since Stan died

A piercing squeal fills the air. I jump. It's just feedback from the speakers. In the run-up to Halloween, Ruby's school, McKenzie Elementary, is hosting a Fall Fair. A section of the schoolyard is full of stalls selling baked goods and crafts made by students and parents. There are simple games like ring toss and croquet. There's a bouncy castle. Kids are performing songs and dances on a portable stage.

Ruby's class is up next. They're doing the Hokey Pokey.

I stand off to one side, where I won't be stuck in the crowd but Ruby will still be able to see me. The weather's cooperating: cool but clear. If it had rained, we'd all be crammed into the school gym.

While the kids wait to go on stage, two teachers issue last-minute instructions. I crane my neck, searching for Ruby. All the kids are dressed as pumpkins, their outfits made from felt and construction paper.

"Mrs. Dykstra?" It's an older man's drawl.

I turn in surprise. Two men stand beside me: Detectives Farley and Morton.

Shit. The cops from the hit-and-run.

What are they doing here? I thought it was weird not to hear from them, especially after Alma died. That must have cranked the case into a higher gear. And there's no way they haven't connected me to Stan's disappearance.

My throat's gone dry. What if they've had me under surveillance? What if they're working with Shergold and Bellows?

"How are you?" says the younger one, Morton. A messenger bag's slung over his narrow chest. He's wearing gray slacks and a tight blue jacket.

"Fine," I say. I clear my throat. "I was very sorry to hear about Alma Reyes."

Detective Morton nods. "Can we have a word?"

I tense up. Now? Surely that's harassment! I'm at my child's school!

I nod at the stage. "My daughter's about to perform."

Detective Farley turns to eye the stage. Ruby's class is getting into position. Ruby's pumpkin-stalk hat has tilted. The music starts. Farley nods. He's sunk in a huge dark-green parka. It makes him look even more like a toad. "After, then," he says. "We have a few questions."

Farley's puffier-eyed than I remember. Beneath his freckles, Morton looks anemic. The skin under his eyes is more shadowed. I imagine them tailing me around the clock.

Throughout Ruby's performance, I'm aware of the detectives beside me. I keep my eyes on her and smile wide. She knows all the words and does the movements with gusto. I should feel proud, but instead, I'm sick to my stomach. I'm also angry that I've been robbed of this precious moment.

When the song ends, I clap and wave at Ruby. All the kids are ushered offstage. Their teacher herds them away for a group photo.

"Let's go over there." Detective Morton gestures off to the side, near a tree, where there are no people. "It'll only take a few minutes."

Gut heavy, I follow.

"Have you found the driver?" I ask, after we stop. Part of me hopes they've nabbed Ryan Reeve.

Morton squints against the weak sun. "Our investigation's ongoing."

I wait. A new group of kids is up on stage, a few years older, singing "You Are My Sunshine." Off-key.

"We'd like to follow up," says Farley. "About this man you say you saw."

Outrage twists my mouth. They don't believe me! "I did see him! Youngish. Sandy blond. Longish hair." My voice is sharp. "Like I told you!"

Detective Farley doesn't react. I press my lips shut. I hate feeling torn. I know who killed Alma but can't say.

Detective Morton pulls a paper from his bag. It's the photo-fit I did with the kindly gray-haired lady. Morton holds it against his chest. "Does this still match your memories?"

I squint at the image. My heart rate increases. The mouth's too wide, as is the nose. And Ryan's hair is less curly. But those eyes! Someone will recognize him. I look away. "I . . . I think so."

Farley rubs his jaw. I feel his eyes boring through me. I must seem cagey. He's picked up that I'm holding back. "Really?" he growls. "What haven't you told us?"

My mouth opens. I glare at him. I mustn't say more. "What do you mean?" I protest.

He sounds triumphant. "You were speeding."

Anger yanks my head up. Cops are allowed to lie. They can pretend to know things they don't to provoke a rise. I jab my finger at the photo-fit. "He was speeding!"

Farley shakes his head. "It's strange, no?" he says. "You being the one to find Alma Reyes after having spent the night with Dana McFarlane the night her husband vanished."

I grip the sleeves of my coat, willing myself to calm down. There's no good answer to this. It *is* strange. I look back at the stage. The kids are dressed in yellow and holding paper cut-out sunshines. Soon, I'll have to collect Ruby.

"Yes," I say. "What a night. It's just . . . awful."

Morton leans closer. "It's been very interesting, speaking with Detective Shergold. She's a legend." His smile is nasty. "Youngest-ever officer to make detective in Glebes Bay. When was it?" He looks at Farley. "Fifteen years back?"

Farley grunts "More. She won the Medal of Honor."

I don't react. I knew they'd connect with Shergold sooner or later. And I already knew she was good.

Detective Morton squints at the stage. "Your current place of employment, Stanton House—do they know why you were fired in Chicago?"

My hands curl into tight fists. I feel faint with fury, and self-pity. On stage behind me, the song draws to a shaky close: *Please don't take my sunshine awayyyy.*

"Those charges were dropped," I say. "Now excuse me, I must find my daughter."

Walking away, I want to cry. It's not fair. This was my fresh start. I'll die if people here find out, everyone at Stanton House eyeing me differently, wondering if I'm guilty. The other teachers. That smug cow of a secretary. Principal Bill. And even Dana.

CHAPTER 25

Jo: Eleven days since Stan died

Today's lesson: discuss deception in *Hamlet*. Nobody handles trickery better than Shakespeare. Normally, I love this topic, but I'm finding it hard to focus. When the bell finally rings, my students race out. Left alone with my thoughts, I collect my books and follow more sedately.

The hall's packed with kids rushing both ways. Sounds bounce to form a muffled roar punctuated by laughter and voices: "No way, man!" "She didn't?" "Meet me or else." "Loser!"

I'm swept toward the back staircase.

Descending, I spy Owen down below, on the zig to my zag. He's moving quickly. Before he slips out of sight, I catch a glimpse of his face: a secretive press to his mouth, the hard set of his fine jaw.

When I swing around the bend, I see him again, on the ground floor, heading out back. I decide to follow. I want to know what he said to Principal Bill.

For his sins, Owen got a slap on the wrist: a thousand-word essay on the dangers of spice and other new psychoactive substances, which yours truly will be stuck grading. He claimed he bought the stuff off some big Black guy at the mall, that this stranger called out in passing, "*Pssst*, hey mon, want to score?" A drug dealer straight out of central casting.

Surely even Principal Bill didn't buy that load, not that it matters—what with Dana and Stan having funded the new science lab. The cops weren't called. Owen wasn't suspended.

Things might have gone differently for the school's two scholarship kids, both brown. Those kids are shuffled out every time a photographer visits so the school can show off its "diverse student body."

Owen exits through the back door. I pause in the doorway.

Out back, it's all but empty, a few kids cutting right across the basketball court toward the library. Approaching from that direction is Emmett Isles, son of Stan's business partner, Ralph.

A year older than Owen, Emmett is taller. He's lanky, though not as skinny as Owen. Clutched to his chest is a big hardcover book. A leather satchel hangs from one shoulder. Fair, floppy hair obscures much of his face.

Owen slows to let Emmett catch up. They exchange greetings and continue on together, quickening their pace.

I'm surprised. I hadn't realized they were friends.

Emmett's far from popular, but he's usually with others. He's well groomed, like his father. Owen's a scruffy loner. What do this pair have in common?

As I follow, they veer diagonally left, toward a stand of pines on the Stanton Street side. If they looked back, they'd see me. Oh, well, so be it. They're on the grass, walking quickly.

The field's wet. My thin leather flats are soon soggy. The boys' postures have fed my suspicion—heads bent, like they're hiding. What's their hurry to reach those pines? I know kids smoke cigarettes back there.

I expect one of them to look back, but they don't. They both slip into the trees.

Just as I think I've lost them, I hear voices. Owen's greeting someone. A lower male voice answers. I stiffen. It sounds like an adult. Is Owen buying more drugs?

I'm not surprised Owen's acting out. His dad's missing. The school—no, the whole damn town—is a hotbed of ugly rumors.

I reach the edge of the trees. Up ahead, a male voice is talking.

Suddenly, I'm unsure. This copse is dank and dark. Despite being near the road, it's secluded. But I can't leave. Those boys are obviously up to no good.

My pace slows as wet branches slap me. I look around, scared *I'm* being followed. The pines press too close, their lower branches dead and straggly. The ground's spongy. It smells rotten. All city sounds have faded. Give nature any space, and it takes over.

A voice makes me stop. "You got it?" Owen asks gruffly. He's closer than I thought.

I wait a beat, then creep forward.

Rounding the next tree, I see them in a small clearing. The boys are facing someone taller and broader. The adult stranger wears a boxy coat and a baseball hat. My breath catches. Is that Ryan Reeve, selling more drugs? But Ryan has long hair, unless it's tucked up, under the hat.

I duck back, crouch, peering between low branches.

The stranger turns. Beneath his hat, he's wearing dark wraparound glasses.

Emmett pulls something from the pocket of his navy blazer. He hands it over. If the other guy slips him something in return, I don't see it. The man mutters words I can't catch. Emmett stays quiet. Owen looks around furtively.

Damn it. What's that boy thinking? Buying drugs on school grounds when he's already in trouble.

Transaction done, the boys turn. I shrink back. Prickly pine needles poke through my sweater. My socks are wet.

Sunk in the brush, I hold my breath as they approach. Owen's so close, I can smell him: slightly musty, like his clothes need washing. I should mention that to Dana. But how? It'll feel like an accusation.

Owen's scowling at his feet. His face looks thinner. Is the boy eating?

His hollow cheeks remind me of Stan. How hard this must be for Owen. To have a loved one go missing would be the worst fate imaginable. Your mind would forever fill in the blanks, painting dreadful scenarios.

We didn't think of the kids when we dumped Stan's body. I can only hope Dana is not tempted to tell them the truth.

Emmett adjusts the bag on his shoulder. I don't trust this kid, his face as blank as a mannequin's. His dad, Ralph, is weird too. Both father and son have pale, dead eyes like Vladimir Putin.

The boys pass me. If they'd looked over, they'd have seen me squatting in the brush. I have two choices: follow them or creep after the mysterious stranger.

Peeking back through the branches, I see this man stride away. Hands thrust deep into his coat, he's headed for the road. I rise and follow. I want to know for sure whether or not it's Ryan Reeve. If it is, I must warn Dana. I can deal with the boys later.

The trees run to a high red brick wall that borders Stanton Street. The man stays in the woods until they peter out, then walks quickly along the wall. The gate's near the backmost school building.

To close the gap, I start to jog.

He must hear me since he looks back. He starts running. His jacket flaps behind him.

"Stop!" I scream. I put on a burst of speed. "Hey! You! Stop!" Anger rockets me closer.

Back in high school, during gym class, out jogging, a passing pervert groped me. I spun around and kicked him hard in the ass. He yelped and shot away like a dog with its tail between its legs. Witnessed by half the class, this episode earned me brief fame.

The intruder is nearing the exit. Two metal rails form the gate, designed to stop bicycle traffic. When he vaults over these, his jacket snags. He arcs forward, headfirst. His hat tumbles off to reveal long, dark gold hair.

Minus the hat, his identity's obvious. It *is* Ryan! That fucker!

For a moment, he lies on the ground, stunned. Then he swings himself upright and yanks his coat free. He darts right.

I stagger up to the rails. Ryan's maybe fifty feet away. "You!" I shriek.

He looks back over his shoulder. His snarl takes me back to that morning, to the intersection of Elm and Marlowe. That thump when his car struck Alma Reyes. Pure rage overwhelms me. "You! Killer!"

At this word, Ryan spins to a stop. I recoil, scared he'll charge toward me. His face is dark with fury. "Shut up, bitch!" he says. "Or you'll be sorry."

He turns and walks away.

I can barely stand, let alone follow. I cling to the gate's railing, gasping.

Leaning out, I watch Ryan saunter down the street. Freed from the cap, his tawny curls bounce. He crosses the road and turns onto a side street.

Still holding the rail, I bend low. I can't suck in enough air. That look in his eyes. He knows who I am! I shouldn't have chased him. If I point the finger at him, he'll tell the cops that I ran that stop sign.

Though I know that I must turn him in, I don't dare.

I can't stop wheezing.

CHAPTER 26

Jo: Twelve days since Stan died

I'm still quaking as I pull up in front of Winderlea. That encounter with Ryan really scared me. I'm sweaty and disheveled. My shoes are muddy. I'll spend weeks picking pine needles out of this sweater.

Ruby's gone home with a school friend. I'll collect her at five thirty. I should be using this time to grade papers. Instead, as soon as school was out, I raced over here. I need to tell Dana about Ryan.

Gloria is standing beside her car, helping Zoe unbuckle her seat belt. The twins, whom she also picked up, are hauling their school bags up the broad stone steps.

I park beside Gloria's Honda and get out of my car.

"Hey, Gloria. How's it going?"

She must notice I'm a mess because her eyes widen. Still, she smiles politely. "Hello, Jo."

In her midthirties, Gloria's a short, attractive woman, curvy but not fat. If I had to guess her origins, I'd wager someplace in Central America. She has a hint of an accent, soft as a lisp. Her eyelashes are so long they could be fake, although I doubt they are, on her wages.

Gloria has freed Zoe, who scrambles out of the car.

"Hi, Jo!" pipes up Zoe.

Like the twins, Zoe's in her school uniform: a pleated gray skirt and white-collared blouse under a navy sweater. With her fair hair French braided, she looks straight out of an old Enid Blyton novel.

Gloria scans my back seat. "Where's Ruby?"

"On a playdate with a friend," I say. "I stopped by quickly to see Dana."

Gloria nods. She shuts the door behind Zoe and walks to the back of her car. She raises the hatchback and bends to collect some bags.

I join her. "Can I help?"

"Oh, no need," says Gloria. "I only have these two." She scoops a bag into each arm. I slam her car's hatchback.

Zoe has run ahead, up the path. Her spindly braids flap.

Gloria and I walk beside each other. I think of the list Dana and I made, people who could know about Stan. Could Zoe have seen something and told Gloria? That would be a stretch . . . and yet. Zoe spends a lot of time with the housekeeper.

"Is everything okay?" I ask. "With Stan gone?"

Gloria looks reluctant to speak, which I get. She's an employee, and I'm Dana's best friend. Anything she says will probably get back to her boss. "It's a hard time on Dana," she says. "And the children."

I nod. "The police—have they talked to you?"

"Certainly," says Gloria. Her dark, full lips tighten. "I could not help them."

I sigh. "Me neither."

She shoots me a glance I don't like. What does Gloria think I might know?

"They asked if I knew he was hitting her," I say quietly.

Gloria's thick eyebrows tilt. "I saw no sign of that."

Again, I nod. "Same." I swallow, worried she might take this the wrong way and think I'm doubting Dana. "Not until that night Stan took off," I add quickly.

Gloria's eyes veer my way. "You were here?" Her surprise appears genuine, but who knows?

"Dana called me after he left. She was upset. I came over."

Gloria stares straight ahead, her brow furrowed. I wonder what she knows. Housekeepers must see a lot.

We've reached the front stairs.

Before taking the first step, I hesitate. The night of the fight, Gloria likely left work around six, as usual. But she might have stayed later or come back.

"Gloria?" I say. "The day Stan left—or before—did you notice anything strange? Like someone watching the house or something?"

Her frown deepens. "You mean like stalkers? Or kidnappers?" She puts the emphasis on *nap*, rendering the word oddly comical.

She rearranges her grip on the bags as we climb the steps. "I told the police," she says sharply, "that someone was watching."

Surprise makes me stop. "What?"

Gloria keeps climbing. I take two steps to catch up.

"Gordon Caballo—he does the garden. He told me," says Gloria. "Someone was hiding in the cedar bushes. He found a mat in there. And cigarette butts."

"The cedars?" Immediately I think of the kids: a childhood fort, re-purposed into Chad's make-out spot or Owen's drug den.

"Over there," says Gloria. She nods toward a cedar hedge trimmed into a thick, flat-faced green wall. It faces the studio's service entrance.

"Oh," I say, my mind aswirl with new images. Was it one of the boys in there smoking? Or something more sinister? "When was that?"

"Some days before Stanley went missing."

We're on the porch. Gloria's gaze is lowered. I know that indoors, back in her place of work, she won't answer any more questions. "Can you think of any reason for Stan to leave?" I ask quickly. If Dana's right and he was having an affair, I want to know with whom.

Gloria shakes her head. Normally, she's smiley, but now she looks sullen. "No. Stanley is a nice man. A family man."

The set of her jaw makes me wonder. Gloria's sexy in a way Dana's not. Physically, she's her opposite: dark, short, and buxom to Dana's fair, tall, and willowy. What if Stan succumbed to the ulti-mate rich-guy cliché: fucking the nanny? I wonder if Gloria resents Dana. She might have told the cops that Dana was cheating with her fitness-freak neighbor.

Since Gloria's hands are full, I shove the door open. "After you," I tell Gloria.

She hesitates, then precedes me indoors. I poke my head in after her. "Dana?" I call. I usually phone or text before coming over.

"Jo?" Her voice floats down the hall. She sounds surprised. "I'm in the studio. Come on in."

I head toward her. The hallway feels longer than ever. I take a deep, steadying breath before entering the studio. Stepping in, I shut the door firmly, making certain to lock it.

The room's cool and fragrant, as usual. Classical music plays softly.

Dana's assistant, Daisy, must be out making deliveries. Dana's alone, bent over an arrangement the size of a standing fan, fashioned from sunflowers and tropical foliage. In her hands is a knife with a sharp, pointed blade. With one expert movement, she slices the stalk of a huge sunflower.

I think of sunflowers as happy, yet this arrangement is sinister. Dark, spiky leaves overshadow the cheery flowers, like something bad is hanging over them. Small red flowers peek through the dark greenery. They look toxic.

"What's up?" asks Dana. She slashes through another sunflower.

I find Dana's arrangements unsettling. She doesn't just make pretty things. She's a true artist; flowers are her medium. Even her prettiest displays contain a hint of menace: the bitter fairy in "Sleeping Beauty," the wolf disguised as a harmless grannie. Her success has surprised me, but people must like that disquieting undercurrent.

I look away from the sunflowers. Trying to avoid bad thoughts is like trying not to sneeze. The more you hold it in, the harder it blasts free. My eyes spasm to the spot where Stan's head lay, that pool of blood on the white floor. The splatter . . .

"Jo?"

I wrench my gaze from the floor. Dana was talking. I've missed it. "Um. Sorry?" I say.

Her oval face swims into focus. The side door lies open. A breeze wafts in, smelling of pine sap and the sea.

"I asked what's wrong," says Dana. She bends low to slice through a thistle, yet another malevolent-looking spike.

What's wrong? I fight back a bitter laugh. What isn't? We used to visit for fun. Now, we're like survivors on a sinking ship, every discussion about what to patch up and how to bail faster.

I turn my back on the spot where Stan lay. "At school, I saw Owen sneak out to meet Ryan Reeve in the woods behind the library."

Knife still in hand, Dana's chin jerks up. Her eyes go round: "What?"

"Owen and Emmett Isles. Ralph's son. They both snuck out to meet Ryan. Emmett gave him something. Money, I guess."

Dana grimaces. "Jesus. You think they were buying more drugs?"

"I guess so."

I hope so, in fact, since it could be something worse. I rub my pants. Why, if not to sell drugs, would Ryan Reeve meet Owen and Emmett?

Before I can stop her, Dana marches to the door I just came through and yanks it wide. "Owen?" she calls. Her voice isn't loud but carries. "Owen, I need to speak with you!"

Anyone in earshot now knows Owen's in trouble.

I wait, half expecting no response. Yet moments later, Owen shuffles into the room, still wearing his school uniform. In one hand is a bowl of cereal. A spoon's clutched in the other. I'm glad to see him eating.

"Yeah?" he asks his mother.

I wish Dana had waited. We should have discussed this and devised a strategy. Now it's too late.

Dana's face is taut. She's still wielding that knife. I see Owen clock it. He's not looking at her but at the silver blade.

"Owen, why did you meet Ryan Reeve at school?" asks Dana. Her voice is soft, but her eyes are hard.

Owen blinks. Behind his long bangs, his eyes flick my way and narrow. He knows I saw him and tattled. "We still had to pay him, didn't we?" He sounds sullen.

"For what?" asks Dana.

"For the stuff that got found in the raid!" He waves his spoon. "I wasn't buying more, if that's what you think!" He sounds offended.

Dana's eyes are narrower than her son's. "So, the big Black guy at the mall?"

"I made him up. I didn't want Ryan to get in trouble."

"Why didn't you pay him before?" I ask. This doesn't sit right. Yet I can't swear that Ryan passed something to the boys. If he did, I didn't see it.

"I didn't have enough money on me," says Owen.

"And Emmett?" I ask.

He scowls; now he's sure I saw Emmett too. "What about him?"

"Why was he there today?" I ask. "Meeting Ryan?"

"He wanted to try it too," scoffs Owen, like it's obvious. Perhaps it is. "Even though the stuff was confiscated, we still had to pay Ryan!"

"Why meet him at school?" I say. "That was risky. He lives right next door." I flick my chin in the direction of the Reeves' mansion.

Owen's lower lip twitches, like he's worried I'll report him and he'll get in real trouble. If he's caught again, he could be expelled. His parents' generosity notwithstanding, even Stanton House must have limits.

He studies his bowl. "Ryan was worried about the cops," he says slowly. "Worried they're watching this place because of Dad." All of a sudden, he's tearful. Is that real?

"Owen," I say quickly, before Dana can interrupt. "The night your dad left—did Ryan come by here?"

"What?" His bottom lip wobbles. He bites it flat, injects some false bravado into his voice. "Why would he? I wasn't buying drugs that night, if that's what you're asking!"

I wait.

"You're sure, right?" says Dana.

He glares at her. "What? You don't think I'd remember?" His frown deepens. "He didn't meet me." He sounds bitter.

I freeze, as does Dana. *He didn't meet* me! The normal answer would be, *I didn't see him.* What was Owen suggesting? Was Ryan here meeting Dana?

I feel hot, then cold. Maybe Dana is lying about everything that happened.

My eyes seek hers. She looks too rattled to respond. I take a quick breath. I'll ask her straight out when we're alone.

I focus on Owen. "Are you friends with Emmett?" I ask.

Some strong emotion warps his mouth. Love? Longing? Hatred? "I . . . No. We just know each other from school."

I don't know why, but I'm sure Owen's lying. Emmett's sixteen and has his learner's permit. Maybe he came over that night in his dad's fancy car and left it on the road. Learners aren't allowed to drive without an adult in the car. Maybe Ralph was lying the next morning to protect him.

"If I find out you've bought more drugs, you'll be grounded," Dana says shrilly. "And you need to stay away from Ryan!"

Owen's answering smile is so contemptuous I expect him to say the same thing back. I hold my breath.

"Yeah, whatever." He spins and sidesteps out the door.

When it's clicked shut behind him, Dana's face crumples. Her eyes meet mine, stricken. "Do you think he's on drugs?" Her voice shallows. "I mean, is he smoking that stuff regularly? Is he"—her hands shake—"addicted?"

I shrug. In Dana's mind, addiction happens to street people and sex workers. Maybe kids living in trailers.

She sets her knife on the counter and rubs her palm. "What would you do if it were Ruby?"

Pre-Ruby, I was sure I'd be the perfect parent. My imaginary kids would love vegetables. They'd have limited screen time. We'd reason things out. They'd never talk back or throw tantrums.

Reality hit hard. For a year, Ruby ate nothing but goldfish crackers and chicken fingers. These days, she's rarely detached from my old iPad.

As for Owen, I'm guessing he's been smoking pot for a while. But this spice stuff is more worrying. "Is he on any prescription meds?" I ask Dana.

"Just low-dose Adderall for his ADHD."

Jesus. *Just?* Adderall is a stimulant. I can't imagine it mixes well with synthetic cannabinoids. "Is he seeing his therapist?"

"Not lately. He stopped last year. He didn't want to go. And he seemed"—she stares at that ominous thistle—"a lot better."

My throat's dry. Normally, I'd advise her to get him straight to a professional, especially with the stress he's under. Yet it's obvious Owen knows something he shouldn't: maybe about his mom's affair, maybe about his dad. We don't need him opening up, even to a therapist.

I choose my words carefully. "Owen will be okay, Dana. He's a smart boy. Just try to keep a closer eye on him. I'll do the same at school."

Dana's still rubbing her scratched palm. Tears well in her lovely eyes. More watching and waiting. I know this is not what she wants to hear.

"This is so hard. I feel helpless."

I bite the inside of my cheek. I don't want to spell it out and say her son's a threat, but he is. He might blab if he knows something, or try to use that knowledge. The boy's smart, possibly scheming. If Dana adds to his anger, she could face retaliation.

"It will be fine," I say. "Just don't push too hard."

CHAPTER 27

Dana: Thirteen days after Stan's death

It's Halloween. Zoe and Chad went to school in costumes, Zoe as a fairy and Chad as a debonair devil. Owen refused to dress up. It was optional.

At just past eight thirty, I'm in the studio with Daisy, who came in early to complete a late order. She obviously went out last night and looks ragged, eyes red and puffy. She's in her late twenties, young enough to be out every other night but old enough to feel a hangover.

I'm stringing white roses onto wire when the front doorbell rings. Gloria gets it. Moments later, she taps on the studio's door. "Dana? It's the police." She sounds apologetic.

I try to hide my dismay. "Thanks, Gloria. Please tell them I'll join them in Stan's study."

I set down my clippers and issue Daisy instructions, then go to meet the detectives.

When I enter Stan's study, they're both facing away, eyeing the Van Dortmund. I doubt they realize its worth. How could they? It looks like an ugly print of three gargantuan gum balls. Ugh. I curse myself for not putting it away. Now if I sell it, they might notice its absence.

I already found the contact info of the art dealer who wanted to buy it last year. He was listed in Stan's day planner. While Stan loved all things techy and had a slew of devices that never stopped dinging, he jotted down appointments and notes in a big black leather binder.

I've pored through it repeatedly, searching for clues of his affair, but the entries are cryptic and seem work related: *Call R re Caruthers. Pay web guys.*

This book rests on his desk, beside where his laptop would usually sit. The cops took his electronics last week and have yet to return them.

"Detectives?" I say. They both turn. "Please, sit." I motion toward the coffee table. "Would you like a drink? Coffee? Water?"

They both decline.

The skin around Detective Bellows's nostrils looks red and raw. He must have a cold or bad allergies. Detective Shergold has a black scarf wrapped high beneath her chin. Perhaps she's poorly too, or trying to ward off her partner's affliction.

I expect them to take a seat. Instead, they both stay standing. I do too. There's an uncomfortable pause. I look at my feet. I'm wearing knee-high boots. The leather's black and shiny. I'm glad I wore them. They're what Jo calls kick-assy.

All things considered, I feel surprisingly decent. Last night, I took a Valium and actually slept. I don't like to do it, especially now, when the boys need watching. Yet it was worth it. If I'd had another sleepless night, I'd be in trouble with the police here. Some beauty sleep didn't hurt my appearance either. Detective Bellows, for one, has noticed.

He shifts from foot to foot. As usual, both detectives are dressed in dark, dull clothes. They both look somber. "Mrs. McFarlane," says Detective Bellows, "I'm afraid we have bad news."

I wait. Maybe they found the hitchhiker in Santa Fe and realized it wasn't Stanley.

Detective Bellows coughs into the back of one hand. His voice is low and sad. "We found human remains."

My head rears back. "W-what?" I stutter.

"I'm sorry," says Detective Shergold. "We have reason to believe it's your husband. We'd like you to ID his body."

I raise both hands to my cheeks. My face feels hot. Or my fingers are cold. I shut my eyes, will myself to calm down. They must be wrong. It's some other man's body. "I . . ." It's hard to speak. "What? No! It can't be!"

"Just take deep breaths," says Detective Bellows.

I nod, eyes still squeezed tight. Beneath my closed lids, I see me and Jo in the boat, feel it rocking. That blue flash when we dropped Stan—a curse upon us.

"Mrs. McFarlane? Dana?" Detective Bellows sounds concerned. "Are you alright?"

I open my eyes but keep my hands pressed to my face. Why do they think it's my husband? Did they contact Dr. Lee, our quietly efficient family dentist?

This thought is horrific, Stan's teeth unchanged, while the rest of him . . . It's been thirteen days. What would be left? Must I really view this dead body?

"We'll accompany you there and back," says Detective Bellows. "It would be a huge help to our investigation."

I force my hands down and rub my wool houndstooth skirt. I can't say no, can I? Detective Shergold steps closer. She takes my elbow. I want to jerk my arm away. Am I being arrested?

"It won't take long," says Detective Shergold. Her voice is sympathetic but firm, as is her grip as she steers me toward the hall.

The city morgue. I've only seen one on TV. Driving here, in the back of the cops' unmarked car, was a blur. Then, walking down long empty halls, riding in a large steel-clad elevator. And now, standing before a wide glazed door.

I'm between the detectives. Shergold still has hold of my arm. Bellows opens the door for us. "After you," he says. We step inside.

The smell stops me. Chemicals and something foul that slithers down my throat. I'm scared I'll retch.

The room's big, but the ceiling's too low. The fluorescent lights are too bright. I stand blinking. The walls are stark white. It's dead quiet. As soon as this pun enters my mind, I want to cry. There's no one in sight.

"This way," says Detective Shergold. She steers me along.

Stainless steel sinks and cupboards line two walls. A giant walk-in freezer runs the length of another. Scales and adjustable spotlights hang from the ceiling. My eyes skate over various metal tools. Near each sink stands a shiny steel gurney. All lie empty but for one. My knees quiver. A human form lies beneath a white plastic sheet. It's too short to be Stan.

The closer we get, the worse the smell. I press a hand to my mouth and nose. I stagger to a stop. "I . . . I can't," I say. "I'm sorry. I just . . . can't."

Detective Shergold's grip tightens. "We know this is difficult," she says. "We'll only show you one small part of him. Only his arm."

"What?" I say, bewildered. Why would they drag me here just to show me Stan's arm? Shergold propels me closer. We're steps from the gurney. An arm span from that covered figure.

Detective Bellows steps around us and walks to the gurney's top end. "You ready?" he asks.

I don't answer. I can't answer. I want to shut my eyes, but my lids feel pried open. Bellows reaches for the plastic sheet. I'm afraid Shergold was lying, scared Bellows will yank it off, force me to face what's left of Stan. His ravaged face would haunt me forever.

Bellows lifts the sheet's edge. He folds it back to reveal a bloated and wrinkled hand. The skin's loose. It's mottled greenish gray. Most of the fingernails are gone. The fingertips look chewed. Here and there, bone shines through.

I shake my head. "No." Those macerated fingers can't be Stan's. Bellows pulls at the sheet. More forearm appears. Then, an elbow and the upper arm.

I jerk back. "Oh my God!" Although the skin's loose and discolored, I recognize Stan's tricep tattoo.

He got it as a college freshman: one of those awful, meaningless tribal armbands that were popular in the mid to late nineties. A ring of barbed lines meant to convey wild masculinity.

I fear I'll vomit.

"Is it him?" asks Detective Shergold.

I shut my eyes. They could have asked if he had a tattoo. They brought me here to see my reaction. To unnerve me. Or to punish me?

"Yes." I bow my head. "It's Stan."

I hear the plastic sheet rustle, and I open my eyes. That's when I realize something is seriously wrong with Stan's corpse. Under the sheet, I can make out the shape of his feet and legs. His torso . . . his arms . . . but . . .

I wrench my arm free from Shergold's grasp. My voice is strangled: "Where's his head?"

"He's been—*ahem*—decapitated," says Detective Bellows. "We haven't located his head yet." I'm too shocked to move. "I'm sorry," he adds feebly.

I spin to look at Shergold. Her pale eyes take me in, her face impassive. She's watching me carefully. She's waiting for me to speak.

I stand, gulping. "W-what? Why?" I whimper.

"There was damage to his neck," says Detective Bellows. "That might have occurred prior to death. But the decapitation was likely postmortem. Wear and tear." Another throat clear, perhaps cold related, perhaps apologetic. "His body was dragged some distance. You know, ocean currents."

I hang my head again. Damn. Where did his head go?

Dead bodies float. Everyone knows that. We gambled on the chain keeping him down. On his being deep enough and far enough out. On the currents going the right way. Jo kept nattering on about decomposition being slowed in cold water, how that helps bodies stay under. So much for that. In fact, the cold helped preserve him. Even his lame tattoo remains visible. What rotten luck. What might his corpse tell them?

I hug myself. The room's freezing. My voice slurs, a sick child's. "Where did you find him?"

"Garibaldi Cove," says Detective Shergold.

I keep quiet. That's not far from Jo's place, not far from where we went to high school.

As kids, we used to party in that cove, sitting on driftwood logs with bottles of warm beer. If we got too noisy, the cops would show up, although they never caught us. By the time they'd parked their cars in the lot, we'd slipped away, across the rocks, giggling and staggering into the dark.

"We've got experts working out the currents," adds Detective Shergold. "To pinpoint where he went into the water."

With a shudder, I start crying. Tears stream down my cheeks and neck, into my high collar. I can't stop them.

The last two weeks, I could pretend Stan was alive—out there, somewhere. That pretense is over. The police aren't looking for a missing person. They've found his dead body. His headless dead body. This horrible rotting corpse is all that's left of my husband.

"I . . . I'm sorry." I gulp. "I just . . . hoped . . ." I bow my head, shoulders heaving.

How can you know something yet not know? I knew he was dead. Even so, there's no need to act here. My shock and sadness are genuine. My one true talent is denial.

Detective Bellows hands me a tissue from a pack in his pocket.

The detectives wait as I compose myself. I mop my eyes and my nose. Despite feeling sick with dread, I have to ask, "How did he die?"

Bellows's eyes meet his partner's. It's Detective Shergold who answers. Her tone is clipped, back to business: "We can't say yet. We need to wait for the autopsy."

I'm not sure I believe her. Are they really unsure or just not saying? I study my feet.

"Mrs. McFarlane?"

I look up to meet her eyes, cool and appraising. "Shall we?" She nods toward the door.

I'm in a daze as we retrace our steps back down the hall to the bright boxy elevator.

As its doors shut, Shergold turns my way. "Don't worry. We'll find out what happened." In her plain, middle-aged face, her eyes shine. Her gray hair is a steely helmet. I imagine her as a matronly knight riding into battle.

And the dragon? It's me, crying crocodile tears.

I nod, feeling freshly sick. I see the way she's watching me, suspicion shining off her.

She zips her plain coat. "His body will tell us a lot." Her smile is smug.

I look away. That's my big fear.

I jump when the elevator doors ping open.

CHAPTER 28

Jo

There's a new girl at Stanton House by the name of Ming, freshly arrived from Guangzhou. Her English isn't great. She's tall, thin, and timid. She walks with a stoop like she wishes she could sink through the floor, straight back to China.

Gemma Costin has launched a campaign of torment against this girl, inciting her cronies to pretend she smells; stage-whisper things that, mercifully, Ming can't catch; and rub condiments in her hair when she eats lunch alone in the cafeteria.

Gemma's behind all of this, but I can't prove it.

Nonetheless, I go to see Principal Bill, who looks extra alarmed to see me, perhaps because I'm dressed as a vampire in a long black wig, plastic fangs from the dollar store, and an old black dress bought for some long-ago New Year's. All the teachers had to dress up for Halloween. Principal Bill's gone all-out cowboy in a checkered shirt, neckerchief, and Stetson. I bet he'd love to wear this full time. He thinks he's John Wayne.

Thoughts of cowboys bring thoughts of Trevor somewhere on the rodeo circuit. What a job: risking your life, day in, day out, to entertain the beer-guzzling masses. We think we've moved on since the age of the gladiators, but we haven't.

I force my attention back to Principal Bill. "This is serious," I tell him. "Ming Lee is being racially bullied."

Bill nods and toys with his kerchief. His answers add up to empty platitudes about adjustment and culture shock, like smearing ketchup into new girls' hair is part of our culture.

I leave his office more pissed than I was going in.

I'm so irate my head's gotten itchy. I need to take off this stupid wig for a minute.

Headed for the staff restroom, I see Ming's locker plastered with blown-up photos of dead, roasted dogs, clearly lifted off the internet. "Oh, for fuck's sake," I mutter, and stomp toward her locker. I consider going back to get Principal Bill but decide not to bother. Teeth tight with fury, I rip down the offending pictures. I ball them up and lob them into the closest trash bin.

Since Bill's no use whatsoever, I decide to change tack and call Gemma's mother. Thanks to the cheating scandal, Gemma's on thin ice. While Angie couldn't care less about bullying, she'd have a fit if her precious offspring were expelled from Stanton House. For one thing, she'd lose a full year's tuition.

I text Dana for Angie's number, then call.

Faced with an unknown number, Angie trills out a greeting. If she knew it was me, she'd sound much less enthusiastic.

"Hello, Angie," I say in my best teacher voice. "This is Jo Dykstra. It's about Gemma. A small issue at school. Can we meet up briefly?"

Sure enough, Angie's tone changes to annoyance: "Jo? What's happened?"

"Gemma's fine. Don't worry. But there's something . . ." I lick my lips. "Look, Angie, it'd be easier to discuss it in person."

A sigh, like she's doing me a favor. "Okay. Fine. How about Felicity's, after school?"

Felicity's is a café popular with Stanton House mothers. It serves gluten-free macaroons and low-fat gelato in pastel colors.

I hesitate. I'll need to fetch Ruby first. Luckily, my last block is free today. I can sneak out a few minutes early. I have pens and a coloring book in my bag. While Angie and I chat, Ruby can color. "Okay," I say. "Three forty-five?"

After hanging up, I get a new message from Dana: *Why do you need Angie's number?*

I text back: *To discuss Gemma.*

Her response is quick: *I need to see you.*

Rather than keep texting, I just call. "Hey, it's me. I'm meeting Angie at Felicity's after school. Want to meet me after?"

"I . . . um . . ." Dana's voice sounds off, like she's been crying. "What's the earliest you can meet me?"

"Four thirty?" I'm scared the police are listening in. The technology exists. I don't dare ask what's wrong. "But I'll have Ruby."

"I'll get Gloria to pick her up and bring her home with Zoe. We really need to talk. As soon as possible." She hangs up.

I stow my phone, feeling shaky.

I cut out at three twenty.

I've ditched the wig and fangs and scrubbed off the makeup but still feel stupid. The dress is ankle-length and uncomfortably snug in the middle. It's too shiny. I'll stick out like a gangrened thumb amid Felicity's bleached boho-chic decor.

Stepping in, I'm surprised to see Dana. She's almost an hour early. She's at a table at the back, wearing boots, a calf-length houndstooth dress, and big black sunglasses. Despite her pallor and obvious distress, she still belongs in Felicity's: a movie star mid-divorce, beautiful but fragile. I hope to God she hasn't done anything stupid.

I look around. No sign of Angie. Figures she'd keep me waiting. After getting my coffee, I walk over to Dana.

"Hey." I set down my decaf and plop into the chair beside hers. All the chairs in here are mismatched yet complementary. Dana's is gold and white striped. Mine's upholstered in faux sheepskin.

I don't take off my jacket. I'll need to move when Angie arrives. "What's happened?"

A quick shake of her head, like it's too hard to talk. I wait. Dana takes a sip of tea. It smells perfumy. She sets her cup carefully back in its saucer. Is she drunk and trying to hide it? She's moving stiffly.

"They found his body," she whispers. "Minus his head. In Garibaldi Cove. It was"—her voice shakes—"the worst thing I've ever seen." She presses a hand to her lips. "I had to go to the morgue to ID him."

I blink. I can't believe it. We went so far out. All that way, past the damn islands. "Are you sure it was him?"

She nods. Her mouth twists as if she's in pain.

She describes his melting tattoo. Despite sips of hot coffee, my insides ice over. The cops have Stan's body.

Our plan hinged on his fate being a mystery. He wanted a new life far away. He was the victim of a botched kidnapping or a drunk who met with an accident . . . Maybe Stan snapped and ended it all.

Dana's cup rattles into its saucer. The last fact dribbles out: the cops are waiting on the autopsy to confirm cause of death.

Hope flickers. "Could it look accidental?" I whisper. "Like he slipped on the rocks and drowned? They can't know he was bashed, right? Not if his head's missing."

Dana won't meet my eyes. "I don't know. Maybe."

I rub my hands to get warm. It's a cold day, and this place is freezing.

It's hard to think, especially in here, everything swirly and soft, from the jazz to the gauzy white curtains and the tufted throw pillows. The place is decorated like Dana's guest cottage, all cream and oatmeal, like Instagram's vision of heaven. The pallor makes it seem even colder. Everything about this place feels as fake as the rubber cacti in miniature pots on each table. Still, it's better than that wretched café in the Oaks Club.

High heels click behind me. The change on Dana's face alerts me: Angie's coming.

I turn to look. Sure enough, she's sauntering our way, a tall glass in one hand, topped with a tower of whipped cream. I bet she asked for skim milk with whip. That would be just like Angie.

Seeing Dana, she grins. "Oh my God, Dana! How are you, honey?"

Air kisses for Dana. A tight-lipped smile for me.

I grab my bag and stand up. Dana's in shock and in no state to be talking to Angie. "Angie," I say quickly, "thanks for coming to meet me. Shall we sit over there?" I point to a window table.

Angie ignores this and sets her drink on Dana's table. She deposits her purse beside it, where everyone can admire its label. "Oh, honey, I just heard." She makes cow eyes at Dana. "How are you?" She shrugs off her jacket and twists into a chair.

I hold my breath. What has Angie heard? The cops only just told Dana about finding Stan's body. It can't have been on the news yet, surely.

Teeth clenched, I reclaim my chair.

"It was on KRAX," continues Angie. That's the local radio station. Pronounced *kay-rax*, not *cracks*—which is how I say it. Angie's breathless. Beneath all that blush and foundation, her cheeks are actually flushed. The color runs into her hairline, where her dark roots are showing. "Oh my God! I can't believe it! Is it really him?"

Like we're discussing hot gossip, not Dana's poor dead husband.

Dana freezes, the proverbial deer in the headlights. Her lips move soundlessly.

Angie rushes ahead. "Foul play!" She shudders happily. "Honey. I'm so sorry!"

Dana blinks at me. "The cops told me they didn't know how he died!" She sounds stunned, although I've warned her that cops aren't obliged to be honest.

Angie frowns as best she can with all the Botox. "Oh, reporters— they get stuff wrong." She toys with the long spoon in her flavored coffee and takes a sip. In their mascaraed nests, her eyes are glued on Dana. "I guess it sounds more sensational, saying he'd been stabbed."

Dana flinches. I hold my breath. Thank God Dana's eyes are hidden behind those massive glasses. Still, the way she flinched. I know Dana's tells when I see them.

Fear and rage hit me. Stabbed? With a knife? Dana said it was self-defense, that he hit her, and she pushed him. She said she lost it and bashed him with a vase. The one we dumped. I feel hot all over.

Dana hangs her head. She looks sick. We're all quiet.

"It might not be true," I manage. "Like Angie said, the news gets stuff wrong." I want to shake Dana the way I did in the boat when she sat there trying to remove her ring after dumping Stan.

A single tear meanders down her white cheek. She doesn't stop it.

Angie's still watching her so intently I want to slap her. I'd like to smack both of them. What the fuck's going on here?

"I should take Dana home," I tell Angie.

Dana looks up, like a spell broke. She shakes her head. "No. I'm fine. Really." She doesn't look it. She blinks slowly. Is she drunk? Or on medication?

I wait, not wanting to upset her further. I'm scared of what she could say with Angie here, listening.

"Dane, I'm so sorry. I thought you knew," coos Angie.

Fury curls my lip. I'm not sure what makes me angrier: Angie's lie or her shortening of Dana's name, like they're besties. Even I don't do that. Her name's Dana.

Dana doesn't react. Angie turns to me. A penciled eyebrow climbs skyward. "Why did you want to see me?"

I frown. Given Angie's news, it takes me a moment to remember: Gemma and her bullying. The persecuted new girl.

I was outraged and eager to save poor, cowed Ming. Now it barely matters. I'm too scared to be righteous.

Throat dry, I reach for my coffee. It went cold ages ago and tastes bitter. Despite a big sip, my voice is hoarse. "Gemma's been bullying a new kid."

Angie snorts. "What? Can you prove that?"

She didn't even try to deny it. "Yes." It's a lie, but Angie won't know. "I just figured I'd come to you first, let you know. In case you can . . . influence her. So there's no need to inform Principal Bill . . ."

Angie frowns, clearly suspicious that I'd try to help. She tugs at her necklace with its big diamond letter *A* pendant.

"Gemma's smart," I continue, in my best earnest-teacher voice. "She has so much potential. I think she could do really well this year, be a top scorer. I just hope she can learn to be a bit kinder. Girls that age, they can be quite—" I shrug. "Well, you remember. We could all be catty back in high school."

Angie releases her pendant to toy with her hair, unsure whether to be mollified or outraged. Am I calling her daughter a bitch or finally acknowledging her obvious brilliance?

"Gemma shows strong leadership abilities," I continue, in top bullshit-parent-teacher-interview gear. "I hope she'll get involved in student government. Try out for student council."

Angie eyes me warily. "This kid you say she's got a problem with. What's her story?"

"Immigrant family," I say. "Newly arrived from China."

Angie's nostrils twitch like she's smelled something off. Her glossy mouth tightens.

In recent years, a few wealthy Chinese families have bought properties in the Oaks. It's pissed off some locals and inspired muttering about being priced out of the market. This is a joke. No one in the Oaks is in danger of being made homeless.

"The poor girl's lost," I say, looking sad. "In a new culture."

Angie's frown deepens. "Did she do something to Gemma?"

"No. That's the point. She's done nothing to deserve being picked on." Inspiration strikes. "Look, Angie, I don't want Gemma to get in trouble or, God forbid, be expelled—not now, not when Chad's grieving." I throw a sad look at Dana. "The boy really needs her."

Angie looks at Dana too.

Dana bows her head. "Oh my God," she moans. "How will I tell the children?"

That stops all conversation, Gemma and her victim forgotten.

For a moment we're three moms contemplating the enormity of Dana's grim task. She must tell her kids their dad's dead. And that the police think he was murdered.

"Want me to come?" I ask after a moment. I need to go to Winderlea anyway, to collect Ruby. And we need to talk about Angie's claim that Stan was stabbed. If it's true, that's another lie of Dana's. My pity gels back into outrage.

Dana pushes her dark glasses up onto her head. Without them, she looks exposed, eyes wide and glazed with tears. Minus mascara, her lashes are pale. I'm transfixed. I haven't seen her with bare eyelashes since she was a girl.

"What can I tell them?" asks Dana.

I start to get money from my purse, but Angie waves it away. "Go. I've got this."

For an instant, I almost like her. But then I see the way she's studying Dana, eyes intent and gleeful above a mouth mimicking pity. "Go!" she says again.

Dana staggers to her feet. I rise too. Before turning to go, I take one last look at Angie, sitting alert and bright-eyed. She brings to mind a scientist peering into a maze, waiting to see which way the rats will run.

CHAPTER 29

Jo

As we cross the café's parking lot, Dana stumbles. She fumbles through her bag for her keys. Is she drunk, on pills, or just in shock? A DUI would be the last straw.

"You're in no state to drive," I say. "Leave your car. You can pick it up tomorrow."

She shakes her head. "No. I'm fine. Really." Moments later, she drops her keys, then her sunglasses. I pick them up and hand them over. She's visibly trembling.

"Come on," I say. I'm in no mood for resistance. "I'm driving."

Her shoulders sink. "Fine."

We retrace our steps back to my sorry Toyota.

I fish my keys from my tote bag. As usual, it's heavy with books and papers. The handles dig deep into my shoulder.

Some cretin has drawn a dick and an arc of spunk on my car's dirty back window. I consider rubbing it out but don't bother. There are more pressing matters.

Beside my car sits Angie's white BMW. Its front window is open, and the keys are in the ignition. Even in this neighborhood, that seems careless. I guess you don't worry about your car getting stolen when your husband's a luxury-car dealer.

I unlock my car, which no one in their right mind would steal, and toss in my heavy bag. I reach across the seats to open the door for Dana.

She crumples in like an old grannie. I turn on the radio as she buckles up, then reverse slowly.

I'm straightening the car when Angie Costin exits the café. Her cell phone's pressed to her ear. No doubt she's busy telling everyone she knows about her coffee with Dana.

I push up my glasses and steer us out of the lot.

We pass the Village Market, where all the Stanton House moms shop for pine nuts, organic arugula, and wild-caught salmon. We pass the Groom Room, where their pedigreed dogs get ninety-five-dollar haircuts. Next comes Core Values, the Pilates studio, where sleek women in yoga gear stand outside guzzling green smoothies.

As I drive, I debate whether to quiz Dana or wait for later. She's facing one of the worst things a parent could deal with. I should let her tell her kids first, then confront her.

Might Stan have been stabbed? For all I know, Angie made it up just to cause trouble. I'd put nothing past her.

The radio's been playing soft rock, the official soundtrack of Glebes Bay. This gives way to a local news bulletin. "This is KRAX breaking news," says the cheesy-voiced deejay. He was a year below us in high school and madly in love with Dana. He gave her a long-stemmed rose one Valentine's Day. She fed it to her pet rabbit.

I hold my breath, listening.

The deejay lowers his voice to sound solemn: "Early this morning, police recovered the remains of missing hedge fund manager Stanley McFarlane in Garibaldi Cove, approximately two kilometers from his home in the Oaks. Police spokesperson Glenda Heath confirmed foul play and stated that Mr. McFarlane suffered multiple stab wounds."

The music resumes: Air Supply's "All Out of Love." Heat blasts through my head. Multiple? Angie wasn't lying.

I veer to the curb without indicating. A horn shrills behind me, and a shiny Town Car honks past. Its driver shakes his fist as he snarls through the window. I know what he's saying: *Fucking women drivers.*

I give him the finger. Sexist moron. There's zero reaction from Dana. I slam the car into park and cut the engine.

We've stopped outside a beautiful two-story Victorian, painted robin's-egg blue. I admire it briefly. Ruby would love a house like that. Maybe someday. My attention snaps back to Dana.

Beside me, she sits rigid. My neck feels hot. I want to scream. I stare at the dashboard. That vase we dumped. Was it all a charade? I'm gripping the wheel so hard my fingers ache. I don't trust myself to let go.

Dana turns my way. "Jo?"

I can't look at her. Have I ever been this angry? Maybe at Trevor, the first time I caught him cheating. I'd only just had Ruby. I should have bundled her up and left.

Against the vinyl seat, Dana's Burberry coat rustles. Her voice is soft but clear. "Jo? That night . . . It didn't happen like I said. That wasn't true. I'm sorry."

I clench the wheel and stay quiet. She's *sorry*? Sorry doesn't cut it. I'm facing jail here. My child sent to live with her deadbeat dad. Or put in foster care. What the fuck happened?

"Stan didn't hit me. He never hit me." Her voice breaks.

I can't help but look at her. What does that mean? Did I help her hide his murder? I let go of the wheel.

She raises a hand to her eye, as if it still hurts, then drops it in her lap. Her voice sounds raw. "He hit Owen."

That shocks me. "What?"

She nods.

I study her face, so familiar, that perfect porcelain oval. Unlike me, she hasn't changed much over the years. She's stayed smooth and glossy. If she's had work done, it doesn't show. She's not like Angie with her over-stuffed lips and stretched-leather forehead. Dana's ageless and as poreless as an oil painting. She's lovely. Her eyes meet mine, wide and transparent. Has she finally told the truth about Stan's death? Or is this another story?

"I didn't know Stan was hitting Owen." Her voice thins. "If I'd known, I'd have left! I swear!" Of everything she's said, this is the most emphatic. She repeats it: "I'd have left!"

Her head bows. I don't believe her.

When she next speaks, her voice is softer: "He'd get so frustrated with Owen. And mad."

I can't breathe. Jesus. *Owen.* Stan's murder was all about Owen. Did the boy see everything that night, his mother covering up her crimes? If so, it couldn't be much worse. My life is in the hands of an unstable teenager.

I try to keep my voice steady: "Was Owen there when it happened?"

Her eyes pop open. She looks through me, glaring at the memory. "No. I saw Stan hit him and ran over. I slapped Stan. Owen ran away, and Stan started yelling at me. He said I was spoiling Owen, that he needed discipline. He started threatening me, saying we'd get a divorce and he'd get full custody of the kids. Stan said he was going to send Owen to one of those teen boot camps—you know the kind? Out in the wilds? I—" Her voice splinters.

"What happened, Dana?"

"I . . . I saw red. I grabbed a knife off my workbench and stabbed him in the chest." She twists her cream silk scarf. "He tried to grab me. I stabbed him again, in the side of the neck." She clears her throat, like something's stuck in it. "He just collapsed. It happened so fast!"

I watch her, unsure. I've known her most of my life. She's my best friend. I trusted her. Is this all or even part of the truth? Did she use me?

My voice shakes. "Where was Owen?"

"I don't know. He'd run off. He didn't see, Jo!"

How could she know? I recall the thick Turkish towel covering Stan's head and shoulders. The inky pool on the floor. A dark smear on the marble bench.

My head swirls with too many questions to catch. "Why was there blood on your workbench?"

She shudders. "He hit his head going down."

I consider her, those clear blue eyes and her pale, blinking lashes. I recall the horror in her studio, the air rose-sweet, a cold draft rushing in. My head throbs. Did I help my best friend murder her husband?

"Why were Owen and Stan in the studio?"

Dana shrugs. "Owen goes in there sometimes. He likes the cool air and the smell of the flowers."

I don't respond. I imagine Owen getting stoned and going in there to sniff his mom's flowers. Perhaps he's drawn to the coolers' blue light. The room has a far-away space station feeling.

I shut my eyes and try to conjure up all the details of that night. I got everything wrong. What other facts am I missing?

Dana lays a hand on my arm. I flinch. Her gaze is imploring. "Please." She grips my arm. "Please, Jo, it's the truth. Please believe me!"

I want to shake her off. I stay quiet.

"Stan was hitting my son! He beat Owen!"

"And your face?"

She looks freshly startled, then guilty. "I did it myself. After . . ." She swallows.

"Why?"

Her eyes sink to her lap.

"Why?" I say louder. Did she injure her face just to trick me? She did. I want her to admit it.

"I was going to call 911 and say Stan hit me. I planned to say it was self-defense." She gulps. "But I'd made our marriage look perfect." She studies her hands, that big shiny ring. "I was scared no one would believe me."

"Except me," I say flatly.

A man peddles past on a bike, dressed in neon spandex and a bullet helmet. Another MAMIL. The Oaks is full of them: middle-aged men in Lycra. Stan's tribe. Dana's watching him too. "I couldn't have asked anyone but you," she says softly.

I sit thinking. I'm too far in. There's no backing out. If she goes down, we go down together. "Okay." I try to smile. "Don't worry."

Dana chokes out a laugh, half relieved, half despairing. "Good old Jo," she says. "What would I do without you?" She peers into the street before turning back. "I owe you so much. Don't think I don't know that." Her voice shakes with emotion.

I shake my head. "That's what friends do. You'd do the same for me." Would she? I hope so.

Dana's still gripping my arm. There are tears in her eyes. "I'll make it up to you. I promise."

I look toward the pretty blue house. I believe she'll try. But what if she can't? What if the cops work it out? That's more likely now that they've found Stan's body.

The enormity of what I've done hits. How rash I was, rushing to help without thinking things through! I acted on instinct, out of old childhood habit. That lifelong sense of loyalty and obligation. Dana gave me a sense of belonging. I was conditioned to help her. And it happened so fast. I didn't think. I just reacted.

The blue house has a red door. It looks warm and festive. Or is that shade of scarlet macabre, too rich and glossy?

Fatigue fills me. I rub my palms on my old evening dress. The zipper's digging into my back. It's too tight to breathe deeply. The fabric's itchy.

"I didn't mean to kill him, Jo. I swear, I didn't plan it."

My voice is flat: "I know, Dana." I want to believe her, but it feels like wishful thinking.

CHAPTER 30

Dana

Jo's anger fills the car, as overpowering as the stinky air freshener that sits on her dash. I sink deeper into my seat, wishing I could vanish into thin air.

To make matters worse, I've started to cry. I dig through my purse in search of tissues.

We make a sharp turn onto Emerald. Jo's neck is ridged with tendons. In those wire glasses and dress, she resembles a mean old schoolmistress, the kind with a grudge and a ruler.

I bite my lip. Jo has a right to be angry. I lied that night and kept lying. I've put her in danger.

I should try harder to explain but can't stop blubbering. It's pathetic. I can't stop remembering Stan's body, his decomposing fingers . . .

For the past two weeks, I've been in and out of denial. I let myself pretend. That won't work anymore. Stan's officially dead. They're doing an autopsy. Just the thought makes me gag.

Many houses we pass are decorated for Halloween. Orange pumpkins on porches. Paper ghosts and black cats in the windows. I usually make an effort but haven't this year, for obvious reasons. You don't celebrate symbols of death and witchcraft when your husband's missing. Or murdered . . .

The decorations remind me of the kids. How will I tell them?

Unless . . . What if they've already heard? It's on the news! I should have gone straight from the morgue to the kids' school. I should have been the one to tell them!

How could the police let the story leak out? Or did they do it deliberately to break me? Are they at the house, waiting to arrest me?

My nose is dripping. I dig deeper into my handbag. A tube of lipstick falls out. Damn it. I know I have tissues somewhere. I bend to retrieve the lipstick.

Straightening, my driveway comes into view. The swirly gates. The gold-lettered sign. The mailbox. That reminds me. It's been six days since I got the last note. A long time. The other two notes were just three days apart. What's the blackmailer doing? My anxiety spikes.

Jo slows and turns in. I lean forward and cry: "Stop!"

She slams on the brakes with a gasp. We jolt to a halt. "What?" says Jo.

I wipe my nose with my hand. "I need to check the mailbox."

She turns and spits out the words: "You what?" Her face is pinched. "I thought we hit something!"

I undo my seat belt. Now's not the time. I know that. But I can't control my compulsion. The discovery of Stan's body has pushed me into a higher gear. My motor's spinning in panic. More bad news is coming. I just know it.

"Just wait!" I say and climb out of the car.

Wet, dead leaves plaster the asphalt. I look around. The pines and spruce press in, dark and claustrophobic.

Overhead a crow caws, mocking. I look up but can't see it. It calls again and hops lower. I spot it, bright-eyed in a crooked Douglas fir.

According to Jo, crows and ravens can recall human faces for up to five years if seen in stressful situations. She read all about it in some scientific journal. Jo loves corvids. She would. They're smart birds. This one might know my blackmailer. I wish I could ask it. The crow cocks its head and croaks out a laugh. Jerk. I doubt it would tell me.

I walk to the mailbox. Its door creaks and sticks midway. I forgot to tell the gardener to oil it. I smush my hand in. I already checked it at lunch. It should be empty. My fingertips brush the metal sides. It *is* empty.

Feeling stupid, I spin back to Jo's car. She's glaring through the window.

I'm near the car when I spy something white on top of the house's name stone. It's a piece of paper held down by a rock. I stop walking.

In the fir tree, the crow cackles. I stagger to the sign and grab the paper. A quick look confirms my fears. I peer up at the CCTV camera trained, uselessly, on the mailbox.

"Fuck," I say. The crow takes flight. I stare up at the camera.

Jo taps her horn to rouse me. I totter back to the car.

I pry the car door open and collapse into the seat. I shut the door. It fails to latch. Jo pulls away. The door alarm beeps as we rattle up the driveway.

Jo glowers at the note, then back at the road. "It's not." She sounds incredulous. "Is it?"

I can barely respond. "Yeah."

She brakes. We lurch to a stop. From here, the house remains hidden but for its roof, dark and steep, over the treetops. "Let me see," demands Jo.

I unfold the note.

MIDNIGHT FRI NOV 2. PUT 3 MILLION $ IN THE OCTOPUS AT MYERS POINT. COME ALONE OR THIS WILL GET WORSE.

The Octopus is a huge cement sculpture in the playground at Myers Point. It's as high as a bus and painted bright Pepto-Bismol pink. Kids climb its meandering limbs and hide in its hollow head. It smells of urine in there, dog and human.

The Octopus wouldn't meet any modern safety standards but has been there since the 1950s. Trying to demolish it would be like trying to wipe *In God We Trust* off the dollar bill. It's part of Glebes Bay. Everyone who grew up here has played there.

The block letters blur. "I can't get it," I say. "Not by Friday."

Jo jams the car into gear. "What about that Russian guy?" Stan claimed the art dealer who wanted the gumballs was pretty shady. I wonder if that's true or if Stan was being a bigot. I called the guy—Oleg something—on Jo's phone after getting the last note, then texted him photos of Stan's entire collection. He's interested in the Cleggs and a few other abstracts.

"Maybe, but it would take time." I refold the note and shove it to the bottom of my handbag. "What if I left some money? With a note, explaining. Like a goodwill gesture?"

Jo snorts. We start to rattle toward Winderlea. "You mean a down payment? Do you really think that would help? It's not a new sofa set on layaway."

I nod, feeling sick. The house looms into view. We round the bend. Gloria's car is in the guest parking lot. As is a matte gray Caprice. My heart stops. That's the detectives' car. There are two people in it, waiting.

Jo slows. She's seen the cops too. "Shit," she says. "If they ask to search, demand a warrant."

I feel too sick to even nod. What if they have one?

"Dana?" Jo's glaring at me. "Is there anything they could find? Anything I don't know about?"

I shake my head. "No. Except if we missed something cleaning up."

Jo parks and kills the engine. For a second, she looks relieved. Then her face goes taut. "Wait!" She speaks through locked teeth. "The knife you used. Where is it?"

I bow my head. "I . . . I don't know."

Incredulity cracks Jo's voice: "You don't *know*?"

"I . . . It was near Stan when I ran to get towels. But I . . . I . . . When I came back it was . . . gone." Stress makes me babble. "It was my favorite knife. Matte silver." Outside the car, a crow caws. Is it the same one I saw by the mailbox? I stop talking.

"Gone?" All color has leached from Jo's face. She stares straight ahead, out the dusty windshield. At the cedar bushes. Like she can't bear to look at me.

When she turns my way, her eyes are hard and flat. If I didn't know her, I'd say she hates me. I've never seen her so livid, not even at her deadbeat ex, who deserved it.

"We're dead meat if the cops have a warrant," she snarls. She unbuckles her seatbelt. "I hope you know *that*."

She shoves her door open and stands. Detectives Shergold and Bellows are exiting their car.

I'm still sunk in my seat, clutching my handbag.

Jo leans back into the car. Her voice is soft but harsh as she says to me, "Dana, you've done enough damage. Look pretty, and let me do the talking."

CHAPTER 31

Jo

I glare at Detective Shergold. The best defense is a strong offense.

Shergold's standing behind her car's bumper, arms crossed, next to Bellows. I ignore him. Her hair's freshly cut, the bangs a touch too short. The effect's a bit dominatrix, especially in her long black trench coat.

Dana's behind me. I march closer to the detectives.

A few feet away I stop and hoist my book bag higher on my shoulder. "Since when do you allow victims' families to learn their loved one's been murdered from the news? Why didn't you tell her?"

"That's why we're here," says Detective Bellows.

"Well you're too late," I snap, scowling at Shergold.

Dana stops beside me. She dabs her eyes with a tissue.

"We're sorry," says Detective Shergold, speaking to Dana. I doubt this. I bet she planned it. She's doing everything in her power to crush Dana. That's her job. "Can we go inside?" asks Detective Shergold.

Dana starts to answer. I cut her off. "What for?"

The last thing I want is the cops poking around now that I know that knife's AWOL. How the hell did that happen? Did someone take it? I think back to the list Dana and I made of potential blackmailing suspects. Most of them could access Dana's house. One of them might have grabbed it. But why? Did Owen nab it? He likes knives, using them for his wood carvings.

Detective Shergold reaches into her purse. I hold my breath. Shit. Did she get a search warrant?

She extracts a manila folder. "We have questions about Stan's injuries," she says. She's still watching Dana. Her tone is pleasant. "Would you like to answer them here or down at the station?"

Dana responds before I can. "On the news, they said he'd been stabbed. Is that true?" Her voice is tortured. Despite my ire, I feel some grudging respect. God she's good at playing the innocent little woman. How often did she pull this on me, growing up?

"Can we please go inside?" repeats Detective Shergold.

Dana nods. "Of course. I'm sorry." She blinks up at the house. Like she's been a bad hostess.

"After you," I say tightly and motion the detectives toward the steps. I take Dana's arm and give her a pointed look, a reminder to keep her mouth shut.

She's still crying, which is good. She should be. The fucking murder weapon's missing! Fresh fury speeds me up the stairs. I release Dana's arm so she can unlock her giant front door.

We all step into the foyer. There's a new floral arrangement in somber blues and purples. Nothing too cheery. The dark blue vase looks suitably mournful. It reminds me of the vase we dumped with Stan's body, the one Dana claimed she'd used to bash him. When all along the knife was missing.

Back then we might still have found it. Anger has quickened my breathing. Why the hell did she lie about that? Stab wounds or blunt force trauma, what's the difference? Either way, she killed him. Although I might not have helped if I'd known. Compared to grabbing some random vase, using a knife seems premeditated. You don't stab someone unless you're trying to kill them.

"The kitchen?" says Dana. She eyes me when she says this. I nod. The kitchen's fine. Surely the knife would have been found by now in the kitchen. Unless it got washed and shoved in a drawer. Or left in the drying rack. Was the blade distinctive? Might the cops recognize it? The police don't need a warrant to collect an item if they're invited in and it's in plain sight.

In the kitchen doorway, Shergold stops. She's blocking our way. "We'd like to speak with Mrs. McFarlane alone," she tells me.

I want to protest, but that might seem suspicious. I don't want to look too invested.

"No," says Dana. She mops at her eyes. "Whatever you have to say to me, Jo can hear it. Please." Her voice wavers. "I just— Right now I need a friend."

Some of my old admiration for Dana resurfaces. She really is a master of persuasion. Shergold is better off with me than if Dana balks and demands a lawyer.

"Fine," says Shergold. She enters the kitchen. The rest of us follow.

The cops decline Dana's offer of drinks. She ignores them and fetches San Pellegrinos from the fridge. I scoop ice into four Finnish mouth-blown glasses. We're buying time to calm down. We all sit at the table. Thanks to Gloria—where is Gloria?—the glass tabletop's gleaming.

Detective Shergold opens her manila folder. The top page is a photocopy. It shows two simple line drawings of a man's body, front and back. Someone's marked *X*s and slashes in various places. I'm horrified and fascinated. It's Stan's autopsy diagram. Lines depict slash marks on his hands and arms. Defensive wounds? Or degeneration, after nearly two weeks in the ocean? There's a cluster of marks on the chest and a big line at the throat. A word's visible here: *decapitation*.

I look at Dana. She's so pale I'm glad she's sitting down. I look back at the paper. If all those marks are stab wounds, the attack was frenzied. Could she really have done that to Stanley?

Detective Shergold flips the page. The next paper bears a sketch of a knife.

"His throat was slashed," says Shergold. "Based on the wounds, we believe the blade was between four to six inches. Short and sharp." Like me, she's studying Dana. "The tip may be curved." She taps the diagram. Her fingernails are short and unpainted. "Have you seen anything like this?"

Dana's sitting beside me. She looks at me, pleading. It's obvious she doesn't know what to say. I kick her gently under the table. I will her to give the right answer. It's not like they don't know.

Maybe she gets it; all those years of teenage telepathy, covering for each other, knowing when to confess what and how much. I keep my face still.

Dana clears her throat. "That looks like a florist's knife."

Shergold smiles, sharklike. "Have any of yours gone missing?"

Dana blinks. *Don't fuck it up*, I think at her. I will the word from my head into hers. *Yes. Yes. Yes.*

"Ah, yes," says Dana. "Some weeks back I . . . uh . . . misplaced one. But I have others, so it didn't really . . ." Fresh tears fill her big blue eyes. "It didn't register."

I pat her hand as if I'm consoling her. I'm not. I'm telling her she got the job done.

The detectives want to know more. When did she last see it? Where might she have left it? With the slightest of head tilts, I give Dana the sign. Time to plead ignorance.

"I don't know," she repeats, apologetic. "I . . . I'm sorry. I don't know."

Shergold concedes. She shuts her folder and slips it back into her bag. "The missing knife," she says. "Do you have any similar ones?"

Dana's gone too still. I kick her ankle again, just hard enough to rouse her.

"Yes." She's nodding like one of those bobble toys that sit on car dashboards.

I hold back my sigh of relief. At least if they do reveal a search warrant, she won't be caught in *that* lie. "I have half a dozen," says Dana.

"May we see them?"

Fresh fear snakes through me. Could one of the remaining knives be the one that killed Stan? Might tests prove that? It's the most logical explanation for where the knife went: back onto her tool rack or in a drawer. Should she demand a search warrant?

My uncertainty feeds hers. I can see it in the way her eyelids flutter. The silence is stretching too long. That in itself is suspicious. Bellows shifts in his seat. Shergold's half smile has turned gloating.

Dana pushes back her chair and stands so swiftly I'm startled. "This way. To my studio."

I push back my own chair much less forcefully. My legs feel weak as I follow the cops down the hall. Does Dana know where that knife went? If she's still lying to me, I'll kill her.

She opens the studio's door and leads them in.

In the doorway, my steps falter. Being back in this room elicits a visceral reaction. The smell. The white lights and bright flowers. The marble, smooth and slippery as ice. And the police, missing nothing. Everything feels treacherous.

I watch Dana lead Detective Shergold to her tool rack.

"We'll need to take these," says Detective Shergold, smoothly. She turns to Bellows. "Can you bag them?"

Dana's face falls. "All of them?" she says. "But they're my work tools. I special order them from Japan. You can't buy them here."

I stay where I am. My ears are roaring. I imagine the prosecutor displaying Dana's knives to the jury. Some expert explaining that a knife like these made the wounds on Stan's body. They're building their case against her. How long until she's arrested?

Detective Shergold looks my way and smiles. "Are you alright?" she asks, too sweetly, just to tell me I haven't been forgotten.

I realize how I must look, hanging in the doorway in my tatty, too-tight long dress. Like some weirdo.

"I . . . I'm allergic to certain flowers," I say.

Shergold nods. Her tone is dead flat. "Oh. Really?"

I fake a sniffle. My God. I'm doing it too: lying for no good reason. In my shrunken dress, I'm sweating. Detective Shergold isn't just after Dana. She's a gray wolf, closing in on the pair of us: two stupid Little Red Riding Hoods who should have stuck to the straight and narrow path of the law.

CHAPTER 32

Dana: Two weeks since Stan's death

I'm in the hall when I hear a thud in the lower level. That's odd. Gloria's left already. My ears strain. Is someone else down there?

That floor houses a home gym, a kitchenette, and two spare bedrooms along with various storerooms and a playroom that opens onto the lower lawn. The twins played there when they were little. Zoe prefers her room. Most of the toys down there are too young for her: giant blocks, old tricycles, a plastic slide. I've been meaning to send everything to charity and turn it into a games room.

The door to the stairs lies just ahead. I edge it open and listen.

Owen's voice floats up, along with another boy's. I didn't know he had a friend over. What are they doing down there? I'm suspicious.

I descend a few steps, listening.

"Here," says the other boy. He snickers.

Sinking onto the step, I can see them: Owen and Emmett Isles, cross-legged on a brightly patchworked plastic mat. They're bent over a single cellphone. Owen's hair is messy, Emmett's smooth as sheet metal. Emmett sniggers again. "Turn it up!" he orders.

I hold my breath. The light's too dim to show their faces clearly, just their postures of nervous excitement. Tinny voices rise up, along with yelping and huffing. A stream of *oh-yeah*s and *harder-faster*s, punctuated by profanities. I recoil. They're watching porn! It sounds violent! I hear only male voices.

I wrap my cardigan against the cold. A gift from Stan, the cashmere's soft and warm. He always found perfect presents.

A moment of sorrow enfolds me. How can you love someone yet hate them? Or does all love grow that way, gratitude intertwined with resentment? Stan was wonderful until he wasn't. I should have left him back when the twins were toddlers.

Clutching my cardigan, a memory rises.

Stan with his back turned, hands clenched into fists, while Owen, maybe three, lay on the floor, shrieking. My son's face was the color of oatmeal, except for one cheek, splotched scarlet.

"Stan?" I said.

My husband turned. He looked defiant.

I wanted to ask but didn't. I was scared he had hit him.

I clutch at my cashmere sweater. What stopped me? Was I just too exhausted—a young mother of twins, one with serious behavioral problems? Was I too selfish, loath to confront Stanley? Or was I just bamboozled? In many ways, he was a good father.

From down below, sounds of fake passion keep coming. I knead the cashmere.

When Owen was little, he'd have fits. He'd kick and screech. Every eye would turn his way. My way. Everyone judged me.

How often had I longed to shake him? Or slap him? But I didn't. I thought that was enough. It wasn't. A good mother would have left Stanley the moment she suspected.

Yes, I was lazy and selfish. Passive, like my mother. She knew Dad hit me. He beat her too. She was dependent on him, both emotionally and financially. She chose to accept it.

I swore I'd be different. Yet here I am, justifying everything, making excuses. How could I have stayed with Stan?

Down below, on that colorful mat, I can see the boys, rapt. The porn voices continue. Could one be a woman? I listen harder. It's doubtful.

I pull my hands into my soft sleeves. Is Owen gay? Has he been struggling with his sexuality? It might explain his resentment and drug use. No, his issues go way deeper, which is hardly surprising given his childhood.

I hold my breath, listening. I don't care if he's gay. I just want him to be happy. He's had it hard enough with his anxiety issues. Sadness fills me. Being gay's a fresh challenge. I want his life to be easy.

The video has degenerated into grunts and shrieks. I hug my knees.

My son's fifteen. I'm not so naive as to think he's avoiding porn. The internet's rife with it, although this sounds brutal. Is this normal nowadays?

I'm wondering what to do, when my phone buzzes in my pocket. The sound's off, and I grab it quickly, yet the boys must have heard something. They both peer my way.

I rise to my feet and pull deeper into the shadows. I retreat, feeling guilty. I'm not avoiding this. I'll deal with it later.

The phone keeps buzzing. Before answering, I slip out the door and back into the hall.

It's Ralph Isles, Emmett's father. I assume he's calling to find Emmett. "Ralph?" I say, still speaking softly. I advance toward the kitchen.

"Dana." His voice is somber. "I just heard on the news. I'm sorry."

"Thank you." My throat's tightened. The hall's wood paneled. I lay a hand on it. It's smooth and cool.

"Dana?" He rushes ahead. "I'm sorry to call now, when you must be overwhelmed, but with Stan gone, there are business matters to sort out." I wait. "Papers you need to sign." He clears his throat. "Has his will been read yet?"

I recall that night, or rather the next morning: Ralph Isles jogging toward his car, parked out front of Winderlea. Was he here that night? I've made no progress toward IDing my blackmailer. None at all. All I have are suspicions. And who isn't a suspect?

I refocus on Ralph: "You should contact Stan's lawyer, Garvin Holloway. Do you have his number?"

Ralph sighs, like he was hoping to keep the lawyers out of it. "Yes." There's a pause. "Dana? Could I come by? We need to talk."

"I . . ." I rub my hair. Rather than answer, I blurt out, "Emmett's over."

"Emmett?" He sounds surprised and indignant.

"Yes. He's with Owen."

There's no mistaking the dismay in his voice. "Really? What are they doing?"

I imagine telling the truth: they're watching violent gay porn down in the playroom. Instead, I say, "Just hanging out."

My head hurts. I'll need to address this with Owen—sometime later.

I consider telling Ralph about Owen's claim that Emmett wanted to buy spice. In normal circumstances, I'd have called Ralph already. It's what a responsible parent would do. If someone suspected my kids were buying drugs, I'd want to know.

Before I can gather my thoughts, Ralph's talking again: "Please tell Emmett I'll be over to get him. He's meant to be grounded." His tone is clipped. "We can have a quick word then."

I'm too surprised to dissuade him. Why is Emmett grounded?

Ten minutes later Ralph is at my front door, dressed in jeans and a button-down shirt beneath a suede jacket. As usual, he looks neat and stylish, his silver beard and hair cropped short and glinting.

I start to lead him to Stan's study but reconsider. I'm not sure what I don't want Ralph to see, but veer toward the den instead.

"Can I get you a drink?" I wave him toward the biggest sofa.

"No." He perches on the edge, ill at ease.

I take an armchair.

"Dana," he says, "how much do you know about Stan's business dealings?"

I bite my lip, ashamed. "I know nothing." How pathetic that sounds. And how stereotypical: the wife too vapid to worry her pretty little head about financial matters. My cheeks color.

Ralph eyes me warily. "Well, things don't look good. Stan over-extended. We'll need a financial audit to sort things out." He licks his lips, choosing his words carefully. "But I hoped police scrutiny could be avoided."

"What?" I blurt. I want to laugh. And cry. Wow. Really? Despite his clean hands and pressed shirts, is Ralph hiding some dirty dealings? Was Stan?

I clasp my hands. "I'm not sure that's possible. Not now, when the police suspect murder." Ralph blanches. "You've met them," I continue. "Detectives Bellows and Shergold. They're very thorough."

Ralph looks crestfallen but doesn't answer. The grandfather clock chimes the half hour. I jump. I didn't want that clock, but Stan liked it. It belonged to my dad.

"How bad is it, financially?" I ask Ralph. "For my family. Are we"—I can barely say it—"bankrupt?"

"It's hard to say." Now that he knows I can't or won't help, he looks peevish.

My head's swimming. How will I support my kids? Or could this bad news have a silver lining? I'd hit myself in the face, hard enough to get a black eye. Could a man stab himself to death? Stan wouldn't do that. Yet he couldn't hack being poor either. He really might have preferred to end it all.

"Bad enough that Stan might have . . ." I study the hand-knotted carpet. "Done something drastic?"

"I don't know, Dana." He squints. "I can't imagine Stan killing himself, if that's what you're suggesting, but"—he rubs his neat beard—"I guess you never know." His mouth curls with anger or irritation. "He was definitely feeling the pressure."

I nod. I hope the police will get stuck on that uncertainty.

It's only after he's left, taking his sullen son with him, that I realize I forgot to ask why Emmett was grounded.

I turn to Owen, still with me in the front hall after seeing his friend out.

Outside, I can hear the doors of Ralph's Porsche slam. "Owen," I say, "what have you and Emmett been up to?"

My son's body tenses. "Just watching video clips," he says gruffly.

I study him, his eyes fixed on the door. Is this the right time to pursue this? There's so much I could say, but it's all caught in my throat.

Owen turns to look at me, like he's wondering what my problem is. "Owen?"

"Yeah." He's wearing black jeans that are frayed at the knees and a stretched, stained gray sweatshirt.

"The night Dad died." The last word feels hard and strange on my tongue, an ugly new language I'm learning. I sat all three kids down last night, in the den, and broke the news that the police had found their dad's body. Zoe cried. The twins didn't. They barely reacted. I need to find a grief counselor. I should have done that already. And yet . . .

Owen's shoulders hunch rounder. "Yeah?"

I'm speaking softly, so no one will hear us. Zoe and Chad are around somewhere. "That night," I resume. "Why were you and Dad fighting?"

He stiffens and straightens, then looks me right in the eye. We're a few feet apart. He shakes his head. "He's dead, Mom. It doesn't matter."

"It does to me," I say. "Please, Owen."

Because he usually slouches, I hadn't realized how much he's grown. With his back straight and his head high, he's almost as tall as I am.

He balls his hands into fists as tears fill his eyes. His face is a hurt child's, yet his voice is a man's: "Dad called me a faggot."

I reach for his arm, but he shakes me off.

"You know what?" he says. "I'm glad he's dead."

CHAPTER 33

Jo: Sixteen days since Stan died

The room's dark but for the soft glow of the night-light. The girls are asleep in Zoe's massive four-poster. It's got a pink canopy, like Dana's childhood bed.

I tug up the embroidered quilt and spread on an extra chenille blanket. A storm's blown in from Alaska. The wind's bone chilling.

I bend to kiss Ruby. Her plump cheek is velvet, her breaths deep and even. If only I could climb into bed beside her.

I turn away and pinch my forehead. Enough with the *if-only*s.

While I don't like leaving the girls in the twins' care, at fifteen, they're old enough. We won't be gone long.

I pad back downstairs to find Dana crouched near the front door. She looks up from a blank sheet of paper. There's a Sharpie in her hand. Her eyes look even bigger due to her recent weight loss.

"You ready?" I say. I can't hide my impatience.

She must notice, because she says, "You don't have to come. The note said I should go alone."

I snort. I hate that martyred tone. "The note also said to bring three million dollars."

Dana frowns haughtily. She bites the end of her pen. "What should I write?"

A blackmailer wants cash, not excuses. We don't have the money. End of story. "Something vague," I say. "In case someone else finds it."

Lips pursed, Dana starts to write, her printing clean and elegant: WE NEED MORE TIME.

She taps the pen to her teeth. "Should I say *sorry*?"

I open the closet. "No."

I'm sick to death of *sorrys*. Most people don't even mean it. Trev was chock full of them: *Sorry I went on a bender. Sorry I lost all that money. Sorry about the Rodeo Queen, but I swear nothing happened! That girl's crazy!*

I should have left him years ago. He never deserved me.

I shake my head. "No *sorry*. It sounds lame."

She sighs. "Lame's how I feel." She folds the note and stands slowly.

I pull my jacket from her closet. My eyes throb. It's Friday night, the end of a long week. Half the school is off sick. I have a cough and was up most of last night. I struggle into my jacket.

Going to Myers Point is risky. Three days back, I saw the younger hit-and-run cop—Morton—at the grocery store. Was that a coincidence? Maybe. But what if I'm being followed? Those two showing up at Ruby's school was unnerving.

If the cops see us creeping around Myers Point, what excuse could we give? A missing dog? They could check that. It's late. A storm's hit. There's no good reason to be there in the dark in this weather. We'd definitely raise their suspicions.

I wrap my scarf and tuck it into my coat's collar. "What if the cops are tailing us?" I ask Dana.

"We'll keep a lookout," she says. She unlocks her colossal front door and drags it open. Frigid air rushes in. "But there's no choice. We need to try." She sounds testy. "We might see something important."

I cough. "Fine. You're right. We should try."

We take my car. A tired gray Corolla is less conspicuous than a spanking new Range Rover or a glow-in-the-dark white Mercedes.

My car's heater won't stop spluttering. It spews burnt stink but no hot air. We don't talk on the drive. Dana keeps her eyes on the rearview mirror. I make lots of unnecessary turns. No one's behind us.

The whole way there, I wish I were home in bed. I wish none of this had happened. Dana didn't deserve my help dumping Stan, not when she didn't trust me. She lied about the way he died. And her affair with that scumbag Ryan. How expertly she played me, even damaging her own face—her greatest asset—so I'd never guess she was lying. I'm furious I believed her.

Dana interrupts my self-pity: "Jo! Park there."

I slow. On one side lies the park, on the other a row of dark houses. I pull up behind a rusted Dodge pickup with an empty boat trailer. From here, it's a short walk to the park's entrance. I dig gloves from my pocket. My throat feels hot and raw.

As I exit the car, the wind strikes me. My nose starts dripping. This can't be helping my cold. I feel freshly resentful. Life was hard enough before Dana's bullshit. If only I'd said no that night and not gone over. Why am I here?

A tall hedge runs beside the sidewalk. We creep in its shadow, out of the streetlamps' orange glow. A small road leads into the park. To our left lies a parking lot, empty but for two parked cars. Maybe couples making out, although what a night for outdoor romance! It's started to drizzle. If it gets any colder, it will snow.

At the end of the hedge, we stop. The Octopus is a good spot. There's little cover, just a few harassed bushes and trees. I check my watch: 11:20 p.m.

"I don't like this," says Dana. "We're too exposed."

I look over my shoulder and think of Ryan Reeve, out back behind Stanton House. That look in his eyes, like he'd happily throttle me. Could he have followed us from Dana's? No, I'm being paranoid. My throat's scratchy. "Now what?" I whisper.

"I'll leave the note." She sounds scared but determined. "You stay hidden, okay?"

A snort escapes, feral. "Fuck that!" I say. "I'm not leaving you out here alone!"

A few months back, a woman was raped near here while jogging after sunset. No one's been arrested. If he did it once, why not again? It's awful that women aren't truly safe anywhere. Not even in Glebes Bay.

For a second, Dana looks set to argue, but she relents. We step out from behind the hedge. The full force of the wind hits. We walk angled forward. The field's soggy.

Besides the giant cement Octopus, there's a slide, a swing set, and a row of posts for leapfrog. Further back lie the beach and the sea.

We're about halfway across the field when I look back, just in case. Nothing moves but the grass and the worn-out trees. I scan the houses and the road. I can't shake the sense that someone's watching.

My foot sinks into a hole. Mud squelches, cold and thick, through my shoe. "Fuck!" I mutter.

Dana twists, big-eyed. "What?"

"Nothing. I stepped in a puddle."

We pass the slide and the swings. As far as creepiness goes, it's hard to top an abandoned playground in the dark. The monstrous Octopus doesn't help. It's a safety hazard. The city's just asking for a lawsuit. I push against the wind.

The Octopus's black head looms closer. Round eyes are painted on. They don't look cute but evil. The door's a jet-black hole.

We stop, and the acrid smell of piss fills my nose.

We left our phones back at Winderlea so they couldn't be traced. I brought nothing but a small flashlight. I free it from my pocket but hesitate, scared of attracting attention.

"I can't see anything," points out Dana.

I click the light on. We step closer to the door.

The room's small, with concave, pink-painted walls. It reminds me of a heart's chamber. I shine the light around. It's empty. There are wood chips and cigarette butts on the floor. A shiny chip bag. A sad, used condom.

Jesus. What's wrong with people? Imagine doing it here.

Dana brushes past me and enters. She sets the note near the back wall on the floor, pinning it down with wood chips.

When she reemerges, she looks ill. "That smell."

We turn and walk back the way we came. I scan the road. Dark houses. Parked cars. The occasional porch light. Nothing out of the ordinary. I imagine normal people leading normal lives. Sleeping. Maybe watching TV. What would they think if they knew what we'd done? They'd view us as terrible people. They would not understand.

Behind us, the waves sound threatening. Wind punches our backs. The drizzle's turned to full-on rain. I clear my throat. It's increasingly sore: "There's nowhere to hide."

"Those bushes?" suggests Dana. A clump of dispirited blackberries grows near the parking lot. We head that way. Rain drips off my hood. My jeans are soaked. The cold's vicious.

The bush is prickly. We sink down in its shadow to wait. Ten minutes. Twenty. It's creeping closer to midnight. In my wet sneakers, my feet are numb.

Crouched next to each other, I'm reminded of our errant youth. Getting drunk in parks. Hiding from parents and cops. Back when we were too young to get into clubs and too stupid to worry. Nights full of promise but nothing to do.

The only time I got really scared was the night Dana's car went off the road.

We were at a party out at Fenton Lake with a bunch of older kids she barely knew. Dana disappeared with some boy. I didn't know anyone else. I sat self-consciously by the campfire, drinking cherry wine coolers.

When Dana reappeared, she looked flushed and mad. Maybe she'd had a fight with that guy. "Jo! Come on!" she said. "Let's go!"

I stood up, happy to be off. Away from the fire, it was very dark. We stumbled arm in arm down a trail, back to her little white car.

Normally, Dana didn't drink and drive. But she was obviously drunk. As was I.

"Maybe we should sleep in the car," I said.

Dana tossed me the keys. "Fuck that."

I shook my head. "But . . . I can't . . ." I'd practiced a few times but didn't even have my license.

Her hands went to her hips. "Come on, Jo! I'm totally fucked up. That guy gave me this punch. It was like . . . laced with something." She swayed on her feet as if to prove her point. "You have to drive."

I did okay on the dirt road but drove us into a ditch on a small country lane about twenty minutes out of town. We didn't get hurt. The car wasn't damaged. It was just stuck, half off the road.

After we crawled out, I got sick—heaves of sour fake cherry.

"Shit," grumbled Dana, as we stood by the roadside. "Now what?"

I was terrified the cops would show up and breathalyze me.

Instead, the first car that came along held a guy from the party. He stopped behind Dana's car and got out with a smile. I recognized him from around town. Early twenties. He ran with a rough crowd. He had a beard and dressed like a biker.

"Well, well, well," he said. "Look who needs help."

Dana gave him her most charming smile. "We'd really appreciate that."

With guys from school, that would have worked. They'd do anything for Dana. But this guy just laughed. "What's in it for me, little girl?"

Dana glared at me. "You got us into this mess."

I shook my head. "I told you I couldn't—"

She cut me off. "Do it, Jo!"

He towed us out for a blow job. Dana sat in the car while I did it.

Next morning, she gave me her new MP3 player. It was her way of saying sorry. I tried never to think of that night again. And as always, I forgave her.

My knees are stiff from kneeling. My toes feel frozen solid. I check my watch. It's 12:30 a.m. I stand up.

Dana jerks me down: "Shhhh! Listen!" She practically mouths the words: "Someone's coming!"

I inch forward and peer around the bush. The wind makes my eyes water.

A figure appears, blacker lines in the dark. They're headed our way, across the field, come from the beach. Or the playground.

Dana's hands cup my ear: "Can you see who they are?"

I shake my head. It's too dark to see clearly. The person's slim. I'm not sure if it's a man or a woman. They pass out of sight. I creep forward, staying low. Dana's behind me.

The figure enters a pool of light cast by a streetlamp in the parking lot. I think it's a guy. He's in a dark hat and green jacket—like Ryan's. This thought elicits a visceral reaction.

He vanishes, blocked by a tree. I crawl further. He steps behind a pale car. Is that an SUV?

A car door slams. The engine starts. Headlights flare. I shrink back, blinded. Can he see us?

The car turns and speeds away.

"Fuck!" I say. "That must have been the blackmailer!" I throw up my hands. "We should have gotten the license plate number!"

"But . . ." says Dana. She looks crestfallen.

I march toward the Octopus. She follows more slowly. By the time she catches up, I've looked inside and stormed out. She sees my face and stops. I spit, "The note's gone."

"Oh shit." She sways. "We learned nothing."

I don't bother to answer but turn and plod toward the car. The wind's hard, from the ocean. The rain's blinding.

Dana doesn't follow. I turn back. She's just standing there, head bent, in the deluge. Her hood's slipped down. I'm scared she's having a breakdown.

I walk back and take her arm. "Come on. It's freezing. You'll catch a cold."

She blinks. "Jo? I'm going crazy! The cops! And now this blackmail! Who saw us? There's nothing worse than not knowing!"

I consider this as I steer her back to the car.

Mom told me my dad didn't want a funeral. She bought an urn for his ashes. It sat on an altar in her bedroom with a scented candle and a vase of fake flowers. I used to go in there and talk to him, tell him I missed him. Light incense. Pray.

At age fourteen, I learned the truth. He didn't die. He ran off to start a new family in San Diego. I have twin half brothers four years my junior. We've never met and never will. It's not their fault, but I hate them. Just like I resented my mother.

It was my dad who betrayed us, but I blamed her. I felt she'd lied for herself, to save face, because she considered divorce less respectable than being widowed.

Since having Ruby, I doubt that. She did it for me, so I wouldn't know he chose to leave us. Wouldn't realize I'd meant so little. Ignorance isn't bliss, but the truth isn't either.

I climb into the cold car and shut my door. Dana curls into the passenger seat and closes her eyes. Her wet hair is stringy.

I start the car and flick on the wipers. The left one starts squeaking.

"Shit," I mutter. "Not again." I only just had it fixed.

CHAPTER 34

Dana: Seventeen days after Stan's death

It's raining so hard the lotus pond's flooding. The weeping willow looks defeated. I sit on the couch, staring out the window. Today's paper is on my lap. Beyond the lawns, the sea's seething.

The detectives just left. They showed up bright and early and were here, waiting, when I got home from dropping the kids off at school. No doubt I looked like a zombie. I barely slept after last night's drama.

The police took another box of Stan's stuff from his study, including his big black day planner. I consented to this. Even Bellows didn't pretend to be charming.

Upstairs, I can hear Gloria vacuuming. I throw aside the morning paper. It's the same old shit. The discovery of Stan's decapitated body has returned us to front page news. Media from further afield have descended. So far I've been treated with sympathy, but the tide's turning. Three days back, I was "private." Today, an unnamed source, purportedly "close to the family," described me as "aloof." So it starts. I've disconnected the home phone.

I check my watch. My stomach's hollow. It's past time. I can't put it off any longer.

I haul myself off the couch and walk to the front hall. It's dark despite the chandelier's twinkle. I imagine smashing it like a piñata.

I march to the closet and yank the door open. In spite of Gloria's best efforts, it's chaos, packed with coats, boots, hats, and umbrellas.

Our house is full of stuff we don't need. A glut of affluence. We keep buying more. It feels overwhelming.

Staring into the mess, I feel strung out: too much stress, not enough sleep, way too much coffee. I'm scared the police might return to search the house. Would they find anything? I've seen enough TV to know about luminol. How clean is the studio? And where's the damn knife? I grab an umbrella and straighten.

It feels strange to fear the police. As a white, middle-class woman, I was raised to see them as allies, the ones you'd call in a crisis. Now I've switched sides. Except the bad guys aren't safer. A blackmailer. Or several! And I don't even know who they are.

It could be Gloria or the UPS man or the guy who fixed our dryer. It could be my son's nasty girlfriend. Or my other son's potential boyfriend. It could be someone I don't know. I'm not sure what's worse: a scary stranger or a wolf in sheep's clothing.

I slam the closet door shut.

I'm near the front door when my phone rings in my cardigan's pocket. I jump and claw it out. Damn. It's another potential wolf in disguise: Ryan Reeve, my ex-lover.

My stomach fizzes, not with desire but misgiving. Ever since Jo saw us in the guesthouse and told me about him selling Owen spice, I've ignored Ryan's texts and calls. It should be obvious, with Stan dead, that I can't see him. Nor do I want to. Why is he calling?

I stare at the phone bleakly. I should speak to him, try to suss out if he's the blackmailer. But I can't face it. The sight of his name has my heart racing. How dare he sell drugs to Owen. I'm scared of him. Jo insists he's the hit-and-run killer.

In the silent house, my phone's as hard to ignore as a screaming baby. I set it to silent and shove it back in my pocket. I'll deal with Ryan later. I unlatch the door. It feels extra heavy.

I want to stay inside and hide away. I want to go back in time, to when my normal problems seemed major. I want . . . I shake my head and recall something my grandma used to say: *If wishes were horses, we'd all ride like kings.*

I trudge through the door.

Stepping outside, the wind whips me. My hair flies into my mouth. It's hard to raise my umbrella. I should get a raincoat but don't. It doesn't matter. I'm only walking to the end of the driveway.

I grip the umbrella with both hands and descend the wet stairs. Rain blows in sideways. The front lawn is sodden. All the oaks lie black and bare. The trees thrash and shimmy.

On days like today, Winderlea comes alive, like it's fed by bad weather. All around, branches creak. And the sea, hissing at my back! It feels too close and angry. The wind drives me faster.

I'm partway down the drive, near the rhododendrons, when a voice says, "Dana!"

I twist and yelp. It's Ryan Reeve, clad in a long green raincoat. A huge hood hides most of his face. He's right beside me.

My heart pops. "Jesus!" I say. What's he doing in my yard?

I think of Jo's claim—passed on from Gloria and the gardener— that someone was hiding in the cedar bushes.

"What are you doing here?" I ask Ryan.

He steps closer. "I need to see you. You aren't answering my calls."

Instead of settling down, my heart pumps harder. Maybe it's his petulant tone or Jo's conviction that he killed that poor nanny.

I look around. My garden's secluded.

For a second, I consider sprinting back toward my door. But that's insane. Ryan's a fitness fanatic. He'd catch me in a heartbeat. And this is Ryan. I know him. He rang every bell but alarm. I'm livid he sold fake weed to my son, but he can't be a killer. Jo's mistaken. My Ted Bundy radar can't be *that* bad.

I start to walk toward the road. I need to act normally. "Why?" I say. "What's going on?"

Hands thrust into his giant raincoat, Ryan strides beside me. "The cops keep coming round, asking questions."

"You mean about us?"

"Yeah," says Ryan. "And the night your husband was murdered."

I'm not sure how to respond. What's he implying? "What about it?" I ask.

He grins. "It's cool. I have an alibi."

"Oh," I say. "That's good."

The slight softening of his tone makes me assume it's some other woman. I should find out. If his alibi's real, he couldn't have been lurking nearby, watching me and Jo, which means he's not the blackmailer.

I clear my throat. "Where were you?"

"On a friend's boat."

My chest ices up. Did he see us from a boat? Is this a hint or a threat so I'll hurry to amass the payment?

"I'm sorry things are so fucked up. I miss you."

I throw him a look. I'm not vain enough to buy this. Given his looks, he must cause traffic jams on Tinder. I'm forty-three, in good shape but past my prime. I've had three kids. There's only so much you can fix with hot yoga.

"I know it was casual," continues Ryan. "But"—his voice is deep and smooth—"we had something, Dana."

I shake my head. What's he playing at?

"Dana?" he says, when I don't answer.

I want to stay cool but can't. I feel a wild urge to hit him. "You sold drugs to my son," I hiss. "He's fifteen!" And a mess, as fifteen-year-olds are. Except for Chad. Although perhaps he's a mess too, dating a girl like Gemma Costin.

Ryan goes quiet. He must have hoped I didn't know.

His voice lowers, contrite. "I'm sorry. But it wasn't a lot. Fifteen's not that young." His raincoat crackles. "What were *you* doing at that age?"

My lip curls. I don't answer. It's none of his fucking business.

Ryan's a total creep, selling drugs to school children. I sidestep a puddle. The wind threatens to upend my umbrella.

Ryan's talking again, about how he's due to come into money, how he'll invest it, how he's stopped dealing.

I interrupt, alert. "How are you getting this money?"

He looks taken aback. "It's a trust fund, set up by my grandpa."

After that, I only half listen. Is this true or is his hoped-for windfall my blackmail money?

We're nearing the end of the drive. I can see my mailbox. I tighten my grip on my umbrella. I scan the Winderlea sign and its environs. Nothing's out of place.

Beside me, Ryan's still talking. For a moment, the sound of his voice takes me back to the guesthouse, his smooth skin, his lips hot and insistent. It makes me sick how much I wanted him. Since when did I get so self-destructive? I'm too old to want bad boys. Was my life really that dull?

My pace slows. The mailbox lies straight ahead. Do I retrieve the mail in front of Ryan? Has he showed up now because I didn't pay up last night?

He cocks his head. "Dana?"

"Um, yeah," I say, undecided.

I check the mailbox three times a day. More than that would look suspicious. It's also giving in to obsession, like checking and rechecking the oven. I'm prone to being obsessive. Like Owen.

"Dana, are you listening?"

My steps slow further. I could bypass the mailbox, tell Ryan I'm going for a walk. But my legs feel shaky, and the wind's ripping through me. It'd be better to grab the mail without looking at it.

I stop beside the box, as does Ryan. There's a weird look on his face, almost amused, like he's watching me do something stupid.

I reach for the door, jammed half open or shut. Glass half empty or full. I don't know what to wish for. Some yellow and red flyers jut out. The ends are soggy.

"What, you don't believe me?" says Ryan. He sounds reproachful.

"W-what?" I ram my hand into the mailbox. There are envelopes further in. I pry them out, along with the flyers. I squash all the papers together and shove them under my cardigan's flap. "Look," I say. "I'm tired, Ryan. I haven't been sleeping well." I clutch the papers to my chest. "What were you saying?"

Beneath that grim-reaper hood, his nostrils flare. "Your friend, the one with short dark hair and glasses. What's her story?"

"Jo?" As soon as I've blurted out her name, I regret it.

Jo insists he mowed down that poor lady on Elm Street. She thought he recognized her too, when she chased him down outside the school. What if she's right? I've told him her name!

I swallow hard. "She's an old friend. From way back."

Ryan shakes his head. "I wouldn't trust her."

The hairs on my arms go up. Perhaps Jo's right and he *is* the hit-and-run killer. Why else would he want to discredit her?

"Why?" I ask.

"I've seen her around here," he says. "Sneaking around. When you're out."

Drips curtain off my umbrella. I squint through them. "What? That's—" I bite my tongue. I wanted to say, "That's crazy."

"I've seen her here." He sounds sullen. He nods at my mailbox. "And messing around there." He points at the Winderlea sign.

My knees loosen. "W-what?" I repeat. "When?"

"Three? No, four days back."

Part of me wants to collapse. That's when I found the last note. Part of me wants to kick Ryan. He's created a crack of doubt in the last solid thing I had: my longest and truest friendship. Jo. Could she be behind it? I think of her interest in Stan's pricey paintings, her encouraging me to call the art dealer.

Ryan reaches for my elbow. I jerk back but relent. I'm scared to piss him off, scared I'm paranoid. I'm just scared, period. "I thought you should know," he says. "There's something weird about her."

I manage a jerky nod.

"Dana?" His voice is low and urgent. "You're under so much pressure. If you need anything, just remember I'm right next door. Maybe when this is over . . . we can . . . ." In that dark hood, his smile's white and canine.

If we were in a busy place, I'd tell him where to go. Even if my husband hadn't been murdered and I wasn't a suspect, there's no way I'd rekindle our affair. Not after he sold that shit to my child.

But here, with no one around, I'm scared. His grip's tight on my elbow. And those teeth. How did I not find him creepy?

Ryan's smile widens. He raises a hand to brush a strand of wet hair behind my ear.

I jerk back, yank my arm free. My heart's thumping.

I step away. "I have to go."

I turn and run home.

CHAPTER 35

Jo: Seventeen days since Stan died

It's close to eleven when my phone rings. I pounce on it, scared it will wake Ruby. The walls are hollow. Sound carries.

"Hello?"

Silence.

I'm in the bathroom, wringing out a bra I hand-washed in the basin. My apartment has no washer or dryer. To save on trips to the laundromat, I wash small things by hand. I stick the bra's shoulder strap around a coat hanger and hook that onto the two other coat hangers suspended off the shower-curtain rail.

"Hello?" I say again. The line's staticky, which makes me think it's a long-distance call. I shut the lid and sit on the toilet.

I imagine Trevor on the other end of the line, in some crappy Midwestern motel, searching for the words to say—what? That he misses me? That he wants to try again? That he's getting remarried?

Or maybe it's some police officer or hospital official who's found my contact information in the system, unaware we're no longer together. Maybe Trev's luck has run out. He's been gored by a bull or thrown off and trampled. Shot in a bar brawl. Stabbed by an incensed girlfriend. My chest shrink-wraps in.

I shake myself. None of this is my problem. I don't miss Trevor. I'm just addicted to missing someone. It feels real, but it's just misfiring neurons, chemicals in my brain. I need to move past my fucked-up childhood.

"Hello? Who's there?"

The silence is thick. It's not Trevor. I should hang up.

I'm removing the phone from my ear when a man's voice growls, "You're full of shit, bitch. Keep your fucking mouth shut."

I freeze. The line clicks.

I sit on the toilet, unmoving. I recognized Ryan Reeve's voice. And the way he snarled the word *bitch*. How did he get my number? Maybe he charmed that silly old cow of a school secretary. I've gone rigid.

Above me, something clomps. I jump. If he could track down my number, he could definitely find my address. I should call the police, but I can't. My heartbeat's gone ballistic.

There's another thud overhead, and another. It's just my old land-lady, Mrs. Simpson, in her heavy orthopedic shoes. Every night, when I'm ready for bed, the damn woman starts clomping like a tap-dancing Dutchman.

The toilet seat's cold. I try to breathe deeply. Drops of water fall off the clothes I've washed and onto the tiles.

I put my head in my hand and recall Ryan's snarl. That flash of recognition when I confronted him out back of Stanton House. I wonder if he recognized me from the hit-and-run. Or from Dana's? *You're full of shit.* Why would he say that?

I recall running that stop sign. If only I hadn't . . . It would never have happened if not for Dana. I feel cold and shaky.

When there's a heavy thump above, my chin jerks up. Some big object's being dragged. I stare at the ceiling. Mrs. Simpson must have knocked something over. The damn woman's nocturnal.

She clomps off. I'm still sitting on the toilet, gripping my phone. I check Recent Calls, but the number's withheld.

I get up and go into the kitchen. There's another weird noise overhead. It sounds like Mrs. Simpson's blender.

I consider sleeping with Ruby but don't. I must stay calm. I'm over-reacting.

Despite my fatigue, I can't sleep. Every small sound—the gurgle of pipes, the slam of a neighbor's car door—signals an intruder. My forehead throbs with tiredness, yet my thoughts won't stop churning.

I turn the clock radio away so I can't see how late it's getting. Or how early. Even Mrs. Simpson's gone quiet. No cars are passing.

When I finally fall sleep, it's lightly. Thoughts of Ryan Reeve break in. That vicious voice on the phone. His laser-like gaze out back of Stanton House. He's a drug dealer and a killer. Utterly immoral. A man without limits, who I fear is out to get me.

CHAPTER 36

Dana: Eighteen days after Stan's death

My mailbox has become an obnoxious obsession. Today I broke my own rule and checked it four times—every time I drove up or down our driveway. The van with the tinted windows was back out front. I thought about asking the people across the street if it was theirs, but stopped myself. It's just a van. Normal people doing normal things wouldn't even notice it.

When we get home, I'll have to recheck the mailbox.

In the back seat, Zoe's iPad pings. "Turn it down," I snap, then regret my harsh tone. But why must kids' games be so noisy, like they're designed to drive parents batshit?

"I can't hear it," counters Zoe.

"Turn it down," I repeat. I'm in no mood for resistance.

School just got out. I drove the Mercedes since it's just me and Zoe. Chad's at football and Owen has chess club. We're meeting Jo and Ruby in Oaks Park. At this time of year, it's bound to be deserted. The girls can run around while we catch up.

Pulling into the parking lot, I study the sky. It hangs low and dreary. We've got maybe two hours of daylight left, if we're lucky. The days are rapidly shrinking.

In three weeks' time, it'll be Thanksgiving, then Christmas—all without Stan. I'm not sure how I'll manage. Will we be able to hold his funeral before then? Tears threaten. I blink them away and bite the inside of my cheek. I'm sick of my self-pity.

Jo's car is alone in the lot, looking abandoned. I pull up beside it.

"Please give me that iPad," I tell Zoe. "And put your hat on. It's really cold out."

The wind hits when I exit the car. Maybe we should have met at the mall or the club. But in those places, I'd risk running into people I know. I'm in no state for casual chitchat.

I zip up Zoe's puffy pink coat. Beneath her red pom-pommed hat, her cheeks are already rosy. I help her into mittens and pull my gloves on. Despite the gray skies, I'm wearing big black sunglasses. Even so, I feel exposed.

I caught a reporter on the rocks out back of Winderlea, snooping by the boathouse. Photos of me have popped up online, on true-crime blogs speculating about Stan's demise. DID THE WIFE DO IT? one headline read. The accompanying photo was recent. I looked guilty and dazed at the end of our driveway. I started to read the comments but stopped. They were savage.

"Ruby's already here," I tell Zoe as she jumps from the car. I take her hand. It feels warm and solid. She hops beside me. Thank God for Zoe.

Rounding a bend, the playground comes into view. As expected, there's no one there apart from Jo and Ruby. This playground's nicer than the one by the Octopus, the equipment newer, the colors brighter. In the summer, this park's packed. There are picnic tables and a kiosk serving ice cream and greasy french fries. There's a softball diamond. The wind's cold off the choppy bay. The pebbled beach is streaked with seaweed. I wish I'd worn a thicker jacket.

Dressed in a big dark coat and a gray scarf, Jo's hunched on a bench near the playground. Her jeans are tucked into knee-high boots. Getting close, I see the boots are badly scuffed. Something—pity? fear?—scuttles through me. She's bent over her cell phone.

At our approach, she looks around. Behind her unflattering glasses, her face is pinched and suspicious. Has she given up on contacts? She could look so much better if she made the least bit of effort. It's like she's trying to appear unattractive.

Her mouth relaxes with recognition, only to retighten.

I release Zoe's hand. "Off you go," I tell her brightly.

Red pom-pom bouncing, Zoe runs to join Ruby on the monkey bars. I set down my bag and sit next to Jo. The bench is cold. Jo looks thinner and sallow.

"How are you?" I ask.

She shoves her phone into her pocket. "Not good."

Her tone scares me. "Why? What's happened?"

"I got a threatening phone call last night." She grits her teeth. "From Ryan Reeve, telling me I was full of shit and to keep my mouth shut."

Fuck. I won't tell her I accidentally let her name slip. "Wow. What makes you think it was him?"

"Who else would it be?" Her voice rises. "The way he looked at me when I caught him round back of Stanton House! It was like he wanted to kill me! He recognized me from the hit-and-run—I just know it!"

I hug myself. Is she overreacting? "He came over yesterday," I say. "He's been trying to contact me."

"Why?"

"He said he missed me."

As expected, Jo snorts. "Jesus. What did you say to that?"

"That I don't want to see him."

She nods, mollified, but her eyes are suspicious. "How'd he get in? What's the use of that great big wall?"

I shrug. "Probably via the beach." That reporter snuck in. As did Gemma. It's not that hard if the tide's right and you're willing to climb along the rocks.

Jo peers out to sea. "What else did Ryan say?"

I follow her gaze toward the seaweed-strewn beach. I won't tell her what he said about her. Waves explode against the offshore rocks. "The police spoke to him again." I adjust my sunglasses. "He has an alibi for the night Stan died. He was out boating."

Her head twists. "Boating?"

"Yeah," I say miserably.

"Fuck."

"And he mentioned coming into money soon. A trust fund."

This elicits another snort. "Wow. Perfect timing."

Through my gray lenses, I watch the girls on the monkey bars. Ruby's in front, swinging from bar to bar, orangutan-style. My daughter's more cautious. She has less momentum and keeps missing the next bar. While it knots my stomach, she's in no danger. There's spongy cladding below her.

I look away. "So you think Ryan is the blackmailer?" I ask Jo.

"He's not a bad bet," she says. "But who knows? I just know he's dangerous."

The girls jump off the monkey bars and sprint for the slide. Ruby climbs to the top and stands up. Jo's on her feet in a shot. "Ruby! Sit down!"

When Ruby does, Jo sits too. "Any word from the art dealer?"

I pull up my hood. "Not yet. It takes time."

This mention of money reminds me. I lick my lips. "There's something else. Ralph Isles stopped by."

Jo's eyebrow lifts. "Ralph Isles? What did he want?"

I consider telling her that I think Owen may be gay but don't. I'm not sure. And there are more pressing matters.

Despite my gloves, my hands are cold. I wiggle my fingers to warm them. "He said Stan was in financial trouble." My voice has thickened. "Major trouble. As in bankrupt."

Jo's lip curls. "What? That can't be right. You're too rich." She waves a mittened hand. "Even when rich people do go bankrupt, they come out okay. It's the little guys who end up with nothing."

I hope she's right. The thought of financial ruin should have me in shreds. There's no way I'll be sending three kids to Stanton House on the profits of Fairytale Flowers. Goodbye, mansion. Goodbye, yacht and country club.

Strangely, I hardly care. Perhaps I've reached my fear limit. This worry's too far down the line, behind the blackmailer and the police investigation.

Jo's voice is low: "Shit, Dana. What will you do?"

"I don't know." It's beyond my control. Like this weather. What can I do? Winter's coming.

She squints toward the slide. Ruby's standing at the top again, showing off to Zoe. This time, Jo doesn't notice. She's got that look she gets when her mind starts to spin. Eyes bright, synapses knitting connections.

"Stan wasn't stupid," Jo says. "He'd have offshore accounts to avoid paying taxes." She yanks off one mitten and tugs at her hair. "Where did he keep his important info? Like passwords and bank account numbers?"

My head feels heavy. "I don't know."

Her eyebrows jump, incredulous. "Seriously? It never occurred to you he could suddenly die, like have a heart attack? Or get in a car crash?" She frowns. "Don't tell me he didn't have a will."

I blink, feeling sick and irresponsible. I'm unforgivably ignorant. Given that Stan wanted a divorce, he'd have squirreled away cash, stashing it someplace so he wouldn't be forced to share.

Jo tuts. "If Stan had secret bank accounts, where would he hide that info?"

"In a file on his laptop?" I suggest. "Something password protected."

"No way," she scoffs. "That's not secure. Stan would know that."

I rub my forehead. Despite his techy ways, Stan was old school. He'd write important stuff down on paper and hide it away. Jo's right: that paper exists somewhere, maybe stuffed in an old book, some first edition he never read. Or tucked into a pocket of an old letterman jacket.

"In the safe?" suggests Jo.

I shake my head. I looked in there, finding only papers from our local bank. Nothing from the Caymans or Panama or anywhere remotely sketchy. They must exist though.

"Think, Dana!" Her voice is gruff, like I'm not trying.

I shut my eyes. "I am!" She's not helping.

My thoughts slip toward Ryan in my garden yesterday morning, what he said about Jo sneaking around when I was out, about seeing her near my mailbox. I want to ask but can't. She's risked everything to help me. Her loyalty's beyond question.

Still, it's hard not to see her reaction through a prism of doubt.

If she were the blackmailer, she'd have selfish reasons to hope I'll recoup Stan's riches. I shake off these thoughts like a wet dog spraying water. Who am I going to trust: the young deadbeat who sold my kid drugs and might have mowed down some poor lady or my best childhood friend?

Jo's right to be worried. I should be frantic.

I stand up. "I'm cold. Can we walk a bit?"

"Yeah, okay."

We trail around the playground's perimeter like we're on patrol. I'd prefer to head down to the beach, to walk into the wind. It might blow some good ideas into my sore head. Yet we can't leave Zoe and Ruby alone. They're too little.

We trudge around the square playground, hands thrust into pockets. My shoulders are up by my ears. I almost step in dog shit.

"Have you talked to the lawyers about Ralph's claims?" asks Jo. "Maybe he's just trying to scare you."

I shrug. I don't trust Ralph Isles, that's for sure. "I'm seeing the lawyers tomorrow morning. But I spoke to Garvin Holloway today." I recall this conversation, dismay and hesitation coming down the line like static. "He sounded pretty cagey."

Jo bends to collect a discarded beer can. She hates litter. "He must know where Stan kept his money!"

"Maybe. But I bet Stan had many lawyers."

"At least you have the paintings," says Jo. "If you think stuff will get repossessed, you'd better hide something, Dana."

I turn to get a better view of the girls. Zoe is seated in what looks like a spinning eggcup. Ruby's pushing her in fast circles. Just watching them makes me dizzy.

I look away. "Assets can't just vanish. There are sales records and insurance papers."

Jo spins my way. Her voice brightens. "Insurance. A couple paintings could get stolen."

I shove my hands deeper into my pockets. It's too bad I let the cops into Stan's study. Two million dollars for that ugly gumball painting.

It'd be enough for a new house, not in the Oaks but someplace decent, plus the kids' education and some security for retirement.

It still would not be enough to pay my blackmailer.

Jo's pace quickens. "Could you say some pieces went missing the night Stan vanished and you only just noticed."

A bunch of Stan's art *could* have gone missing that night without my having noticed. I hate most of it and try not to see it. But Gloria's another story.

"Our housekeeper might know. She has to dust it."

Jo walks closer to a bin and tosses the beer can. "You think? Your house is full of paintings that all look alike." She has a point, at least with the abstracts.

I shut my eyes, trying to remember. "There are three small abstracts in the upstairs hall. I think they're worth a few hundred-thou each." I shrug. "And there's a Gustav Cleggs in the dining room, which we never use, unless we have guests. Which we haven't since . . . You know. There's a big one in the guesthouse. Just a bunch of green scribbles. It's by some French guy who died in a plane crash." I frown, struggling to remember. "Something Mueller?"

Some hair has escaped my hood. The wind throws it into my eyes. I shove it out and turn to see the girls. They've traded places, Zoe pushing Ruby in the eggcup. Ruby's shrieking with terrified glee.

Jo stops to rewrap her scarf. Her eyes are shining. I know exactly what she's thinking.

"Forget it," I say. "Insurers aren't stupid. Wife learns she's broke, and *ta-da*, her dead husband's pricey art goes missing. Not one bit suspicious."

She ignores me. "What were the artists' names again? Cleggs? And who else? Mueller? I'll check them out." Her tone hardens. "Don't you google them, whatever you do. The cops will check your browser history."

"They might check yours too," I point out, "if they suspect we're in cahoots." Cahoots. It makes us sound sassy and rebellious, members of an all-girls Victorian pickpocketing gang, hiding the loot under our hoop skirts. We'd have nicknames. Cutthroat Jo. Diamond Dana.

Jo nods, her face serious. "You're right. I'll do it at the library. They have public computers. I promised to take Ruby later."

I study our laughing daughters. Another kid has joined them, a younger boy in a green coat and yellow boots. He's watching the girls, who ignore him. He's too young to interest them.

I look around for his parent, see a red-haired woman with a poodle. The dog's pulling toward the beach. The woman keeps tugging it back. "Five minutes!" she calls to the boy. "It's too cold out."

I look back at Jo, who's waiting. I shake my head. "Look Jo. I just can't. Insurance fraud . . . I'd be worried sick about getting caught. It'd be too stressful."

A corner of Jo's mouth tics up. "News flash. Being poor is stressful too." She sounds grim, despite that quick smile.

Guilt tugs at me. If Jo needed help, I mean desperately, she'd have asked, right?

"God forbid it happens," continues Jo, "but if you *were* arrested for Stan's murder, you'd need a lawyer." I can't meet her gaze. "Good criminal lawyers don't come cheap." She gives a dry laugh. "What's a little insurance fraud compared to the other charges you might be facing?"

My breath catches. She's right. Yet it's not just that but the realization I'm trapped. I don't for one second think Jo's the blackmailer. Even so, how can I ever say no to her again? I'm forever in her debt. Is real friendship possible when your power's so unequal?

Jo squints back at the girls. Her lips thin. "My grandma's things are in a storage unit. You could hide some art in there."

I stop walking. Jo's grandma's been in a care home for years, ever since Jo's mom died. Would Stan's art—my art—be safe there?

The wind blows a plastic bag across the playground. It snags on a bush. Beyond the playground, the sea's an ugly gunmetal gray. Waves batter the rocks. From here, I can just see the islands where we dumped Stan.

I recall Ryan's warning that Jo can't be trusted. Maybe she saw Stan's death as a chance to improve her lot. If she took the paintings, sold them, and refused to pay me, what could I do? I couldn't report her.

I never did ask why she got fired from her last school. Didn't want to upset her. Maybe I should have.

Jo's stopped walking too. She spins to face me. "What's wrong, Dana?"

"I . . ." I cough. I can't breathe. Is this a panic attack? I've never had one.

"Dana?" She grasps my shoulder.

I think of Ryan and my reaction when he touched me: that curdle of revulsion and fear. This is more complex. I freeze, unsure whether to fold into Jo's arms or jerk away.

Her eyes narrow, a hand still on my shoulder: "Dana, what's wrong?"

I keep wheezing. It's too late not to trust Jo. I'm just paranoid after yesterday's encounter with Ryan.

"We'd better go," says Jo. "It's getting too cold."

CHAPTER 37

Dana: Nineteen days since Stan's death

Tonight will be three days since I missed the blackmailer's deadline. Three more days of looking over my shoulder.

The police haven't released Stan's body—or his "remains," as they call them.

Sometimes I truly believe I'm a grieving widow. I forget my role in his ending. I forget I wanted him gone. It sounds crazy, but I miss the good in him, the hard worker, the pragmatist who could solve any problem—except the ones *he* created.

I want to bury him and have a grave to visit. It also might help the kids mourn.

It's Gloria's day off. I'm in the kitchen, cooking, although that's too grand a term. I'm sliding a tinfoil-wrapped slab of salmon, bought pre-marinated from the deli, into the oven. I'll make a salad. Zoe's at the table, drawing a princess. The twins are upstairs, doing their homework. At least I hope so.

When the doorbell rings, I jump and slam the oven door shut. Zoe looks up. "Who's that?" she asks me.

"I don't know." My first thought is the police, come to arrest me.

What would happen to the kids? Would they be taken into care? Family's not an option. Stan's parents are dead. His sister, an accountant, lives in London and is proudly childless. He and his brothers weren't talking. Even if my mom weren't so frail, she's shown zero interest in my offspring. I wouldn't trust her. I might get Jo to stay, to act as guardian, unless she's arrested with me.

I wipe my hands on a tea towel. It can't be the police. They don't know my gate code. Surely they wouldn't creep around on the rocks. "I'll be right back," I tell Zoe.

There's a peephole in the door. Squinting through it yields a fish-eye view of Jo. Her head is big, her body tapered. She raises a fist and raps loudly.

I unlatch the chain and swing the door wide.

Jo tumbles in, Ruby behind her. Jo's pale and wild-eyed.

I slam the door and lock it fast, as if more bad luck could follow.

"Ruby," I say with forced brightness, "Zoe's in the kitchen. Why don't you both go up to her room?" I look at Jo. "You'll stay for dinner?"

She doesn't respond. It's like she didn't hear me. She's already striding down the hall.

Zoe's happy to take Ruby upstairs. They ascend the staircase hand in hand, straight off a Hallmark card.

I follow Jo to the kitchen.

"Wine?" I ask, reaching for the red I'm drinking. No response. She's staring out the window. I pour her a glass.

From the fridge, I grab a bag of mixed greens, two cucumbers, and a vine of tomatoes. I start to wash the tomatoes. They're some heirloom kind, smaller and lumpy. Imperfection now costs more.

"Jo?" I say. "What's happened?"

She turns from the window and sets her bag on the counter.

"Look," she says. She pulls a piece of paper from her bag and shows me.

YOU FAIL TO PAY AGAIN YOU LOSE ZOE AND/OR RUBY.

The tomato falls from my hand. It thuds into the sink. I stare at it. Bright red and heart-shaped. My heart. Zoe's my heart, my baby.

I tip forward, over the sink, feeling sick. You lose bets and keys. You lose weight and sleep. You don't lose your children. The thought's a tightening noose.

"It was in Ruby's bedroom!" says Jo. "Under her fucking teddy!"

My mouth opens and shuts. Finally, I manage to take a breath. "How did they get in?" I whisper.

Jo starts pacing the length of my counter before she snaps back, "My spare key's missing from under the plant pot."

The faucet's still running.

"They must have watched us!" says Jo. "They know Ruby's name!" Her voice is shrill. "Is it that creep, Ryan?" Her red eyes are staring at me.

I grip the counter. The note's like the others, plain office paper, red block letters. No clues. Nothing. Just rising panic.

I twist off the faucet. Could someone really have entered Ruby's bedroom in broad daylight? When this thought sneaks in, I sway, wondering what my brain is suggesting. That Jo planted the note? That's absurd. Look at her! I've never seen her looking so frantic.

Jo keeps pacing. "What do we do?" she snarls. "He was in Ruby's bedroom!"

A noise makes me turn. Chad's in the doorway.

Jo leaps forward and swipes the note off the counter. She jams it back in her book bag.

Chad frowns, then smiles. "Hi, Jo." He doesn't seem to notice her lack of response. He's changed from his school clothes into jeans and a blue sweater. It brings out his eyes, makes his skin still more golden. He's barefoot. "Mom, can Gemma come over, after dinner?"

I respond on autopilot: "No. It's a school night."

Owen would scowl. Chad's smile widens. "She won't stay late." He sniffs, appreciatively, buttering me up. "That smells great. What's for dinner? I'm starving."

I realize he's right. The kitchen has filled with the smell of baked salmon and ginger. I love this dish, yet now it turns my stomach.

"Fish. It's almost ready. And yes, fine. Invite Gemma." I lack the energy to fight him.

Chad looks from me to Jo. He must have noticed our tension. Jo's eyes are bugged out, and her neck's rigid. I doubt I look much better.

My son rubs his chin, suddenly watchful. "Is everything okay?"

I take a deep breath. I haven't discussed this with Jo. She might get mad. Yet it feels worth a try. We have nothing. Less than nothing. And someone's threatening our daughters.

"I've been getting threats ever since Dad . . . that night. And now Jo got one."

Chad looks at Jo. He has his dad's height but my face: dark blue eyes; straight, fine nose; high cheekbones. "Threats?" He frowns my way. "What does that mean?"

I don't look at Jo. I don't need to. I can feel her fury.

"Notes," I say. "Asking for money."

Chad squints. "What?" His tone suggests I'm joking.

"Blackmail notes, threatening to go to the police and say I'm to blame for Dad's murder." The words stick in my throat. "That I killed him."

He blinks. "But . . . but you didn't."

"But I'm a suspect."

My son slowly nods.

"Look," I say. "You don't need to worry about this. I just—" I study the picture windows. "You haven't seen anyone lurking around, have you? Anyone suspicious?" The windows are big black squares. From outside, looking in, we'd be players on a lit stage. Players in a family drama. I forgot to draw the curtains.

I cross the room and yank them shut. Window after window. This room is a fish tank. What were we thinking with those renovations? How smug we were, convinced of our safety, sure no one was watching. Should I hire a security guard? The alarm system might not be enough. Chad hasn't moved. I refocus on my son. "Have you noticed anything off lately?"

For a second he looks like Owen, his face twisted in an incredulous scoff. I get it. Everything's off. His dad's been murdered. We're all suspects.

Chad shrugs. His face smooths out. Chad could enter politics. He's remarkably good at appearing unruffled. "Uh, no. Nothing." He opens a cupboard to retrieve a glass and walks to the fridge. After pouring some milk, he turns back to me: "Have you told the police?" he asks.

I hesitate. I can feel Jo's displeasure, a new note over her panic. If I were innocent, I'd go to the cops. Surely Chad will wonder. I shouldn't have mentioned this. "No," I say. "I'm afraid it'll stoke their suspicions." I look at Jo, pleading.

"Your mom's right," she tells Chad. "The police seem increasingly hostile."

My son takes a swig of milk. "Maybe it's some crazy person who heard about Dad on the news." He rubs his smooth forehead.

"Maybe," says Jo, "although they know details about your family. And mine. They left a note in my apartment."

From the way she's watching him, I know she's searching for clues. Jo's not convinced my boys aren't behind this blackmail scheme. I'm not stupid. I know that. I know her.

Chad's forehead furrows. Even Jo must see his confusion. "That's crazy," he says. "I haven't seen anything." His nose wrinkles. "Do you smell something burning?"

As soon as he says it, I do. The salmon!

I lunge for the oven and click it off. When I lower the door, black smoke roils out.

I slam the door shut and stand, head in hands. This feels like the final straw, proof I'm a failure as a woman and a mother. I can't even feed my kids. It's not just the smoke that makes my eyes water.

Chad sets his empty glass on the counter. "Want me to order pizza?"

I inhale and nod, trying to keep my voice steady. "Yes, please."

As Chad goes off to call, Jo catches my eye. "What the fuck?" she whispers. "Why did you tell him? What if he tells his girlfriend, huh? And she tells her gossipy mother?"

I rub my sore eyes. For all I know, Gemma's behind the notes. I recall the slim, dark figure at Myers Point. They got into a big car, some sort of SUV. The Costins have one.

Even as I think it, a voice in my head scoffs: Everyone in the Oaks drives an SUV—as if climate change will only affect people who don't bring their own cups to Starbucks. Still, it could have been Gemma. Was Chad in the car? My brain slams this thought shut. It could have been Gemma, but there's no way it was Chad. He would not blackmail his own mother.

I glare at Jo. "Chad won't tell Gemma! Don't worry."

She rolls her eyes. "Jesus, Dana, things are bad enough already!"

I'm about to snap back when Chad reappears. If he notices our tension, he pretends not to. "I got two pepperonis, one veggie, and a four-cheese. All extra-larges."

I ignore Jo's simmering fury and fake a smile. "Wow! That's a lot of pizza! Chad, could you help me make a salad?"

He hesitates, then relents. "Sure." Maybe he's trying to stay on my good side so I'll be more likely to let Gemma stay later. Or maybe he's giving me a break, having realized Jo and I have unfinished business.

"Thanks," I say. "Jo? Let's go into the dining room." Without waiting for her answer, I head toward it. She follows.

The room's still and formal. It's got a long, polished oak table and twelve high-backed chairs. We rarely use it. It was decorated to impress Stan's clients. Three large handblown glass orbs hang over the table. When lit, they glow an eerie blue.

I shut the door.

We don't sit. We're too wound up.

Jo walks to the back wall. She stops before a pale canvas in a thin silver frame. The painting's mostly white, crisscrossed with swaths of beige. There's one red dot, a bit misshapen. Like my heirloom tomatoes.

She clicks on the angled spotlight. The painting flares to life. It's the Gustav Cleggs. I walk up beside her. We stare at the canvas. The red dot pulses.

I've never looked at this painting, not really. To call it white is unfair. It's white like a forest's green, every leaf different. And the beige. There's sand and camel. Caramel. Gold. Sunlight. But it's the dot that gets me. It's like a heart, not a love heart but a real one: the kind that beats in a fetus on an ultrasound screen. It's magic. How can a red dot seem fragile and vital?

Focused on the painting, I fail to realize Jo's crying silently, her shoulders shuddering.

"Jo?" I say, aghast. All anger leaves me. She doesn't suspect my boys, not really. She's just scared. We both are.

"It was such a shock," she rasps. "That note. In Ruby's bedroom." Her voice shakes. "My God. What if she'd been there?" She swipes under her glasses.

I imagine a stranger in Zoe's room. Jo's right to be petrified. And livid. Right now, the girls are upstairs. Safe. At least we think so.

I think of the last note, the one before this, stating things would get worse. That was true. "I'm so sorry."

Jo cleans her glasses on her shirt. Her face is pinched. "They got into my house! Anything could have happened. Anything." She replaces her glasses. "Whoever's behind this is dangerous. We've been in denial."

I nod. She's right, but what can we do? We don't even know who we're fighting.

"This painting," says Jo. She rubs under her nose and nods at the canvas. "One of Cleggs's sold in June for three point two million." I blink. "He's been discovered," she continues. "Posthumously. The poor guy died broke. He was gay, Black, and bipolar." She squints at the canvas. "What did Stan pay for it?"

"Dunno. But way less than that. Typical Stan." He had an eye for a bargain.

We both stare at the canvas, unappreciated for so long. My throat's dry. "You think I should sell it and pay the blackmailer?" My voice sounds secondhand, passed down from some older, hard-living woman.

Jo grasps her hair. "Fuck, I don't know." Her anger's passed. She looks spent. Shoulders sagging, she turns her back on the Cleggs. "I'm scared for Ruby. Scared to go home. Scared to let her out of my sight."

I hang my head. It's all my fault. "You can stay here," I say.

"I know. And we will. But we can't stay forever."

I nod. If Ralph Isles is right, that's not even an option. I once thought this house was mine. Forever, like my marriage. Once upon a time, both seemed rock solid.

I stare at the Cleggs painting, its red dot pulses.

Like Jo, I might soon be in some cruddy rental. Stan's will won't be read until after his funeral, after the coroner has released her findings. Until then, Stan's lawyer, who I thought was *our* lawyer, won't discuss his estate, except to say that things look "messy."

Despite hours of searching, I have yet to find any evidence of other assets. No secret offshore bank accounts, safety deposit boxes, stock certificates, or property deeds. Nothing. I know they exist. Stan might risk a lot but not everything, not financially. There's money—surely a fortune by most people's standards—tucked away somewhere.

I refocus on the Cleggs. Would the housekeeper notice if it vanished?

"I'm going to sell it," I tell Jo. "I'm not sure if I'll pay the blackmailer, but it'd be better to have cash than this painting." This thought cheers me. At least I have options.

Jo nods, drawn and unsmiling. She turns back toward the canvas. "You know what?" she says. "It's weird, but the more I look at it, the more I like it. Maybe Stan's taste wasn't that bad."

"The rest are still shit," I say. "Especially the gumballs."

Jo tilts her chin toward the Cleggs. "Does the housekeeper know what it's worth?"

"I doubt it." I didn't, until Jo told me.

She chews the inside of her cheek. "If the cops find out, you'll have to explain what you did with the money."

My resolve wavers.

Jo spins my way. While her mouth's grim, her eyes have that spark. She licks her lips. "Do you have any oil paints?"

Despite myself, I smile. When you're friends long enough, you become like an old married couple. Without her spelling it out, I know what she's thinking. "Owen has some," I say. "In the garage." God, Jo's brilliant.

She eyes the Cleggs. "Any canvases?"

"Yeah, but I'm not sure about the size."

She nods. "Can you get a tape measure?"

I retreat to the kitchen to find one in the junk drawer.

"Here," I say, rejoining Jo. I toss it to her.

"Thanks." She unfurls it and starts to measure.

Watching her, I'm relieved. Even if we're doing the wrong thing, at least we're doing *something*. It feels better than just waiting and hoping.

Jo looks up: "Can you paint it? You're more artistic."

I almost laugh again but nod. Owen's the artist in our family, but I can hardly ask him. Forgery is a felony. Something to add to my rap sheet. "Okay," I say. "I'll do it first thing in the morning."

The doorbell rings. We both freeze.

I hold my breath, waiting, until the smell of cheese hits me. Chad must have buzzed them in. My mouth fills with saliva. When did I last eat? Maybe breakfast.

"Don't worry," I say, relieved. "It's just the pizza."

Since I couldn't sleep, I got up to paint.

At 5:30 a.m., I'm sitting on the floor, drinking coffee. It's still dark. These days, it doesn't get light until after seven.

The dining room's dark but for the spotlight on the Cleggs painting.

To clear the odor of fresh paint, I've got the windows wide open. It's freezing. I'm wearing a jacket. While this room doesn't face the sea, I can hear the ocean. I swear the red dot's pulsing to the waves' rhythm.

Some other noise rouses me: footsteps coming up from downstairs. I twist to listen. "Jo?" I call cautiously. The footsteps pad closer.

"Dana?" She sounds worried.

I get up and open the dining room door. "I'm in here."

The hall's dark. Jo's clad in her flannel pajamas. "I heard you were up," she says. Her eyes dart around the room. "What are you doing?"

"I couldn't sleep. I did the painting." I point to my canvas, on the floor. I switch on the overhead light.

In the bright light, Jo looks even worse than she did last night. The rings beneath her eyes could be branded. She walks toward the two paintings. I follow.

"Did you get any sleep?" I ask.

"Not much." She sits down and stares up at the Cleggs, then down at my copy.

I settle beside her. "I called the dealer. He offered three million flat."

Jo frowns at me, then nods. "He's ripping you off. The one that sold in June was smaller. And this one's nicer."

I shrug. Now that I've really looked at this Cleggs, I'm sorry to sell it. And sorry to be the kind of person who only appreciates stuff when it's gone. "Now's hardly the time to quibble," I say. "And maybe I can buy it back when I find Stan's money."

"If," she says darkly.

I take a gulp of coffee. "I'm trying to stay positive," I say, studying my canvas.

I did a decent job—beige scuffs in all the right places, red spot fine in terms of size and color. Yet my canvas inexplicably lacks soul. Why is there a spark in Cleggs's work but not in my copy?

I recall Stan's lifeless body. My throat constricts. I turn to Jo and nod at my canvas. "What do you think?"

"It'll do, Dana."

I nod. It will do. A few days back, I'd have sworn the Cleggs was just white with some swipes of beige and a glob of scarlet. I'll switch the paintings before Gloria gets in. She won't notice. Nor will the kids or anyone who's ever dined here. Would Stan have noticed? I doubt it.

An expert, on the other hand, would pick out my forgery in a heartbeat. Were this painting to be repossessed, I'd face unpleasant questions I should fear but don't. There are too many bridges to cross before that one, all of them rickety and precariously perched above sharks and piranhas.

Jo gets up and approaches my painting.

"It's still wet," I warn.

She looks up and down, between my work and the Cleggs. She turns with a tired smile. "You did a good job, Dana. You're ahead of your time. A misunderstood genius. I read it in the *New York Times*."

I smile too. "Then it must be true."

CHAPTER 38

Jo: Twenty-two days since Stan died

Wine and firelight have soothed my nerves. Heat wafts across me. It feels wonderful to be warm. We're in Dana's living room, stretched out by the fireplace. It's late at night. The kids are all in bed. Jazz plays softly on Stan's fancy-ass sound system.

Dana's on the sofa, staring at her tablet. I'm on the floor. She passes down the tablet. "Check the account again," she orders.

I type in the details. The money from the sale of the Cleggs painting is supposed to show up in my grandma's account. She's got dementia and lives in a care home. I have power of attorney. It's a risk, but Dana and I couldn't work out how else to do it.

I lean back against the sofa. I press Account Balance.

"Holy shit," I say. Dana shipped the Cleggs two days ago. The guy actually paid. I wasn't sure he was legit, not that we had much choice. The police know about Stan's regular art broker. I look up at Dana and smile. "The money's there."

She leans over to stare at the tiny screen and smiles in relief. "Thank God." She raises her wine glass and clinks it against mine. "I'm not broke anymore."

"To Stan's art." I take a sip of wine. It's delicious, from Stan's wine cellar. Dana's husband may have bought a bunch of shitty art, but his taste in booze was stellar.

I squint at the small screen. "God, it's weird," I say. "To see my grandma's name and all those zeros."

Dana sighs. I look back at her. The firelight's lent her face some color. I expect her to look happy, but she doesn't. Her forehead's creased with worry. She upends her glass. "I still don't know if I should pay the blackmailer or not." She's had a lot to drink and is slurring slightly.

I turn to watch the fire again. The urge to stare into flames must be wired in our DNA, passed down from cavemen. Fire's a threat and a comfort. My eyes feel heavy. "Maybe we should just run away," I say. "Head for Mexico, become outlaws."

"I wish," says Dana. She snorts. "Chad would give us away by texting. And imagine Owen. He doesn't cope well with changes. If we run, the cops will know we're guilty."

I nod. I didn't mean it for real. It's just nice to imagine. Maybe this is how my dad felt before he took off; like he was trying to swim in heavy clothes that kept dragging him under.

"Three million dollars," I say. My cold's gotten worse. My voice is throaty. "Jesus. That's a lot of money."

"It is and it isn't," says Dana. "If Stan left me broke, it's a small fortune. But he must have some secrets accounts. I just have to find them."

I yawn. "I'm wrecked. I'm off to bed, Dana." I stand and pass her the tablet.

Her face tightens. "Shit. What happens if the police check this? If they get a search warrant. Will they see the link to your grandma's account?"

I should have thought of that. They can trace everything, can't they, these days? If they get a warrant, they'll check all her devices. "Damn," I say. "I guess so." The wine and this cold have left my brain numb.

"It's old anyway," says Dana. "I need a new one. It'd be better to get rid of it."

"How?"

She shrugs. "Smash it? Or toss it in the ocean?"

I twist to stare at the windows facing the sea. More junk in the ocean. The broken vase, Stan's plastic tarp and iPhone. Now this. We're the opposite of eco-friendly.

When I look back at Dana, I see her pretty mouth twisting like she's chewing on some dilemma. "Dana?" I say.

She won't meet my eyes. Instead she stares, glassy-eyed, at the tablet.

I hold my breath. I know her so well that I know what she's thinking: she has no proof the cash in my grannie's account is hers. She'd have no recourse if I took it. She couldn't go to the police.

My stomach feels hollow. She doesn't trust me—not entirely. It's a bad feeling, like being unwanted. Doesn't she know how much I've sacrificed for her, how much I love her?

She sits up, decision made. "I'm tired," she says. "And I've had too much wine." Her smile's pretty. "Please, Jo, can you get rid of it for me?" She hands me the unwanted tablet.

———————

I walk onto the back patio. Dana's tablet is in my coat's pocket. It's a cold, clear night. The ocean is black satin. Stars dot the sky. Despite my quilted jacket and scarf, I'm freezing. I can't get over this cold. I should be in bed, not clambering around Dana's dark garden.

Rather than head for the dock, I walk to the guesthouse. I pick my way across the rocks that separate it from the ocean. Below the high-tide line, they're slippery with seaweed. I drank less than Dana but am far from sober.

At the water's edge, I smash the tablet with a stone. It takes several tries before its screen shatters. I pry the motherboard out and break off all the pieces. I throw the remains into the sea. My heart pounds.

I retrace my footsteps back to the top deck.

I should go to bed, but I'm wired. And those stars! I sink onto a deck chair. I lie down and stare up. The stars are pinpricks in black velvet.

I let my eyes soften until constellations take shape: the W of Cassiopeia, named for the vain queen whose boasts unleashed a sea monster and forced her to sacrifice her own child. Ursa Major, transformed into a bear by the jealous wife of her lover. Orion, the rapist god of the hunt, plus his loyal dog, its heart Sirius, the brightest star in the sky.

Down the hill to my left, there's a noise. I look sharply toward the Reeves' mansion. Its chimneys rise over the treetops. The sound comes again: rustling down the path to the boathouse. I think of Ryan.

Moving quietly, I swing my legs off the deckchair and stand. I step off the deck and cross the first terrace. My legs feel unsteady.

The slope's steeper, the path slippery. A koi plops in the pond. I stop, startled.

The fish keep getting picked off by herons and crows. Dana wanted to net the pond, but Stan refused, saying it would look bad. I must remind her to net it. Those poor fish must live in terror.

Somewhere closer, a twig snaps. I spin in panic. Something's in those black bushes. Dry leaves rustle. It's too loud to be a mouse or frog. It's coming closer . . .

Panting, I stagger back up the hill.

Back on the top deck, I can't stop shaking. Why am I out here, putting myself in additional danger? I keep digging myself in, deeper and deeper. All for Dana.

I recall her face in the firelight. Her hesitation. No matter what I do, deep down, she mistrusts me. Do I trust her?

It takes all my strength to pry open her back door.

CHAPTER 39

Dana

I wake up in snarled sheets, stiff with panic. Did some noise or another bad dream rouse me? My eyes feel heavy, a hangover brewing. I set the house alarm, didn't I? I wince. A sour taste coats my tongue. I had a fair bit of wine tonight. I could have forgotten.

I lift my head off the pillow to listen. Is that the wind? Or Jo maybe? She's sleeping in one of the lower-level spare rooms. She might be up and about. Like me, she's been having trouble sleeping.

I push back the duvet and sit up. My skin prickles with goosebumps.

My windows rattle. Maybe that's what woke me. Winderlea's old, despite its modern veneer. Old houses aren't quiet.

I'm lying back down when I hear a sharp click. Was that a door? I sit up and reach for the bedside light. Its glow hurts my eyes. The clock reads 3:03 a.m. I squint toward Zoe's room. Ruby's sleeping with her. Did something wake them? Or could it be one of the twins, up to no good?

I should check. It'll only take a moment. Cold wraps around me as I get out of bed.

The hall lies dark and smells of wood polish. I tiptoe past a row of Stan's abstracts. They look like smears of mud and are aptly titled *Brown 1*, *2*, and *3*. Might the art dealer want them?

I stand outside Chad's door first and listen hard. All's quiet. Owen's room is equally silent. I tiptoe to Zoe's door. The energy feels different here, like the air's been stirred up. I hesitate, then open the door.

To my left stands a playhouse, painted white, and strung with lights. They twinkle faintly, serving as a night-light. Zoe's canopy bed rises to my right. I creep across the polished floor.

The duvet has slipped, exposing the two sleeping girls. Zoe's curled on her belly, hugging her pillow. Ruby's on her back, arms and legs star-fished. In the sparkly light, Zoe's hair is brassy. Ruby's shines like molasses.

I smile. They're sound asleep. I tiptoe closer.

I'm near the bed when fear grips me. They're too still.

In the newspaper, some years back, I saw a photo of three children who'd been gassed to death in Syria. They looked angelic, a plastic sheet folded neatly beneath their chins. They lay side by side, as if asleep. Like this.

I jerk forward and prod Zoe's shoulder. Her face is bone white. I stare at her chest. It's not moving.

I grab her wrist. It's cold. My throat shuts.

No! There's no way. I'm seeing things. It's just that note . . .

I reach for her chest and press my palm flat. Nothing moves. Dread piles down on me. An avalanche. I can't breathe, my eyes and mouth frozen wide.

My daughter's head rolls sideways. Her blue eyes open, wide with worry. "Mommy, what are you doing?"

Relief blooms hot in my throat. I lean back, open-mouthed. My voice is a croak: "I . . . I was checking on you."

Her eyes dart behind me. She sits up. "Why?"

"I . . ." I shut my mouth. I've alarmed her. "Everything's f-fine," I stammer. Holy shit! I could have sworn she'd stopped breathing. "Go back to sleep, hon."

I bend to hug her. I inhale her warm, beloved scent. Jesus Christ. I've lost the plot. Those threatening notes, the police—it's all too much. Nothing feels safe.

"You're shivering," she says. "You're cold, Mommy."

I nod and stagger upright. "Yes," I say. "I'm going back to bed. Sleep tight, Zoe."

I'm turning to go when I see the note on her bedside table. I lunge forward and grab it.

Fear blasts my chest open. The blackmailer was here. In Zoe's bedroom!

"What's the matter?" asks Zoe.

"Nothing." It comes out a breathy squeak. "Go back to sleep."

With a yawn, Zoe reclines. Her eyes shut.

I stand by the bed, clutching the paper. Even in the dark, the writing's clear: block letters. Next Monday's date and a string of numbers and letters. A bank account and a Swift code. Plus the words "NOT PAYING IS NOT AN OPTION."

I spin to look behind me. Nothing. I crouch to peer under the bed. It's bare but for a used tissue.

On quaking legs, I rush to the closet. I swipe an arm under the hanging clothes. Fabric rustles.

In full-blown panic, I stagger to the closest window. I claw back the drapes, sure I'll find someone hiding: Gemma, looking smug yet sullen. Ryan, oozing sex and danger. Ralph or his smirking son, Emmett Isles.

I yank each drape in turn. Each tall window stands empty.

Feeling sick, I lean against the cold glass. Down below, my yard steps down to the sea. Here and there, pools of light break the darkness. The giant willow flails in the wind. The dock's a tear in the sea's gray fabric. My teeth clack. The islands are ink stains: a Rorschach test I will fail.

I want to stay with the girls but can't. I must check on the twins. Search the house. I need Jo.

I'm near the door when I realize I missed a hiding place: Zoe's wooden playhouse. I teeter toward it, note in hand.

Square, symmetrical windows frame an open door about as high as my chest. I peer in. The floor's covered in soft, flowery mats. In one corner lies a sprawl of stuffed animals: watchful glass eyes, soft limbs, and snouts.

In the other corner lie two dolls, both naked, pink limbs askew. I blink and shrink back. The dolls are headless.

I stand and spin to see the top shelf near the door. Two decapitated heads sit side by side, smiling vacuously. One's fair, the other dark. I gag.

Those dolls are new and precious, the girls' latest obsession. There's no way they'd break them, nor could they reach that shelf. Bile fills my throat.

Was it Owen? I sway, hating that I had that thought. It's not fair.

As I lock the door to Zoe's room, I picture Stan's severed head on the seafloor: mouth agape, eyes empty.

CHAPTER 40

Jo

Dana's ragged voice finds me: "Jo, wake up!" I can hear her outside my room, stumbling down the stairs to my level.

I sit up with a jolt. The room's dark. My stomach knots. I shove back the covers. "Dana?" I'm hoarse. "What's wrong?"

The door flies open and the light flicks on. Blinded, I shield my eyes.

"Jo?" In the doorway, Dana is ghoul-faced. "The blackmailer!" With one hand she clings to the doorframe. There's a piece of paper in the other. "Look!" She shakes it. "Right next to Zoe's bed!"

I stagger over, dizzy from standing up too quickly. It's another note, written in thick red marker. "Where are the girls?" My voice is loud with panic.

"In bed. Sleeping."

I exhale. "And the twins?"

"They're fine. I locked the doors to all the kids' rooms."

"Okay," I say. "Good thinking."

Dana's trembling. "We need the police, Jo! Someone broke in! They could've—"

"What? No!" I'm near enough to smell her lemony lotion—and her breath, sour with wine. "What does it say?" I snatch the note from her hands and read it. Bank details and a threat: NOT PAYING IS NOT AN OPTION.

"Fuck," I say. I peer into the hallway. "We need to search the house. Now."

She doesn't react. I grab her arm and push her into the hall. "Where are Stan's golf clubs?"

"What?"

"His golf clubs!"

"The, um, storeroom." She looks to the end of the hall.

I rush toward it. "Come on. Hurry." There are three sets of golf clubs. I extract two large drivers and hand one to Dana. "Should we split up?"

This gets her attention: "Hell no!"

She grips my arm as we search this floor of the massive house. There's nothing here.

We quietly climb the stairs. Halfway up, Dana stumbles. I yank her up. Is she in shock or just drunk? We reach the main floor.

I go to switch the lights on but stop. I recall the back patio, and the sounds in the bushes. If Ryan were outside watching, with the lights on, he would see us.

And if he's inside, the lights won't help us.

———————————

In the hall closet, I find a flashlight. We move from room to room. In a house this big, there are a million hiding places.

"I think they're gone," says Dana. She's got the golf club in one hand and the note in the other.

"Maybe," I say. I push open the door to Stan's study. We both step inside.

Something moves in the darkness. I yelp, ready to swing. Dana grabs me. "Stop!" she squeals. "It's the cat!"

Toonces advances and slinks around her ankles. I scan the room's windows. The one facing the cedar bushes lies open. "Look!" I say. The sash is raised a good five inches.

Dana shakes her head. "But it can't be! I set the alarm."

I push past her and stride to the window. I look out. It's too dark to see anything. I yank the window down and lock it. "You can't have," I say flatly. She's drinking too much, getting careless.

"I did," she cries. "I . . . I . . ." Her voice wobbles to nothing. I feel like screaming. Now's not the time to give her shit. That can come later.

Heart hammering, I peer under Stan's desk. I swipe my golf club under the sofa. Toonces leaps onto Stan's chair, fat but agile. His tail swishes, indignant.

It's past five by the time we're done searching all the rooms. Morning, although it's still dark. Dana looks limp. I lead her down to the kitchen. It's freezing. Not one single room in this house feels safe or cozy. I almost miss my shitty apartment.

"Want tea?" I ask tiredly. Tea was my mother's cure-all.

"Coffee, please." Dana leans her golf club against the counter, sinks onto a barstool, and sets down the blackmail note.

I don't answer. This is all her fault. She should be making *me* coffee.

I brew some coffee, then sit beside her. I feel wrung out: overtired and hung over. Last night's wine was so tasty. I'm not much of a drinker. Or maybe stress has caused this headache. "Who knows your alarm's code?" I ask.

Dana stares at her mug, slack faced.

Anger pounds through me. When I found the note in Ruby's room, she didn't seem that perturbed. Now it's happened to her, and she's catatonic. "Dana?" I say sharply.

She hangs her head. "The boys know the code, but . . . I . . . I'm sorry. The alarm . . . I thought I set it, but . . ."

I take a sip, force myself to calm down. *But.* That means she didn't. I grit my teeth. "I'm not mad at you." This is untrue. "I'm just . . ."

She nods, eyes downcast. "I know." Her voice quakes. "Who could do this? First your place and now here? It's so brazen." She bites the inside of her cheek. "Do you think it was Gemma Costin?"

I stare at the note on the counter. The red marker has bled into the paper. "Could a sixteen-year-old pull this off?" I ask. My sinuses throb. "Why a bank transfer this time?"

"Last time was a test," says Dana. She sounds bitter. "A game. They just wanted to watch us creep around in the dark. To get off on our panic."

I'm croaky. "Yeah. We should've realized." I sip hot coffee. Black-mailers have moved with the times. "Paying in cash seems outdated."

I scan the room. Everything's white and silver. The chrome counters belong in a morgue. And I hate the tall dark windows. Anyone outside could see us huddled at this counter. I cough. Anyone—like Ryan Reeve.

I try to stare outside but see only our reflections. We look pale and insubstantial, a pair of ghost women.

Dana's reflection shudders. "They were in the girls' room, Zoe! I thought she was . . ." Her transparent face collapses.

I look away from the window, back to my friend.

Her head's in her hands. "I can't not pay," she says. "I just can't. This dread's killing me. What if they'd hurt them?" She peers at me, hollow-eyed. "What should I do?"

I set down my mug sloppily. Coffee sloshes onto the shiny counter. It's not fair, her asking me: it's not my money. I'm scared too. I want to cry. I know I sound resentful. "No idea. It's your decision."

She takes a deep breath. "No. We're in this together."

I push back my stool and stand. I'm too wound up to stay still. I walk to the picture window and breathe deeply. The stars are still out, so vast yet so small. They shine, cold and pure.

I turn back to Dana. "What if paying doesn't help?"

She stares at her hands. I don't think she even heard. "I'm going to pay," she says. "I need to do *something*!"

I don't respond. What's there to say? It's her choice, after all.

Dana's voice shakes. "Our girls! This was the last straw." Fresh tears fill her eyes. "Who could hate me this badly?"

I shake my head in frustration. "It's about money. People do terrible things for money! Kids get killed for their sneakers!"

Dana shudders. "That's—" Her voice breaks. "Awful."

She sounds indignant, so out of touch with reality. But then she is—in the exclusive Oaks, behind the tall walls of her mansion.

"Three million dollars should keep them happy for a while." I scan the yard, looking for movement, then spin back to Dana. "And who-ever it is will start spending."

"So we watch and wait?" she says. "See who's had a windfall? Like Ryan?" She looks toward the Reeves' mansion. Her voice thins with fury. "If he's behind this, I'll kill him! Pretending to miss me. What a wacko!"

I shrug. I don't want to think about Ryan Reeve. I recall the sounds in the bushes. Probably just a raccoon or Toonces. But what if it wasn't? I won't feel safe until Ryan's in jail.

I'm gazing at the Milky Way when a shooting star flares by. I gasp, momentarily joyful.

"What is it?" says Dana, freshly anxious.

I turn and smile. "A shooting star."

She rubs her forehead. "Did you make a wish?"

"Not yet."

"Well, don't tell me," she says. "Or it won't come true."

I look back at the sky, thinking of all the people who've wished on stars over the millennia. Most of them are long gone, along with their wishes. And shooting stars aren't really stars, just chunks of rock burning up. We're witnessing their demise.

And yet I recall the bright gash where that star sliced the sky. I deserve a wish.

I shut my eyes.

CHAPTER 41

Dana: Twenty-four days since Stan's death

I raise a hand to my brow and squint out the picture window. That dinghy. What's it doing?

I'm in the living room, coffee in hand. We made the transfer yesterday, as instructed, from Jo's granny's account to the blackmailer's. I woke up feeling optimistic. For the first time in ages, I actually slept well. I figured my luck was turning.

But something's wrong. The black dinghy keeps coming closer. Close enough to read the letters on its side: GLEBES BAY PD.

Dismay grips me. Three people are onboard, two of them clad in black wet suits. Are they coming to moor on our jetty? But the dinghy stops, just short of our dock. One man lowers an anchor. My gut shrinks. I shouldn't have drunk that extra coffee.

I set my cup on a side table and walk to the patio door. I unlock it and stride onto the terrace. Two divers shrug on their oxygen tanks and check their equipment. They toss out a dive flag. One diver steps overboard, then the other. The tide's low. Where they are, the water must be shallow.

I cross the terrace and take the path toward the jetty. Like my stomach, my thoughts are churning. Sour coffee burns up my windpipe.

I push back my hair and remember my tablet. Jo tossed it out back.

Damn. What if they find it? How could I explain? Could I say someone stole it? No. I'm getting wound up for no reason. I take slow breaths. I mustn't panic.

I continue down the path toward the boathouse.

Near the back of the dinghy a head pops up, black and slick. It's one of the divers. He passes something up to the man still on board. My belly flip-flops. Jesus. What the hell is it?

I'm nearing the rocks. I stop, unsure whether to keep watching or to flee back indoors.

Turning, I spy Detective Shergold off to my left. She's in front of the Reeves' place, standing on the rocks exposed by the low tide. Everything's public property below the mean high-tide line.

I freeze. She hasn't noticed me yet, her gaze fixed on the dinghy. She's speaking into a walkie-talkie. The man onboard holds one too. I can't hear what they're saying.

Detective Shergold lowers her walkie-talkie. The guy on board nods and does the same. She turns and walks my way, intent on where she's stepping. The rocks are slippery with seaweed. On a bedrock base, some loose stones are shaky.

I'm turning to go when she looks up. Shit. Our eyes meet. I can't slink away. It would look bad, like I'm guilty and can't face her.

She walks faster, with more confidence. After a moment's more hesitation, I walk her way.

"Morning," she says when we're about twenty feet apart.

"Morning." I stop and shove my hands into my pants pockets. I didn't plan on coming outside. I'm wearing a sweater but no coat. Despite the sun, it's cool. The breeze off the water is chilly.

Shergold keeps coming. She's clutching the walkie-talkie.

"What did they find?" I blurt. "I saw them recover something!"

She squints at the dinghy. "Nothing relevant. Junk. Just a broken car headlight." In the morning light, she looks tired. Older than when we first met, the skin around her eyes more crinkled. She's been putting in long hours trying to catch my husband's killer.

I don't answer. I hope my relief's not too obvious. Not that relief's warranted. It's not like they'd tell me if they did find something useful! The only reason they're here is because they suspect me.

Does she really think I dumped Stan right out back of my own house? Do I really look that stupid?

I hunch against the wind. One of the divers pops up, nearer the guesthouse.

I recall the role I'm meant to be playing: the grieving widow, desperate for answers. "Will you tell me when you know who's responsible—and why? My children and I—" My voice breaks. "We need to know."

I expect her to show me some sympathy, but her frown deepens. Her voice is flat as she says, "All I can tell you is that we're getting closer. And you'll be the first to know. That much, I promise." Her iron eyes spear me.

I shrink back.

With a nod, I spin away. I can't maintain my pretense any longer. That sounded more like a threat than a promise.

CHAPTER 42

Dana

I've barely had time to calm down when I get a call from Jo. My anxiety surges. She's at work. Her phone's usually turned off at this time.

I set down my florist's knife and the white camellia I was cutting. The police have yet to return my good Japanese knives. This replacement slices less cleanly.

I accept Jo's call. "Hey, Jo?"

Her voice is low and anxious: "Dana! Owen's locker's been searched again. They found pills. Oxys."

"Jesus." I lean against my worktable and squeeze my eyes shut. How much worse can things get? I can barely get the word out: "Oxycontin?"

"That's what he says," says Jo. "But it could be worse. No one's sure what they're buying anymore. And that's not all." She's talking fast, her voice low and urgent. "I found a cell phone."

Her tone signals danger. I don't get it. "A phone?" I parrot. All I can think about are the pills. Oxycontin. There's a freaking opioid epidemic. Kids are dying in record numbers. We've all heard those tragic tales: a good kid tries something once and drops dead. An allergy. The wrong dose. A bad batch.

"A burner phone," says Jo. "You know, the cheap kind, without contracts. You can't trace them?"

I touch my abandoned camellia's waxy leaves, unsure where's she going.

"I was on the search team. Thank God. I managed to snatch it before anyone else saw."

I feel cold all over. Why? What, besides increasingly dangerous drugs, has Owen been doing?

Jo's voice tugs me back: "Look, Dana. You'd better get here. Deal with Owen first, then come find me. You won't believe this. I need to show you in person."

The camellias' scent rises, overpowering. The fragrance is fine out of doors but all wrong in here. They reek like cheap perfume.

CHAPTER 43

Jo

I'm teaching when I get her text: *Where are you?*

I text her back and assign my class some reading. Bag in hand, I speed-walk to the closest washroom.

Leaving this lot alone is a risk, but there's no choice. If something goes wrong, I'll claim food poisoning and a mad dash to the toilet.

Meeting in the school bathroom takes me back to my school days. I'm not sure how we worked it, pre-texting. Handwritten notes? Whispered commands in the hallways? Sign language?

I look both ways before shoving the door, feeling furtive and adolescent.

Stepping inside, I'm hit by the odor: bleach and bad drains offset by Dana's perfume. It's a clean, citrusy scent. She never smells girly.

Sure enough, she's near a sink, arms crossed tight, like she's freezing. She looks drawn, her face shadowy in the fluorescents. Seeing me, she steps forward: "Jo, what's happened?"

I study the stalls behind her. While they look empty, you never know. I brush past her and give each door a hard push. This sets them all clanging.

Satisfied we're alone, I spin back. Dana's arms hang limp at her sides. She looks strung out. "What happened with Owen?" I ask.

"Two weeks' suspension. And mandatory counseling. He's clearing out his locker."

I nod. Two drug offenses in two weeks. And an escalation. He got off lightly. I extract the phone from my bag and tap it to life. It's a small, blocky red Nokia, more like a toy than a cell phone. "Here. Look." I pass it to her.

She takes it tentatively, looking scared and puzzled.

"Start there," I say. "And scroll down."

The screen's small, the light watery. Dana squints. The lines around her mouth look deeper.

I move closer to reread the exchange over her shoulder.

It's a series of WhatsApp messages between this phone and another number, not linked to a name. It starts innocuously enough.

Night!

Night.

Morning. How r u?

Good. You?

And so on.

I've had time to digest it and reach my own conclusions. I wonder what Dana will think. She keeps scrolling, her forehead wrinkled.

I miss u.

Same. Today was great.

Uh huh. U r so hot!

She swallows. This sort of stuff goes on for a while. Compliments, XXXs, and love hearts.

Dana looks up, confused.

"Keep reading," I tell her.

Tonight BB?

Can't. D's home.

Pleeeeeeeeease. I miss u.

When I first read it, I figured the phone was Owen's. I wondered if *D* was for Dad. The lines bracketing Dana's mouth are getting deeper.

What u doing BB?

Out with twins.

This gives Dana the same zap it gave me, her body tensing. Twins? What are the chances that this refers to some other twins? She licks her lips. The phone isn't Owen's.

Dana looks up, her eyes a hurt puppy's. I can't hide my impatience. Who knows what my class is up to? "What do you think?" I ask.

She sweeps a hand through her fine hair. "I don't know."

I tamp down a snort. "Keep going."

U free?

Can't. D's getting suspicious.

What?!?

Yeah. She asked me.

About us?!?

If I'm cheating.

Whatcha say?!?

NO, of course.

Stop worrying LVR. Wanna come here? House
empty all day. 🔫 💥 😊

You sure?

Yessssss! 😵 😵 Remember? Lame car show?

Dana lowers the phone. Her face is stricken. When she meets my gaze, I know she gets it. Dana is D, and her son had her dead husband's secret phone in his locker, the one Stan used to conduct the affair she knew he was having.

Dana rubs her forehead. "These texts were Stan's."

"Yup." I cock my head, waiting. "And?" I prompt.

"Car show." Her nostrils flare. "Angie Costin."

I almost smile. Angie's husband, Walt, is a car dealer. They run Costin Motors. Still, it's hard to fathom Stan cheating on Dana with Angie, like learning a Ferrari owner has been taking secret joyrides in a Hyundai. But some guys like trashy.

I nod. "It's Angie's number. I checked. I thought it looked familiar."

I've only called Angie once, to arrange that rendezvous at Felicity's. Yet I've always had a good memory for numbers. "She was just using her normal phone, not a burner."

Dana's eyes have turned hard and bright. "Stan was cheating on me with Angie Costin?" From the look on her face, you'd think the phone is covered in dog shit.

I understand how she feels. Stan was fucking an old high school rival. Except Angie wasn't a rival. She's too inferior: not the first runner-up, or even the second, but a contestant who got weeded out before the pageant even started.

Dana's eyes narrow. "Ew! How could he?"

For a second, I think she's forgotten that Stan's dead, forgotten the past few weeks.

"She's so—" Dana's lip curls in revulsion.

"I know," I say. "You don't have to tell me."

Stan wasn't ugly. He was mega-rich. If he wanted to fuck around, he must have had options. So why go for Angie, a woman with no charm, whose looks are as convincing as cheap clip-on hair extensions?

Yes, she's thin and blond. She's white of tooth and red of claw. She bares an expanse of perma-tanned cleavage. From a distance, these things signal sexy, but up close they're false advertising. Yet Stan got suckered in. Or maybe her appeal was that she was the anti-Dana? Perhaps Stan had tired of gourmet and wanted a greasy Big Mac.

I recall Angie back in Felicity's, her avid eyes upon Dana. How she must have savored that secret, the sense of one-upping Dana. I wonder how long the affair lasted. For all his financial smarts, who knew Stan could be such a moron?

Dana shakes her head. "Stan told me he found Angie vapid."

I roll my eyes. He probably did. Lots of men prefer vapid. It lets them be lazy.

Dana turns to study herself in the mirror. Her cheeks have reddened.

For the past few minutes, it's as if we were back in high school, high on outrage. If only cheating lovers and frenemies were the true extent of our problems.

Distracted by her ire, Dana's failed to see the real problem. It's time to return to reality. I clear my throat: "How did Owen get Stan's phone?"

Dana's face hardens. "I don't know. He must have found it some-where." Her voice is brittle.

Out in the hall, someone yells. This reminds me of my class, left alone. Is that one of my students running amok in the hall? I need to get back.

I nod at the phone in Dana's hand. "There's more. Give it here. Let me find it. I need to get back to class before all hell breaks loose."

She hands the phone over.

I scroll through a blur of XXXs and love hearts. LOLs and firework emojis. Jesus, they were nauseating. Whose taste in lovers was worse, Stan's or Dana's? Angie versus Ryan. It's like trying to decide between eating a slug or a laundry pod. Both unappealing. Both possibly toxic.

"Here." I hand back the phone.

Dana bites her lip. She's seen the date. The night.
It's a cluster of messages, all from Angie.

U there BB?

I miss u 2 much sexyyyyyyy

Meet 2night?

I got a surpriiiiiise 4 u

And then one from Stan:

Midnight. My guesthouse?

The phone goes down. Dana's head jerks up. Her narrowed eyes go round. "Fuck," she says softly.

I nod. Well put. Turns out Dana wasn't the only one taking advantage of the secluded guest cottage. It was practically a love hotel.

"Fuck," she says again. "Do you think Angie saw us?"

Instead of answering, I nod at the phone.

Dana's eyes dip downward.

The next texts are all from Angie:

I'm here

Were r u? [*sic*. It's a wonder she graduated
high school.]

BB? U r SO late! I'm getting sleepy.

Hey!?! U coming?

"Look at the times," I say. All sent between midnight and 12:20 a.m.

Dana runs a hand over her eyes. Her voice is raw. "What time did you come over?"

"Twelve thirty?"

Her eyes bug out. "Fuck. She could have seen us on the dock."

A bell rings out in the hall. Its buzz penetrates the walls. I look up sharply. "I have to go." But I stay put. "Scroll down," I order.

She bends back to the phone. I watch her closely.

The next message comes at 1:14 a.m.

I fell asleep here . . . LOL. Y u not answering?

This is followed by three missed calls. Then, twelve minutes later:

S? Whats going on?!?

WTF Stan?

Not funny. Were are U?????

CHAPTER 44

Dana

I don't feel up to having this conversation, but it has to happen. I should have broached the subject ages ago.

I wait to exit the school parking lot. Owen's slouched in the Range Rover's passenger seat, his backpack on his lap. He fiddles with a strap. Head down, his hair hides his face. He's obviously waiting for me to berate him.

There's a gap in the traffic. I edge out.

Owen's drug use is terrifying: first the spice, now the oxys. Did it start with Stan's death, or did I miss the earlier signs? I'm obviously failing as a mother, his sole remaining parent. I'd be terrified to send him to rehab.

I'm so preoccupied I fail to notice we're barely moving. A sharp honk rouses me. I glance in the rearview. A blue BMW is riding my bumper, its driver glaring.

Jo would slow further to spite him. I speed up a little.

Beside me, Owen shifts in his seat. I sense his eyes on me. I feel jittery, unsure where to start. My thoughts keep squirming free.

What do I know for sure? My husband of sixteen years was fucking Angie Costin, who was in our guesthouse on the night he died. She could have watched me and Jo lug his corpse down to our dock. A woman I wouldn't trust to feed my fish knows my worst secret.

You can't actually see the dock from the guesthouse, but it's a short walk. If Angie heard something, she'd check. She was born nosy. I picture her hiding in the trees, trying to work out what she was seeing.

Anyone decent would have called 911. But not Angie. So it's clear who's been blackmailing me: fucking Angie Costin. I'm amazed she had the balls. Or the brains. I underestimated her.

I should be relieved. She's not that smart, just lucky. Surely Jo and I can outwit her, maybe get the money back. As far as adversaries go, we got lucky.

Yet I don't feel relieved, because a new can of worms just got opened. When Jo asked me why Owen had Stan's burner phone, I changed the subject. But she's no fool. I'll need to explain how Owen grabbed it that night. I'm scared of Jo's questions.

I shift. My seat belt is digging into my hip bone.

Stan's secret phone is now stashed in Jo's car, in case the cops search my stuff. I wonder what else it might reveal. For all I know, Stan had a whole other life. Like Jo's duplicitous dad.

"Mom?"

I squint through the windshield. I'm not fit to drive. The guy behind me is still tailgating. His BMW is a small two-door with a soft top. If it hit my Range Rover, I'd come out fine. I try to ignore him.

My son twists my way. "Mom?" he repeats.

"Yes?"

"I'm sorry."

I wait. A city bus has pulled out just ahead. I slow further to keep a suitable gap. The guy in my rearview throws up an irate hand. I wonder what his hurry is. Is he late or just habitually angry?

People—men especially—seem more impatient of late, even here in the picture-perfect Oaks. Stan was like that—railing at stupid drivers, complaining about idiots on social media. Contempt was his default setting. He wasn't that way when we met. I don't understand how it happened. He had it all, by anyone's standards: wealth, prestige, a family who loved him.

I shift in my seat. The guy behind me is glaring.

My son's breathing is broken. "I'm really sorry." Head bent, he's started crying.

His tears start mine. There's nothing worse than to see your child suffer and not know how to help. I don't have answers, only questions.

I surprise myself by voicing one out loud: "Why was Emmett grounded?"

"What?" He swipes his hand under his nose.

"Emmett Isles. His dad said he was grounded."

My son pushes his hair from his eyes. He looks my way, confused but careful. "He, um, he got caught sneaking out."

"Where to?"

A blush creeps up Owen's neck. It's so transfixing I forget to look where I'm going.

"Mom!"

I look up and hit the brakes. The bus has stopped just in front of me. We jolt to a halt right behind it. I exhale shakily. My son's hands are braced on the dash. They look too big for his thin wrists, which stick out of his school blazer.

The bus starts up again. I hardly dare tap the gas.

Owen's gaze is fixed forward, like he no longer trusts my driving. The flush on his neck has receded.

"Was Emmett at our place?" I ask.

His head jerks my way. His whole face colors.

I'm squeezing the wheel, my voice just as tight. "Was it the night Dad died?" It comes out in a whisper.

"Yes." Tears trickle down his pale cheeks.

Without thinking, I stomp on the brake. The car behind me blasts its horn. I pull over and park. I can't drive. I cut the engine.

Owen's hands are splayed on the dash. He's staring straight ahead. His lower lip quivers. "Mom, I'm gay," he says softly.

I release the wheel and turn to him. I clench and unclench my hands to loosen my stiff fingers. "I wondered."

Owen cups his face in his hands. His voice is rough. "It's weird."

I shake my head. "Why? Lots of people are gay."

"Dad saw . . ." His face crumples. "He saw me that night. Me and Emmett kissing."

I reach for him, only to be stopped by my seat belt. I undo it and bend his way. I put my arms around him.

I'm scared he'll pull back, but he leans in, like he did when he was tiny. Back then, he was small and compact. Huggable. Now, he's long and bony, all ungainly angles. I rub his back, unsure how to comfort him, still a boy, but not little. Nostalgia rips through me.

When he was younger, problems could be solved with a kiss or a song or a toy. But no, I'm remembering things wrong. That was Chad.

I've forgotten Owen's screaming fits. Strangers' disapproving stares and embarrassed-for-me pity. Stan's frustration, blaming me for Owen's outbursts.

Beneath my arms, his narrow shoulders shudder. "Shhhh." I rub his back. "It'll be okay, hon."

"Dad hated me." His voice is muffled.

I hug him. "No! I'm sure he was just shocked. He'd have come around and accepted it. Me and Dad, all we want . . . wanted . . ." I trip over the tenses, stagger on. "We just want you to be happy."

My son shakes his head. "He would not have!" The anger in his voice kills my reply. I stroke his hair. It could use a wash. He's stopped crying.

Bent close to my son, I fear my heart will crack open. For three weeks I've avoided this moment, as if by not voicing the truth, I could change it.

Jo said we were in denial about the blackmail. If only she knew the full extent of my denial. I've been like a kid with my fingers in my ears, eyes shut, and screaming so I wouldn't hear.

Owen leans back. He scours his face with his sleeve.

I straighten too. There I was, thinking our house was a private oasis when it was Grand Central Station. There's no choice. I must ask.

That night, Angie may have seen us. What about Emmett Isles? "The night Dad died. Did Emmett see . . ." My throat shuts, the words poison. I swallow. "Did Emmett see . . . everything?"

Owen bites his lip. "What do you mean?" His confusion looks genuine.

I wait. Does he really think I don't know? I start to talk but stop. My lips feel rubbery.

What I want is a drink—something stronger than wine. Whiskey. Or vodka. Straight from the bottle, like when Jo and I were teens. She'd down cheap booze straight to show how tough she was. I mixed mine with whatever was on hand—apple juice, root beer, Slurpees.

Beneath his shaggy hair, Owen's watching me, his eyes dry and wary. I can't avoid this. Half knowing isn't enough. Or rather half not-knowing. I need to know the whole truth before I can bury it so deeply it'll stay down.

I lick my lips. "Did Emmett see you and Dad fight?"

A tight nod. "Yeah. Dad was screaming at us. I tried to talk to him, but he kept yelling at me."

"Did Emmett see Dad hit you?"

My son studies the backpack in his lap. "No. He left before that." A single tear trickles down his cheek. While his eyes are angry, his bottom lip quivers.

Tears fill my eyes. Does he blame himself? My heart twists. "It wasn't your fault! None of this was your fault! You must know that, Owen!"

Another tear snakes down his thin cheek. "It's all my fault," he says.

"That's not true!" My voice is shrill. I take a long breath. I need to get the truth, not doctor it, not yet. "So, Emmett didn't see?" I ask.

Owen's forehead crinkles. He swipes the wetness from his cheek. "See what?"

"The . . ." I try again. "The rest of the fight."

His head turns, dark eyes fixed on mine. "What do you mean?" I have his full attention.

"The fight. You and Dad fought . . ."

The heat's on, but I'm freezing—just like that night in my studio with the AC blasting. From that first instant I saw Stan's body, I knew two things: Owen had snapped and killed him, and Stan deserved it. I force down a shiver, force myself to hurry on. "It was an accident, I know that. You didn't mean it." My voice wavers.

Owen's mouth twists open. "What? Really?" His laugh is bitter. "For real, Mom? You think *I* killed him?"

CHAPTER 45

Jo

I wrench the shower's faucet to turn up the heat. Dana's house has much better water pressure than our hovel. Hot water pummels my head and shoulders. My neck's knotted. I sense that I'm missing something. Something important, related to Dana.

I crank the heat higher. I revisit our rendezvous in the school bathroom this afternoon. Jesus. The truth hits like a blast of ice water. Dana's been lying through her perfect teeth. I should have realized sooner.

When I asked why Owen had Stan's burner phone, she claimed not to know. Then noise in the hall distracted me; I had to get back to my class—I let it go.

But thinking back, her voice should have tipped me off; how hard and thin it got, a crust of ice over a pond, easily shattered. I've heard Dana lie before. I've watched her tell whoppers. Her face gets still, her eyes wide and innocent.

I snap the faucet shut. How dare she lie when she needed my help? How dare she keep lying!

My spine's rigid as I step from the shower. My toes find the soft mat. I yank at a towel, drag it over myself. Struggle into sweatpants and a hoodie.

I find Gloria alone in the kitchen, chopping broccoli. The air smells of roast chicken.

"Where's Dana?" I ask.

My tone must be off because she frowns. In her hand, the knife flashes. "In her studio." She sniffs, resentful. "Working."

I know Gloria wants me gone. It's more work for her with me and Ruby here. She's aware I'm not rich and feels I'm no better than she is.

I speed-walk down the hall. The door to Dana's studio lies open.

She's at her workbench, bent over a blue and white flower arrangement. Cornflowers, delphiniums, irises, and anemones rise from clouds of chrysanthemums, peonies, and daisies.

Hearing the door, she looks up and smiles. "Hey, is dinner ready?"

Seeing my face, her smile dies. "Jo?" She puts down her knife and straightens.

I barely dried my hair, which drips cold down my collar. As always, her studio's frigid. The overhead lights are bright, the tiles icy. I march closer.

In Dana's hand is a single blue iris. Her favorite flower, named for the Greek goddess of rainbows and sacred oaths.

"Jo, what is it?"

Storming down here, I felt loaded with fury. Now, faced with her fear, my rage misfires and fizzles. Flower clutched to her breast, she looks baby-bird fragile. I'm more disappointed than angry.

"I just realized why Owen had Stan's burner phone," I say quietly. "You didn't kill Stanley."

She sets down the flower and grips the counter. She tilts forward. Her hair falls into her face, a perfect, shimmery curtain. Owen uses that trick too.

I wait, my resentment rebuilding. I deserve an explanation.

"I'm so sorry."

I shake my head, hard bullets of anger clicking back into place. "No, Dana!" I hiss. "Fuck your *sorrys*!"

She blinks, fingers splayed on the counter. She's got lovely hands, her fingers long, white, and slender. Beneath her bright work lamp, those preposterous diamonds sparkle.

I step to the edge of the bench. Only the counter lies between us. "Tell me everything. I want every detail."

Dana inhales, pulls herself together. "Okay." She stares at that single iris, laid flat on the counter. "That night. Stan and I fought."

"What about?"

She hesitates. "About you."

"Me?"

She nods. "Chad got a C-minus on his *Antigone* essay." I wait. I remember that essay, a half-baked examination of sibling love and rivalry. It should have been a D or a D-minus. Chad's smart but lazy, like many beautiful people. The world's kinder to them. They get used to making less effort.

"Stan was mad," she says. "He wanted me to talk to you."

I cock my head. Huh. Stan felt he owned me.

Dana looks sheepish. "I know. I told him that's not how it worked. Chad deserved a C-minus. He had to try harder. Stan just went on and on about how his grades mattered, how he had to get into Harvard." She clears her throat. "He'd given up on Owen. But Chad was the son he could brag about. Football star. Yada yada." She rubs her forehead. "I couldn't take it anymore. He was being such an ass. We argued. I slapped him. He caught my wrist and twisted it." She touches her wrist, as if it still hurts. "I left the room."

"Where was this?"

"The den," she says. "I went upstairs and had a shower to calm down."

"Then what?"

"I heard more yelling: Stan super loud, and someone else softer. I . . . I just stayed in the shower. I was upset. I had to calm down. Then I'd go down . . . try to sort things out. When Stan got worked up, he could be a real dick. Not just with me but with the twins. Chad could handle him, mostly, but Owen . . ." She bites her lip. "I should have gone straight away to help." Her head bows.

I stay silent, waiting.

"I thought they were in the den, but when I got there, it was empty." Her voice softens. "I looked everywhere, in the living room and the kitchen. I didn't think of the studio until I'd checked everywhere else." She blinks repeatedly, like there's something in her eye.

I grit my teeth. We don't have time for her dramatics. Who knows what the cops have surmised? All this time, I thought I knew the real story, that *that* was the basis for our lies. Now I'm learning the starting point was a world away, like I was dropped in the Gobi with a map for the Kalahari. "Then what?" I ask.

"I found Stan dead on the floor in my studio, with blood everywhere." Her eyes latch onto mine. "A knife was sticking out. Here." She touches her throat. "I ran over and pulled it out."

I grip the cold counter. "Who else was there, Dana?"

Her head tilts, eyes full of horror. "No one!" She looks toward the service entrance. "That door was open."

I follow her gaze. That door exits onto the side of the house. I'm not sure I believe her. My jaw hurts. We can return to this later. "What next?"

"I figured . . ." Her voice slips away.

I won't let her evade me. "You figured what, Dana?"

Again, she hides her face. Her voice is tiny. "When I saw the knife, I knew Owen did it."

I nod. That's what I thought. "Why would he?"

"Stan saw Owen kissing Emmett and lost it. You have no idea, Jo! Stan could be awful! Hateful! He'd get after Owen and . . ." Her eyes squeeze shut. "He'd torment him! Say horrible things! Even hurt him." She shakes her head, as if to shake off her memories. "But Owen denies killing his dad. He swears he didn't do it!" She sounds frantic and pathetically hopeful. She's still in denial.

I tug at my hair. My God. Emmett was there too? "Then what, Dana?"

"I ran to grab a towel to stanch the blood. But there was so much . . ." Her voice drops. "I went to find blankets."

I blink. Had she already decided to wrap him up and dump him?

She's hoarse. "When I came back, the knife wasn't there."

"Did Owen take it?" I ask. "Or Emmett?"

"I don't know," says Dana.

I turn to her tool rack. Pruning shears. Wire cutters. A long knife for cutting foam. Short, sharp knives with pointed tips, all bought to replace the ones the cops took. "Did you ask Owen?"

"He said no."

She attempts a smile, like that will win me over. "I panicked that night," she whispers. "Owen would be bullied in juvie. Or in jail, if he was tried as an adult. He'd never survive!" Her eyes are pleading.

Despite myself, my chest softens. She looks tragic, and beauty is compelling; we're wired to respond to it. Those big eyes blinking at me. Dana looks like a scared, pretty baby. Or a kitten.

She wrings her hands. "I couldn't let Owen go to prison! He's so . . ." She gives up. "You know him, Jo! I couldn't call the cops and turn in my own son! I . . . I just couldn't."

"So you called me."

She doesn't respond. Her face is so pale it's translucent, like the petals of her white flowers. Against that blanched background, her eyes seem even bluer.

If she'd told me the truth, the whole truth, would I have helped her? "First you hit yourself so I'd believe Stan beat you," I say. Bitterness has left my voice flat. How brilliantly she played me, ruining her own perfect face so I'd never doubt her. "Then what?"

"I was frightened." Her lip trembles.

I nod. I get that. If it were Ruby—not that Ruby would kill someone, but *if*—would I have done the same thing?

"He's my baby! The one who needs the most help. The one who struggles."

I recall her back when Owen was little, taking him to therapists and doctors. He seemed much better lately. Until this.

I look away. It's hard to think with Dana's pleading baby-gaze on me. I stare into a cooler ablaze with bright flowers. I don't blame Dana for lying to protect Owen. Good mothers defend their children. But how dare she lie to *me*! I put everything on the line for her, including my daughter, yet she didn't trust me.

I inhale slowly, then exhale. I must stay calm to find a way through this mess. Yet I'm not calm; I'm buzzing.

"Jo?" Her voice is petal thin and equally fragile. "Do you think Owen killed him?"

My jaw clenches. Her question, so full of false hope, leaves no doubt. She knew it was Owen from the get-go. This is worst-case scenario. The boy's fifteen and troubled. He killed his own father. What's to stop him from talking—if he hasn't already? Teenagers talk. We're fucked if he confesses.

Fresh anger rises in me. I tamp it down. I need to focus. We're rats on a sinking ship. If Owen goes down, Dana and I drown with him.

CHAPTER 46

Jo

There's no time to lose. I tiptoe down the dark hall. As well as being suspended from school, Owen's grounded. This makes searching his room a challenge.

Luckily, after dinner, he went downstairs to watch a movie with Chad. Dana's in bed with a headache. She barely touched her food.

I left the girls in Zoe's bedroom, both glued to their iPads. All my good mothering intentions have gone out the triple-glazed windows. What's some extra screen time compared to your mom going to jail? When all of this is over, I'll make it up to Ruby. We'll bake cookies and read together. We'll visit museums.

I fear Owen's door might be locked, but it's not. I slip inside and lock it. His room smells like a thrift shop, musty and stuffy. I flick on the light.

I brought latex gloves, just in case, lifted from the nursing station at school. I tug them on and wiggle my fingers. My hands look pale and creepy.

I'm not sure where to start. I scan the neatly-made bed and a tall bookcase. Its bottom shelves are full of mostly sci-fi and natural history. The upper shelves display plastic models of monsters, Lego spaceships, and a chess set, while the middle shelf bears Owen's weird wood carvings. The sight of them sets my fury refizzing. Dana even lied about the murder weapon so I'd be less likely to suspect Owen.

A dozen mobiles hang from the ceiling, some bought and others handmade from wire and natural objects. They sway in a light draft, casting shadows, rustling, and ticking. The sound is unsettling.

I walk to Owen's desk, stacked high with books, papers, and comics. I leaf through them and find a sheet of paper in a physics textbook. I turn it over. Jesus. It's a pencil sketch of a man with a knife in his chest. Blood spurts everywhere. Owen's done a fine job with the shading. Detective Shergold would be orgasmic.

I fold the drawing and shove it into my jeans. I slow down and leaf through every paper. Nada. Maybe I'm wrong, and there's nothing here. Owen probably tossed the knife, although he'd have wanted to keep it. He's a hoarder. I walk to the chest of drawers.

I start at the bottom. The lowest drawer holds ancient stuffed animals. I pull out a lumpy dog, which reminds me of one my dad gave me when I was small and how fiercely I loved it. I shove the dog back in the drawer.

Next come old Lego catalogs, picture books, and music sheets. There's a drawer full of shells, pebbles, and twisted wire for his mobiles. Another holds playing cards, stickers, and broken electronics. He's got enough to build a bomb.

I check my watch. It's been twenty minutes. I'm worried Owen will tire of his movie. Throat dry, I move to the closet.

I find a half-smoked joint and a Bic lighter in his raincoat. No surprise. I shove the joint into my back pocket and keep looking.

When I'm done with his hanging clothes, I grab his desk chair and carry it over. A shelf at the top of his closet holds hats and folded sweaters. I climb onto the chair. My fingers wiggle between layers of wool. Nothing.

Behind the sweaters stands a blue plastic tub. I tilt it, hearing the instantly recognizable rattle of Legos. Keeping the box tilted, I use my other hand to rake through the sharp blocks. Something smooth finds my fingers.

It's long and hard, wrapped in plastic. I hold my breath and extract a knife. It's shaped like a dagger. The tip is curved. Holy shit. There are flecks on the blade. I can't believe it. Could he really have failed to wash it? It's inexplicably stupid.

As a teacher, I've seen plenty of teens make dumb choices. Teenage brains suck at risk assessment. Apparently, their prefrontal cortex remains undeveloped. But this— My breathing quickens. Still balanced on the chair, I glance toward the door.

Who in their right mind would keep the knife they'd used to stab their father? I am Owen's teacher at school. He's far from stupid. Is this some sick sort of trophy?

My eyes dart about the room. Have I misjudged him entirely?

I push the knife into my hoodie's pocket. My hands are clammy. It feels vital to leave this room ASAP. I clamber down, feeling shaky.

Dana and I have been luckier than we deserve. No. *She's* been luckier than *she* deserves, considering her lies. If the cops had thoroughly searched Winderlea, our lives would be over. They'd get the truth out of Owen. I'm as jittery as his mobiles.

Dana was blind about her husband. Why not her son? I should have guessed sooner.

I drag Owen's chair back to his desk and switch off the light.

Before opening the door, I listen hard. All's quiet but for my heartbeat and the click of his mobiles.

I look both ways down the dark and empty hall. I can just make out a trio of Stan's heinous abstracts. All in brown, they look like shit.

I creep quietly past Dana's bedroom.

I'm descending the staircase when I see Owen coming up. The knife in my pocket feels heavier. The staircase seems much too narrow.

I must look odd because he shoots me a suspicious frown. I will my voice to sound normal: "You off to bed then?" It comes out croaky.

This boy, now within feet of me, killed his father.

"Yeah." He frowns. "Why are you here?"

I don't think he just means here right now. But here in his house, with his mother. I stop walking. It's a good question. "I . . . I'm going," I say.

As soon as I say it, it's obvious. I'll pack up and leave. I'll sever all contact with Dana.

All those years and all those lies—I can't take it anymore. I don't need her. Everyone has a limit. I've reached mine.

Owen shrugs. Maybe that's not what he meant after all. "Goodnight, Jo."

"Goodnight."

I stay where I am until I hear his bedroom door shut. I feel the knife in my hoodie's pocket.

Back in the guest room, I shove clothes and toys into my suitcase. I'll take it out to my car, then come back for Ruby. Leaving tonight, while Dana's asleep, feels essential.

Above all, I must not panic. I need a good plan. One that doesn't involve Dana.

CHAPTER 47

Dana: Twenty-nine days since Stan's death

It's been five days since Jo up and left. No note. Nothing. I know she's pissed that I lied. I get it. But still. She's never not answered my calls. She even unfriended me on Facebook.

I reach for my phone and dial her number. It goes straight to voicemail. Damn. How long will she keep this going?

Trying to shake off my irritation, I bend back to my flowers. I'm working on a bridal bouquet, an orb of tiny white roses. It's the choice of the bride. I'd never choose roses for a wedding. They're too conventional, even dull. Jo carried a single protea—a spiky hot-pink flower the size of a soup bowl—when she married that bum, Trevor.

The front doorbell sounds. Gloria calls from down the hall: "I'll get it."

Minutes later, there's a tap on my studio's door.

"Come in," I say. I expect it's Gloria, come to ask about something.

The door opens. "Mrs. McFarlane?" My stomach drops. It's Detective Shergold. She walks in, followed by Detective Bellows. They're both unsmiling, in similar long, dark coats. Men in black, except one's a woman.

I'm the first to speak. "Detectives? What is it?" I sound guilty.

Detective Shergold unbuttons her coat. Detective Bellows answers: "We need to speak with you, Dana."

I nod, incapable of speech. They're here to arrest me. This is it. I can feel it.

I look down at the bouquet. I'm gripping the stems so hard a thorn's jabbed me. I thought I got them all but must have missed one.

"We wanted you to be the first to know," says Detective Bellows. "We've made an arrest."

I look up, not computing. He's not smiling, but his eyes are triumphant. "W-what?" I stammer.

A moment ago, I was sure they'd come for me. That spark of panic flares into a fireball. My insides warp and flap. Owen. Oh my God. Owen. Would they arrest a minor at school? Could they do that?

Detective Shergold coughs. Beneath her blunt bangs, she eyes my butcher-block table. "Can we sit?" she asks.

"Yes. Yes of course!" It comes out as a squeak. I motion them toward the table.

"This won't take long," says Detective Shergold. She sounds scarily cheerful.

I follow the detectives toward the table. While I prefer to work on my arrangements standing up, I use the table for admin. Besides my MacBook, it's strewn with papers, books of color swatches, stacks of magazines, and towers of rolled ribbon.

Every step takes effort. I feel dazed. An arrest. What led them to Owen? Or is it Jo they've arrested? Is that why she's not answering my calls? Are they trying to hammer out a plea deal?

Yes. They would take her in first and offer her immunity or a reduced sentence for testifying against me. I grip the bouquet.

A big black bag is slung over Detective Shergold's shoulder. When she sits, she places the bag on her lap. Bellows sits beside her. He pulls a tiny recording device from his pocket and places it on the table.

I'm moving slowly. Seeing that recorder makes my heart pound harder. Everything I say will be used against me. I fold into a chair, facing Bellows. I clasp my bouquet, penitent and waiting.

Detective Shergold pulls something from her bag and sets it carefully on the table. It's a phone, wrapped in plastic. "Do you recognize this item?"

I freeze, aghast, then shake my head. It looks like the red Nokia

Stan used to text Angie Costin. But how can it be? Jo has it. Where did the police find it?

"I . . . I'm sorry. No. Stan had a black iPhone." Jo and I tossed it into the sea, after dumping his body.

Beneath her sharp haircut, Detective Shergold smiles. "We found this phone the day before yesterday in Norman Gaynor Park, not far from where we located Stan's jacket."

My brain feels caught in a current. Thoughts smash like waves.

Jo must have left it there, but why didn't she tell me? Has she turned on me? I squeeze the stems of the roses.

Detective Bellows rubs his sharp nose. "You had said that you suspected your husband was having an affair."

I nod and clear my throat. "Yes, I thought so."

"You were right," says Detective Shergold, a glint of steel in her tone. "Do you know Angela Costin?"

I manage a small shaky nod. Has that bitch double-crossed me—taken the blackmail money *and* turned me in? How could she?

Bellows shifts in his chair, waiting.

"Yes. From high school. We're old . . . f-friends," I venture. This feels like a lie. Yet you can't call someone you've known thirty-plus years an acquaintance. Time turns you into more, even if you have nothing in common. Because you do: you have that shared past. You're the same generation.

And if you're enemies? Time's meant to wear down grievances, to rub off their rough edges. Clearly, it didn't. All these years, Angie's been biding her time, the wicked wolf in soccer-mom clothing. I misjudged her as horrid but manageable if kept in check, like mildew.

My throat's dry. "Her daughter's dating my son, Chad. They're at the same school, Stanton House."

Bellows nods, like I'm confirming what he already knows. His close-set eyes look somber. "We believe this woman, Angela Costin, was sexually involved with your husband." He sounds like a newscaster reporting some tragedy. Professionally sensitive.

I blink, like I'm shocked. I am shocked, just not by this. What has Angie told them?

Detective Shergold's eyes dip to the burner phone then veer back to mine. "Angela Costin was here the night of Stan's death. In your guesthouse."

She pauses. Some response is expected.

"W . . . what?" I stammer.

"She texted him," explains Bellows. "And we traced her cell phone movements."

I loosen my grip on the flowers.

Angie must have told them she saw me and Jo move Stan's body. Maybe all of this is subterfuge, a decoy, so I'll lower my guard. Do they know about the blackmail?

"We need your permission to search the guesthouse," says Detective Shergold. Her voice is smooth. "And the grounds of your estate."

I can't respond. This is the real reason they're here.

"Angie tried to blame you," continues Detective Bellows. He sounds disappointed, like Jo discussing some underperforming pupil. "And your friend, Joanna Dykstra—Ms. Costin suggested her involvement."

He pauses, as if to let me refute this. I stay quiet.

"Ms. Dykstra was staying here, correct?" adds Detective Bellows.

I want to cry. I don't know how to answer.

Detective Shergold tilts her head. "Are you alright, Dana?"

I nod, breathless. "Yes. Jo stayed here for a few days, helping me. I . . . uh, I've had trouble sleeping."

Detective Shergold's voice is smooth: "That's normal, given the circumstances. Your sense of safety has been shattered. Have you considered counseling?"

"I . . . Not yet," I say. "But, um, Jo helped a lot." As I say it, I realize it's true. I feel bereft. Why did she unfriend me?

"That's good," continues Detective Shergold. "Having an old friend." Is she trying to win me over? She frowns. "This must add to your shock, to learn of your husband's infidelity. Especially with another old school friend. It's a double betrayal."

My head throbs. Talk about rubbing it in! Are they waiting for an answer? I've lost track of their questions. I should probably ask for a lawyer.

Detectives Bellows and Shergold exchange concerned glances. "Do you need a glass of water?" asks Bellows.

I shake my head. "No. I'm fine. Really."

Shergold nods. Her tone's all back to business. "We suspect but can't yet prove that Mrs. Costin's daughter was an accomplice."

I bleat out, "What? Gemma?" They've got this all crazily wrong.

Detective Shergold looks back at my workstation. "About your missing knife." She lets these words settle. Her smile is chilling. She pulls something else from her handbag and sets it on the table.

My chest locks. It's my missing silver knife.

"Is this item familiar?" asks Detective Shergold.

I recall the moment I last saw it. It was in Stan's neck, the handle glinting in the light of the coolers. Owen got angry when I asked where it went. Did the police divers find it?

"Mrs. McFarlane?" Detective Shergold's voice drags me back to the present, to the white blooms in my hands and the trickle of blood in my palm. The thorn I missed. How careless. It could have injured the bride.

She sounds stern. "Please state if you recognize this item."

Finally, I squeak out a reply: "Yes." Where the hell did they find it?

"Please acknowledge that it's yours, for the tape."

I have no choice but to admit it. My voice is feeble. "Yes, that's my missing work knife."

Bellows sounds smug. "We found it in Angela Costin's walk-in closet."

I stare at the squashed white roses. So pretty but dead. Cut flowers are dead. How strange that we display and admire them. "I don't understand."

"We also found sheets matching the ones used to wrap up your husband's remains," says Bellows. "We've arrested Angela Costin for the murder of your husband."

None of this sinks in. The words bead off me like raindrops off flowers. I stare at him blankly.

Bellows doesn't seem to notice. "Mrs. Costin arranged to meet your husband in your guest cottage, where we suspect they argued."

I rub my eyes, trying to imagine it. Could this possibly be true? Could Angie—and not Owen—have killed Stan? Imagine if Jo and I inadvertently cleaned up Angie's mess! I'm on the brink of hysterical laughter.

"The daughter's not talking," says Detective Shergold. "But might she have said something to your son?"

The urge to giggle dies. I shut this down, fast: "If Chad suspected Gemma was involved in any way, he'd have said so. He loved his dad."

Bellows shifts, bringing us back to the key topic. "Your knife," he says. He nods to the knife on the table. "Do you have any new memories as to where you last saw it?" His head turns an inch toward the side door. Both detectives look expectant.

I blink and drop the bouquet onto the table. The blood on my palm has dried. I rub my hand on my dark trousers.

A flood of warmth spreads through me as the truth slides into focus: Jo did this. She made sure that burner phone would be found. And she set up Angie to take the fall for Stan's murder. Jo somehow planted the knife at Angie's place—just like in high school with the shrooms in her cheerleading jacket.

I picture Angie back then, despondent, slouched before the principal's office before being led away by her angry, abrasive parents.

"Mrs. McFarlane? Dana?" Detective Bellows's voice sounds far away. "Are you sure you're alright, Dana?"

I grab the diamonds on my ring finger and squeeze. I press the stones into my flesh. I need to wake up *now*.

Jo did this to save me. To save me and Owen. To save us all. Even though she now hates me. Is she still my friend, after all? I feel weak with gratitude and admiration. Good old brilliant Jo. I can't fuck it up.

"I . . . I sometimes take a knife outside," I say, thinking fast. "To cut flowers or foliage. There's a holly tree by the side of the studio. And ferns by the guest cottage. Plus ivy. The day Stan went missing, I was out there, cutting holly and ivy. I must have left the knife out there. I haven't seen it since."

Detective Shergold tilts back. Her eyebrows relax. They're the same steely gray as her hair. "Right," she says. She scoops up the plastic-wrapped items and sticks them back into her bag.

Bellows clicks off the tape recorder and smiles. "Thank you, Dana. We'll be in touch. We'll need you to come to the station for a fuller formal interview." They both scrape back their chairs and stand.

I follow more slowly.

Detective Shergold smooths down her dark trousers. "All the tox results came back on your husband. The medical examiner should release his remains shortly. And we'll return most of his personal effects within the week." She looks almost kind. "Then you can bury him. And settle his estate." She slings her black bag over her shoulder.

"Thank you," I manage.

My knees are weak as I walk with them out the side door. I see Detective Shergold turn to look for the holly tree. She smiles when she sees it. Lush ferns grow nearby. There's no shortage of ivy.

I lean against the doorjamb and watch them walk to their unmarked car. Detective Shergold grasps her bag tightly, like it holds her life savings.

Except it's my life that stuff is saving. And I owe it all to Jo.

CHAPTER 48

Dana: Seven months later

Professionals would normally pack up the art, but with this work, I'm taking no chances. I sink back on my heels to admire my copied Cleggs. I tried to buy back the original, but the owner declined to sell.

I touch the red dot. Perhaps my shoddy replacement means more.

Some movement behind me makes me turn. Toonces has hopped into a cardboard box, curious as ever. Cats don't like moving. He won't be happy. He leaps back out, his gaze disdainful. He's gained more weight, eyes small and piggy. Toonces always preferred Stan.

I gaze around the den, littered with junk and half-packed boxes. I've spent the morning sorting and packing up valuables. We need to vacate the house by the end of the month.

My stomach growls. I should stop for lunch soon. On cue, the grandfather clock starts to chime twelve.

Three months ago, I found Stan's USB banking keys hidden in that clock. It was a relief, to say the least. While Stan lost a fortune, he still had a fortune. Now it's mine. His art collection's smaller, minus all the ugly pop art and abstracts.

I don't *need* to sell Winderlea, but I want to. It's time for a fresh start, still in the Oaks, but not on the water. The ocean creeps me out. Stan's empty-eyed skull is somewhere on the seafloor.

I rummage through a drawer. It's full of junk.

I pull a garbage bag off the roll and slide it between finger and thumb. Opening found, I start to toss in unwanted items. It's amazing how things build up. The new place we're moving into is smaller: just four bedrooms, with a shed I can use for my studio. It feels good to downsize.

When the bag's full, I drag it out the front door.

I sniff appreciatively. The lilacs are in bloom.

I consider leaving the bag on the porch for the gardener to toss tomorrow, but I don't want to leave things half-done. I carry the bag toward the road. I refuse to fetch the wheelbarrow. It reminds me too much of that night when we dumped Stan.

By the time I lug the bag down the driveway and through the gates, my breathing's heavy. Beneath my quilted vest, I'm sweating. I stop on the sidewalk to unzip it.

I'm turning to go when I spy a police car parked out front of the Reeves'. Two uniformed cops emerge from their driveway. Ryan staggers between them, head down. Hair hides his face. His hands are behind his back.

I stand transfixed. Ryan's being arrested! Was he caught selling drugs again?

Two other men appear behind Ryan. One is in his midthirties, the other closer to sixty. The younger one has red hair. I recognize them from Jo's description: the hit-and-run detectives.

Ryan's head swings my way. He glares at me. I can't move.

After Angie's arrest, he tried to relaunch our affair. I rebuffed him. Like the spoiled child he is, he took it badly.

I recall Jo's fear of him. He does look scary: snake-eyed and shaggy like a fairer Charles Manson. My former attraction to him is inexplicable, like *I* was on drugs. What the hell was I thinking?

The uniformed cops bundle him into their car. They shut the door.

I rub my palms on my jeans.

A tow truck pulls up behind Ryan's parked Audi. Its driver gets out. He joins the detectives as they examine the Audi's left front headlight. They're clearly excited, leaning close and nodding. The younger detective snaps photos.

The dots connect in my head. Detective Shergold told me the police divers found a broken car headlight in the ocean out back. Ryan must have tossed it!

I watch the tow truck driver hook up Ryan's car.

The marked police car drives by. Ryan's hunched in the back, white-faced. He looks scared, a small boy trying not to cry.

I feel a moment's sympathy but remind myself that he killed that poor lady! If Jo hadn't stopped to help, she might have lain in the street for hours in the rain.

Jo. Did she turn Ryan in? Or did the cops finally crack the case on their own?

I check my watch. Jo should be on her lunch break. I should phone and tell her. She'll be thrilled to hear of Ryan's arrest. If only she'd answer my calls.

I walk up the drive. The trees have bright new buds. The rhododendrons are in flower, a party of hot pink and orange. Spring. I breathe deeply. The air smells fertile. Everything feels possible, except another grim winter. And what a winter it was! I really must talk to Jo. Ryan's arrest marks the end of a dreadful chapter.

I spent months worrying the truth would wash up, like Stan's corpse. I feared a trial. Luckily, thanks to Jo, the case against Angie was too strong. Her lawyers convinced her to plead guilty to second-degree murder. In exchange, the DA dropped the obstruction and illegal disposal of a corpse charges against Gemma. They didn't have that much on her, although Gemma did herself no favors by insisting she'd never been in my guesthouse, which was smeared with her DNA. She and Chad were obviously sneaking in there.

With no prior record, Angie will be up for parole in fifteen years— *if* she behaves.

I stop to admire the Chinese wisteria, heavy with blue blossoms. I knew Jo was smart. Just not that smart. Or that ruthless. She stitched Angie up so neatly you couldn't even see the thread.

The police found traces of Stan's blood on the driver's seat of Angie's car. The murder weapon was stashed in her closet. Sheets matching the one used to wrap Stan's body were found in Angie's garage in a bag meant for Goodwill. Two menthol cigarette butts were retrieved from the bushes outside my guesthouse. A third was wedged into a crack in my dock, somewhere Angie swore she'd never been. All three bore her DNA.

I touch the wisteria, such a delicate lilac blue. I should buy a tree for the new place.

Staring up at the blooms, I feel sorry for Angie. There are no flowers in jail. She'll be close to sixty by the time she's freed, if she's lucky. That's pretty harsh, given that she's innocent of murder.

Except she's not innocent, I remind myself—not of blackmail. Or of fucking my husband. It still rankles, her stealing my spouse *and* my money. Luckily, I'm not broke. She can't spend it in prison. Wherever she's stashed that cash, by the time she gets out, she'll be ancient.

I walk around the driveway's bend. The wind rises off the sea, swishing through the pines and cedars. Winderlea appears, dark and austere.

A Chinese family bought it. Apparently, they made a fortune in poultry. I cross my arms against the chill and wonder what the old coal baron would think. I reckon he'd approve. He was an immigrant too.

Staring up at the house, I recall that night in Zoe's room. My sleeping daughter, too still. The ripped-off dolls' heads . . . Shergold was right about one thing: my sense of safety *was* shattered. Even now, I don't sleep well.

I think of Angie in a jumpsuit and a cell. She's not innocent. She threatened me and my children.

Fury quickens my footsteps. Who knows how far she'd have gone? Angie deserves this. Thank God she's in jail.

Entering the house, I double-lock the door. I walk to the kitchen, where Gloria is kneading sourdough.

I'm pouring myself a glass of Chablis when I spy her phone on the counter. "Gloria, do you mind if I borrow your phone? Mine's dead."

This is a lie. But Jo won't pick up if she knows it's me. I've tried everything. Notes. Gifts. She looks right through me when I go to Stanton House. I feel awful for Zoe and Ruby too. They didn't deserve to lose their friendship. Jo's being selfish and petty.

Gloria looks up. "No problem," she says. "There's no passcode."

I carry her phone into the hall. I know Jo's number by heart. I hold my breath as it rings. Once, twice. She picks up. "Hello?" She sounds tired.

"Hey, Jo. It's me! You won't believe what I just saw."

She hangs up.

I lower the phone. Shocked tears cloud my eyes. I had good news—news she'd want to hear. It's been seven months! I can't believe she hasn't come around! After everything we've been through together. And things turned out fine. How could she dump me?

I tell myself it doesn't matter. Who does she think she is? I don't need her. But that's bullshit. I stare up at the chandelier's feeble twinkle. This house feels too big and quiet. Too lonely. The cat swishes past, evading me when I try to pet him.

I miss my best friend.

CHAPTER 49

Dana: Six days later

In desperation, I yank Owen's iPhone from its charger and dial Jo's number. I'm scared her phone's off, but it rings.

"Pick up!" I beg. It's late. It could be on silent. "Please! Please!"

Five rings. She picks up. Her voice is throaty: "Hello?"

"Jo!" I cry. "Don't hang up! I need help!"

There's an exhale that's almost a laugh. Jo sounds incredulous, like this is a joke. "What? Fuck, Dana, it's two a.m.!"

I sink against the wall. It's hard to get the words out. I'm sure she'll hang up on me. I've started to cry. "I . . . It's Owen."

"What?" She sounds alert. "Dana? What's happened?"

Down the hall, Chad yells. I start to run. The hall's dark. "Chad, don't go out there!"

"Dana?" says Jo. Her voice is a nail, rusty but sharp.

"He's—" I careen down the hall. A sliver of light shines from Owen's opened door. "Oh my God! I . . . I have to go," I tell Jo.

Chad yells again. I hang up and run into Owen's room. The only light shines from his desk lamp.

Chad turns at my approach, his hair tossed by the wind. He's standing by the open window. The curtains billow. Wind and rain blast in. "Mom, what do we do?"

I stop beside him. Rain stings my eyes. I raise a hand to shield them.

"Did you call for help?" asks Chad.

I don't answer. I don't dare call the police or the fire department. What if Owen confesses to killing his father? I've repeatedly told him that Angie belongs where she is, but he feels guilty. The wind yanks my hair. I lean out the window. I just wasted time calling Jo.

The roof's dark and steep. Rain snakes down the tiles. Treetops thrash. The ocean's seething. Owen's crouched on the roof, below. "Owen!" I scream. My knees buckle. "Come back here!"

His shoulders shake. He ignores me.

I swipe wet hair from my eyes. Looking up, I see two tall chimneys; looking down, the sharp, black roof edge. Owen crawls lower. For a good five minutes, I stand there, uselessly pleading. Owen ignores me.

"Stay here," I tell Chad. His mouth is slack with panic.

I climb out the window and start to crawl. I'm barefoot. The slate tiles are slick. Wind shakes me. I'm soon sodden. The rain's freezing.

I start to slip and squeal in panic. I lie flat on my belly. Time stops. "Owen," I croak. My voice is lost in the wind. "Honey. Please! Come back here."

He doesn't turn. He's moved even closer to the roof's edge.

Moving slowly, I slither sideways on my belly. I try to talk to him but get no response. Perhaps he can't hear. He's squatting near the edge, peering over.

A yell comes from above: "Dana!"

I turn. Two figures are silhouetted in Owen's window. The shorter one's Jo. I can't believe it. She actually came! And so quickly. She must have sped the whole way here.

"Dana! What the fuck?" she yells. "Come back here!"

I turn away and keep inching downward. I can't leave my son.

"Owen!" yells Jo. "The roof's wet! What are you doing?" She's got her teacher's voice on—calm but stern, like she's discussing late homework. I pray Owen will listen. Kids respond to Jo. She's an excellent teacher.

Owen turns to peer up at the window. He's crying like he did when he was tiny, his face scrunched with resentment and fury. He yells at Jo: "Go away! You understand nothing!"

"Okay," calls Jo. "Tell me."

Owen leans closer to the edge. I bite back a whimper.

"What's the point?" he yells. "When no one believes me? Everyone at school still thinks I did it!" He glares my way. Through his sobs, his words are garbled: "Even you don't believe me!"

I can't breathe. I have no answer. What triggered this breakdown? I thought things were fine, that Angie's sentencing would help. I thought we were safe, that this was over.

Owen keeps sobbing. He turns and yells into the wind: "I didn't do it!"

In the window, Chad jolts as if tasered. He starts to clamber over the sill.

"Chad! Stop!" screams Jo. She tries to grab him, but he shakes her off. He's strong and nimble. I scream too. Chad's on the roof. He starts shimmying toward me.

"Chad!" I shriek. "Go back!"

He keeps coming, on his feet but crouched low, arms outstretched like he's surfing. He creeps closer to me and Owen.

My throat shuts. What do I do? Both my babies are out here. If I reach for Owen, he might jerk away and topple over. If Chad slips, he'll start a domino effect. I look back and forth between them. "Please, stop!" I rasp. "Both of you! No!"

"Owen!" says Chad. "Don't worry!" He's getting closer.

I try to crawl his way and block him, but he evades me. His eyes flash. "Mom! No!" His voice is flat but fierce. "Let me do this." His calm is unnerving.

I'm shaking so hard I'm scared I'll roll off the roof. I shouldn't have come out here. I cling to the tiles, watching Chad's progress.

Back when the twins were small, they were close. Chad had a knack for soothing Owen. Now they're rarely together. Still, might Owen listen? I hold my breath, hoping.

"Owen, it'll be okay," says Chad.

Owen spins. His mouth twists with scorn. "That's bullshit! Gemma's mom pled guilty, but everyone still thinks I did it! Mom can't even look at me." He claws wet hair from his face. "I scare her."

I gasp. "That's not true! I knew how Dad could get! I should have left years ago! When you were little . . . This is my fault! Not yours!"

He ignores me.

Chad stops sliding. His head snaps my way. "What?" he says. His lips are curled and disbelieving. "You think Owen killed Dad?"

"I . . . No!" I say. "I don't . . ." I can't get the words out. It's obvious I'm lying.

"Jesus," says Chad. He turns back to Owen, then to me. "You've got it all wrong, Mom. It wasn't him, it was me!"

I can't speak.

Chad looks right through me, his eyes unfocused. "Dad kept yelling at Owen. And he hit him." He sounds unnaturally calm, like he's in a trance. "I went into the studio." He frowns. "But Owen wasn't there."

"I ran out the side door," says Owen. "I hid in the cedars." His voice softens. "You know, our old fort?"

Chad nods. "Sure. Our old fort." He shimmies closer to his brother. "When Dad saw me, he grabbed me. Asked why I hadn't told him you're . . . gay." He swallows. "I told Dad to stop, but he just laughed. He said at least he had me to be proud of, that I'd go to Harvard." Chad's voice cracks. "I said no. Never. I told Dad I hated him." Chad's eyes shut. "He pushed me and I fell . . . It hurt." His jaw clenches. "He said—" His back straightens. "Dad's dead. It doesn't matter."

All around there is howling wind, waves, and rain. Only my sons and I are silent.

I dig my nails into the roof, feel the house hunched beneath me. At any moment, it might wake, and shake us off.

"I saw the knife on the bench," says Chad. "And I grabbed it." He grits his teeth, half grin, half grimace. "I stabbed him." His eyes shut. "There was so much blood! I just lost it . . . Oh Jesus, my life is over."

I can't stop shaking. Tears and rain blind me. How can this be true?

"I went back inside," says Owen. He blinks as if to unsee the memory. "Dad was dead. His neck was peeled open . . ." His face scrunches up. "I grabbed the knife off the floor. And a phone. It must have fallen from his pocket." He laughs in despair. "I thought Mom did it." Owen's voice quakes. He sounds very young: "I . . . I kept the phone. And hid the knife in my Legos."

I sit up. A wave of dizziness fells me. I look down at the swaying treetops. Rain gushes toward the eaves. My sons hunch like gargoyles, framed by the sea.

Rain blasts my eyes. I duck. The roof shakes. Someone screams.

I squint into the wind. I don't believe what I'm seeing. On the roof below me there's only one figure.

CHAPTER 50

Jo: The night of the fall

I run outside, clumsy with panic. The grass is wet. The rain's hard as
hailstones.

He's on the side of the house, snow-angeled on the lawn. I slide to
a stop.

His head turns. "Jo?" He's smiling, angelic.

I fall to my knees. It's a miracle.

I kneel and lay a hand on his shoulder, as I had with Alma Reyes.

"Chad?" He looks good. Joy pings through me. Typical Chad! The
boy was born lucky. I grasp his hand. It's cold. "Are you okay?" I manage.

"Jo?" His face shadows.

My fear returns with a vengeance. Something's wrong. Logic dictates
it. No one could fall that distance unscathed. Not even him. I croak:
"Where does it hurt?"

"You know what I said about Dad and Owen? About why I did it?"
He looks dreamy. "That was true but . . ." He frowns. "There was more."

I should break away, call for help. I can't. I sit frozen. His gaze holds
me, pleading for understanding. I can't let go of his hand, can't break
eye contact. What if he's dying? He wants to say something. His grip
tightens.

"When Dad pushed me, I tried to hit him." He grits his teeth. "He
laughed and said one son's a fag and the other's too pathetic to satisfy his

slutty girlfriend." Chad blinks. "He laughed!" He has started to shake. His eyes bore right through me. "He laughed about how he . . . you know . . . with Gemma."

I'm too shocked to respond. Oh my God. I remember now: Angie confiscated Gemma's phone as punishment for cheating on my English exam. Gemma sent those texts, from her mom's phone. I feel sick. That means Stan wasn't fucking Angie but her teenage daughter. Gemma's sixteen! His own son's girlfriend. As for Gemma, I shouldn't be surprised, earning props at school with her football-star boyfriend *and* snagging luxe gifts from her doting sugar daddy. She wouldn't see herself as another victim.

"How could he?" says Chad. "And Gemma?" The betrayal in his eyes is crushing.

Chad stares up into the rain. He releases my hand. It hurts where he's gripped it.

Behind me I hear running footsteps. It's Dana, ghost-faced, her pajamas vacuum-wrapped to her skin.

Chad grabs back my hand and yanks it, eyes bright with alarm. "Please Jo," he says quickly. "Don't tell her! Don't tell anyone! Promise!"

Dana's almost upon us. Seeing Chad, she starts keening, a horrible wail. I can't look at her. My best friend, whose whole life seemed charmed. All her luck has rubbed off, like cheap gold plating.

"Promise!" mutters Chad.

I nod at him. "I promise."

With a sharp exhale of relief, his eyes shut.

CHAPTER 51

Jo: Next summer

Ruby stares out the car's window. "Is this it?" She sounds suspicious.

I nod. "Must be."

I park behind the realtor, Susan, a pleasant-looking woman in her midfifties. Behind me, in her newly purchased booster seat, Ruby unbuckles her seat belt. Her hair's freshly bobbed. I've had mine done too, cropped into a cute pixie cut. It feels light and modern.

Like Ruby, I peer out at the house, an unremarkable two-story, neatly painted in neutral colors. There's a box elder in the front yard that would be perfect for a tire swing. Nearby stands a For Sale sign. "Let's go look," I tell Ruby.

The realtor waits on the curb, smiling politely. Despite the heat, she's wearing a green blazer.

We walk up the path together. Ruby's hand feels hot in mine.

Boulder's sweltering, in the mideighties. The sky's high and blue. I spent a week here one winter years ago with Trevor. I loved those dazzling snowy days. Many people prefer the sea. I like the mountains.

A breeze lifts Ruby's new sundress. We bought it yesterday, along with new school clothes.

The realtor pulls a key from her handbag. In her smart sandals, her toes are glossy red. This reminds me of Dana, who favored that color. I can't think of her without thinking of Chad.

Through former colleagues at Stanton House, I hear he's home from the hospital and doing physical therapy. Dana has reverted to alpha-mom mode, tackling Chad's paraplegia with the same energy she once devoted to Owen's behavioral issues.

Chad. My chest locks. It still hurts to think of him, star quarterback, Dana's golden boy, confined to a wheelchair for the rest of his life. And Owen: how wrong we were, blaming the troubled son, the one with all the labels. I was his teacher. She's his mom. We should have known better.

I squeeze Ruby's hand. I try not to think about the McFarlanes, especially not Stan.

Susan unlocks the front door. "It's empty," she says. "The owner moved out a few weeks back and went into assisted living. She kept the place immaculate." She holds the door for me and Ruby. "Take your time," she tells me.

Ruby and I walk through the echoing rooms. The house feels bright and airy.

I've always loved empty houses. I enjoy their stillness, their blankness. In a way they feel sad, full of what once was. But there's room for what could be.

I turn to Ruby. "Do you like it?"

She looks serious, tongue flicking through the hole left by a missing tooth. "Which one would be my room?"

"Let's go upstairs."

The house has three bedrooms. There's a big back deck and a big-enough yard. Ruby's new school is a short walk away. My new school, where I'll start next month, is a ten-minute drive.

Excitement thrums through me. The decor's old-fashioned. Fussy wallpaper in the bedrooms. In the kitchen, someone went wild with a stencil. Yet overall, there's a good feeling. As they say, it's got good bones.

The bedroom at the back has a small balcony overlooking the square yard. "What about this room?" I ask Ruby.

Her face lights up. She was sad to leave Glebes Bay. She misses her school friends. But this. She spins around. This makes up for a lot. "It's so big," she exclaims, grinning.

I nod. It's at least double the size of her old room in the basement. She runs to the window. I follow and gaze out at the back garden.

When I told Principal Bill I was leaving Stanton House, he seemed genuinely dismayed. I guess he changed his mind about me. I ran a tight ship. My classes listened. On the whole, my students scored highly.

Maybe I misjudged Bill. Maybe he never disliked me. He gave me a glowing referral. I can finally stop worrying about being fired in Chicago.

I stare out the window. My thoughts circle back there.

The principal was a woman. Black. Early fifties. Hyperefficient. Not the sort of person you'd want to fuck with.

"Jo?" She peered at me over her purple glasses.

"You wanted to see me?" I said. I followed her into her office.

She didn't ask me to sit and didn't sit either. Just swiped a paper off her desk and shoved it at me. She looked like she'd happily smack me. "How long have you been doing it?"

My stomach dropped out. I looked at the old exam, tried to bluff. "What is that?"

She snorted. "Don't bother."

That's when I saw the cops at the door. They didn't cuff me but escorted me from the building in front of everyone. Staff. Students. All gawking.

It was just an exam scam! Could they actually charge me? I'd let it be known that extra help was available, then blackmailed those students who took me up on the offer. I only targeted entitled assholes, the ones too lazy to study. They deserved it.

The cops led me to a police car. One opened the back door. "Mind your head, ma'am."

I balked. "Am I being arrested?" I said. "On what charge?"

"Get in." His voice was iron. "Academic fraud."

Ruby's voice breaks through. "Mommy? Mommy?"

I shake myself back to the here and now. Ruby's staring up at me, jigging in place. "Um, yes, hon?" I say.

"Can I use the bathroom?" asks Ruby.

"Oh. Sure thing." I lead her in.

After checking the other bedrooms, I follow Ruby back downstairs.

I'm still feeling wobbly. That memory shook me up. I reach for Ruby's hand. It's time to stop beating myself up, to look forward instead of back. I'm able to do good things now, like paying the school fees for Alma Reyes's three children in Manila.

Susan's waiting on the deck, gazing out at the garden. The backyard's neat but plain, just grass and a few trees. I could add a playhouse. Plant vegetables in the far corner. We could adopt a dog from a local shelter.

Susan smiles when I join her. "What do you think?" she asks.

I smile back. "I like it. How much are they asking?"

Her answer makes me smile harder.

The next morning, after having the house inspected, I make an offer. That afternoon, it's accepted. My whole life, I've longed for a house of my own. Someplace safe. Now I have it.

"You're going to love it here," says Susan when I'm back in her office, filling in more paperwork. "There's so much for kids in that neighborhood. Boulder's ideal for young families." She pauses, as if the word *family* might be fraught since it's just me and Ruby. Or maybe it's *young* that tripped her.

I smile back. I'm not that old. And families come in all shapes and sizes.

"For the down payment," says Susan, all back to business, "twenty percent is standard. Do you need a referral to a good mortgage lender?"

I hesitate. It's tempting to say no. I could buy the place outright. But that's unwise. Who pays for a house in cash? Certainly not a teacher. That's how people get caught. It's never smart to stand out.

I've been frugal, partly to avoid suspicion but mostly since that's my nature. By some estimates, a staggering 70 percent of lottery winners end up broke, stupidly wasting their windfall. There's no way I'll do that.

"I can pay thirty percent up front," I say, hesitantly. "And yes, please recommend a good lender."

Susan's smile widens, a hint of relief in her eyes. Perhaps she'd feared that amassing that 20 percent down payment would be difficult for a single mother. I smile. If she only knew! Money's no problem.

Susan hands me the banker's card. "I can call her, if you like, and make you an appointment."

"Please do," I tell her.

As she calls, I turn my attention to Ruby. She's seated beside me, coloring in an image from *The Little Mermaid*. Ariel's hair is hot pink, her tail orange. I'm glad she chose her own colors instead of copying the ones from the movie.

We've been in Boulder for a week, looking at houses and doing touristy things, getting to know our new city. Beneath her yellow sundress, Ruby's tanned.

After this, because she's been patient, I promised her ice cream.

Susan puts her hand over the phone. "Does tomorrow morning at nine suit you?"

I nod. "Yes. Thanks."

She goes back to her conversation. My thoughts wander.

A 30 percent down payment adds up to $190,000. My hands are sweaty. Despite the AC, this room's warm. I'm excited, nervous about buying my first home.

I think of my mother, how it's something she never managed. Could she have imagined me now, buying a three-bedroom home in a respectable, middle-class neighborhood? I'm a teacher, not exactly a top job, but it sure beats being a cleaning lady.

I rub my hands on my shorts. I wish my mom had lived to see this. There's an extra bedroom in the new house. I wish she could live there. Sit on the back deck. Putter in the garden. She worked so hard for so little. She rarely complained. I never appreciated her efforts. Kids don't, I guess, until they have their own children.

Tears press behind my eyes. My throat has tightened. Listening to Susan's cheery small talk and the swish of my daughter's crayon, I feel awash with bittersweet emotions.

I stretch out my legs. For the first time in a long time, I feel safe. A safety my single mom never knew. She was forever in danger of being fired. In danger of being evicted. In danger of unforeseen medical bills. We were always hanging by a thread that any minor setback could sever. How precarious our life was!

My mom thought a life of drudgery was a woman's lot. Unlike her,

I expected better, thanks to teenage Dana. She taught me to set my sights higher.

After Trev fucked me over, I had no choice. I wouldn't let Ruby have a childhood like mine. I couldn't. She deserved better.

Again, I think of the exam scam. It kept me afloat until I got busted.

Small-time hustles are stressful. I regretted that one. Now I know: nothing's wasted. The experience helped prepare me for the big time. It was my apprenticeship for blackmailing Dana.

Susan hangs up. "Okay. The loan officer, Lisa, expects you at nine." She straightens papers on her desk. "She's great. You'll love her."

"Thank you," I say, and stand up. We shake hands. I help Ruby collect her crayons.

Leaving Susan's office, I feel buoyant. New house. New job. New town. Glebes Bay was full of sad, guilty memories. I do have a conscience, but doing the right thing is a luxury we can't all afford.

I lead Ruby toward our car. The breeze blows hot off the sidewalk. My phone buzzes in my pocket. I pull it out, surprised. What timing! It's Dana.

Phone in hand, I stop walking. I could answer and hear her news. And her excuses . . .

For a second, I'm tempted. We have so much shared history. I know her better than I know anyone. And she knows me. Has she figured it out? My belly lurches. But no. Facing my betrayal would force Dana to examine herself. She'd have to question how she drove me to it. She's too conceited to admit she was a bad friend.

I didn't set out to screw her over. The idea never crossed my mind on the night we dumped Stan. I helped out of love and duty because I thought we were friends. Then I learned that Angie knew about Dana's affair with Ryan Reeve and I didn't. Something snapped. Did she see Angie as her social equal while I was—what?—there to clean up her shit?

I hit decline and return my phone to my pocket. I pry it out again and block Dana's number. This feels revolutionary. I'm finally free of her! Free of the past. I don't miss Dana and I don't miss my lying father or Trevor. Something's shifted in me. That aching void's gone.

I can't stop smiling as I pocket my phone.

Ruby climbs into the back seat. "What will it be?" I ask her. "Regular ice cream or soft serve?"

Her mouth purses. "Can we go back to the same place as yesterday?"

I hesitate. It was one of those trendy artisanal places where ice cream costs seven bucks a scoop. Yet Ruby's been so patient. "Sure," I say. It was delicious.

She smiles slyly. "Can I get two scoops?"

I laugh. "We'll see." Why not? We're on vacation. And today's special.

"Chocolate chip mint and strawberry," says Ruby, clearly sensing my weakness.

I hop into the driver's seat. This car's a rental. Maybe tomorrow I'll go and buy one. My smile widens. "Just for today. Two scoops. To celebrate our new house."

"Yay!" cries Ruby.

As I drive, I'm smiling. Life is so much easier with a $3 million safety net. I do the math in my head. $2,810,000 after my home deposit.

The ice cream shop's on a busy street. Yet there's a parking spot right out front. I zip into it, feeling lucky. Some days, the universe sweeps you in your chosen direction. I park and start whistling.

I shouldn't get cocky. Luck can turn in an instant. Just ask Dana.

Do I feel guilty? I grab my purse off the passenger seat. Sometimes, but not really. Not about the money.

God knows I earned it.

Ice creams in hand, we go back outside and sit at a round sidewalk table. I pull Ruby's coloring book and crayons from my bag and lay them before her on the terrazzo. She doesn't notice. She's too busy licking her overpriced ice cream.

She's finished the strawberry when she spies her coloring book. "Can I get a Little Mermaid blanket for my new room?" she asks. "One like Zoe's. Remember? I used it the night her daddy died."

I stop licking.

"When you and Auntie Dana went out in the boat," says my daughter. "In the dark!" Her tone suggests we were naughty and silly.

There's a man by himself at the next table. He must see my face for his eyebrow arches. I freeze. There's no good way to respond. Do I try to explain? Do I tell Ruby she's mistaken?

The man bends back to his phone, smiling. Perhaps he didn't notice me at all, his eyebrow lifting at some text. My stomach has shrunk. All the ice cream I just swallowed is threatening to reappear.

Beneath her bangs, Ruby's frowning. "Mom!" Her eyes are bright with alarm. "Your ice cream's dripping!"

"Oh," I say, rousing myself. I grab a tissue and dab at the drips. "I'm, ah, I'm going to toss it." On shaky legs, I stagger to the nearest trash can. I feel like crying.

Small kids' memories are soft like their skulls. Easily squashed and fragmented. While Ruby's memories of that night might get warped and buried, they'll stay in there—like a splinter. Splinters fester.

I shut my eyes. A fresh start. That's all I wanted.

"Mommy?" Ruby sounds distraught.

I spin. She looks pale. "Mommy, I don't feel well!"

Just as I reach her, she vomits pink and green splatters all over me and herself. All over the sidewalk.

Kneeling in front of her, covered in vomit, I'm reminded of Stan's ugly abstracts.

Ruby starts to cry. I pull her head to my chest. "It's okay, baby," I say. "Get it all out." If only she could. She spits some more into a napkin.

When she's recovered enough, I pull her to her feet and guide her back to the restroom. I wash her face and help her blow her nose. I pull off her sundress and toss it in the sink, then do the same with my T-shirt.

She peers up at me, dressed in nothing but panties and sandals. "Mommy?" Her eyes are red. "Are you mad at me? For what I said about Zoe's daddy?"

"No!" I say, stricken and scared. "I'm not mad at you, honey!"

Her frown deepens. "Then who are you mad at?"

"Myself," I say quietly.

She doesn't answer. How could she? She's six years old.

I squirt hand soap into the basin and start to scour her dress. Strings of greasy vomit float to the water's surface. Tears press against my eyes. I bow my head and scrub harder.

Tonight, when Ruby's asleep, the dam will burst. I can already feel the pressure building.

I think of Angie in jail. No parole for fifteen years. Walt divorced her and moved the kids to Texas, where he's from, to escape all the gossip. It was the talk of Glebes Bay. Still is, I bet.

Despite all the proof I planted, I was worried until Angie pled guilty.

I got the cigarette butts from her car's ashtray. It's lucky she never kicked that filthy habit. While I was at it, I scraped blood off the murder knife onto her driver's seat. DNA testing has come so far. They can detect even minute traces.

Getting into her house was harder but doable, thanks to Gemma. I lifted her house key from her schoolbag and got it copied. After that, it was just a matter of finding the right time to plant the knife and the bedsheets. I worked fast: five days from start to finish.

I knead Ruby's sundress. The fabric's slimy.

The only way Angie could have saved herself was by proving she wasn't there that night with Stan, which would have led the cops straight to Gemma. Angie must have read Gemma's texts to Stan and realized what they'd been up to. At that point, I bet she wished she *had* killed him, that scumbag—taking advantage of her teenage daughter.

What I'll never know is whether Angie believed that Gemma killed Stan or just feared that she'd be blamed. The cops did threaten to charge Gemma as an accomplice after the fact. Without witnesses or a confession, I seriously doubt they could have made that stick, but how was Angie to know? She couldn't take any chances.

The new girl at school, Ming, attempted suicide last December. She got pulled out of school. I heard the family moved back to Guangzhou. Maybe I should have framed Gemma for Stan's killing instead of her mom. Despite her youth, that might have been fairer. Gemma gets off on hurting people. I bet she's bullying new kids in Texas.

I add more water to the sink. A sob takes me by surprise. Fuck. I hate feeling guilty.

Angie sacrificed herself for her kid in the same way Dana tried to. As I'd give my life for Ruby. Angie is a silly cow, but I respect her for protecting her daughter, even if Gemma doesn't deserve it.

The smell of vomit is making me sick. Or maybe it's me. I'm making myself sick. I spit in the toilet. Fifteen years. My gut heaves. I can justify things all I want, but Angie didn't deserve that.

I unplug the sink and let the tap run.

When the water runs clear, I extract Ruby's dress. As I wring it out, I study us both in the mirror.

I'm in shorts and a bra. Ruby's in aqua *Frozen* panties. She's less green than before but still pale. In the fluorescent light, I look jaundiced.

My eyes flick back and forth. Same dark hair. Same strong nose and high forehead. Same big, anxious eyes. Wringing Ruby's wet dress, I think of all the traits that pass down through generations. All things good and bad.

What have I passed on to my daughter?

ACKNOWLEDGMENTS

Writing's a solo sport, but publishing demands a team. Huge thanks to Jackson Keeler, who didn't just sell this book but greatly improved the story. My editor Dana Isaacson—a.k.a. "Good Dana"—made my prose sound way smarter. Everyone involved at Blackstone—including Daniel Ehrenhaft, Josie Woodbridge, and Michael Krohn—deserves a massive and heartfelt thank-you. As for the cover—thank you to Larissa Ezell.

Industry people who've generously helped and inspired me include Amy Tipton, Sharon Bowers, and Deborah Goodrich-Royce.

Closer to home, huge thanks go to my longtime friend and writing mentor A. D. Scott, head honcho early reader. Another early reader who gave insightful feedback is P. J. Peraza, randomly found online, proving you don't only find crazies on the internet. All the friends—especially you, Saeko Ando—and fellow writers who've supported me both IRL and online have my enduring gratitude, with a special nod to my crew on Instagram. (Look me up at elka.ray and say hi.)

This book was inspired by two of my best childhood friends, Dr. CK and Dr. Jessica Ringrose, both incredible, successful women I'm proud to call friends.

There's no way I'd have managed to survive and write without the support of my patient, ever-optimistic, and hilarious husband, Thien

Nguyen. And I would not be a writer at all were it not for my brilliant and adventurous parents, Gisela and Dr. Gerry Ray, who always found money for books and travel—even if it meant we only had stacked books to sit on. Finally, thanks to my grade twelve English literature teacher, Lana Simpson, who convinced me that studying arts wasn't definitive proof that I was too dumb to study science.

AUTHOR'S NOTE

Some time back, I saw a meme going around social media: a drawing of two women in faux-antique dresses, wielding shovels. The caption read, "Real friends help you hide the bodies."

It got me thinking: Who would I help?

My best childhood friends sprang to mind—not that they'd wind up in that situation. But if . . . I'd race right over, no questions asked. We're formed by our earliest friendships.

What emerged from that meme was this novel about old friends, loyalty, and the corrosive power of dark secrets.

Jo and Dana are far from perfect. It's easy to claim they're bad people. And yet. The characters that materialized charmed and scared me.

I hope you enjoyed *A Friend Indeed*—my exploration of moral dilemmas, social disparity, and complex female friendships.